W

work of the
Angels

⚨ ⚲

Kat Goldring

BERKLEY PRIME CRIME, NEW YORK

This is a work of fiction. Names, characters, places, and incidents either are the product of the author's imagination or are used fictitiously, and any resemblance to actual persons, living or dead, business establishments, events, or locales is entirely coincidental.

WORK OF THE ANGELS

A Berkley Prime Crime Book/published by arrangement with the author

PRINTING HISTORY
Berkley Prime Crime mass-market edition/December 2003

ISBN: 0-425-19214-8

Berkley Prime Crime Books are published
by The Berkley Publishing Group,
a division of Penguin Group (USA) Inc.,
375 Hudson Street, New York, New York 10014.
The name BERKLEY PRIME CRIME and the
BERKLEY PRIME CRIME design
are trademarks belonging to Penguin Group (USA) Inc.

PRINTED IN THE UNITED STATES OF AMERICA

10 9 8 7 6 5 4 3 2 1

ACKNOWLEDGMENTS

Hau, k'ola. Hello, friends. With the first book, *All Signs Point to Murder*, a magical world of new friends opened up through meeting librarians, booksellers, bookstore liaisons, and readers. These wonderful readers came to signings and enjoyed talking about books and characters and all the life lessons they had learned through books. Ah. These new friends from Ohio to Florida, from New Hampshire to California, and certainly those from my home state of Texas catapulted that first novel into a best-seller on one of the three major mystery lists. To those delightful readers—new friends—I say *pilamaya ye*—thank you.

As I write this third book in the series, the second novel, *Death Medicine,* is four weeks away from the bookshelves. This third novel, dealing with a juxtaposition of American Indian spiritualism and ancient Celtic divination will be out a year from my penning this. So, to those who've read the first and are coming back for the second and third, and for new readers I will be meeting for the first time, I dedicate this book to you all. It is my sincere hope that each of you can enjoy them not only for the mystery-murder plot and subplots, for the fun characters and nefarious villains, but also for learning something new and for finding valuable life lessons. I've always believed in Coyote Medicine—the ability to learn through opposites—meaning, through humor you can learn serious lessons. Through serious situations, you can see a hint of humor and earthiness.

In American Indian lore, the storytellers were called

Acknowledgments

Twisted Hairs. I'm proud to be one and to be able to share stories with all of my old and new *k'ola* -friends. Thank you for your encouragement and support. Happy reading.

To Aunt Norma and Uncle Steve, Cousin Marc, Cousin Betty Williams, my brother Tony Goldring, special brothers and sisters of the spirit—Claudia, Peggy, Shirley, Mac, Truman, Cathy, Linda, Sandy, Cathey Lynn—thanks for your special support.

K'eya Kimimila Win
(Butterfly Turtle Woman)

Kat Goldring ☺

CHAPTER

I

Druids. Murphy's chowder. Irish sourdough bread. Banshees, war maces, and recipes for Irish ale all fought for Willi Gallagher's attention. Her head swam with all the details gleaned in a meeting of the Celtic Irish Fling Committee. Now, in her car, something else caught her attention.

Bird poop. All Willi Gallagher wanted was to slow the pace of her hectic day, get into her comfort zone at home, but droppings from her feathered friends on her windshield put the last nasty touch to an already foul day. She turned on the wipers and pushed the windshield wash button. "Damn," she said, as the last three drops smeared the mess. She repeated, "Well, damn if that's not the worst-looking barf. And heaven knows I've seen plenty of samples while teaching high school." She sighed and peered at Quannah Lassiter in the passenger seat.

In a Western-style shirt that strained across his broad chest, raven ponytail tied back with a beaded band, he appeared fierce. His deep frown added to the look. She said, "I guess you don't care if I can or can't see through the windshield?"

He tapped the speedometer. "Gallagher, do you think you might speed up? I'd like to bathe and pack before you have to take me to the airport."

"Well, that's fine, just ignore—"

He leaned forward within her sight. She pretended not to notice his hooded eyes considering her. "If The Winged Ones choose to drop a message, perhaps you need to pay attention to it. That doesn't mean you can't drive at the speed limit. I can't afford to miss the last Friday-night flight out."

She squinted to see through the streaked green baby-poop color. "I," she said with slow emphasis, "am just trying to follow your advice and use Ant Medicine—mellow out, slow the pace—that's what our aborted day at the lake was supposed to have been—relaxing—remember? I'm the one who had to attend the Irish Fling Festival meeting. I'm the one who should be stressed out. So, where's your patience today, Big Chief? And what possible message could this uck signify, anyway?"

"Winyan," he said, "you must decide for yourself what the message is, but it certainly smacks of an uncertain situation of some kind, perhaps—"

"Yes, there certainly has been that today," she tilted her retroussé nose in the air.

"I think, Gallagher, you're trying to pick a fight, but I don't have time right now to calm your ruffled feathers."

"Don't have . . . don't have time?" She ground out the next words between gritted teeth. "First. We have hours. Sun has just now disappeared. There's no reason to rush. Secondly . . . secondly, if you hadn't gone swimming with Miss Tits-in-the-Air and so gallantly saved her from that mass of underwater vines, we'd have even more time."

"Ah," Quannah said, leaning back and sighing. "Her name was Loraine Zimmerman, not Miss—"

"And how interesting that you first felt it necessary to save her bikini top. Came waving it around like some prize ribbon."

"I merely threw it clear of the brambles she'd caught it in, and she freed herself."

"Sometimes men are so unbelievably stupid."

"Willi, would you really have wanted her to drown?"

Willi peered at him sideways and slowed to ten miles below the speed limit. "Let's just say, it happens again, neither one of you better come back up to the surface." Out of the corner of her eye, she caught the quick movement of his fingers wiping the grin off his face.

"Oh, I may have found a way to get even," she said.

"And just how—?"

"You said you'd help and just to volunteer you wherever we needed you."

"Willi?"

"So—"

"So?"

"The two-stepping jig contest. You and a couple of others."

"Who?"

"Dan Oxhandler and—"

"Isn't he the one you went out with—?"

"Before I met you, Lassiter, and we didn't date, just had a meal or two together."

"Hmm."

"Okay?" Willi peered up into Quannah's hooded eyes.

He said, "Okay, past history. Now back to this revenge you're exacting for that innocent lake scene."

"Nothing about that woman and her bikini is innocent."

He reached over and rubbed his thumb along the back of her right hand and changed the subject, "Today, Smart-Teacher-Woman, your mind is controlled not by your Indian blood but by the Irish warrioress in you."

"And what is that supposed to mean?"

"The Irish are known for their fits of jealousy. Must come from dealing with little leprechauns and wanting their gold."

"Big Chief Know-Not, you pulled that false statement out of thin air. For love of the ale, for Celtic divinations, for dancing, for the mystery surrounding their Druidic beliefs, yes, for those and many other things they are well known."

"Right now, *Winyan,* your mind is as confused as one of those intricate Celtic knot drawings."

Willi smiled. "Considering that those are referred to as 'works of the angels,' I'll consider that an apropos compliment."

"My mistake."

"You—" She stopped when she turned her head to see an ornery grin on his face. "You just get a kick out of aggravating, don't you?"

"*Winyan,* only when I know it'll be taken in the right spirit."

When he used the tender Lakota word for *woman,* she melted considerably. He used it to let her know he appreciated all her feminine strengths, wisdom, and beauty, as he had finally explained. Of course, he'd also said it was sometimes his way of showing exasperation for times when she was too curious and bound for trouble and ignored his manly advice. It was a simple word, but one that carried so much when spoken to her. It was, along with the continued gentle touch of his thumb, a most sweet apology. "It's okay, Lassiter."

"I get to wear feathers and ceremonial paint in this dance?"

"Noooooooo. Black slacks, Irish vest, and buckle shoes."

"Grrrrr."

Someone behind her honked, she tugged the steering wheel and swerved back into her own lane. "Good Granny's goose, no one can be in that much of a hurry in Nickleberry." Deputy Sheriff Junior Beans glared as he passed and whooped his siren once to prove her wrong.

"What's his big hurry?"

"Maybe," Quannah said, "he has a plane to catch, a criminal to transport to Fort Worth, perhaps before the life sentence has been completely served."

Willi sniffed and tried the wipers again. "Just because he's got a uniform and a souped-up cruiser doesn't give him the right to run law-abiding citizens off the road. I am not going to be rushed. I wanted a relaxing day, a slow day. It's not too late to get my wish." She pushed a strand of her dark hair back from her cheek and glanced at Quannah. "And furthermore—"

"Gallagher!"

"What?"

"Watch the road. Stay in your lane."

"I was barely touching the line. See? Here's how far over I was."

Another cruiser passed her, sirens and flashers on full. Quannah pulled on the steering wheel. "Great coyote balls, Gallagher."

She pressed down on the accelerator only to regret the move when blisters shot a reminder to her feet.

"Now, you speed up?"

She sat straighter. "They're turning off at Worchester." She pushed her single dark braid back over her shoulder and again brushed the loose curls near her eyes.

"*Winyan,* what are you doing? Don't take this corner at that—" He gripped the dashboard. "Slow down."

"Won't take a minute to see what's happening, then I'll drop you off at your place. You'll have plenty of time for a dip in the Jacuzzi before I come back by to take you to the airport. I might join you in the Jacuzzi even."

Her tires squealed on the hot tarmac as she tailed the two cruisers. "I won't even wear a top you'll have to retrieve."

He raised one finger to make a point, obviously thought better of it, and said, "Hmmm."

She swerved the car to a stop before revolving lights, flickering red and blue against the high school's brick surface. Some contended the old building must have served as a fort at one time or a prison, due to its square-box architecture. Green lawn sloped downward toward a concrete perimeter that would have been the perfect place for a high fence with guards posted. A bevy of vehicles, lights revolving, sat in a circle—a modern-day wagon train in the middle of a laser show—looking as if the encampment expected an Indian raid. Willi slapped the dashboard. "I bet it's some more of those lewd racist remarks. Townsfolk have finally had enough, and they've caught the little creeps."

Quannah sighed and folded his arms. "Yes, I know, but if I miss that flight—"

"You won't. You can stay here while I check this out."

"Last time you said that, I found you leading a protest march in Dallas." He threw open the door so hard that when he turned to shut it, the door caught him soundly on the wrist. He rubbed the wound and said, *"Hiya, hiya. . . . Ptebloka tatungca."*

"So," Willi said while crossing the parking lot, "is *pet's bloated tongue whatever* a new name for me?"

He growled and slammed the door. "Perhaps. *Ptebloka* is the word for *bull*. You can guess the other one."

"Be nice, Lassiter."

Sheriff Brigham Tucker reached out and grabbed her elbow just as she neared the area cordoned off with yellow crime tape. "Howdy, Miss Willi." Turning her loose, he sneezed, brought out a green bandanna—handkerchiefs not being of a size to accommodate his great honker—and blew. "'Scuse me, Miss Willi. Quannah, boy, thought you was flying out today?"

"My intent exactly, Uncle Brigham." He held on to Willi's other elbow. "Now that we see everything is in your capable hands, we'll be on our way."

Willi smiled sweetly while pulling her arms free from uncle and nephew. "Has there been an accident?"

Sheriff Tucker stowed away his bandanna and opened a Benadryl packet. He popped a tablet into his mouth before wiping his watering eyes with the back of a massive paw. "Could be something like, I guess. We just this minute come on the scene ourselves."

Willi stood on tiptoe to peer behind the tight circle of officers. Her blistered foot protested so badly that despite her curiosity, she wished again to be at home and comfortably floating in the Jacuzzi, water cascading and bubbling away the aches.

Quannah sighed heavily and crossed his arms. He gave a curt nod.

"Obviously," Willi said, "with this many of the county's men, this isn't just some vandalism. How can we help?"

Sheriff Tucker worried his left earlobe and sniffed. "Got us an unidentified . . . corpse."

"One of the staff . . . or a student?" Willi asked. She closed her eyes. She'd dealt with the deaths of students before, and she didn't think she wanted to see that ever again. Tears stung her eyes at the thought.

Uncrossing his arms, Quannah put his hands in his jeans pockets. "Not more mutilated animals from those satanic cults? We've been there and done that in Nickleberry already."

"Nothing like that. This is a lady with no ID, but seems like I've seen her before, so she's got to be local. Save us time if we could ID her before the coroner takes her away."

Sheriff Tucker led them carefully through a narrow, cordoned walk to a second barrier that neither he nor other officers could pass by until the coroner arrived. He said, "She might have been to the lake today, seeing as how she's dressed like you, Miss Willi. Swimsuit and a terrycloth robe. Sandals. Cool and comfortable looking."

Willi said, "If you enjoy the sensation of kiln-heated knives pricking your flesh and sandy grit grinding into burst blister wounds."

"Mayhap looks can be deceiving."

When Sheriff Tucker instructed the officers to shine more light into the circle, Willi concentrated on breathing to calm the fearsome lurching in her stomach, a reaction that did not in the least lessen the fact that she wanted to *know*. The last officer within her path moved aside. A photographer still blocked her view of the body, but the lights swirled and glinted off the yellow Cadillac's chrome. Willi expelled the breath she'd been holding. The only person she knew with such a vehicle was about to retire: Superintendent Bernie Fritzpatrick Burkhalter. Flashes from Dole Manley's camera strobed in cadence to the smack of his gum. Also keeping carefully out of the inner area of the tape, he nodded in her direction. Five years ago he had worked on the high school annual staff. Now he took pictures of dead bodies. She couldn't see that as a step up, but Dole's happy features belied this thought. When he shifted his stance, she leaned nearer to see the body.

"No, no . . ." she whispered. Her knees trembled as if the bevy of circled wagons had been trampled over by a stampeding herd of buffalo, making the ground reel and buck beneath her, creating a cacophony of thunderous sound. She gasped and cleared her throat, tried to yawn to pop her eardrums, but with each attempt the pounding blood in her temples increased. She swallowed. Maybe she was mistaken. She bent down and peered closer.

The victim's legs were still in the confines of foot pedals and twisted floor mat, whereas the torso hung suspended at the hips by the bottom half of the seat belt. The head touched the gravel, and the whole body looked like a marionette slung aside, abandoned with half the strings severed. The face had none of the circled cheeks or pin-sharp lashes painted in place, but the glow of ebony skin immediately caught Willi's attention. One of the detectives picked up a piece of green cardboard to bag it. Flashing bulbs and undulating lights reactivated the stomach lurches she thought she'd controlled. She shut her eyes. So much for her damned curiosity. She wanted to go *home* and to all the comfort that word afforded. Yes, she wanted home and Quannah. Warm bath, soft socks, sweet-smelling pillow, smooth summer blanket up to her chin, perhaps she could talk Quannah out of his trip and his arms could enfold her and—

"Ahhh-choo!" Sheriff Tucker stifled the second outburst in his green bandanna. " 'Scuse me. Well, Miss Willi?"

She forced herself to open her eyes and really study the poor creature before her. The left side of the face, burned bright pink and crenulated with welts, had oozed viscous fluid and blood, now dried.

Okay, enough. Willi swallowed and willed her limbs to

move away, but her traitorous feet seemed held in place with superglue. *Stay calm. Detached. Professional. Absolutely no reason to get hysterical.* She could handle this. She pinched the bridge of her nose. Questions flooded through her. How was Willi going to explain to India Lou? And why was Tessa—there, she'd said the name—*Tessa,* in Burkhalter's Cadillac?

A strangled whimper escaped, and her bottom lip trembled. Tears spilled over her bottom lids and onto her sunburned cheeks. Sheriff Tucker handed her a clean purple bandanna.

She said, "It's Tessa Aiken, India Lou's niece. She's a lawyer in Austin. Tessa's been home ... home for ... a holiday. This will kill India Lou. She raised the girl and her brother."

Some minutes later, outside the circle of tape, Willi sniffled while Quannah kissed her on the top of the head. "Uncle Brigham will get you home after he's questioned everyone."

"He can talk to me later. I've got to go home now. Or ... I could go to your apartment and help with the packing. I should never have turned off—"

"Gallagher, now listen—"

"If my damned curiosity didn't get the better of me, I wouldn't do such things."

"I know, *Winyan.*"

"And I don't think you folded yesterday's wash since you left it on top of your dryer, so you'll have to dig through it. I was going to help you later, but—"

"Shush, Gallagher. I'll find everything." He tilted her chin up. "*Winyan,* go into The Silence. Think before you are questioned. You mentioned at the lake that a lot of unusual things had happened this week while I was gone."

"But ... nothing to do with this accident, and I need to see you off—"

Quannah narrowed his eyes and shook his head. His expression became stern.

"Okay," she admitted. "Not an *accident.*"

He grabbed her around the shoulders and squeezed.

"Cold-blooded murder. You be careful, *Winyan;* you be aware. Think."

"Why," she asked, "does life do this to me for absolutely no reason?"

"There's always a reason, but it's up to us to interpret the messages."

"Oh, right, like . . . like . . . bird poop."

CHAPTER
2

In the circle of classrooms called The Mall, willi sat on a hard bench much like those found at bus stops on city streets. These sported the school colors, royal blue and yellow. The Nickleberry mascot, a bright yellow paint horse with blue spots, careened across the backs of the seats. Good grief, even two weeks before school, the cheerleaders had been busy. Willi eyed the footballs hanging from the ceiling with players' names emblazoned on each. She glanced at her watch. Nine-thirty already, and she probably couldn't hope to see home and bath until about midnight as slowly as things were moving. Oh, how good it would feel to sink her aching limbs into a hot bubble bath.

She shook her head. She, along with the rest of the faculty members, gazed at Deputy Sheriff Junior Beans. Willi had a soft spot for this past student, not one of their brightest, but good-hearted and courageous. His eye patch attested to his going into a melee of bikers to save one of Nickleberry's own. He did just that but lost his eye when one of the bikers literally ran over his head. Since then he'd been really slow in words and actions, yet no one complained. He'd saved the

Methodist minister's daughter, and that set plenty fine with folks in Nickleberry, Texas.

Willi nodded to those around her and pulled her bathing robe a little tighter. She supposed Sheriff Tucker would explain in his own good time why she was being kept here with the suspects. Those here now, according to the high school guard—Mortimer Tackett—at the front shack, were on campus at the time of the murder. It had been easy for him to keep track with so few entering during these two weeks prior to school opening. No sir, nobody could fault Mortimer Tackett. He had everyone listed, even those he'd buzzed in and out the back entry. The shock of Tessa Aiken's mutilation and murder kept them quiet for a few moments, but grumblings started as the hours ticked away.

"Damn it all to hell! What kind of a son of a bitch could do this?" Neeper Oxhandler blurted. Willi grimaced. Nickleberry's Oxhandlers never said anything in less than a stentorian yell as if encouraging their namesakes to come in for supper from a mile away. Neeper had on his lab coat, since he'd been called from the science lab. He and his cousin Dan shared the lab as two of the three science teachers on staff. "Damned cold-blooded son of a bitch that could use acid in—"

"I don't want to think about it." Samantha Yannich, the school secretary, screeched this and with jerky movements stumbled from the bench. She ran red manicured nails through her short gray bob. Under a no-smoking sign she lit a cigarette and inhaled as if she were breathing fresh oxygen. The haunted expression veiling her features relaxed.

Willi put a hand on Sammie's thin wrist and pulled her down and hugged her. "Sammie," she said in a low voice so only the secretary could hear, "if you're worried about Tessa being found in Bernie's car, don't. I overheard Sheriff Tucker telling Deputy Beans that Bernie Burkhalter had been questioned, and his alibi was unshakable."

"What?" Sammie asked, and her eyes finally met Willi's gaze. Sammie licked her lips. "What's it to me? What do you mean?"

Willi explained that Superintendent Burkhalter had been in his office talking to Jarnagin Ventnor, the incoming superintendent. She said, "Bernie had left his car in the parking lot. He admitted to a bad habit of leaving the keys, too. But he had no clue as to how Tessa was put in there or whether she got in by herself, perhaps intending to use the car as a means of escape."

Willi imagined the horror of Tessa's last few moments and blinked back tears. She beat her fist on the bench. "I know how Neeper feels. I'm on that angry edge, too. I want to know who could *imagine* doing this to such a fine young woman, much less *doing* it and why. Why?"

Sammie blew smoke in her face. "You wish it had been Bernie Burkhalter, don't you? Why won't people mind their own business and let bygones be bygones?" She stubbed the cigarette out on the bench and started to throw it behind her, but chose the trash can instead. She ran her fingers again through her gray, bobbed hair, clasped her hands behind her back, and walked toward the end of The Mall, away from the benches and the other suspects.

Willi momentarily frowned at the thought of her colleagues as suspects. If she could just get home before the mental and emotional turmoil totally crushed her, she'd never again stick her nose in where it didn't belong. Absolutely not. Ever.

Oh, right. Sure, and nobody in the Lone Star State chewed Red Man tobacco. Might as well be truthful with herself. This wasn't the first time her curiosity had catapulted her into an uncomfortable situation, and it probably wouldn't be the last. So she'd better use her time wisely and put the proverbial thinking cap on. At least the mental exercise would keep her mind from floating to the comforting scene of scented candles, warm waves, and gentle music that *would* have been waiting at home.

Okay, on the opposite bench from her was Neeper Oxhandler. Next to him sat the newest member of the faculty, Saralee York. With not a red hair out of place and long-sleeved creamy pants suit, she could have been a model on break rather than an English teacher. And—Willi rubbed her sun-burned arms—how in Hades did Saralee stay so cool-looking in long sleeves in this Texas heat? Willi admired the intricate old-world ring on Saralee's hand that by means of numerous golden chains connected to a bracelet at the wrist. Tiny emer-alds danced along the chains. Willi pursed her lips. A most unusual but beautiful piece of jewelry.

On the other side of her, Vic Ramirez, legs stretched out and arms behind his head, leaned back against the wall. Willi supposed he'd been at the school in his role of fireman to check the building for fire code violations before the start of classes. Did it on his own and weeks before classes in order to give the principal time to correct any problems. Willi had to admit that some of the previous students like Vic and Neeper and Dan were among those of whom the district could be proud. A shiver ran down her arms. Unless, of course, one of them was capable of mutilating one of their classmates, Tessa Aiken.

Willi peeked along her own bench. Bernie Burkhalter sat beside another former student who worked at one of the local papers, Kassal Heberly. Hortense Horsenettle, the librarian, pushed her red-rimmed glasses up her long nose. She hugged a box of Kleenex tissues to her chest and swiped at her eyes. Obviously, being the one to discover the body, Hortense was more upset than anyone. Sammie Yannich stumbled near, grabbed a tissue, blew her nose, and wiped her eyes.

Willi tilted her head. Odd for Sammie to carry on so about Tessa, considering that when Sammie's child attended Nick-leberry High Sammie had hated the sight of Tessa and her kid together. And it was—Willi recalled—narrow-minded big-otry against the color of Tessa's skin. Sammie had been made to attend a number of special classes on ethnic differences because of her nasty comments. Willi knew, sure as she knew Texas bubbas loved long-neck beer, Sammie still held to her abhorrence of anyone different than herself. So, why the tears? Had to be worry over Burkhalter, despite Sammie's denial.

Willi rose from the bench to get a drink at the water fountain near Sammie, who suddenly turned and hissed. There was no other word for the vitriolic whispered words she said. Sammie repeated again, "Well, guess this brings back fond memories?"

Willi wiped away water that had shot from the fountain onto her forehead.

Neeper said, "What?"

"My kid's accident years ago. You know."

"Surely, you don't compare that accident with . . . with . . . this horrible . . . on purpose . . . No, Mrs. Yannich, don't go there." Neeper backed away from her.

Willi inched closer to the two while pretending to study some of the football artwork hanging nearby.

Sammie plopped herself on the bench. In a more normal volume, she said, "No, no, not really. And the party responsible for that accident is long dead and gone. Let the past alone. You're right. " She got up after only a few seconds and stood in front of Junior Beans. "I need a breath of fresh air, and I need a *full* smoke. Outside. *Now.*"

Junior walked her to the end of The Mall and opened the glass doors, instructing her to stand right outside so he could keep an eye on her and those inside at the same time.

Willi sat in the place Sammie had vacated.

Neeper sighed. "You heard her?"

"Yes, but you could tell she was sorry she'd brought the matter up."

Neeper shifted his muscled legs. "Why are you being asked to stay, Willi? You weren't on the campus today, were you, until you and Quannah drove up after the . . . the atrocity?"

Another officer came down the stairway and approached Willi. A man, perhaps in his late thirties, older than young Beans. Willi had seen him many times but didn't know him. His badge gleamed. She had to squint to see his name: Jon Piedra. Willi smiled as she followed him upstairs. "Unusual spelling of John."

"Yes, ma'am."

"And Piedra?"

"Ma'am?"

"It's Spanish for *rock,* isn't it?"

"Yes, ma'am."

"You're a man of few words, Jon Piedra."

At the landing he turned to look her in the eye. "Might account for me still working in this business after eighteen years." He added a quick smile that disappeared faster than a diving swallowtail.

Willi snapped her fingers. "I've seen your name . . . now where . . . yes, in the *Nickleberry News.* In the art section they print your poetry."

"Yes, ma'am."

"Would you present some of your work to my classes someday?"

"Why, yes ma'am."

Willi blinked, not sure she'd even witnessed the grin. He seemed to have that inner strength she so much admired in Quannah, totally sure of who he was and his purpose in life and focused 100 percent. Often when Quannah's intenseness became awesome, she envisioned him as a bird of prey, a tiger on the hunt, or a wolf. This Jon Piedra put her in mind of a less colorful but no less fearsome creature. Quannah would have said he had Badger Medicine.

"Maybe you'll get to go home soon," he said and opened the door to the upstairs teachers' lounge, annexed for the duration by Sheriff Tucker. The officer nodded, and with a clear, "Ma'am," Deputy Jon Piedra shut the door, walked to a corner where he sat down, crossed an ankle over his leg, and took out a notebook and pen.

Willi walked toward the sheriff, sitting under a ceiling fan, where the scent of Luden's cherry cough drops wafted upward and back down toward her. He rose and offered her the chair next to him. "Miss Willi." A coughing spell interrupted him, he placed another drop in his mouth, got out his green bandanna, and wiped his bulbous nose. "Care for a pop?"

"Pardon?"

He jingled pocket money into the drink machine.

She said, "No. Thanks anyway. I'm so tired and just want to get home and to a bath as soon as you can let me go, which," she said, raising a finger, "shouldn't be long, since I wasn't at the school this afternoon."

He popped the top of his 7UP and peered at her. He leaned forward so only inches separated her tilted nose from his great tuber. "You know, Miss Willi, I've often found your talents useful."

She smiled. "Well, I could do a little research on blood splatter, poisonings—"

"Whoa, hold that galloping horse. You know better than that. Now just dampen that flair of yours for spurring right out of the chute." His beefy finger tapped the end of her nose. "Last February when we had that death over to the construction barns out near the hospital, I had Marty Mason help out some. He's the dispatcher. An insider. See what I mean? You sure came up with the goods months ago during the spring break by getting us authorities on the right track of catching those murdering satanists."

"What does that have to do with me helping now with—"

"You, Miss Willi, are the *insider* here. Mayhap you could give me some background on folks you work with here at Nickleberry High." He grabbed his bandanna in time to catch what must have been a small internal explosion, wiped his watering eyes, and folded the green cloth away.

"You want me to be a snitch?"

"Not a'tall. Piedra, did I say anything to do with being a snitch?"

Willi looked over her shoulder. Jon Piedra said, "No, sir."

The sheriff patted her shoulder with one hand and worried his earlobe with the other as if that would conjure up the needed word. "Consultant. Yep, that's what I need, so's I won't step on these touchy scholastic toes and souls."

"Yes, Sheriff, I could do that. I might need to come into the office now and again, touch base with your investigators, your deputies, and we'll all pitch our findings in together, and—"

"Miss Willi." Sheriff Brigham Tucker's tone of voice dampened her enthusiasm.

"Okay, just what do you want?"

"Sit in on the interviews. Speak up and say things another way if you see I'm a-getting on the wrong side of folks. If after a talk with these folks, I have questions, may-hap you can supply the answers without having to call them back in again. Things like that, Miss Willi." He leaned back in the chair and sighed, seeming to give her space and time to think. To Jon Piedra, he said, "And we do know she's innocent of this here horror herself, right?"

Jon Piedra nodded. "Yes, sir. Twenty-five or more wit-nesses accounted for her being out at the lake since early morning. Then she was in a meeting for . . . uh . . . the Celtic Irish Fling fair. Most of the day was in the company of your nephew, sir."

"See, Miss Willi, no reason you can't help us out this eve-ning. You've helped on a couple of other cases . . . uh . . . in one way or another."

"Sheriff, you know my bent is toward getting so involved, you'll soon be barking at me to get off your terri-tory, but this time . . . I'm hesitant because . . . well, these are my friends, and—"

"Knowed you were a loyal friend to them, but to my way of thinking, I reckon one is the culprit. Wouldn't you want to help me get the right critter with as little inconvenience to everyone's lives as possible?"

"Well, since you put it that way, I—"

"Mighty fine. I'll treat you just like Marty Mason. Going to deputize you. Makes it more legal like to have you sit in on interviews, you see? For later court purposes and what all. Simple, that's what it is, simple."

"Simple." *Sure.* Mentally picturing the scales of justice, she placed her friends' and colleagues' feelings on one side. They weren't, after all, likely to appreciate her being privy to personal tidbits. On the other side, she imagined her students who had over the years become bound to her with something akin to the umbilical cord, and her rage was strong as any natural mother's. Blue blazes and hades, she wanted to know who had scarred and left the young attorney to die, who had abandoned a life so heartlessly. "Simple," she repeated and nodded.

Sheriff Tucker deputized her and told Deputy Piedra, "Escort the next lady in."

Willi moved her chair to the side and back to be less obtrusive. Saralee York smoothed the jacket of her cream-colored pants suit and smiled timidly at Willi before she sat down in front of the sheriff.

"Mayhap," Sheriff Tucker said about a half-hour later, "you'll be patient, Ms. York, and just let me make sure I understand." He worried his left ear with his huge paw. "You were in your classroom all afternoon. You left it long enough to get a Coke from the commons area, what you all call The Mall."

"Yes, Sheriff Tucker," Saralee answered in a low monotone. "Actually, you know, I picked up materials from the office afterwards. Remember, Ms. Gallagher? Those papers—the ones from the Irish Fling Fair Committee— were in the office. Something about reading Irish stories or serving the shepherd's pot pies."

Willi considered the new English teacher and sighed. Again the thought that Saralee would never hold the kids' attention more than three minutes running with that monotonous voice made Willi cringe. "That's right. I did leave the information. We hope you'll participate." *But not reading the cards. The young woman's voice would put the most persistent metaphysics hunter into a trance all right, a snoring trance.*

"Perhaps." To the sheriff Saralee said, "You recall, I've told other officers all this three or four times." Saralee's voice actually had a tinge of exasperation. Maybe there'd be hope if those kids got her riled enough. Willi shook the meandering ideas away and concentrated.

"Yes, ma'am." Sheriff Tucker pulled out a fresh red-checkered bandanna in time to save Willi from the aftereffects of his sneeze as he turned his head. "Sorry." He refolded the cloth. "Now, Ms. York, I have to say I admire you."

"Oh? Why?"

"You're so calm. Most young women would be nervous as a chili pepper in a stir-fry skillet, having to see such a thing, answer questions and what all."

Saralee's burnished hair fell forward across a face Willi considered too heavily made-up, but attractive nonetheless. The redhead ducked her head so Willi scooted closer to hear better. Saralee said, "Actually, you know, I'm more shocked than . . . than emotional. I've only met Tessa Aiken once, in fact. Of course, her manner of death was so . . . unnatural." She wrapped her arms around herself and shivered like a cat having a bad dream.

"My understanding is Miss Willi introduced you all."

"Miss Willi?"

"Sorry, ma'am, my name for her since she was a young-gun'. Ms. Gallagher."

"Yes, she's been kind that way."

Willi knew a cue when she heard one, nodded at the sheriff, and said, "No problem, Saralee, it's been my pleasure. Just so I can figure out the details—you know me and exact details—what were the times you left your room today?"

Willi glanced at the perspiration trickling down the side of Saralee's cheek, taking a rivulet of the thickly applied matte makeup toward her roll-neck collar. Willi got up and pulled the chain on the ceiling fan to increase the speed. That young woman was going to have to learn to dress as if she were in Texas, not the North Pole, for Pete's sake.

Saralee said, "Thanks, Ms. Gallagher."

"Willi, Willi, please."

"Certainly. Willi."

"And so you left the classroom when?" Willi asked again.

"This isn't going to be very helpful," Saralee said in her lackluster voice. "I chose today, Friday, to do some prep work, knowing that everyone would be out at the lake all day and evening and tomorrow for the opening of the Irish Fling.

I was so busy, you know. Actually, I lost track of time. Didn't even stop for lunch. I'm sorry, Willi. Sheriff Tucker, I'm really sorry."

"Like me, I guess," Sheriff Tucker said, "Miss Willi was expecting a mite more from a scientific type of mind."

Saralee's auburn hair swirled as she turned back to face Tucker. "Pardon?"

Willi said, "Saralee is going to teach sophomore English, right?"

"Well, yes, but—"

"But," Sheriff Tucker said worrying his earlobe, "you got some degree in science, too?"

"A minor. I've never taught in that field. After this many years, probably forgot all I learned in those college courses."

Willi tapped her foot and crossed her arms. Oh, she ought to know by now; Sheriff Tucker was wily enough to know some of the answers before he asked the questions. And he claimed to know so little about the staff. Right, and west Texas winds never blow dry. Willi glanced around at Jon Piedra. Yeah, he probably brought that info to the sheriff during one of his many trips back and forth. As if reading her mind, Deputy Piedra peered up from his notes and nodded. Willi huffed and glared back around at the sheriff. Great. So that was how it was going to be helping out with the interviews. Token female, that's what she was serving as tonight. Ornery men. All she was likely to get out of this was a lot of frustration and unending suspicions about all her coworkers.

Considering Saralee's bent head, Willi sighed. There'd been no reason for the instructor to let Willi know earlier about the other degree. Willi had subjects she was qualified to teach but didn't, since they had so many students in the English courses. Well, she wasn't going to be pushed to a shadowy corner. She got up, shoved her chair right next to Saralee and right smack-dab in front of Sheriff Tucker. He wanted help, he was going to get it . . . and she was going to do it her way, thank you very much, and move over Colombo, Magnum, and Kojak.

"Are you sure," she asked, "you didn't meet anyone while outside your classroom?"

"Yes. Earlier I'd been out at the lake with two other teachers. Dan Oxhandler and his cousin, I think . . . can't remember his—"

"Neeper?"

"Neeper Oxhandler, yes. Aren't they the two cousins who teach some of the science classes?"

"Right. And this was what time?"

"When I went to get a soft drink. Well, they came back from the lake maybe two, three hours after I returned."

"Around two o'clock, maybe three?"

"Ms. Gallagher . . . uh, Willi, actually, you know, I don't remember the time. I'd been out at the lake before lunch and then rushed to get some work done here. I'm not sure."

"Didn't mean to upset you, Saralee. The reason," Willi said, "is I know it couldn't have been earlier because both Neeper and Dan were in some of the prelim boat races at the Nickleberry Lake. We're calling those the Galway Bay Relays, and each of the boats has to have an Irish name, at least for the day and—"

Sheriff Tucker cleared his throat and stared pointedly at her.

"I'm a bit wound up about the Irish Fling festivities."

"Understandable, seeing these cultural fairs are bringing the different communities together to work, sort of like we're all doing here."

"Yes, and it's just our second one, the first being the Latvian Night of Lights last year. But, as you say, we've more important things here," Willi said. "Anyway, the Oxhandlers came to the high school to work in midafternoon sometime after the races."

Tucker sat back and pursed his lips, but nodded—a sign to keep going. Darn right. There just might be a few smidgens of info of which neither the sheriff nor his deputy were as yet privy. She patted Saralee's sleeve. The redhead flinched as if Willi had grasped her hard. Willi turned loose, saying, "I'm sorry."

"I guess . . . I guess . . . I *am* a little nervous."

"Saralee, I am, too. Not to worry. Let's face it; we'll all be jumpy until this is cleared up." Willi maintained eye contact with the brown-eyed teacher but didn't reach out and touch her again. "When you met the Oxhandlers, how long did you all stay together? Until you finished your soft drinks?"

"Just a minute, maybe two. They already had their drinks in hand and were heading toward the office. I continued through The Mall toward the Coke machines."

"Yep," Sheriff Tucker said, standing, "seems right clear."

Saralee stood also and walked toward the door.

"Dangnab it, Ms. York, I just remembered. One more thing?"

"Yes, sir?"

He wiggled his earlobe with his massive paw and yawned. " 'Scuse me. Where is your classroom? Thought all the English classes was downstairs and science and computer labs up here."

Like a *Vogue* model on the runway, Saralee made a 180-degree turn toward him. "Actually, there's a mix since we're at over-capacity student-wise. My room is a door down from the main science lab."

"She's right," Willi offered. "Enrollment skyrocketed with the Terraceland additions of hundreds of HUD tracts and mobile homes out east of town. We've filled every nook and cranny. One of the math teachers is on this floor, too, and most of them are in the other of the high school's two blocks of buildings. You know, Sheriff Tucker, the other one is part of the old school, now connected by a covered walkway."

"A-yep, yeah, I recall that. Well, ladies, makes sense to use every bit of space, economy being what it is nowadays. Makes sense to let this young lady go for now, too."

Saralee again pivoted and had her hand on the doorknob. Willi spoke up quickly. "Wait. One more question. How'd you hear about . . . about the incident?"

Saralee sighed and peered over her shoulder. "I heard the screams. Hortense's screams, like everyone else."

"You were," asked Willi, "back upstairs by then?"

"Yes, yes I was. I remember that. Now, I'm really tired. It's close to midnight. I am sorry I'm so little help, really, and I do want you to find whoever killed Tessie Aiken."

Deputy Jon Piedra rose and placed his hand on top of hers on the doorknob. "Don't worry. He won't be bothering any other women if Sheriff Tucker has any say-so, but . . . keep your doors locked, be sensible with precautions, and let us know if you think of anything else."

His soft cadence was so soothing to the ear, Willi wanted to hear him talk more. She noticed his hand atop Saralee's. Hmmmm. That young woman could do worse than a well-educated man, a law officer of the highest standing in the community. Willi would have to remember to mention that he had poetry periodically published as well.

Jon Piedra said, "I'll see you out to your car before I get the next person up here."

Sheriff Tucker nodded. "Good idea, Deputy, as always thinking a step ahead. Guess it'd be fine to walk each lady out tonight. Might cut down on the worrisome jitters. Show Dan and Neeper Oxhandler in one at a time when you return."

"Yes, sir."

Rather than alleviating the nervousness, Deputy Piedra's and Sheriff Tucker's reassurances seemed to have the opposite effect. Willi gasped at the shock on Saralee's face. It struck folks like that sometimes—*delayed shock,* wasn't it called? Perhaps the possibility of personal danger brought the realization of her own vulnerability home to Saralee.

Certainly, Piedra's remarks made Willi taste bile. Her mind must have circled around the facts like turkey buzzards—floating, drifting with the wind, swinging gently down from the sky to finally stand upon the prize of dead flesh—the reality that a killer—a *cold-blooded murderer*—was among those here in Nickleberry High. When she blinked and looked up, Dan Oxhandler sat in the chair vacated by Saralee, Neeper pulled up another after asking if the cousins could both be together, and Piedra dropped a note in front of the sheriff before again perching in his corner roost.

Dan took a long sip of water from a bottle of Evian. He wiped his mouth with the back of his hand.

Sheriff Tucker took the Oxhandlers through the same type of questions the others had had to answer. Sometimes he seemed slower than a hound dog after the chase; other times that bloodhound got on the scent. Never taking his eyes from them, he tapped the paper on the desk. "This here, gentlemen, indicates from the first brief prelim look-see the burns were caused by sulfuric acid." Tucker stretched, yawned, and tilted the rear legs of his chair at a forty-degree angle. When he suddenly crashed the front legs to the floor, Willi jumped and Dan flinched. The sheriff spat the question in Neeper's direction. "Where might you get such a substance here on campus?"

"That's no secret." Neeper sucked on his upper lip, glanced at Willi and back at Tucker. "No secret. We keep some in the science department stockroom."

"And where, Mr. Neeper Oxhandler, might that be?"

Willi sat up straighter. Why did Tucker call him *Mister* in that cold voice as if he'd taken an instant dislike to a man who was one of her coworkers and former students? A cold brick seemed to settle in her stomach, rough corners grinding at her innards. She blinked her gritty eyes and tried to think what she could do to change the frightening turn of questioning into something less threatening for her comfortable world and for the cousins.

Neeper answered the sheriff. "The stockroom is a long, narrow area running directly behind all the science labs on the north side of the hallway."

Sheriff Tucker drew forth a plastic bag containing a bottle, not a small vial, as Willi had expected. "Mayhap this bottle come from your stockroom? What might *your* thoughts be on that?" he asked, turning his attention to the other cousin.

Dan, his ever-present baseball cap settled on his knee, said, "This container resembles those we have, but it's a common type and could be found in any lab."

"And did you have reason to get this bottle out today?"

"No, I did not. The stockroom isn't exclusively mine, Sheriff Tucker."

Willi licked her lips. "Sheriff, all the teachers—the science teachers, that is—have keys to the lab, not just the Oxhandlers."

Sheriff Tucker worried his earlobe and nodded. "Good point, Miss Willi, surely is. I just thought one of them might have the only key, but I understand you all would need access. I'm just glad this kind of stuff—acids and what not—are always kept under lock and key, yes sir-ree-bob."

Neeper sighed. "Under normal circumstances that's true."

Willi and Tucker said in unison, "Normal circumstances?"

"It's two weeks before classes start. We're lax during these weeks. Lots of deliveries being made, we're in and out checking orders, reshelving items, trashing out-of-date or broken equipment."

"No students on campus now, then?" Sheriff Tucker asked in his most dangerous on-point bloodhound bass.

Dan lowered his chin to his chest. "A few office aides. But those students are chosen because we trust them. Good kids."

"Uh-hmmm." Tucker let that hang in the air so long Willi could hear Piedra's scribbling behind her. The sheriff took an agonizingly long minute to run his hands through his gray banty-tipped red curls. "Let me just do a recap here. Not only could each science teacher unlock his individual door and wander through the whole length of the stockroom, but also so could anyone else who traipsed in while all this shuffling of beakers and poisons was a-going on. Mayhap another teacher or one of the board members on campus going to get a Coke or just looking for one of the science instructors? That about right?"

Like their yoked and paired namesakes, the cousins nodded in unison. Willi slumped her shoulders, the tired just washing all over her. Sheriff Tucker's concern was justified. Anyone in the building, *anyone* had the opportunity to get the sulfuric acid.

"Miss Willi, you got some questions?"

"One or two. So, as far as you two are concerned, all these questions are a moot point since you didn't arrive until *after* the body was discovered." The weight of the heavy brick seemed to lighten, and she smiled at her colleague.

Neeper said, "Willi, we came back before the discovery but not together. Dan's been here most of the afternoon, but I first went to lunch at uncle's place."

Sheriff Tucker patted his stomach. "Oxhandler's Barbecue and Emporium. Your Uncle Ozzie knows good vittles, he does. Sure am partial myself to Friday's special; fried venison and quail pie. Would set mighty fine about now, I can tell you."

Neeper said, "You're right about that, Sheriff. It was delicious."

"Yes-sir-ree-bob. Bet you're some tuckered, and I got more anxious folks waiting downstairs. Keep yourself to home and town in case we have questions later."

The giant cousins stood. Dan said, "Absolutely. Couldn't leave town anyway. I've been roped into being one of the dancers in a competition at the Irish Fling Festival. Perhaps the same person who got your nephew involved volunteered me." He stared at Willi.

With a smile full of sunshine and goodwill, she said, "Do tell. What are friends for? Wouldn't want to leave my *amigo* out of things."

"So appreciated." Dan sighed and added, "After all, Tessa Aiken was in my graduating class. I'll do whatever I can."

"Me, too," Neeper intoned.

When Jon Piedra escorted them outside, Willi peered at the sheriff.

"Now, what," he said, "do you make of that?"

"Pardon?"

"Never on a Friday, nope, never."

"Never what on a Friday, Sheriff Tucker?"

"Ozzie hates venison, don't believe in shooting little quail, even if he is from the clan of the Oxhandler hunters."

"You mean—?"

"I mean Neeper Oxhandler, who ought to know better, didn't eat no venison nor quail on this Friday or any other day at his uncle's Emporium."

The brick in her stomach developed into a chunk of heavy concrete. "Do tell." Shocked by Neeper's lie, she opened and shut her mouth like some catfish thrown on the riverbank. Finally, she managed, "Perhaps a local hunter brought some in, and Ozzie made an exception."

"You always have had that quality."

"What?"

"Ability to stick to something even if you don't like it. You don't never take the road of least resistance. Curiosity gets you into a heap of trouble as we both know, but that bulldog quality gets you through the mess." He pulled his earlobe. "Ain't got curiosity, can't get passion for learning things. Ain't a bulldog about the learning, curiosity won't be nothing but a frustration." He frowned and wiggled around in his chair, peered at the door as if wishing Jon Piedra would walk through, and coughed.

"Sheriff, was there something else? You've changed your mind, maybe, and just don't know how to tell me you don't want me to help anymore with the interviews?"

"No. No, no, not a'tall. In fact, wanted to tell you for a long time how fine you are. Especially, now that you and that rambling nephew of mine seem to be fanning your tail feathers at each other. The short of it is, Miss Willi, you got integrity. Big word for an old country boy, one who got to be sheriff before they started all these regulations about advanced studies and degrees. Didn't say *honesty. Integrity.* Difference there, you know?"

"Confucius noted some slight distinction."

"That old feller was right smart, then. Honesty is telling others the truth of a matter. Integrity is sometimes harder."

"I think I know now, Sheriff. Integrity is telling the truth to oneself."

"Yes, sir . . . ah-choo . . . I mean, ma'am." His bandanna was again put into service. "Ain't going to be easy being truthful with yourself, with your coworkers and close friends involved."

"I managed just fine when I helped with the Wiccan murders."

"You were pushed into that because you were on the scene at most of them."

"I see, Sheriff. You're giving me a way out. If I stop now, I won't have to ask my friends obnoxious and intrusive questions nor worry about small white lies that don't amount to a pot of chili beans."

The sheriff's hound dog eyes drooped. He sighed. "I do want your help on this one, but only when I say . . . like in these here interviews. I don't want you a-doing stuff on the side and getting into any trouble. Quannah's up in Tarrant County and elsewheres. I can't say as I'm always available . . . if . . . if . . ."

"If I were to get into trouble?"

"Mayhap, you won't, but considering your record . . ."

"I am not backing out. Tessa Aiken was one of our finest students. She made Nickleberry proud. Sheriff, she was one of those beautiful black women who could have chosen any path—modeling, TV work—but she chose the law in one of the toughest of Texas cities—Austin, the capital. She chose law work because she believed in the ultimate victory of good over evil. I'll do whatever I can to help, to show her the value she held most dear was a star worth trying to catch."

"And what if you find out she wasn't as . . . good as you want to believe?"

"All of us have a shadow side. Quannah often tells me the story of the White and Black Wolf."

"Yes, life at one moment in time may depend upon the one we feed the most—the pretty or the ugly side." He nodded. "Mayhap it'll work out fine. So, you don't mind getting to the truth of that venison and quail pie story?"

"Uh, well . . . no. I'm sure there's a reasonable explanation."

He worried his left earlobe. "Then, we're gonna talk with these other folks in the morning. Right here again. I'll have Jon Piedra tell them. You get along home, Miss Willi. We'll see you bright and early. Always keep that story in mind, now, hear—that one about the two Wolves, the Black and the White? Hear now?"

CHAPTER
3

By one in the morning Willi's eyes were grainy with lack of sleep, but her nerves were so taut she could have been strung on a rock guitar. She squinted while driving the last miles toward home. And the story of the Black and White Wolf played over and over in her head just as Quannah had told her one night last week while they sat on a blanket together underneath the stars. Because he had been angry at the injustice of a felon being let loose due to a technicality, she had thought the moments beneath what he called the Star Nation would be soothing for him.

He said, "Ah, Willi, you would have loved my grand-fathers."

"Grandfathers as in two, three?"

"Tunkasila," he said, "like the name of your stone, can refer to any older one who guides you. I had a special *tunkasila* who taught me so much through his stories." Quannah's voice and heart drifted back to those childhood days as he related the words of his older advisor:

"Son, we've all held hate in our hearts for those who

have taken much from us. But such an emotion will wear a heart down. The hate does not hurt the wrongdoer."

"Grandfather, I cannot think of anything else."

"Little one, is it like you have a poison inside you?"

"Exactly, yes. You understand such hate?"

"You wish your enemy would die, yet you are the one taking the poison."

The young Quannah bowed his head. "But, it is like two wolves, one beautiful and white snarling against one dark and evil and—"

"Yes, my son, you have the answer. You just aren't interpreting it well. The White Wolf is good. He lives in harmony with all. He will fight when and only when he must and only in an honorable way. The Black Wolf is angry and fights all. He cannot even reason due to his hate, and yet this great anger changes nothing."

"Grandfather, it is hard to live with both of these snarling within. I am afraid. Which one inside me—the White Wolf or the Black Wolf—will win?"

As her car's tires spun along the tarmac, she smiled and relaxed. She still remembered the answer the *tunkasila* in Quannah's story gave.

Who will win?

The one you feed. The one you feed.

Willi understood how Quannah had felt. Such a battle drove her now to work with Sheriff Tucker. She sighed. Perhaps two snarling wolves were fighting within the heart and mind of a certain killer, too. As she had told Sheriff Tucker earlier, all had a shadow side. Now, they just had to discover that Black Wolf hidden within someone, a colleague, a friend, perhaps. She drove over hilly Licorice Lane to the farm some twenty minutes outside of Nickleberry proper. A network of twists and curves, it had years ago claimed the lives of her folks. She drove the ten miles carefully. She had to calm down so she could sleep when she got home. Oh my gosh, and she had to get up in less than five hours. Her worst dilemma was to decide whether to bathe and go immediately

to bed or to prepare the Irish apple and potato cakes she had
promised for tomorrow's retirement picnic for Superintendent Bernie Fritzpatrick Burkhalter coupled with opening
night festivities of the Irish Fling Festival. He'd offered to MC
for the opening night ceremonies, one—if she'd also make
it his going-away dinner and, two—if Willi would do the
daytime water races and such. The new super, Jarnagin
Ventnor, had asked her to host an Irish cook-off contest at
her home the next day to introduce him socially and to help
the Kachelhoffers with the tearoom out at the lake tomorrow
evening. Ought to be an entertaining Saturday fete with everyone's mind on the murder. Willi changed position to ease
the ache between her shoulder blades. "Oh, yes, I definitely
need my Calgon bath beads and warm water."

She rolled her window down, the better to take in the
heady scents of oak and pine, rich loam and smoke from
someone's fireplace. Mesquite scent meant someone was
barbecuing. When she drove into her gravel drive, lights
shone from the old two-story farmhouse she called home.
Freshly painted a country eggshell with speckled brown
trim and roofing, the house offered welcome respite underneath its guardian cottonwoods and huge oaks.

She grinned as she pressed the control to raise the garage
door, an electronic convenience Quannah had installed for
her one weekend. Said he didn't want to worry about her getting in and out to open the thing. She shook her head. Texas
Ranger, city police, or county—they all had cop minds. Bless
them. She had protested. The only things likely to attack her
while opening would be a possum, armadillo, or skunk. Ah
well, he'd won the battle and seemed to take such pride in
doing the job for her. She'd gained far more than the convenience; she'd garnered a special warmth from the knowledge
that he cared, really cared about her safety.

That comfort zone continued as she went into the kitchen
to check on that bit of fur, her dachshund Charlie Brown.
She continued through the dining room and into what she
called her nookery—her small library where a soothing
light above the aquarium highlighted her finned friends,

Beowulf and Chaucer. After feeding them, she headed up the stairway of thirteen steps. She took an extra long stride so as to step on only twelve of them. She blamed her superstitious daddy, Phidias Gallagher, for that eccentricity. For a nanosecond she considered going back down the stairs to put the apples and potatoes to boil for the cake mixture. But with one humongous yawn, her dilemma ended, she poured rose-scented Calgon beads in the bathwater and sighed with contentment underneath the sweet-smelling water.

At last snuggled beneath soft flannel sheets, she glanced at the recently installed phone—another insistence of Quannah's. *Winyan, you need a phone upstairs, too. An intruder could have you blocked off from downstairs.* The cop mentality at work again. And that protective streak, which Willi enjoyed so much, although she'd not let him know that it mattered. Big Chief's ego was in mighty fine shape as it was. Oh dear God, how she missed him. The message light blinked. She punched it and heard his voice. "Just letting you know my flight was fine. I'll pick the perp up in the morning, *Winyan*—Woman-Full-of-Curiosity. Don't know how long booking will take ... so you'll see me when you see me. I will be there in a couple of days, in time for the jig contest. I *have* been practicing with the tape the Oxhandlers made." There was a pause and then a quickly stated, "See that star twinkling outside your window? That's me winking at you, Gallagher."

She sighed and drifted into deep slumber only to be disturbed about three hours later.

"Ohhhhh," she groaned and pushed at some monstrosity. Willi opened one eye. What had awakened her? Uck. Felt like wet sandpaper on her face. She turned on the light and received another lick in the face from a long, pink snout. "Rose Pig? What—?" Willi finally got her mouth unstuck from sleep's hold, but she couldn't seem to get her other eye open. "Elba forgot to lock you in again, didn't she? Okay, okay, we can handle this. Just got to get you back home."

She imagined the Kachelhoffer sisters' place about two miles away. Yes, the two good-hearted white witches were probably sitting around their table with Clyde, Agatha's cat familiar, staring at the tarot cards. Elba's more eccentric familiar, Rose Pig, should be snuggled across Elba's round feet. Yet Rose Pig's bristly pink form gyrated around Willi's bedroom.

Willi rolled out of bed and sat with her head in her hands. "How did you get in, much less upstairs?" She reached for the phone to call Elba. It was a moment slower than what it took to boil a three-minute egg before it seeped through Willi's fogged brain that the phone line was dead.

"Aha. We've had a storm. You broke out of your pen. You ran wildly. Scared, you came to the first recognizable place. Well, Rose Pig, you aren't a little piglet anymore, and I'm not pig-sitting. We'll have to get you back to the Kachelhoffers'. I'm not going to change clothes just to put you in the pickup for a three-minute ride." Willi grabbed her robe and stumbled around like a one-eyed robotic creation with all the chips malfunctioning. Rose Pig's squeals escalated into a high vibrato that could shatter any respectable crystal. Above the piggish caterwauling, something downstairs crashed. Willi stood still to face a quieted Rose Pig with ears at attention and pink snout in the air.

Willi sighed. "You brought a friend to the party, didn't you? If that damned cat Clyde is down there doing unspeakable things in my library nookery . . . I'll . . ." She could have held on to that idea if she hadn't glanced outside and seen the stars twinkling in a clear sky with the trees standing still and stately. No storm clouds. No high rain. "So no wind blew open the door."

Her bedside light flickered once—twice. Darkness wrapped around her. Willi inched her bare foot toward the stairway to try that light. The click sounded as loud as a firecracker going off in a church sanctuary, but she received no illumination from Heaven on high or on the stairway.

She whispered, "This is not good." She wished she had grabbed her *Tunkasila* stone—her Teaching-Protecting Stone Quannah had given her long ago. Just its touch calmed and centered her.

Rose Pig didn't care for the dark either. Screeching as only a frightened sow can, the pig hurtled into Willi, knocking her down the steps—all thirteen. A sickening bolt of pain shot through her funny bone; a knee went instantly numb. Why the rest of her abused body didn't succumb, she had no idea, since she landed atop the entire three hundred pounds of Rose Pig. Another item crashed to the floor to Willi's left, definitely somewhere in the living room.

Rose Pig staggered upward with Willi astride her. Her royal pinkness careened into the lamp table. Framed photos and knickknacks clattered, glass tinkled into tiny pieces. Willi rolled off the pig's back and plopped onto the floor facedown. Moonlight coming through the open front door allowed her to see as Rose Pig gifted her with a sandpapery kiss. With ham haunches moving like pistons on drive speed, Rose Pig bolted for the great outdoors.

Willi pulled air into her lungs, whimpered, and rubbed her backside. On hands and knees, she touched the hardwood section of the entryway, located the carpeted area of the living room, and blindly reached her arms out to get her bearings along the edges of furniture. Silence surrounded her. That and a breeze coming through the front door. She held a slender hand over her heart. Everything had happened so fast. Clambering off her knees, she stood. More than likely Elba or Aggie, who did the housework, forgot to lock the doors. Rose Pig had done the rest.

But . . . the lights? The phone line . . . dead?

Willi's heart fluttered beneath her hand. She groped along the living room wall for the switch.

Click. Click.

Nothing. Nada. Kaput.

A rustle melded with the sighing wind. She froze, ears straining. Now her heartbeat fluttered like a full-winged monarch trapped beneath her hand. Poe's words rose eerily to mind: *"And the silken sad uncertain rustling . . . of each curtain."* Was it her overdeveloped imagination, or was someone in the room with her? Her eyes widened to take in

as much moonlight as possible to still her "fantastic terrors
never felt before."

Thump.

Thump? Curtains don't thump. A shiver ran down her
spine. Her only weapon, her father's pistol, lay upstairs
underneath lacy panties and teddies. "Useless," she whispered. Both the lace and the ancient firearm. Next time
Quannah offered to give target practice, she'd bet all her
lacy finery before she refused. Thinking of him brought the
idea of balance and Sacred Breath to mind. She breathed in
slowly and out a number of times. No more rustling, no
more thumps. Probably just a magazine with pages ruffled
by the wind finally toppled off the coffee table.

As her muscles relaxed, the butterfly tappings diminished. Okay, she had to think what to do next, and the most
logical—

What was that?

Something . . . someone knocked into the couch; she
could feel the tremble of the furniture against her knee.
Willi turned toward the door. *Get out, get out, get out. Run
to the Kachelhoffers'.* Her hand touched the cold edge of
the doorframe. Behind her a vase crashed to the floor,
splintering despite the cushioning carpet.

A body, hard and lean, crashed against her, pushed her
backward and down toward the carpeted stairway steps.

A swoosh, a slam. Quiet reigned, and her head hit against
step number thirteen. She managed to stumble out to the
porch in time to see one lanky figure in clothes so bright she
looked like a low-flying parrot. Beside Agatha stood her
sister Elba, short and round, and a sight for teary eyes. Willi
grinned as they tromped onto the wraparound porch. "I suppose," Willi said, "you're looking for one wayward sow?"

With hands on her hips, Elba yelled out into the first
light of dawn, "Sue-weee." Gentle oinks and the tapping of
hooves announced Rose Pig's arrival from the south-side
porch by the kitchen. "I was worried as an elephant in the
graveyard, as bothered as a tick without no dog, near concerned as a gator watching them little 'uns wiggle away

forever." She grabbed Rose Pig, put a huge collar around
the sow's neck, and led her over to Willi. Then and only
then, did she reply. "You okay?"

Willi recounted the pig tale while Elba located the
breaker box and switched the breaker. By the time Willi finished the story, she had boiled the potatoes and apples, set
out the sultanas, sugar, butter, and eggs. Agatha had somehow placed orange juice and a Mexican omelet in front of
her while Elba called the phone company. She said, "Nope,
nobody else's phone is off. They's sending a feller round
about to check, but I done looked at the box aside the house.
Somebody cut them wires sure as grass grows green, taters
grows white, and turds comes out—"

"Sister!"

"Elba!" Willi exclaimed over Agatha's admonition.
Nothing they had said seemed to change Elba from spout-
ing out some of her more earthy comparisons. Willi took
a deep breath. "So someone cut the lines. That's not good."

Elba stood with arms akimbo. Agatha crossed hers. Her
polka-dotted chartreuse scarf used as a belt between purple
skirt and green blouse, slapped and snapped in the morning
breeze. Both Kachelhoffer sisters glared at her. "Willi,"
Agatha said in her softer, more refined tones, "what have
you gotten yourself into now?"

"Nothing." She opened her eyes wide and splayed the
fingers of one hand across her chest. "Nothing."

"Nothing." Elba snorted. "Your nookery's torn to Hell
and back. Phone line cut. Door opened. Glass broken.
Someone knocked you down. Nothing?"

"Willi," Agatha said, "someone purposely let Rose Pig
out and took her old leash. We think someone led her here,
maybe to make you think it was an accidental break-in.
I've already called Brigham."

Willi finished her omelet and stood up. "I wish you
hadn't. It was probably kids playing pranks or, worst-case
scenario, someone looking for money tucked away or looking for something to sell for quick money."

"I suggested as much to Brigham, but he said this was

way too far out in the country to attract that sort." Agatha smiled each time Sheriff Brigham Tucker's name passed her lips. "Brigham said something about you helping with another murder case, that poor Tessa Aiken girl."

"Grown woman and now an attorney . . . *was* an attorney in Austin. She's India Lou's niece. You all remember her, don't you?"

"Oh, no, poor child," Agatha said.

"Poor India Lou," Elba said.

Willi nodded. "Anyhow, the sheriff just wants me to visit with folks, nothing more. Now, I've got to get these cakes made for the Irish Fling Festival today. We're doing a double-header with the super's retirement activities at the same time. I'll make an extra couple to take to India Lou, too. She was going to bring Irish currant tarts and a carrageen pudding, but I'm sure she won't now. Tessa was her only kin in the state, but I believe there's her older brother in the army or navy somewhere. Yes, Terrance."

Elba said, "We'll go out with you when you get ready. We made rhubarb fool and farmers loaf. Like you, we made extras to take to India Lou. Family or no, she'll have a passel of her church folks and neighbors in the next few days."

Agatha said, "We know someone who might very well help with the Fling if you were to help her." She fluttered her scarf over one lanky shoulder.

Elba said, "Not now. Willi has too much on her mind. But . . . soon."

Agatha played with her dangling earrings. "Don't know what got me on that tangent anyway."

"I do," said Elba. "I was telling you about the poor toothless lady out to the Meadowbrook Senior Citizens' Home. I wish they wouldn't take their teeth away. Something like that changes the whole way a body looks. We think she could be the same girl we knew so long ago. We'll find out for sure before telling Willi more."

Willi stepped in. "Excuse me, but could we go down memory lane later? I have a lot to do, and so do you all before we can pull this together tonight."

Elba and Agatha, Rose Pig in tow, wandered off to their disreputable pickup. Willi wondered how she was going to get through all the details she needed to attend to and somehow pay attention to everything everyone said. All she really wanted was that Calgon experience with one Lakota-speaking Texas Ranger beside her. And for Quannah she'd give up the Calgon in less time than it took to say, "Rodeo riders run rampant in rough riding terrain."

Just before Elba reached the pickup, she turned around and said, "Oh, yeah, that handsome gun-totin' lawman called us about ten minutes afore we started out. Just had one of those feelings, he said, that you's in trouble, worried 'cause he couldn't reach you by phone."

Willi groaned. "And you said?"

"We seen the trouble around you in the cards and the crystal ball ourselves. Told him we'd go check. He'll ring us again, he said." Elba hefted herself up into the pickup. She slammed the door. "When you gonna let that man move in with you here? Half the time he's here, half the time in that apartment. He'd be a mighty nice comfort to have around."

Willi's cheeks pinked up. She turned away and ignored Elba's question. Under her breath she mumbled, "Mainly, because he hasn't brought up the subject, and by damned I won't ask, if he doesn't."

An hour later, the phone wires repaired, the Irish apple and potato cakes ready, she got in her diesel pickup rather than her car figuring it would hold the Kachelhoffer sisters and all the picnic paraphernalia better than her small car. Never comfortable driving the big vehicle, she roared down the drive and the two miles to the white witches' domain, a cottage they called Frogs' Feet.

Every foot of both miles her mind kept colliding with the fact that her good friend, Neeper Oxhandler, had lied, not just to the sheriff, but . . . but to her . . . and about something so insignificant as what he ate on Friday. She could call him and just out-and-out ask him when she reached the Kachelhoffers' or tackle him at the picnic. Sitting straighter to see over the hood of the monster truck, she groaned.

Either way would be uncomfortable, but . . . but eyeball to eyeball was the right way. That decided, she wrestled with the steering wheel.

At last she drove down the short but enchanting driveway of Frogs' Feet with a wooden water wheel and brook cascading over rock on one side and weeping willows on the other. She killed the engine and sat a moment enjoying the sweep of the trees. Quannah would have insisted the willows be shown honor as one of our Standing People by mentally capitalizing the Willow. And today, they seemed as if they were comforting, were bending over to embrace and give shadow to confusion and grief. Mercy, she hadn't given in to the grief she harbored, only to the anger. Hell's bells, anger would serve her just damned fine right now. Guess she'd be feeding the Black Wolf for today. She blinked back the burn of tears and honked the horn.

After depositing all the food in the backseat of the truck cab, Agatha and Elba clambered into the Ford. Elba snorted and crossed her arms under her ample bosom, giving it a push here and a shove there to better accommodate her comfort zone. "Willi, don't want you going and getting yourself upset and in a dither—"

"I don't dither." Willi glared across Agatha's fluttering scarves and at Elba in her overalls.

"Well, now that's not meant unkindly, a young woman like you living all alone."

"So lonely," intoned Agatha as the chorus backup.

"As alone as a whippoorwill singing at night, lonely as that old bum on North Main, lonely as a young woman without no man can be."

Willi sighed. "What is it this lonely, dithering woman is going to be upset about other than your triple-whammy comparisons?" She started the motor.

"You had that break-in last night." Elba pointed a finger across at Willi. "But that ain't all. People coming and going where they ain't got no right to be coming and going, not just in your house. We can see better from our place that old cabin where your mama used to paint. Lights going on and off, all kinds of hours. Guess you ain't turned off the electricity yet?"

Willi let the question hang in the air. No, by dadgum, she hadn't turned off the electricity, nor the water or gas or phone. Sometimes, she'd go spend a spring morning there and remember her mama happily dabbling in her oils, her father piddling around the rosebushes and the wisteria. Quannah thought Wisteria a truly magnificent Standing Person, its roots being obviously deep as its bower spread over thirty feet supported by steel posts. Fall called her there, too, and she would fix a light meal, enjoy the outdoors, her mother's paintings, which were along the walls and floors, her daddy's tools neatly stacked in the corner. And one winter, she stayed there for four days when her house's furnace failed. The old space heaters kept her toasty warm. Elba broke into her reverie.

"There you are off again into one of them daydreams of—"

"I do not daydream—"

"Do crickets rub their hind legs?"

"Elba!"

"Turn right here and go back towards your place. You need to see what's going on, I tell you."

Agatha patted Willi's arm. "She's right. We've both had signs and dreams, dreams about a black wolf and a white wolf." Agatha frowned. "We don't understand those."

Willi slammed on the brakes.

"Good Lord alive." Elba yelped. "What'd you see? Charlie Brown in the road?"

"Did you say black wolf?"

"And white wolf, yes." Elba patted the dashboard.

Agatha said, "Have you had dreams, too?"

Willi stared at the two. "No . . . no, just . . . nothing, just coincidence. I had just remembered Quannah's tale about . . . wolves last night. Just coincidence."

In unison the sisters said, "Nothing is coincidence."

"You're being given double whammy signs. Ought to be aware," Agatha added.

When they reached Willi's farmhouse, Elba said, "Here's what we'll do. Let Aggie go on with the vittles in your diesel Ford. We'll go check on the cabin and follow along in your car, Willi. Ain't that a plan? Then you can drop me off at the lake whiles you shake a leg and get back to Sheriff Tucker and those morning interviews."

"Couldn't we check after the picn—?"

"Nope."

"No. Time is important in this instance." So Willi drove around to the cabin. Forcing Willi out, Agatha scooted over to the driver's side. "You two take care. May blessings and goodness follow you."

"Now, Agatha," Willi said, staring at the pickup. "You know, you don't have to speed in this diesel. It'll pick up speed all by itself practically, and I just got the ding from your last trip fixed, so—"

"Not to worry. I'll treat this big beauty like a beloved darling." Agatha pushed the automatic button, and the tinted window shushed upward. She backed out, gunned the motor, and varoomed out of the driveway like a sixteen-year-old with a first set of wheels. Willi ducked as gravel spewed in her direction.

Within a copse of thick-trunked oak trees, Willi smiled at the brambles and roses covering the cabin. Another dirt track led off to the left of the cabin, which led to the Kachelhoffers' land about a quarter mile as the track went. The sisters' place was actually much closer to the cabin than Willi's home was. There was a rough-stone fireplace, and the chimney stood strong and straight. Willi looked for the key hidden within the false water hose spigot. "Uh-oh. It's not here."

CHAPTER
4

Elba shoved the door open. "Don't need it. Somebody done broke the lock and the latch on the screen door. See?"

Willi followed her inside. The modern, compact kitchen glowed with the sunshine streaming in through white lace curtains. A small microwave oven peeked from behind a stenciled door covered with bluebirds and cardinals, some more of her mother's handicrafts. But on the cabinet, a couple of plates, food congealed but not yet rotting, attested to someone's recent presence. In the living area, chintz sofa cushions were strewn across the floor as if folks used them to lean up against here and there. The fireplace had the makings of a half-burned fire in it, ashes and wood scrambled, obviously to put it out quickly.

Tears sprang to Willi's eyes. To hide them, she bent over, picked up one of the pillows, and hugged it. "How could anyone . . . these were my folks' treasures . . . no one, no one should—"

"I know, Willi, but someone has, and now you got to deal with what is."

"Right." She shoved open the bedroom door. Her mother's

embroidered rose quilt lay rumpled on the floor. She backed out of the room and slammed the door. "They won't get away with this. To enter my home was bad enough, but to break in here, where my parents had such happy . . . well, damn it to Hades and back."

"Ought we to call the law?" Elba shoved her balled fists in her overalls.

Willi wrung her hands while she stomped back to the kitchen area. "I guess. No, wait a minute. Sheriff Tucker already had one of his deputies out this morning to check on the break-in. He's pulling in volunteers as it is for the festival starting, and he can't do anything about this. Maybe tell me to get better locks, which I will daggum well do come Monday. Oh, no. Look. They've opened the root cellar. A lot of Mama's paintings were packaged and stored down there. They'd better not have—" Willi rushed down to take a look. When she was satisfied that nothing was missing she returned upstairs.

A half hour later, they had nailed the outside cellar door shut and put the tools away. Willi preferred to wait for the locksmith to fix the front door rather than nail it closed. Elba handed Willi the *Playboy* magazine. "Did you see this here?"

"Where in heavens did you find that?"

"In there. It was on the floor next to the chair. I figured it wasn't your usual reading material. . . . There's an address label."

Willi turned the slick magazine over. "Right you are, but the name isn't there, only an address." They walked back to her farmhouse and got her car.

"Well, for one so hell-bent as you are sometimes to do some investigating, seems like that there would set your nose to twitching."

Willi rolled the lurid pages. She stuffed the book into her shoulder bag. "I might look into it."

"Or you could turn it over to Sheriff Tucker."

Willi grimaced. "Or . . ."

"Or not," Elba finished. She grinned and patted the herbs she kept in a pouch around her neck. These represented to

Elba and to her sister, Agatha, talismans against some of the evils in the world. She and Agatha were professed white witches, Wiccans who practiced only what they referred to as the white arts of doing good one for another. They also attended the United Methodist Church and seemed to have no qualms about the mixture of beliefs, and certainly the congregation loved them in return. The Methodist minister often said to those first encountering the eccentric Kachelhoffer sisters, "I've only witnessed them doing good and loving their neighbors. If something other than that is harbored within their hearts, you'd have to go a long mile to prove it to me." Wise man that he was, he never tried to explain their uncanny psychic abilities or their use of the less conventional means—the tarot and the crystals—for seeking inner knowledge.

"Did you hear me or was you daydreaming again?"

Willi tilted her retroussé nose in the air. "I do not—"

"Save that for some who don't know you so well. I said, trouble seems drawn to you. Aggie and I figure it's partly 'cause of that wild blood of yours."

"The Scotch-Irish?"

"Well, that's a pretty strong duo, but I was referring to the Indian blood. You got to admit, taken all together, those three ain't the most gentle of our species. Might find out more if you was to let us do a past lives regression session."

"I've answered that a dozen times. The answer is no."

"Well, one of these days, one of these days."

"Elba?"

"Yup?"

"I've always loved this place tucked fifteen miles from Nickleberry."

"Sure, and why not, what with the pines and oaks to give it that peaceful feel."

"But, now . . . after two incidents . . ."

Elba said, "You know better than to go there. You are a survivor. Got good folks around who care about you and gonna keep an eye out for you. Be nice if you didn't go hunting for trouble, though."

"I don't. I didn't invite intruders, and—"

"And, so, you're going to turn that address over to the sheriff?"

"Well, in time, of course, in time."

"Me and Aggie should have done a follow-up read about you before leaving this morning. Too late. But, you listen to me now. I got one of those feelings, so I got to speak up. Can't deny the messages, or they'll stop being sent."

"And the message you're getting?"

"One I get a lot when you're concerned."

Willi drove onto the gravel entry leading down to the lake plaza area.

"Third time's the charm," Elba said.

"Third time's the charm? As in, there's going to be another break-in?"

"Don't know about that. All I'm getting is third time's the charm."

Willi stopped and pulled on the emergency brake.

Elba folded her arms and lowered her chin toward her ample bosom. "And, there's the dreams, too. The ones about the black wolf and the white. So's, just be careful, hear?"

"I just want to get through this retirement dinner for Superintendent Burkhalter, get the new one welcomed with appropriate fanfare, and then crash somewhere quiet."

From out of the heavens a menacing rumble grew, followed by a few raindrops from what looked like a beautiful clear sky. "No, we don't need rain today," Willi said.

A small gathering of clouds swooped into the sunlit sky.

"Only in Texas. You don't like the weather," Elba said, "just you wait a minute, and it'll change on you." She hefted two of the picnic baskets. "Best be setting these up in the lake clubhouse. Using it for the Tea and Scones Room. Going to be mighty crowded in that bitty space. Only holds about seventy bodies at one time. Everybody gets here it's gonna be like mice in an overcrowed maze, like a rabbit hutch in season, like a shoulder-to-shoulder sale at JC Penney on the day after Thanksgiving."

Willi quirked her mouth up on one side. "No doubt. I'll

have Neeper and Dan Oxhandler to set some tables right outside to help with overflow." She sighed.

She got through her articulate and amusing speech for the morning and left everything in Agatha's capable hands. "I'll be back to help this evening." With Elba, Willi walked among the winding paths of booths having to do with Celtic dress, drums and harps, jewelry, and books. "Don't guess I can put off the interviews any longer. Sheriff expects me there. Let's go."

Willi arrived in time to get a cold Dr Pepper in the teachers' lounge before Sheriff Tucker stomped in. He no more than said a hi howdy before Deputy Jon Piedra escorted Hortense Horsenettle, the high school librarian, inside the room. Morning sun streamed across Hortense's long face and glinted on her red-rimmed eyeglasses. No amount of sun could find any shine within her overly frosted hair. A shapely figure was her one positive asset, and the forty-five-year-old librarian made the most of it when sitting. She crossed her legs and hiked her skirt up at the same time.

Willi sighed. Oh, now they'd be regaled by Hortense's problem. When people were kind they referred to it as her sinus situation. But most agreed it was simply like a mule's bray. Even that would be fine, if Hortense would not insist on her method of improving her vocabulary with the word of the day, one which had to be used sixteen times before she *owned* it. Hortense said, "Willi, so glad you're here. Heard about the vandalism?"

"Hmm. A lot of that going around," Willi murmured.

Hortense said, "Some *boodler* is going to ruin my circulation."

Oh my gosh. Well, at least the word of the day was out. "Sheriff, you remember our high school librarian, Ms. Horsenettle? I believe she's referring to book circulation, right?"

"Yes, and things were stolen yesterday. Some trophies kept on the top shelves and some old yearbooks. A horrible *boodler* is responsible."

Willi raised an eyebrow. "Boodler?"

"An opportunist. One who augments their income with under-the-table thievery."

"Aha," said Sheriff Tucker.

"Hmm," chimed in Officer Jon Piedra.

"So, with boodlers about, I must get back to the shelves and see if more has been taken."

"That is serious, Hortense, but perhaps this situation is more so?"

Hortense lowered her glasses down the slope of her long nose. "Oh? Well, of course."

Tucker said, "If you'll just scoot over there beside Deputy Piedra, we'll chat a minute. Then maybe he'll go along with you and check on the uh . . . boodler on the premises."

Hortense let out a giggle that ended with her characteristic hee-hawwh bray. She fluttered lashes over her myopic eyes and grinned at Jon Piedra. "I hope," she said, "this close proximity won't be an unwelcome impingement?" Deputy Piedra hurriedly opened his notebook and concentrated on the written page.

Hortense shoved her red-rimmed glasses up her nose. "I suppose boodlers are better than finding that poor woman."

"Tessa Aiken. Did you know she was a former Nickleberry High grad?"

"I know now, but didn't when I found her."

"She was India Lou Aiken's niece," Willi said.

"How tragic. I do remember now, India Lou raised a niece and nephew as her own children."

Sheriff Tucker said, "Yep, this whole town likes India Lou. And we all want to help her out now. You can be part of that, Ms. Horsenettle. Here, have a Luden's cherry drop while we talk."

Hortense snorted to clear her sinuses and took the drop.

"About what time would you say you discovered Miss Aiken?"

"Four-thirty, maybe five o'clock. We've had long days lately. I'm not real sure of the time." Her fingers inched up and down her thighs, hiking her skirt up with each movement. "No, I'm not positive."

"You placed the 911 call, right?"

"Yes, that was the responsible thing to do, but the exact time . . . I—"

Willi leaned forward. "Hey, that's no big deal. We can find that out later, I bet, from the 911 tape. Why don't you just tell us in your own words what happened. It must have been one of the most awesome and frightening experiences."

"My, yes. You've been there and done that, but this was a first and horrific encounter with . . . with a body . . . for me." A telltale bray and snort gave truth to her nervousness with such an experience.

"Sammie Yannich had to run to the bank and needed some go-for errands run on campus. I put mail in the teachers' boxes, then took erasers and two packages to the Ag building across campus." Hortense beat a silent tune upon her leg to the tempo of something approaching the Macarena. "Let's see. Ah, yes, then I dropped those items off inside the door, because nobody was there. On my return across the parking lot I see this yellow Cadillac. Everybody knows it belongs to Superintendent Burkhalter. But the door is open, and something is hanging out." In a rush now, Hortense blurted, "I thought maybe he was in a hurry, and I intended to do the proper thing and pick up the dropped item, put it in the car, and shut the door."

"Yes," Willi encouraged.

With a deep sigh, Hortense nodded. "I go around the front of the door and hear these little sounds like a puppy. I'm thinking, *Awww, how precious,* but it's not a puppy, it's this black lady, really pretty figure and legs . . . but . . . her face . . . it was like eaten away . . . oh, awful."

Tears pooled in Hortense's myopic eyes. "I just stood there. I didn't know what to do. I just stood there until she gestured for me to come closer. I couldn't not bend down. She mouthed something. I could tell she thought she was saying a lot, but only one thing came out. Understandable. By that, I mean I could see the inside of her mouth was oozing and eaten up, too, just like her face." Hortense took off her glasses and wiped at her eyes. "That poor woman."

Gently, Willi pulled her hands down and stared into Hortense's eyes. "What did she say?"

"*Win* or something about *winning* and then *señor*. She was Spanish-speaking, right?"

Willi frowned. "No, don't believe so."

"Both those words could have been part of some other word. Like I said, she was mouthing, but nothing but those two things came out. Her head lolls over, and I scream. I couldn't stop. So very unprofessional of me. I don't remember getting back inside or . . . or anything for hours. I appreciate you not questioning me until today."

Sheriff Tucker peered at Jon Piedra, who nodded, evidently indicating he'd gotten everything down. Hortense confirmed her story a second and third time before Deputy Piedra escorted her downstairs. Hortense reminded him as they went out the door, "Deputy Piedra, I do expect you to help me with these . . ."

"Yes ma'am. *Boodlers,* yes, ma'am."

After the last interviews, Sheriff Tucker said, "Guess with that vandalism last night and getting ready for the beginning Irish Fling Festival today, you ain't had the wherewithal nor time to check on Ozzie Oxhandler's vittles. Mayhap I ought to get Deputy Piedra to run around and—"

"No! I mean, there's no reason. I'll take care of it." She smiled while mulling over whether or not to mention the second break-in at the cottage.

"Is there something else, Miss Willi?"

"Uhmm, no. Nothing that pertains to the matter at hand. Nothing that can't wait until later." She pushed a dark tendril of hair behind her ear. "What do you think *win* and *señor* were meant to signify?"

"Being as I don't know, I can't say. My bet is you'll put your thinking cap on, seeing as how you knew her better than me." He eyed her sternly. "Just remember no going off on wild-goose chases. You let me know your thoughts. I'll decide what we hunt and what we don't. Consultant, remember?"

"Hell's bells, Sheriff, of course. That was our agreement. You know me."

"Yep, yep, I do, and that's a mite worrisome at times."

CHAPTER
5

At the Nickleberry Lake clubhouse, Willi got stuck behind the serving table, backed literally up against the rough wood of the rustic room. Scents of fresh breads, cinnamon, and frying meat pasties permeated the area. Five teapots and an equal number of industrial-sized coffeepots steamed beside Willi. A table next to her held chowder redolent of onions and garlic. Grit from all those who'd rushed in from fishing and swimming floated over everything. Booths were crowded three to a seat. Chairs had two each perched on the edges. Others stood, fingers wrapped around the slices of the Irish apple and potato cake or one of the three dozen other Irish taste treats.

Within the surrounding glass on all four sides, music from the pennywhistle group with singer swept through the room, but at pleasant decibels where conversations could be kept at comfortable levels. In fact, most listened attentively to the rendition of "Danny Boy."

All in all, the retirement picnic and festivities for outgoing super Burkhalter were going well. Speeches had been made; the flame of trust had been passed to the new superintendent in a flourish of Texas hoopla and Irish jokes.

In another hour, the fireworks display and the lighting of the shamrock lights around the lake would herald the official opening of the Celtic Irish Fling Festival. Retiring Superintendent Bernie Fritzpatrick Burkhalter sat at a tiny table with the new top dog, Jarnagin Ventnor.

Agatha, in her rainbow of swirling skirts, said, "What do you think they're talking about?"

"Do I look like an eavesdropper?"

"Do Nickleberry Oxhandlers bellow?"

Willi sighed. "I might have overheard something when I walked a scone tray over."

"And?"

"And they're both kind of like those ice cubes: frozen. Only their anger at each other melts them, but into isolated little pools."

"Willi, oh literary teacher, wax less poetic."

"Burkhalter is accusing Ventnor of not delivering the goods, whatever that means. Ventnor made a few less-than-kind remarks about Bernie's on-again-off-again romance with our Sammie Yannich."

"Interesting. I always thought there was a Mrs. Burkhalter somewhere in the background. But, then, I've only been around here less than a year."

"Oh, right, Agatha. Years ago when he worked for another district, there was one. Must've been a divorce before he came here, what . . . , four, maybe five years ago? So what's your interest, Agatha?"

"None, none really. They looked like two tigers circling the same prey, and I had this uneasy feeling. You know those feelings Sister and I get now and again."

"Now who's waxing poetic?"

Neeper Oxhandler walked up. "Willi, I'd sure like some more of that Irish apple and potato bread. Mighty good. Uncle Ozzie will be after you for that recipe."

"Ozzie's Barbecue Emporium has plenty of better recipes,

but thanks." Out of the corner of her eye, Willi watched him as she said, "I especially love Ozzie's Friday special."

Neeper pointed to the beet salad. "That, too, thanks. Oh, yeah, everybody loves Uncle Ozzie's fried clams and onion rings."

Willi faced him, "But, gee, I thought you said the Friday special was—"

"Oh my God," Neeper said, staring at the doorway. "I can't believe *she* came."

The conversational decibels lowered as India Lou Aiken, Tessa's aunt, walked through the room and to the dessert table where she deposited two cakes. She came over to Willi and said, "I promised two cakes, and the bottom line is I always keeps my promises." Her usual beautiful ebony skin tones were ashen and her intelligent eyes sunken and red.

The door opened again and Saralee York sauntered in wearing long white pants, a long-sleeved blouse to match, and white tennis shoes. She turned as pale as her clothes when she noticed who stood beside her. Willi approached both. "Come in, Saralee. There's a place right over there where you can sit and have a cup of tea. India Lou, let me help you with those cakes." She took hold of India Lou's arm and guided her to the sideboard of pastries and teas surrounded with shamrock and rose displays. "India Lou, there's a rocker behind that table with your name written on it. Have a seat between Elba and Agatha."

"Child. Stop your fluttering and fussing. I be all right. Came to see you, anyways. How about we take these two rockers out to the back under the trees a minute. I gots something I want to get off my chest."

Outside away from the pennywhistle group's rendition of "The Humors of Whiskey," the last rays of the sun dappled a pattern through the oak leaves. Sitting beside India Lou, Willi reached over and grabbed her hand. "I'm so very sorry. There aren't ever the right words, but you know that I'm here for whatever you need. Aunt Minnie, too."

"Appreciate the kind words. You always encouraged Tessa. Her brother Terrance graduated before you came to teach, or you'd have done the same for him. Because of you, Tessa speak so fine, not like her old aunt."

"You taught them the important things, India Lou. Strong work ethic. To believe in themselves. This whole town has the greatest respect for you and for them."

"They was able to go out in the world and get fine jobs. Terrance—he out in the middle of the ocean in a dangerous part of this old world."

"He won't be here for the funeral?"

"Nope, Terrance did get to send an E-mail through the sheriff's office. They's kind enough to pass it along. Real sweet boy. He is, yes ma'am."

"Did you have something special you needed me to do, India Lou?"

"Two things I need to say. First one I should have told Sheriff Tucker, but couldn't bring myself to do it. My pride of Tessie got in the way, yes ma'am, it did. No matter what I say, you remember how fine a young woman she was, yes ma'am."

Willi squeezed her old friend's hand. "You've every right to be proud of Tessa. She accomplished so much in such a short time."

"You right about that, yes, Miss Willi, you are. Finished university and got on with that Austin law firm. Mighty proud. This . . . this is something just since last time she was to home. Drinking. That's what I thought. Being with that fancy law firm means doing that socializing scene. Figured she just let it go too far, the drinking." She sighed. "I worked with them high school kids, just like you, too long not to knows the signs."

"Drugs?" Willi asked.

"Hmm. I watch Tessie this last time to home. She here about two weeks before . . . before . . . hmm. She just left her makeup case a-laying open, stuff spilling out. Needles. A heating *apparatus*. Heard it called that on *Sixty Minutes*, yes ma'am. *Apparatus*."

"Definitely drugs."

India Lou turned loose of Willi's supportive hand and

sat up straight. "Number two reason. Find out who done this . . . this most awfulest thing to my Tessie. Might be because of the drugs, but . . . if it's not, there's no reason to go talking that part around, is there, Miss Willi?"

"I'll do all I can but will have to share the info with Sheriff Tucker."

"Yes ma'am, but only if and when necessary?"

"I'll do my best. Do you have any idea who supplied her here in Nickleberry? What friends she was with while here?"

"Same as in high school. She run with Vic Ramirez and Dan Oxhandler, Neeper some, too. Guess you taught *her* not to see color, either."

Willi sensed rather than saw the smile on India Lou's face.

"She was some interested in one of the men with her law firm in Austin. He a handsome young black man, but he been in Europe for a month for the company. I guess the firm will let him know."

India Lou hefted herself from the rocker, and Willi rose, too. India Lou said, "I was out here fishing yesterday—that be Friday—and Tessie come out with Vic and Dan to swim. Neeper, too. She was paged while at the lake clubhouse, just before she left. Miss Willi, she didn't say nothing, just kissed me and left. Kissed her old aunt for the last time, and she left."

"I was here, too, remember? We had to work on the quilt for the raffle. Tessa helped for awhile, too."

"My mind going in so many directions. Yep, you right as rain in April. She grabbed some of those pieces of the other quilt we couldn't finish in time."

"Yes, the Irish double-chain pattern. She used it as a kerchief around her head."

"Yes ma'am, she did. Mighty pretty in it, too. She drove off by herself in her own car. Dan and Neeper left earlier, but Vic Ramirez, he stayed a while longer."

India Lou moved along toward the rustic clubhouse now lit with the green and crystal lights, the loudspeakers operating on the outside so all could hear the pennywhistle group now performing "Guilderoy." Two hours later, when Elba and Agatha helped Willi clean up the last of the teapots and scones, she stopped for a moment, dumbstruck. Head tilted, she stood very still until the thought bubbling up came to the surface and then she whispered, "Oh, no . . . then where was it?"

Elba ran into the back of her. "Wish you'd get your tail-lights fixed or not stop so sudden like."

Agatha placed a hand on Willi's shoulder. "Where was what?"

"The Irish double-chain square, of course."

The Kachelhoffer sisters peered at each other. "Of course."

Sheriff Tucker strode in the door. With a duck of his head and a hand around Agatha's waist, he said, "How about a mosey around the festival grounds before they turn out the lights for the evening?"

Agatha tucked a few strands into her wispy bun and nod-ded. "Could I talk a certain lawman into giving a lady a ride home to Frogs' Feet afterwards?"

"Believe we might can arrange that." He pointed a finger at Willi. "Bet I know what you'll be getting come your next birthday or whatever. A cell phone."

Grinning, Willi said, "I take it that your nephew has rung up the sheriff's office when he couldn't reach me at home?"

"Yes, Miss Willi, and he said if you was of a mind to, he's got a four-hour layover starting in about two hours at DFW Airport. Not long enough to come in, not long enough for a night's stay there, but long enough for some fine Italian restaurant. Here's the name and address. I told him I'd call him back if you couldn't make it."

Willi grabbed the sheet. "Oh, I want to, but I've still got to clean up here and haul all this—"

Elba crossed her arms and shifted her ample bosom into a comfortable position. "You drive on home so's you can pretty up. Lord knows a good-looking hunk like Quannah deserves a woman sweetened and soaped off, powdered and primped, panting and—"

"Would you please?"

"Sure, I was just a-telling you. Me and Aggie and Brigham can deal with this here. With four hours, you got more time than's needed for a simple meal. A smart-like woman on the edge of old-age spinsterhood might ought—"

"I'm going out the door, Elba. And thirty-two is not old spinsterhood." Outside she ran into Saralee York, who walked up holding onto Neeper Oxhandler's arm. He boomed out, "Sure is a shame that special investigator feller isn't here to show you around. Pretty sights tonight with the lights and all."

In her monotone voice, Saralee said, "The lights and sights will be here all week. Isn't Quannah competing in the men's jig dance contest against Dan and Neeper in a couple of days?"

Willi said, "Yes, and my shillings are on him. Sorry, Neeper." She peered closer. What was wrong with him? He kept ducking his head as if he were still in her class and in trouble. "Oh, Neeper, when you and Dan were here yesterday with Tessa Aiken, do you remember her wearing a green and white kerchief?"

In his booming Oxhandler voice but more refined speech than his cousin's, he said, "Yes, Ms. Gallagher, she did have it wrapped around her head. We kidded her about her looking like a kid again and a tomboy at that."

"Knowing Tessa, I bet she didn't let you get away with that. Is that where you got that shiner you're trying to hide?"

He looked her straight in the eye. "You're right, she didn't let me get away with it. I believe that may have been when she threw me over her shoulder into the lake."

"And the shiner?"

"The cousins," Saralee said, "had a little misunderstanding tonight, and Officer Piedra just got them parted."

"You and Dan fighting? Fistfighting?"

Neeper waved his huge hand. "Ah, it happens now

and again. Stupid argument about Tessa and what she was doing. Doesn't matter now. I'm . . . I'm gonna miss her, Ms. Gallagher. Doesn't seem right. One minute, she was like we were in high school ten years ago, and then found—"

Elba walked out with a clean coffeepot. With an elbow, she nudged Willi and explained in loud tones about Willi and Quannah's rendezvous. "Well, it's a perfect night for lovers, young and older, that's what I say."

Neeper, always respectful as he'd been in Willi's senior English class, grinned. "Good thing tomorrow's Sunday, Ms. Gallagher. Seeing as how you're having a late night out."

Willi growled. "Grrrrr."

"What?" Elba asked.

"Small towns. You can't keep anything a secret in a small town. Especially—"

"What now?"

"Especially when I have my own Nickleberry Sisters' Advertising Agency."

"We are good, aren't we?"

"Bye. Grrrrrr."

At the farmhouse she got a similar growl from her four-legged friend, her dachshund, Charlie Brown. His growl lacked ferocity, probably due to his limpid brown eyes, velvety skin, and whirligig tail. She gave him a five-minute run in the yard while she entered her library nook. With floor-to-ceiling backlit shelves on two walls, it offered a calm respite. She glanced at Chaucer and Beowulf bubbling happily in the aquarium. "Here, fellows, here's your food. Come up to the surface for a kissy face. Come on. Hurry, guys, this girl's got a hot date."

While waiting for this maneuver, she glanced at the shelf above and behind the aquarium. Last night's intruder had slung some of the books to the floor. She caressed the leather binding of a yearbook that she had bought one of the first years she taught. As she thumbed through pages of photos, she mused. Seemed like the events of the past few days had drawn those of the class of ten years ago into the eye of a hurricane. The Oxhandler cousins—Dan and Neeper. Vic Ramirez, the fireman, had graduated with them and, of course, Tessa Sheenala Aiken. Two of the yearbooks had fallen between the dark wooden shelves. They blended so well with the wood, she almost missed seeing the edges peeking up. Each one had been there so long, the covers stuck to the wood, and she had to pry them away.

"Yes, here's the one with Tessa's graduating class."

Bubbles plopped on the surface of the aquarium. Chaucer ducked in and out of the underwater castle. He wriggled his body back and forth, creating a frothy swirl around his fins.

"Right you are. I don't have time to peruse yearbooks and go on a trip down memory lane." She tucked four books, the ones from Tessa's freshman through senior years, under her arm and fled upstairs for a quick shower and change. Elba was right about one thing. Quannah just might appreciate a powdered and perfumed lady who'd taken a little time with her appearance. She intended to make him entirely forget Miss Tits-in-the-Air Loraine Zimmerman, by daggum.

Willi smiled at the Italian quartet of roving singers and violinist as they finished a rendition of "O Sole Mio." They moved off toward another couple's table. "I love this old-world charm, the rich woods, the crystal candle holders, the plush carpet and linens and the music and—"

"And?" Quannah's eyes glinted with mischief.

"And . . . uh . . . the view." From high atop the Fort Worth Bank One Building inside the Grotto Restaurant, they looked over the gorgeous lights of the city where the West began.

"Ah. And I was hoping absence made the heart grow warmer."

She flirted back with a wink. "Well, that *might* be true." Her breathing quickened.

"Ever cautious in affairs of the heart, that's Willi." Quannah licked the red wine from his lips, crossed his knife and fork over the plate, and pushed it back. "What was the end result of the two break-ins, one at the cottage and one at your house?"

She cut another piece of veal. "Nothing really happened. I didn't even call about the second intrusion beca—"

"What? Willi, I can't belie—"

"Wait a minute. The sheriff's department couldn't do a dangblame thing about my house ransacking. What could they have possibly done about the old cottage?"

"Woman-of-Stubbornness, you must report it as soon as you return. You never know what might turn up in one or both places that might connect the same culprit. Promise me, *Winyan.*"

She brought a forkful of veal to her mouth and stopped. "Okay. I see your point. I'll turn it in, but they won't find anything." *Especially since I took that magazine with the address. Uh-oh.*

"Why?"

"Why what?"

"Why won't they find anything? Have you removed evidence?"

Get out of my head, Lassiter. "Me?" She gulped. "Evidence?" She wouldn't lie, but she wasn't going to tell him about the *Playboy* magazine that would in all likelihood not amount to a spoon of fried frijoles. "I straightened the pillows and such. Like I told you, Elba and I boarded up the cellar door and the locksmith will make a new key for the front door, maybe already has."

He glowered at her a moment. "Someone wants in badly, they'll rip off the boards." Finally, his features relaxed. "You are aware of the rule of three."

"Only where Elba's pithy sayings are concerned. What is the rule of three?"

"Third time's the charm? That rule of three."

"Now, you're getting scary, Lassiter. That's something Elba does always say."

"She's right, Gallagher. The universe seems to work with that three more times than not. And then, sometimes with us more reservation types, there's that magical number of the more sacred *four.* I'm wondering if there hasn't been a third or fourth break-in to tie with these two. Maybe you aren't even aware of them yet."

Willi snapped her fingers. "Hortense."

"Ugh."

"Don't be that way. Hortense is a good person. A little eccentric but a good person."

He rolled his eyes. "And she came to mind because—?"

"Because of the rule of three. The school library had an intruder the day before or maybe the night before mine showed up. Could that be connected?"

"Perhaps. Best let Uncle Brigham know about all three when you return."

"Oh, I will soon as I see him." Willi smiled. Of course, she might not see him before she got to talk to Hortense again and checked out the address on that magazine. After all, she wouldn't want to run to Sheriff Tucker with every little thing unless it was important. Before Quannah could do a brain-drain on that thought, she folded her napkin. "So, how long is your layover?"

He grinned and folded his arms in his Big Chief stance. "Not long enough. Not nearly long enough."

The intensity of his gaze left her breathless. Yes, Elba and Agatha were correct. Something would have to happen soon between them if she were to ever breathe right again. But, damnnab it and back, every time she was ready to leap over that line of no return, he retreated. Each time he closed in, she jitterbugged.

With one finger he stroked the outline of her chin. Back and forth, back and forth, sending tingling sensations to every nerve. "Someday, *Winyan,* we'll both cross that abyss at the same time, won't we?"

Oh my gosh, there he was again, in her head. She pulled in air. "Abyss? Oh, yes, that abyss where . . . where we can both work on a case together without being uncomfortable with each other . . . yes, someday."

He drew his warm hand away. The patter of her heart slowed a little, as if a hypnotist had snapped his fingers. He said, "Yes, that, too. Right now, we have time for a walk downtown. Fort Worth by night should be experienced many times over. It's a beautiful city anytime but magical at night."

She shoved back her chair. "That's high praise from one who doesn't care for concrete and skyscrapers."

"Somehow, the city seems like all of Texas, brash and arrogant but at the same time comfortable with what it is and all it represents. By night it blends with and seems truly a beautiful extension of Mother Earth. Maybe the water gardens and the botanical spots around the city help. For a metropolis, it is one of the most earth-friendly I've encountered. Care to share a little of it with me before I fly the skies?" He held out his hand.

After seeing Quannah off on the American flight, she sat a moment in her car to allow the AC to cool the warmth of her cheeks. By the time she'd maneuvered the Airport Freeway traffic and headed south toward Nickleberry, her nerve ends had calmed to a less heightened intensity level. She turned off the AC and opted for lowering her window to receive a cool breeze. As she drove into the edge of Nickleberry, she passed the plastic red-white-and-blue banners blowing before the Worchester Used Car Lot. Ah, then she smelled the mesquite at Oxhandler's Barbecue and Emporium. After inhaling the teasing aroma, she met the comforting woods.

Pine needles and oak tree mulch exuded a pungent aroma. Must have been a rain shower while she visited Quannah. At the curve of the Maple Leaf Bridge, she slowed down. Only wide enough for one car to cross at a time, the rickety wooden span had been a site for many accidents. The hill past the bridge curved sharply to the left. She sighed. Just had to hope anyone descending knew the danger and would slow down. On her side of the bridge, Willi checked for oncoming traffic and accelerated. When she was a third of the way across the dangerous structure, a yellow Cadillac whirred around the bend. Willi's breath caught on the tail end of her yelp. Her heart did a quick mambo as she swerved toward the right and floored the accelerator.

Just as the mustard monster made the edge of the wooden span, Willi, just barely off the bridge, jerked the wheel even more sharply to the right toward the bar ditch. Her car landed hood-first in the spongy loam. Jumping out, she struck her hand against the door. She stomped her foot. Her left heel broke off and went flying into the darkness. Tail-lights winked in the distance.

"Damn you, Bernie Burkhalter. I hope all the rest of your offspring are . . . are . . . spud farmers." Tears stung her eyes, and her knees were shaking, making a nice coun-tertempo to the heaves of her chest. "Now, I'm gonna be stuck in this muck. I should have gotten a cell phone. At least I could have called someone." She spent another few minutes sniffling through her pity party. "Enough."

She got back in the car. "Just got to do the best I can with what I have." Coaxing the wheels one way then another, she finally eased the vehicle out. For the last few miles home, the cool breeze and Wilson Pickett's lyrics, "I'm gonna wait 'til the stars come out . . . 'til the midnight hour," kept her company. By the time she reached the sanctuary of her garage, she had a plan in mind. After all, she was too hyped up from being with Quannah, too unnerved from the near crash, and too worried to simply sleep. Yes, she had a plan to chase down one clue, and this would be the perfect time of night. She peered at the car's clock: 12:03 . . . uh . . . okay, perfect time of *morning* to do just that.

CHAPTER
6

As far as a marina went, Nickleberry Lake Marina was
limited and hosted only craft that could navigate the connecting tributaries that finally joined with the Colorado
River. The Colorado, navigable only to Austin, continued to
flow southeast to Galveston and the Gulf of Mexico. She
wished herself somewhere along that sun-drenched coast
rather than where she was now: at the quiet end of the lake in
darkest shadows. But Quannah had ended the evening with a
challenge. Not directly, no, but his attitude showed when he
told her only to do what Sheriff Tucker said, not to go out on
her own and get her nose into things. Well, she was perfectly
capable of deciding for herself what was and was not good
for her nose, thank one Lakota-speaking Ranger very much.
The opposite end of the lake still glowed with twinkling
green lights that looked like minute Irish fireflies.

The adrenaline high Willi had after leaving Quannah's
side had carried her this far. Then renewed anger over
Tessa's death fueled her resolve. She would have to be convinced all these strange happenings weren't related. What
better way than to eliminate one by one, each one. The least

likely incident to be associated with the murder was the
break-in at her cottage. She had the means of learning about
that through the abandoned magazine. The address was the
Comanche Raider, Berth number seventeen. So, here she
was at the Nickleberry Marina. Now, reality shook her until
her proverbial teeth chattered. Her dry tongue seemed to
swell in her mouth until she couldn't work up a spit if a fire
loomed before her. This was not good.

Not at all *in balance.* So, what Medicine would Big Chief
Lassiter have called forth to help in this situation? Opossum? Playing dead until the enemy showed no interest?
Nah. That didn't seem to suit. Ant Medicine of patience?
Ditto: meaning, *No way, José.* She snapped her fingers.
Sure. Yeah, Medicine of Weasel. She shut her eyes while she
tried to remember what the book of Native American totems
said about Weasel's gift. She lay down on the pier edging
boat dock number seventeen, the address on the *Playboy*
magazine. Weasel could slink into enemy camps and gather
information, sneak out unseen, and bring back valuable
information to the tribe.

She sighed. Damned if she wasn't doing things backasswards again. Probably, to invoke the qualities of the animal,
she should have done some ceremony. Then again, Quannah had said he often called on the *Wamaskaskan*—the
Animals—when in need. Somehow, some way, they would
bring help either in a physical sense or an intuitive knowledge needed. Okay, guess it wasn't all that much different
than calling on angels, which lots of folks did. Just seemed
like calling on the animal totems was just more . . . more
specific. She could handle that.

Whispering to the lapping water, she said, "So, Weasel, if
you can help, I'd appreciate it. Perhaps let me see a person's
name outside the boat. If not . . . well, help with plan B.
Maybe show me how to break and enter, seeing as how I
didn't have the foresight to bring any tools, as if I would've
known what tools." She grimaced. "I truly may be in over
my head . . . so I really do need some help."

A light flickered within a cabin window. She tried to

slither farther out of sight into darker shadows. Her foot
caught on a rope, and she fell on the decking with a thump.
In a half crouch, she held her breath. Guess those inside
hadn't heard. She licked her lips, grasped a taut rope, and
eased herself quietly into the water. Must have been an intuitive action because she didn't know what prompted her to
dive in. Surprisingly warm, the water lapped comfortingly.
Of course, now her tennis shoes were more like two washing
machines with full loads attached to her feet. The cabin door
of the *Comanche Raider* opened. A feminine figure in heels
strode past, followed by the scent of musky violets.

Willi executed half a dozen strokes to go around to the
other side of the boat but stopped as the man turned, locked
the door, and sauntered in the same direction Kassal Heberly
chose. Wonder what story the news lady was looking into?
Or maybe this was *her* place? Or she could just be visiting a
friend. Willi waited a good three minutes before easing herself, dripping clothes, and washtub feet, onto the deck.
Hell's bells, what madness made her do these things, forced
her to tread where angels wouldn't flap their wings in a
strong gale, much less some wise Weasel spirit of the animal
world? Maybe she should just have faced the owner with the
torn porno magazine.

*Stop it. You know you've come too far to backpaddle
now. Grit your teeth and see what's what.*

Everything happened for a reason. She wasn't a quitter.
Start something, finish it. She always preached that to her
students . . . so . . . so best get on with it. The heart was back
into reaching the goal, but her shaky knees let her know she
wasn't and never would be cut out for illegal maneuvers.
She straightened her shoulders. Someone broke into her cottage—what amounted to a very sacred part of her past with
her family—and she had a right to discover who and why.

"Okay, Weasel Medicine, help me to find a way in, locate
answers, and slink back out safely." Crouching, she
approached the locked door, slid past and around the cabin
to the window through which a dim light shone. Hoisting
herself on top of a metal deck chair, she eased one leg

through and stuck. Her heart pounded so hard her rib cage hurt.

Blue blazes and Hell.

What kind of totem had she called on? Someone would think she was a big flying wahoo, half in and half out the window. Certainly, she didn't resemble the sleek Weasel. The leg she balanced on shook. *Okay, just back out, get down, and run.* She grunted and twisted. After no results, she whispered under her breath, "Damn, damn, damn, damn, shit!"

This was definitely not behavior becoming a lady, a respected English teacher. *Calm down. Think. Think like Weasel.* That little animal would be very relaxed, muscles easily rippling so he could twist around tight spots. She breathed in slowly and blew her breath out until she literally seemed to shrink. Arching one shoulder, she eased it inside, bent her neck just a fraction of an inch. Ah, now for the other shoulder. Yes, yes, yes. With torso inside, she balanced on a built-in cabinet and lifted her left leg through the opening. Her left shoe caught on the sill and plopped somewhere on the deck, and she landed spread-eagled on her stomach on a furry, undulating area: a tremulous surface that threatened her with seasickness.

She blinked. The cabinet was the headboard to a king-sized waterbed. The fluted light shade allowed plenty of illumination. She turned over on her back, screamed, and quickly stifled her outburst. Suspended above her was a madwoman, long, dark tendrils of hair cascading across the tiger skin throw, clothes wet and askew and with the left tennis shoe missing. Her shocked reflexes reacted. Her foot kicked sideways. Now her right tennis shoe went flying. In the process, her head hit one of the myriad control buttons on the headboard. Well, damn.

The gentle waves became a frantic vibration and music—"The Stripper"—bounced and hummed through the area. If one of these buttons started the song, one should be able to end it. She shoved, and a video on a ceiling-mounted television ground into action. "Oh my gosh." She punched the same knob. The groaning from the screen stopped. She tried another button. "The Stripper" ended.

"As Quannah would say, *aho*—amen."

Her toes touched thick carpet. She scrambled toward her tennis shoe. The muted light shone into a bathroom in black and red marble. Okay, so the door to the left should be the galley and living room—whatever boat folks called that. The bar, wooden with lewd carvings, greeted her by way of jumping out and hitting her on her funny bone as she turned the corner. Hell's bells. A wall clock ticked, and her heart beat a fast syncopation. The owner could be back any moment. She wanted to know whom before she faced him.

She scrabbled her way through cabinets and drawers. "I must be going through some early life crisis time. Thirty-two is far too young for menopausal shenanigans. What am I doing here?" To get info about the cottage break-in. She wanted to know *who* and *why*.

Keep focused. Keep your goal in mind.

Be a lot easier if she could stop trembling. A magazine, a rival to the one in her cabin, lay on the polished countertop with an electric bill. Well, yeah, made sense, the lights and all. She glared at the address label on both. "I don't believe this."

She edged down on the arm of a love seat. Oh, what the hell. What if she did get their nasty little den wet. She slid down to sit comfortably. She glanced from one address to the other. Dan Oxhandler's name was on the magazine. On the electric bill was Neeper Oxhandler. They . . . well, they'd said they batched in a place together. They just never mentioned it was a boat.

"Damn both their stinking hides. What was their magazine doing in my cabin? What were they doing there? If they had this place, why would they need another rendezvous spot?" She slammed the offending slick work to the sofa. The bill fell between the cushions. Retrieving it, she grabbed something else and pulled it out along with the UCS notice.

Tessa's scarf. The quilt square. The Irish double-chain design in green and white was unmistakable. Tears sprang to Willi's eyes. Her fingers trembled so badly, she dropped the scarf. "Oh my God, ohmygod, my God." The words were a prayer, one of those unintelligible to other human ears in its request, but clear to the speaker and the receiver. She jumped up and hid the scarf between the cushions, returned the mail and magazine to the countertop. She again pulled out the cloth and stuffed it down her sweater top. She grabbed a fistful of hair on both sides of her head and pulled.

"No. No, no, no. There has to be some explanation."

Hey, the Oxhandlers had folks visiting. Someone else could have borrowed a magazine. That could explain one being at her cabin without the intruder being one of her coworkers, one of her former students of ten years ago. Her teeth chattered, and she just couldn't seem to calm the erratic beat of her heart.

Okay, face it. She was out of her element here. She needed time to sort, time to think. *Get out, get out, get out.* A quick rush through the bedroom, atop the bed, foot over the sill, slink . . . think of the sleek *We . . . eeeeeeee . . . asel . . .* slide out the window. A police cruiser edged along the lake road. The directional high beam hit the edge of the *Comanche Raider.* Willi hit the deck so hard she swore she'd wear a different cup size after the impact. Some Weasel Medicine she turned out to have. She pictured her bedraggled self behind bars, thumbs inked from the booking, begging the officers not to let Quannah know. The beam of light flashed back and forth across the deck. Highlighted for a moment was her tennis shoe up on the edge of the banister. The cruiser drove on by. She eased herself into the water on the far side of the *Comanche Raider* and stroked across the water for all her little country ass was worth.

Dead tired after the events of the day, night, and early morning, she wanted nothing but to fall asleep at the wheel. Her damp clothes kept her awake along the trip across treacherous Licorice Lane. Sharp pin turns, sudden hills and valleys made up the road where her parents and a number of others had met their deaths. She shook her head. *Don't go there. Not while you're driving along this stretch.* Her neck muscles tightened into hard knots.

George Morgan's "You're the Only Star in my Blue Heaven" played on the Nickleberry country western station. The music reminded her of Quannah's message on her answering machine and his touch as they walked around the bright lights of downtown Fort Worth. Instantly, a great comfort stole over her. She was beginning to think she might like to be the only star shining for him. Oh, nonsense. He was a rambler, a rover, a Texas Ranger on the move, and had no intention of settling down. She had a busy life; probably they'd be very incompatible if thrown too much together. Sure, and . . . and, oh, damn. She sighed. She glanced at the clock readout. Only 1:45 in the A.M. "Thank you, Weasel. At least, you helped get me in and out quickly."

Red eyes glared at her from the middle of the road. She braked sharply. A rabbit, caught in the beam of her lights, dashed into the underbrush. She straightened the wheel, and high beams of a diesel truck made her change her rearview mirror angle. At least she was on the one straight part of Licorice Lane. Surely, he'd go on around. She narrowed her eyes and studied the vehicle in her side mirror. Looked like Neeper's double-cab Chevy. Neeper's and half a hundred more within a five-mile radius. Texas country equaled truck country, by daggum. Whoever drove backed off and kept a distance of about four car lengths. Even though she varied her speed, the distance never changed. Rather than making her relax, the exactness made her nervous. "Why is that jerk following me?"

She rubbed her gritty eyes. Okay, get the reality kick. In the last day and a half she had seen the horrible mutilation of a favorite student, had a break-in in her home while she was sleeping. A second intrusion of her cottage. Worst of all, she had lowered herself to the same tactics—not a proud moment—and had learned only enough to form more questions. She sighed. She was seeing killers and bogey-men in someone who simply operated his Chevy in a safe way. The radio crooned out Conway Twitty's "Slow Hand," and her neck muscles relaxed.

When she turned into her driveway, the vehicle stayed at the Y of the road. It just sat there, its great diesel engine pounding pistons loudly in the predawn hours like a fire-breathing dragon building up steam to lash out and devour in one horrendous flash. In a nervous jerk, she locked her car door. In the movement, her hand hit the station buttons and the rap song, "Who Let the Dogs Out?" erupted. After three lines she switched back to the Golden Oldies 98.5.

The lines "I want to tell you how-ow-ow much I love you. Do you remember when we met . . ." came softly across the airwaves, but were interrupted by the DJ. She flicked the radio off. "Great. Now, those lyrics will bug me until I figure out the song." When she drove around the back of her house to the garage, she could then see the truck at the Y facing her. Hairs on her arms rose. She tapped the garage door opener and whispered, "Thank you, Quannah Lassiter, thank you."

Inside, she quickly set her purse on the kitchen table, ran through to the living room, and peered out. She checked her front door. Oh my gosh, she had left it unlocked in all the hurry of getting things hither and yon this morning. What the heck did it matter if she locked the garage if she forgot to lock the front door? She turned the dead bolt. Well, no harm done. She pulled the curtain aside again.

Slowly, the Chevy backed up, its high beams pinpoint-ing the very window at which she stood. Her heart simply stopped, and she couldn't move. As if satisfied at her reac-tion, the great roaring beast turned, backed up, and ponder-ously disappeared. When the taillights twinkled into nothing, she sighed. Probably just someone lost. No reason to really think anything else. Unless . . . unless someone had seen her leave the *Comanche Raider,* someone like Dan or Neeper or a certain visitor who knew they'd left a green and white quilt square there. She shook her head.

"Stop it."

She kicked off her shoes, turned on lights, and from underneath the fish tank pulled out a box of food. She hummed the two lines to the song before singing the words out loud. "I want to tell you how-ow-ow much I love you. Do you remember when we met?" She sprinkled grains on top of the water. "Come on, cuties. I need some help here. Beowulf? Chaucer?"

Willi bent down to see if they were hiding in the grotto behind the undulating greenery. "What?" She thought she was seeing things and rubbed her eyes. As the awful truth hit home, she fell on her knees in front of the aquarium. No bubbles rose to the top, no flash of golden fin grazed the window.

"What? Why?"

She sat and crooned to them for the longest time as if they were still capable of hearing her. Their bodies lay in the castle moat, skewered there forever with two green swizzle sticks. "Oh, my pets. I'm so sorry. I left the door unlocked. It's my fault."

As she peered through teary eyes, she gasped. On the far side of the tank, taped to the outside was a strange plastic-coated playing card. Sort of like a tarot card, but not. Such an intricate banding of whirls and swirls decorated the outside edge. Through the movement of the water it was hard to see what was depicted in the middle. She reached around, pulled it loose, and stared at it. A tree. Some kind of tree?

Perhaps the Kachelhoffer sisters could help her. She wasn't about to call them out at early hours two mornings in a row. After she gently took care of the remains of her finny friends, she set the card carefully by her bedside. Reaching underneath the bed, she drew forth one of the yearbooks from when Tessa Aiken attended Nickleberry High, but her fingers dropped away after only five minutes. She fell into a deep sleep.

The alarm jangled her awake, announced Sunday in bright neon, beeped seven times, and jangled again until she hit the Off button. The day's planned events rolled out in a mental announcement board while she showered, put on makeup, and dressed. What in Hades ever made her volunteer her spacious kitchen with two ovens, her ample dining area, and wraparound porch for the Irish Fling Sourdough and Meat Pasties Contest, she couldn't imagine.

Before she got downstairs, the phone jangled. She jumped over the last two steps, dodged around Charlie Brown, and grabbed the kitchen receiver. "Ah, Sheriff Tucker. Morning."

Tucker sneezed, excused himself a moment, and finally said, "Been reading over all the notes. Seems there might be a connection years past over in Tyler School District. Yep, let's see. Tessa Aiken, Dan Oxhandler, and the Caddy owner."

"Bernie Burkhalter?"

"You write down what I want, hear now?"

She did and frowned when she hung up the phone. "Odd. Dan never mentioned he'd worked in another district."

Somehow, she had to get a few questions answered today. The first one about *why* someone got into her home again to take the lives of her finny friends as well as leaving a calling card of sorts was answered. She knew the *how*. Her own stupidity in leaving the front door open. Secondly, she wanted to know if Dan or Neeper or both were responsible for the cottage break-in. And thirdly, why was Tessa's Irish quilt square in their boat? Willi pushed the last hairpin into her sleek chignon with only a few tendrils dangling. She frowned. Seemed like there was something else she needed to focus on. She tapped her cheek with the blusher. Guess she'd think of it later. Meanwhile, she tucked the unusual card inside a baggie along with the quilt square. She placed all the evidence into her purse.

She attended the eight-thirty rather than the ten o'clock services at the United Methodist Church. Reverend Jordan Farmer had so earnestly supported the Irish Fling Festival, despite his recent injury, that she dared not miss today. Playing football with the youth group had earned him a stint on crutches. But with robes flowing, he hobbled up to the dais and took his seat. His youthful eyes twinkled in the backdrop of freckles, not diminished even by his fifth decade.

Elba sat on her right, Agatha next to her. Try as she might, Willi could never understand the mix of the white witches' philosophy and religion. They seemed to have no problem reconciling their white witchcraft with Sunday excursions into middle-class Protestantism. On the far side of Agatha sat the sheriff.

Sitting in the same pew with the Kachelhoffer sisters and Sheriff Brigham Tucker posed a problem. Double-dang blast it, she had planned to show them the card during the service, let them mull over its meaning, and by the time they sang the last hymn, she would have had a few answers. But if she showed it to the sisters now, the sheriff would see it. Of course, he would eventually. She planned to share with him about the third break-in at her home, but not until she had more facts. So much for the moment for that plan.

Her Aunt Minnie and her sweetheart, Rodrigo Vivar, sat in the pew in front of Willi. Those in both pews exchanged hand squeezes and air kisses. Aunt Minnie leaned her head over on Rodrigo's shoulder. Willi always smiled at his resemblance to Charlton Heston, albeit a shorter Charlton Heston, in the role of El Cid. In fact, Aunt Minnie often called him her El Cid, meaning her own hero.

Suddenly, Elba got up, motioning for Willi to move over into her vacated space. Willi whispered, "What's going on?"

" 'Peting."

" 'Peting?"

Elba crossed her arms under her bosom. "She gets mean when she 'petes." She thumbed in Agatha's direction, barely missing Willi's nose in the process.

"Hmmm." Willi hoped Elba wasn't picking up Hortense's habit of a new word a day. She had no idea what '*peting* was.

Agatha's sharp elbow caught her in her right rib. "Sister is the one who gets miffed and out of sorts. It's the pressure, of course, knowing her goods can't touch mine."

"Hmmm." Willi was glad the minister called for a prayer about then, and she knew just what to pray for.

At the reverent amen, Elba said, "I've 'peted with the best in this here county and three others aside. Ain't nobody, Sister included, can put the *p* in prize, pride, or 'petin like I can."

Willi groaned. Guess the Lord hadn't heard her last prayer. "What," she asked, "is—?"

"What I'm saying is, the judges are going to be looking for authentic. Irish all the way. She's planning on using a ton of garlic and basil and all kinds of stuff that ain't got a thing to do with Irish flavoring."

Agatha leaned over just as the choir's opening song began. "I can beat you out any day. No meanness meant, Sister, it's just fact. Judges are going to love my sourdough bread dipped in sweet onion sauce. The competition should not cause a problem between us, though. We have more important things to discuss with Willi, remember? The Nickleberry Home. Remember? A matter of life or—"

"Shush," Elba admonished.

Willi sighed. Ah, *'peting*. Competing. Elba and Agatha were in both the Sourdough Bread Contest and the Irish Meat Pasty competition. "I have something I want you all to focus on, too." She reached into her purse.

Just as she pulled out the card, Sheriff Tucker leaned around Agatha and said, "Song is about to end. You all quit your chirping."

Quickly, Willi shoved the card back into her purse and snapped it shut as the choir finished "Morning Has Broken." Reverend Jordan Farmer intoned in his rather musical voice about the church activities before launching into the sermon for the day: "Togetherness on the Spiritual Plain." He was doing a wonderful job with the extended metaphor of plain and plane, and yet Willi's mind zoomed off at jet speed toward an American Airlines craft with one Quannah Lassiter aboard.

Ah, he was strangely dressed in white buckskins with beaded fringe work. His hair, combed down over his broad shoulders, glistened as morning light broke through the small window along with twisting vines in an intricate pattern. Willi smiled at the sight of what she could only describe as so beautiful they had to have been twined together by the angels. The light caught the sparkle in his dark eyes as he stared down at her, the woman by his side.

Willi, too, wore white in a fringed shawl. Her blue-green eyes danced while she twirled a strand of her curly hair between her fingers. He leaned down as if to kiss her, but instead laughed. "Winyan, you never bore me," he said. "You make me smile at unexpected times. Your Tweetybird Medicine is strong. You make me laugh. You give me joy."

She sighed, closed her eyes, and waited for the kiss. And she waited. And waited. At last she opened her eyes and gasped. Brother Turkey Buzzard, neck feathers ruffled out in anger, glared at her, reached out, and snapped a fringe from her dress. His breath was foul like poison. She drew back as far as the aircraft's window would allow. He snorted out the rank death odor; she turned her head. Outside the plane, darkness caressed the craft, and only starlight glittered.

A face appeared outside the window, from which the green vines had disappeared. Quannah's voice came through clearly. "Winyan, don't get in the way of the birds of prey, the animals of prey, don't get in the way. . . ." His face drifted out of sight, but the words continued. "Don't get in the way of the wolves or the birds of prey . . . prey." The armrest gouged her on one side, the sharp-taloned bird struck her in her ribs on the other.

Reverend Jordan Farmer intoned, "Let us pray."

Agatha's sharp elbow landed another blow to Willi's midriff. Elba poked her in her left arm. "Stop that woolgathering. You daydreaming again sure enough. You'd think you'd grow out of that."

"Now, Sister," Agatha whispered. "It's not that with her. Quannah agrees with me. She has the visions, you know. Course, she has to learn how to interpret them. A sacred place like this would be the perfect ambiance to have one. Now don't go picking on her about that."

Elba grunted by way of apology. "Yes, seems you're
right. She's done that since a child. Can't help it, I guess."

"Excuse me," Willi said, "did you two notice that I was
sitting right here between you?"

"Now if that ain't a silly question, I don't know what is
unless it's Misty Sue's new baby, poor little ugly thing, or
maybe Ben Porter's new beard—all three hairs of it—or
maybe it's the silly look on Reverend Farmer's face right
now. What you suppose he's looking at us for?"

Willi shuffled behind the Kachelhoffer sisters but left
them to do the hand-shaking ritual as she rushed to her car.
When she parked at the farmhouse, she smiled. Everything
was going great. Students, hired for the day, had already
placed the shamrock-covered cloths on tables beneath the
spreading oaks and along the three sides of the wraparound
porch. One rushed out the door with green napkins. In a few
minutes, Elba arrived and hustled to the kitchen to help
India Lou with last-minute details. As Willi passed through,
Agatha came in the back door. She had her two entries in
beautifully woven green baskets with green checked covers. These she set along with the rest of the entries on the
dining room table. All the chairs had been removed to allow
the judges to eventually go around the table and taste as
they desired. India Lou had backed out of the competition
but had supplied the beautiful garland of roses and vines
woven between each of the seven contestants' offerings.

After Willi changed into a flowing white ankle-length
dress with a white lace shawl, she returned to help. India
Lou pinned a rosebud and shamrock corsage in Willi's hair.
"Ah, shame your feller ain't here to see you looking so
pretty, Miss Willi, it sure is. I gots my camera. Smile. Ah,
that's pretty. He'll like that, yes ma'am, he will." She
shoved her camera in an apron pocket.

Willi grabbed her friend's hands between her own.
"How are you?"

"'Bout well as can be 'spected, I guess. They don't give

me Tessa yet. I can get past anything with the good Lord's help, yes ma'am, I can, but can't move on until . . ."

"I understand. You just keep yourself busy here if that helps. You'll find plenty to do with just keeping the Kachelhoffer sisters from squabbling over the sourdough."

"Bottom line, Miss Willi, I'll do the bestest I can with what I gots, but you asking lot out of me to watch those two, yes ma'am."

Willi strolled out to the porch where the scent of roses surrounded her while the breeze lifted the white lace around her shoulders. Perfect weather, perfect day. She frowned. Right. If you discounted all the frustrations. She'd not yet told anyone about Chaucer and Beowulf nor about Tessa's scarf found aboard the *Comanche Raider*. And there was this niggling worry about one Lakota-speaking lawman. Surely, her vision, as he would call it, didn't mean he was in danger on the flight home. She shook her head. No, that didn't feel right.

Trust the feelings. The knowing is inside you. Be aware. Think.

Yeah, but if he knew some of the left fields her knowing took her, he'd probably advise her to get a double dose of Valium quickly. What she truly thought was that some jerk of a turkey was going to pick on her in some way, maybe nudge her out of the way so he could get to better prey than she. Now, that was a crazy thought that had absolutely no basis in reality, right?

She tilted her head and peered at her reflection in the bird-bath. She touched the bloodred rose in her hair. Wait just a cotton-picking minute. Perhaps there was reality in that thought process. Her home had been ransacked, someone had trespassed at the cottage, her finny friends had been skewered. Oh, yeah, and don't forget Burkhalter or someone in his yellow Caddy running her into the ditch and the monster truck that had stalked her. Hairs on her arms rose, and she shivered. Okay, just put those ideas on hold. Enjoy the moment and try for just a smidgen of the courage shown by India Lou.

Do the best you can with what you've got.

The first cars rolled into the drive. Two sophomores directed the drivers through the gate to the freshly mown field. Willi put on her best smile to greet the contest judges and the guests.

Something caught her eye near the grape arbor. She squinted and brought the two people into focus. Sammie Yannich, hands on her hips, shook her head against whatever the new superintendent, Jarnagin Ventnor, was saying.

Elba approached and considered the couple, too. "They arrived in the same car. Wonder what old Bernie thinks of them together, huh?"

"It's none of our business."

"Well, it don't seem like no romantical get-together. Can't imagine what business they'd have with each other, though."

"Elba, you're worse than I am. They work in the same school district. Could be a hundred subjects to be discussed. Now, let's get back to our other guests."

India Lou's tall figure loomed over both Elba and Willi. She waved her ebony arm and pointed toward the bower. "Whatcha think about that there now?"

"Willi said it ain't none of our business," Elba grumbled.

Superintendent Ventnor disappeared in the crowd, but Burkhalter stood now with Sammie. She grabbed his arm and leaned her head against his shoulder. The couple disappeared into the deeper foliage.

Willi nudged both Elba and India Lou away from the rendezvous.

Agatha, in a bright yellow blouse and Irish green skirt flowing about soft yellow boots, came dancing up and touched Willi's chin. "Sugar, your cheeks are bright red. You might ought to get out of this dry wind and sun." Her look took in Elba when she said in a theatrical whisper and exaggerated roll of her eyes, "We have to meet in the library nook."

Willi sighed. "Fine. We have a half hour before the judges start tasting. I have a tarot card or something like one to show you all anyhow."

In a breathless voice, Agatha continued, "Only chance we'll have to make plans for tonight. It's a matter of life or death. We have to be brave, be strong. We can do this!"

"Do what?" Willi said, her hands on her hips. "Just what wild schemes are you two Kachelhoffer sisters into now?"

Elba crossed her arms. "My crystal ball gave a vision last night. All kinds of wild vines twisting and turning around the wolves and around the trees. We got to act, or somebody is a goner tonight."

Agatha added, "My, yes, Sister, and the tarot cards laid out a horrible plight if we do not intervene for the good."

Willi shut her eyes, breathed deeply, and hoped when she opened them, a cauldron of newt's eyes and monkey's tails wouldn't be bubbling.

CHAPTER
7

Willi sat in her Herculon recliner. she straightened her flowing white ankle-length skirt and shawl. The Kachelhoffers wore fierce frowns. She said, "What?"

"You've got to understand," Agatha said, twisting a lavender cloth around her waist. "You've got to understand that this is serious and truly life-threatening."

"More serious than a wart on your nose, a cold sore on your lip, or a pimple on your—"

"Elba!" Willi sighed. "Who? What tragedy? And maybe you should be telling this to Sheriff Tucker."

Agatha shoved a gray strand into her bun. "Well, truth to tell, we did already approach Brigham."

"And?"

Elba snapped her fingers. "Told us to forget it, don't get involved, that in due time and by due process it'll be looked into. Now, Willi, if Agatha, the love of his life, can't sway him otherwise, the rest of us don't have a hope."

Willi peered outside at the revelers in various shades of green. A cardinal flew among them to settle on a branch. No one but she seemed to take note of the beautiful flash of color. She turned her attention back to the sisters. "What?"

Elba said, "They're planning to kill that old lady."

Willi raised both hands out, fingers splayed. "Whoa. Who are *they?* Who is *she?* Where did you hear all—?"

"That's what I'm trying to tell. Meadowbrook Senior Citizens' home."

Elba shoved her bosom up and wiggled a little. "In particular that dang head night shift nurse, Inga Rufflestone. I care for folks there twice a week, you know. Take 'em baskets of goodies, do their hair, take walks with 'em, play checkers, whatever. They been keeping her drugged."

"*She* being?"

Agatha said, "She is Mrs. Ventnor."

Willi frowned. "Ventnor? Any kin to our new superintendent? Older sister perhaps? Aunt?"

Elba nodded. "Yep. Wife. And our old friend. Way back when we's teens. She was Viola Fiona McPherson then moved off to Kansas and attended college. Think that's where she met up with *him.* They went on visits to Ireland now and again."

"Whoa, ladies, he's not married."

"According to him, he was divorced years ago. But she says otherwise," Elba said.

"And," Willi said, "she's saying these things while on drugs. Uh-huh, well—"

Elba pulled out a much-creased and worn paper. "She's been acting like she swallows the meds but spits them out. That's why she can talk now, but she don't let them know she can." Elba eased each fold open. "Bless her, she kept this hidden, even when they stuck her in there. Look at the proof."

Willi carefully held the sheet near the sunshine streaming through the window. "Marriage certificate. Well, I'll be. But, ladies, maybe she has some early onset of dementia. Perhaps he put her in there and—"

"And?" Agatha asked. "Put her in there, but claims he's not married to her? Doesn't sound like what a loving

husband would do. She says he's wanting her dead. She's
the one with the money, and he's wanting her a goner.
Now, if you don't have a loving spouse or child to check on
you, things can happen in those places. Most people are
good and take care of the old ones like they're babies, but
this Nurse Ingastone—"

"Rufflestone," Elba corrected. "Inga Rufflestone don't
have the warmth of an Antarctic ice cube. Viola Fiona says
Inga's in cahoots with Jarnagin Ventnor." Willi held a hand
palm outward, but that didn't stop Elba.

Elba said, "We just know what we seen with our own
eyes and overheard Sunday two weeks ago. We'd a-come
to you sooner, but we tried to convince Tucker. Lost cause.
Men."

Agatha twitched a loose hair behind her ear. "Now, Sister, don't be so hard on Brigham. It does sound fantastic.
You know the male of the species has a harder time trusting the intuitive knowing than the female."

"Yes," Willi agreed. "Even Quannah, though he talks
about it and strives toward it, admits it's a harder concept
for him than for me." Willi shook her head. "And you want
me to do what?"

Elba said, "Allow us to bring her here for a day or
maybe two, seeing as how you've room galore, and help us
get her here all comfy-like."

"Why," asked Willi, "are words like *kidnapping* coming
to mind?"

"No such thing," Elba said. "No such thing. It is sort of
a . . . a sneak attack—"

"Because?"

"Because if we sign her out for a three-day pass, which is
the most a body is allowed, that Rufflestone woman will
alert the husband. If we can sneak her out, might be they
won't check on her for a couple days, and she'd have time to
meet with her attorneys. If they check on her and push
comes to move the mule, we'll tell them we thought we
signed her out proper. We'll say they lost the papers. They're
always losing paperwork."

"So . . . she's not going to be killed tonight as you two so melodramatically claimed?"

Agatha played with her silky sash and looked at the ceiling. She said, "We might have stated it with dramatics just to get your attention. You can't let Elba and me do this alone, Willi. A couple days to see her lawyers, that's all we're asking. Viola Fiona says if that husband of hers hasn't had her sign away her rights while on all those drugs, then she can turn the tables on the sorry thing."

Agatha again spoke while swishing her bright skirt with one hand, one of her endearing habits that made her seem so much younger than her sixties. "We may be overreacting. However, Viola Fiona Ventnor does feel strongly that it's this week she's in danger. We only get to converse with her in bits and pieces, you understand, when others aren't around. It has something to do with the Irish Fling Festival. She truly feels before the end of it, she'll be dead if she doesn't get out and see about her affairs."

"Yep, and we both been having them bad dreams," Elba said. "Nasty as a harlot's johns, darker than the reaper's breath, frightening as a killer's knot."

Willi held up her hand. "I get the picture."

"Dreams of a white and black wolf fighting, snarling, bringing blood, slinging it all over," Agatha said. "Most frightening. Nightmares about the wolves and the trees, strange trees that bring death with all these vines or . . . some kind of ropes." She shivered.

"Wolves? Strange trees?" Willi whispered. Seeing Quannah's face outside the aircraft window and hearing his words might have been a warning. She shivered and repeated, "Trees?"

"You've had dreams, too? Maybe one of your . . . uh . . . visions?"

Willi chose not to go in that direction but pulled out the card. She told them about finding Beowulf and Chaucer skewered in the moat. Then she handed the plastic-coated card to the sisters. "Is it a tarot card?"

Elba tapped the forest green back side with gold design in

the middle. "This here's a Celtic cross. So, guess we got us another link to this Irish Fling Festival, the first being Viola Fiona's fear she'll not be here to see the end of it." She turned the card over. Two words, one at the top—*Coll*—and one at the bottom—*Hazel*—seemed smothered by an edging of woven and twisting vine designs in gold and green.

Agatha said, "Work of the angels. That's what those designs are, right, Sister?"

"Yep, them's fancy Irish knots, Celtic designs. That is what they was called—work of the angels—because it took such a lot of patience and love to create them. Now this here in the middle is a Hazel tree."

Underneath the tree was a depiction of a salmon in stylized waves of water. "I suppose," said Agatha, "this part is why the card suited being placed on your aquarium. Possibly the lady at the fair, the harpist who's the Landises' cousin, could tell you more. She knows a lot of the Celtic lore."

"So why did someone skewer two goldfish and leave this for me to find?"

Elba said, "We don't often use them, so we may be missing the right interpretation." She wiped her hands on her oversized apron. "If it has to do with land and such, a lot of boundaries round hereabouts been broken into." She held up fingers as she counted them off. "Your house two times and the cottage."

"Usually things come in threes." Agatha frowned. "Breaking and entering. So unlawful."

Willi sighed. Hmm. It was her turn to look at the ceiling. Thank goodness there was no mirror overhead to show her guilty features over her little excursion into so called deeper waters.

Agatha snapped her fingers. "Brigham told me not to say anything. I wasn't supposed to see something in his office the other day. Goodness knows, I wouldn't want to mess up the investigation, but you are his sworn-in deputy. You two will be sharing information, right?"

Willi chose not to mention that the swearing-in was only

for interviews when she was with Sheriff Tucker. Such small details needn't be given out to everyone. She merely said, "Okay."

To help matters, Elba said, "And it ain't like Sheriff Tucker was into aiding us with Viola Fiona. Spit it out, Sister."

"That card, the tree and vines, that's what I saw."

Willi frowned. "You saw this card at the sheriff's office?"

Agatha twisted the ends of her sash. "In a little plastic bag."

Willi nodded. "An evidence bag."

"I rushed into his office. So rude of me."

"Anxious to see her man," Elba teased.

"I saw the file out on the desk. Tessa Aiken's name big as you please with the little bag aside it. Quickly, he shoved it into the file. Why he felt he had to do that, I don't know."

"Grrrrr." Willi ground out the words. "Because, obviously, he didn't want folks to know about it. Not even his trusted, sworn-in deputy. When I ID'd Tessa in the parking lot, the deputy bagged a piece of green cardboard. Oh, I've been a fool. This was Sheriff Tucker's tactic, probably cooked up between him and one Big Chief Lassiter, to keep one little lady out of the real details of the case." Willi stalked around the small nook. "Agatha, the card you saw had to be the same one found at the murder scene. So there's a tie-in with everything that's going on."

Agatha said, "That card. It was different. Something like *Straight,* but that isn't quite right."

Agatha looked up at the ceiling. *"Straif.* I bet it was *Straif."*

"Well, Sister, what in Hell does that mean?" Elba asked.

"Blackthorn. In witchcraft, the thorns of the blackthorn are used to pierce—kill—wax images."

Outside the window, screams erupted. Willi ran, the others on her heels. Dan Oxhandler landed a blow on Vic Ramirez's shoulder that knocked him sideways. Green sherbet punch splashed over both men and Saralee York. Gaining his balance, Vic elbowed Dan in the chin. The impact was hard enough to make Willi's knees turn to taffy. Dan's ever-present bottle of Evian water flew into the flower bed. Dan lowered his head, just as his namesake would, and slammed into Vic's midriff. This sent both sailing over another table, upending more punch, tea, and finger foods. Jarnagin Ventnor danced out of the way, but not before his blue shirt was soaked. Vic, after a blind swing that only punched air, bent over and held his hands to his knees. Dan, in the same position, stared at him.

Willi strode up to them and stood with hands on her hips. "Both of you. Apologize and leave. Right now." Her cheeks were hot, her heart pounding. *Damn the two.*

Neither man gave an inch. After a moment of silence stretching out longer than the Rio Grande, Vic Ramirez straightened his back. He looked at Willi. "Ms. Gallagher, I do apologize to you. He threw the first punch. You want me to stay and clean up, I will."

Her cheeks flamed. She spat out the words. "I don't care who threw the first punch or what was said to cause this. You are a respected fireman of the community. Dan is a teacher at the high school, for heaven's sake. Neither of you are in my sixth-period English class anymore. It's unforgivable behavior at . . . at my home." She took a deep breath. "I accept your apology, Vic, but maybe you'd better go on back to the firehouse for the day. Dan, I'm sure, will want to go cool off elsewhere. Now." She picked up the blue-capped Evian water bottle and slammed it into his hand. "Now."

In the hullabaloo of cleaning up, soothing hurt feelings, and seeing all the guests and workers off, she never found out the reason behind the fight. She was merely thankful that the contest entries had been in the dining room. Elba's sourdough bread won, hands down. She gloated over it considerably until Agatha's Irish meat pasties beat her out in that category.

One of the last guests to leave was Saralee York. Her white pant suit, ruined by the green punch, looked bruised. Her face, overly made-up as usual, also seemed bruised around the eyes as if she'd already been staying up nights grading papers. Her red hair fluffed and pulled forward left very little of her face showing, but still the tiredness showed. Mercy. Willi frowned. What would happen when they actually got into classes and started the paper load?

"Saralee," Willi asked, "are you getting enough rest?"

"Oh, the move from my former district took more out of me than I thought. I've been keeping late hours, too, with the Irish Fling Festival happenings."

"I noticed," said Willi, "you had a Celtic cross necklace and earring set on the other day."

"Yes, I'm very interested in the old ways, having visited some of the Druidic ruins in England, Ireland, and other areas. They had a simple philosophy."

"Anything in particular come to mind?"

"Oh, I was thinking of things like 'an eye for an eye.'"

Willi cleared the last tablecloth off. "That's a belief found in many faiths."

"True. I suppose the old ones seem more clean with their revenges."

"If," said Willi, "you're partial to fighting with maces and such. Lots of people lived hard lives full of battles. As a result, many must have been maimed. Goodness, what dark thoughts one fight between two good old boys has brought about."

Saralee wasn't turning loose of the subject so easily. "Ah, if getting rid of our enemies were only as easy as swinging a mace or cudgel." Saralee's voice, usually so monotone, rose an octave in passion. Her brown eyes flashed.

"Good grief," Willi said. "You are far too young to have any enemies. Been steeped into the dark Gaelic studies too long, perhaps? You'll have to attend the Irish Jig Contest. That's a far lighter side than the old tales of war and bloodshed that, to tell the truth, still separates folks in the old countries. We also still have the children's Leprechaun Costume Contest and lots of music. We'll put the pink back in those cheeks, yet."

Saralee glared with anger so palpable Willi could feel it hit her, and she couldn't imagine what she'd said to deserve such a look. She tried to soothe the younger woman.

"Uh . . . and I'm so sorry Dan and Vic ruined your lovely white suit."

The fierce look disappeared. Saralee, in her more normal monotone said, "I'm sorry. This heat, the long hours, and the fight—I guess I do need some rest, and don't worry about the suit. It's an old one anyway." As she turned to leave, she waved. The sun glinted off an enormous emerald crest ring with chains and smaller emeralds running in a spider web over her left hand.

Willi called her back. "By the by, I know Officer Piedra is a few years older than you, maybe eight, ten, or so, but he's got some similar interests."

In a cold voice, Saralee said, "Excuse me?"

"Please, don't get upset. I just wanted you to know he writes poetry about Ireland's legends. He's intelligent, a nice man, a good job—"

Saralee sighed.

Willi did, too. "Sorry. I hate when the Kachelhoffer sisters matchmake for me, but with your being new in the town, I thought . . . I'm so sorry."

"It's okay. Who knows? I might at least talk to him if we meet."

She laid her hand on Willi's arm a moment. The sun caught at the stones again and winked. She must have one of those rings or an enormous bracelet for every outfit. Willi sighed. You'd think with such youthful hands, she'd want to go with simple to show them off. Well, variety makes the world go round. Willi waved and walked off to bid the rest of the guests a good-bye.

At fifteen until eight, Willi met the Kachelhoffer sisters at Frogs' Feet. Surely, she'd be able to help them with Viola Fiona Ventnor without having to resort to the actual abduction. Their cozy front room, with fireplace and candles alight, welcomed her with scents of bayberry, black cherry, and vanilla. Polished wood walls gleamed. Cornbread baked on the side of the fireplace, and in a small cauldron broccoli cheese soup, redolent of onions, bubbled. She grinned at the two seated at a round table, brocaded burgundy and forest green corduroy cloth hanging to touch the woven rag rugs. "Thanks for the supper invite."

"Oh, Willi," Agatha said, "it's the least we can do." Agatha's familiar, the longhaired white tom named Clyde, wound round Willi's ankles before he pattered to his basket by the hearth.

"One more thing, too," Elba added. "We are a-going to do the reads before chomping on the vittles." She sat with her feet atop Rose Pig. The porker lowered her white lashes in a languid welcome as if to say, "See? This is the way to run a comfortable home."

Willi drew up a chair between the sisters. Okay, these two wanted to talk about something that was bothering them. She would humor them, agree to just about anything other than accompanying them into the Meadowbrook Senior Citizens' Home on a kidnapping jaunt. They often used the tarot deck and the crystal ball to warm up to their subject. After offering thanks to the Universal One and all the helpful spirits, Agatha shuffled the deck. She then had Willi cut the cards a number of times. When Agatha turned up the cards, she and Elba exchanged glances and sighed in unison.

With her slender fingers, Agatha tapped the first cards. "Three queens again. You're being deceived by many women."

"Tell her about this one." Elba's gnarled finger pointed at the significator card, the queen of swords.

"Yes, Sister. Well, this represents you, Willi, and the one laying across you is the obstacle you have in store for you." She placed the third at the top of the queen. "This is to tell us what you can hope for in this situation, and this fourth and last one indicates what or *who* you can use."

Willi considered the brightly colored pieces of cardboard. After surrounding the first queen, they lay in a cross with four other cards in a straight line to the right. Willi grinned. "Hey, this one is a handsome knight; *what* I can look for, you said. Not so bad, right? Maybe it's Quannah?"

Elba and Agatha looked at her with pity. "First off," Elba

said, "considering the surrounding lay, this here could be a younger female. Whether female or male, there's a dark secret what could do you great danger in some way." The two good witches exchanged pointed looks.

"What?" Willi asked. "What are you not telling me? Not that I take this all seriously, exactly, but . . . what?"

"You are stubborn about trusting the reads, but you've got to admit we've told you true more times than you can count on your fingers and toes. Been guiding you right, we have."

Willi frowned. "Well, between you all's guidance and Quannah's insisting I learn to follow my Native American roots and teaching, there are times when confusion sets in."

Agatha patted her hand. "Confusion is the way to self-discovery, and the path is different for each person. Sister and I know that you are on a most unusual life span. Part of our job in this lifetime is to help you through."

"By getting me involved with a confrontation with my new super when he finds out about my harboring his wife?"

Agatha drew her attention back to the layout of the tarot. "One of the three queens isn't who they seem."

"Sister is right on the mark. Makes me as nervous as that old Easter bunny with an empty basket, as skittered as a dangblame frog on the freeway, as—"

"Elba!" Willi hadn't meant to raise her voice, but the cuckoo clock over the mantel always took her by surprise. The seven dwarfs marched out whistling their work song as Snow White clanged on a triangle eight times. When finished, the dwarfs went inside the cottage, Snow White stood guard with her broom, and the bluebird hands of the clock clicked a notch over.

With a nod, Agatha took out a half-used bound writing notebook with an attached ribbon to hold the place. She took pen in hand.

Elba said, "Guess we're ready." Settling her ample form more comfortably, Elba concentrated on the crystal ball in front of her. Willi was amazed at the change that came over the old woman when she brought out this divination tool. Elba grew quiet, and she never went on and on like the typical shyster fortune-tellers. Usually her messages were cryptic and had to be interpreted by the one for whom Elba did the divination. Candles flickered.

A log crackled, causing Clyde to jump up, hackles raised. He didn't settle down but kept his eyes on Elba. Rose Pig, in great agitation, flicked both ears in opposite directions. Wind came up unexpectedly and wheezed underneath a casing, and still Elba remained silent. Her breathing had grown shallow.

Willi shivered as if a winter wind had seeped into her bones. She pulled her white shawl from the chair back onto her shoulders.

The spitting fire died down, Clyde settled, the hog sighed, and at last, in a quiet voice, Elba said, "Black wolf in white. Eyes hidden. Poison wrought the nemesis unbidden." She repeated it four times.

Agatha wrote the message in the notebook. Willi peeked at the entry and saw Agatha also made notation of the date, exact time, and who was present during the read, including the familiars.

When Elba covered the crystal ball with a blue cloth and pushed back from the table, she sighed. The fire glowed warmly, Clyde licked his paw before stretching out, and Rose Pig oinked contentedly beneath her lady's feet.

Willi said, "Do you know this is the first time you've actually let me witness a divination all the way through other than the fun ones at the fairs and parties?"

Elba laughed. "Those are more for fun, but approached seriously, too. This here was a . . . spiritual experience. Happens when you come to the read with a true concern and ask for help. Sometimes the message is clear as a Colorado river, other times as muddy as a pig wallow, no disrespect, Rose Pig."

Willi asked, "Why do you write all that down?"

Agatha handed her the notebook to study while explaining. "As Sister said, sometimes we get strange messages, hard to interpret at first. But, if you are patient and aware of all the signs the universe offers you, you will be given clarity and confirmation about the message as time goes along. Seems the spirits sometimes have a very military outlook, telling us in a need-to-know mode and a little at a time."

She showed Willi a read some months past. "See? We did this read and kept getting messages about peacocks. Next day, Elba tripped and bruised her ankle. The following week, we saw a peacock run across the yard. An hour later, we saw a show on peacocks on the television. The next day, out of the blue one of our old friends came thousands of miles to visit. His name was—"

"Let me guess. Peacock."

Elba snorted. "Yep. Cody Peacock."

"So . . . I still don't understand."

Elba took up the tale again. "We was a might hard-headed on that message ourselves. Then Cody told us about his latest job, bronc riding in Wyoming. He took a mighty tumble and broke both his ankles."

"You hurt your ankle, right? And he broke two ankles?"

"Now you're beginning to see. So we read up on them peacocks, the birds, I mean. Seems them dang birds, what are so pretty to look at tail-wise has the ugliest feet in the land. Some lore says that's why they run around with that raucous cry, 'cause they're lamenting their ugly feet."

"So?" Willi asked.

"So, finally we were *aware*," Elba said. "We knew to be watchful and to consider anything real careful concerned with long walks or such that might mean foot trouble."

"And?"

"Sister's feet," Agatha said, "swelled up like a matching pair of beached whales. She was in such pain. We used herbs. Nothing was strong enough. We took her to the doctor. That's when all the warnings clicked in."

Totally immersed in the peacock tale, Willi leaned both elbows on the table. Both sisters' faces seemed much more like friendly gnomes, rather than witches, in the candle-light. "So the doctors were able to give her a diuretic and all was well."

"Absolutely not," Agatha said. "The specialist's name was Dr. Phillip P. Cockerel."

"P. Cock—"

"Exactly, and he was," Elba said, "as obnoxious as a strutting bird, as full of himself as a dang stuffed turkey, and as flighty headed as a dingbat."

"He insisted," Agatha said, "that sister needed an operation right then and there to the monetary tune of fifteen thousand. Said he would put her in the hospital that day."

"But them alarm bells were going off by then," Elba said. "We took our leave of Dr. P. Cockerel lickety-split, got two more opinions, and got them tootsies taken care of. Just a change of diet and more time off the feet for a couple months, and I was righter than a newborn baby."

Agatha pointed to the story written in the notebook. "If we hadn't taken the read seriously, if we'd not received so many confirmations and been aware, we'd not have recognized the danger when walking into his office. We would have been crying over the financial loss, the horror of what his operation might have done to her . . . oh, we've been blessed and protected so many times."

"And," Elba added as the half-hour bluebirds chirped and Dopey peeked out of the cottage, "we're going to have more blessings when we save Viola Fiona tonight."

"Save?"

"After that Peacock story, you willing to ignore all the warnings concerning her safety?" Elba asked.

Willi said, "Tonight?"

Both sisters nodded. Agatha said, "It's best. We have a plan."

CHAPTER
8

The moon, ducking behind a heavy bank of clouds, seemed to wink at the two nurses and the driver. Willi hated the starched costume with white hose. Elba wasn't too fond of it either, twisting and turning it here, pulling it down there. Agatha, in her usual bright plumage, drove.

Willi winked back at the moon and shook her head. "Why the getups if this is not an abduction?"

"Done told you," Elba said, "these uniforms just make things easier. They don't allow any but emergency visitors after hours. We can go up and down the halls unnoticed."

"They are bound to have a small night staff, and I'm sure everyone knows everyone."

"Oh, they're used to seeing me lending a hand. As for you, some of those folks have private nurses come in when a loved one is taking a turn for the worse. There are also hospice ladies who are in and out. But everyone is dressed right, and so we're going to be, too."

"Agatha looks like Spain's flag on parade!"

"I could only get two uniforms, one short and your size,

one short and my size. Sister is going to stay out in the car in the darkest corner of the parking lot next door."

"That's a mechanic shop. Rick's Wrecker or something."

"Which means," Agatha said, "no one will be there this time of night. I'm going to drop you all off in front of the portico drive and leave immediately. You all walk right in the front door, clipboards in hand, stethoscopes at the ready."

"And when we're ready to leave?"

"That's the tricky part," Elba said. "If we get a hurry on, we can get to Viola Fiona and push her out in a wheelchair at nine-thirty."

"I'm surprised you didn't say the witching hour."

"Here that is the witching hour."

"Meaning what exactly, Elba?"

"Meaning the doors automatically lock. Only way we can get out then is to go out the back, which can be opened but which sets off an alarm that would wake folks in three counties over."

"If that happens—us having to run out the back—where will Agatha be?"

Agatha drove underneath the lighted portico. Elba pushed Willi out the door. "Enough questions. It's nine on the dot. She'll drive through every fifteen minutes. Let's go."

Elba led her down one of six corridors—this one labeled Hansen Hall—branching off a nurse's station. They had taken only half a dozen strides when from one of the offices on the left Jarnagin Ventnor walked out. With him was a nurse who for size and muscle could give Arnold Schwarzenegger a run for the bodybuilding medal. Before the duo saw Willi, she grabbed Elba's elbow and stomped briskly back in the direction they had come. At the hub, she chose the next corridor over, Lattimer Lane. Willi grimaced. What could you expect from a place called Meadowbrook Senior Citizens' Home?

Elba said, "Fast thinking. You see? Maybe we're too late. You just got your first and hopefully only gander at

Nurse Inga Rufflestone. This way. We can cut through the cafeteria, which has entrances on both these wings."

Willi glanced at her watch. "Almost three minutes gone." She hurried to catch up. For a short-legged, round lady, Elba could get the pistons smoking. She made record time across the darkened cafeteria. At the doorway arch leading back into Hansen Hall and its muted, recessed lights, Willi peeked around the corner. She slammed back against the wall. She whispered, "They're still there."

"Makes no nevermind. We go to the left down the hall to Viola Fiona's room. They can't tell nothing from our backsides. We'll decide what to do there."

"Right." The broccoli soup was doing unpleasant things in her tummy. She checked the wall clock this time. "Five minutes. Already, five minutes."

"Don't go mental on me, Willi."

With backs to the dastardly duo, they walked slowly but purposefully. Behind them, Jarnagin Ventnor said, "Then this time give her a hypodermic, not a pill. Make sure she's . . . uh . . . comfortable. I'll be back in about two hours, near eleven, so do it soon; then she'll be totally relaxed for the trip."

Willi cut her eyes over to Elba, who was doing the same. "Uh-oh."

"We better go into a couple rooms just to make things look right, you know?"

"Okay," Willi said.

"Girl, are you breathing?"

"I'm . . . I'm fine. Obviously, I would never be a comfortable criminal."

"Well, now don't go judging yourself so harshly on a first time out."

Willi swallowed back a confession that somehow needed telling about a certain cabin cruiser on Nickleberry Lake.

Elba said, "We'll go down to the end room and work our way back to Viola Fiona's when he's gone."

Inside room thirty-seven, they paused. Loud snoring emanated from the two beds, surrounded by flowing pink curtains. The rest of the room was like walking into a floor display of *House and Garden*. One side was done in ginghams, ivy plants, and gewgaws of every sort, while the far side was done in a Southwestern motif of cactus and pottery. *Shower to Shower* bath powder vied with Camelot perfume. Night-lights winked on both sides of the room. Neither occupant was in danger of being awakened unless workers started sandblasting in the next few hours.

Elba peeked outside. "She's seeing him out. Come on. Time's a-wasting."

Willi followed her to room forty-six. Only one occupant here, but she, too, was sawing those proverbial logs, and they had to be the size of the great sequoias. The room had hundreds of framed photos on the walls and even a couple of trophies. Willi studied them. "Women's golf champ in 1953. Here's an award for best pool secretary at Lockheed, 1967."

Elba wrung her hands and pulled at the tight uniform. "Maybe it's too late."

"No. You heard them. She hasn't yet been given the sedative."

"How long we been here now?"

"Almost eight minutes. We've got plenty of time. Let's wake her and go. Like I said, though—"

"I know, I know, you got to hear from her own lips about her a-wanting to get out to her lawyers."

Willi drew back the pink and white striped blanket. A cadaverous face with a gaping hole for a mouth lay on the pristine pillow. The empty mouth was explained when Willi glanced at the glass beside the bed. Gleaming dentures smiled at her. A snore stirred the occupant, who licked her lips and made smacking noises. Suddenly all the smells associated with hospitals and like institutions hovered around Willi's nose. Light-headed, she took in a deep breath. Her wristwatch seemed to tick louder than the Kachelhoffers' cuckoo clock. *Twelve minutes.*

"Agatha will be driving through in just a few moments."

"This ain't her."

"Of course, it's not Agatha."

"You *are* going south on me, Willi. This ain't *Viola
Fiona*." She pinched Willi's arm.

"Well, what was that for?"

"Don't want you fainting on me. Seems you'd have the
strength for some work with that broccoli soup and cornbread sticking to your innards."

"Don't remind me. What do you mean this isn't her?"

"Must've been forty-five, not forty-six. Sorry. Let's head
to that one."

Willi opened the door. Inga Rufflestone, with her back to
Willi, was just saying good night to the occupant of the
room across the hall. Elba heard, too, and pointed to the tiny
bathroom. Damn and double damn. No night-light even, but
the door didn't shut all the way. The odors here almost made
the broccoli do a repeat performance. If Willi's nose were
any judge, someone had tried to mask the odors with Lysol
and Mr. Clean. She studied Inga through the crack.

Nurse Rufflestone pulled the covers up over the women's
golf champ of 1953. She spoke into a small walkie-talkie.
"Get the hypodermic ready for Mrs. Ventnor. I'll get it after
checking these last two rooms."

When she turned to peruse a chart, the night-light gave
Willi a vision—a frightful one of Rufflestone's face. Huge
eyes, almost three times the normal, which bulged, studied
the drug dosage. Willi raised an eyebrow. The woman was
much younger than Willi had thought at first glimpse.
Probably in her early thirties, like Willi. Inga's thick, long
hair, which could have been pretty, was simply stuck up in
a rubber band in a twisted mess. Tiny beauty spots adorned
her face but in such profusion that as a child she would
probably have been nicknamed Warty by peers. Her lac-
quered nails, obviously the twenty-five-dollar salon fakes,
were chipped. Willi grimaced. All in all, Nurse Inga
offered an unkempt persona.

Nurse Inga reached toward the bathroom door. Her
scent, old perspiration and coconut oil, made Willi wrinkle
her nose. When Inga touched the doorknob, Willi froze.
Cold sweat oozed between her shoulder blades. Her knees

trembled. Nurse Inga grasped the handle and closed the door so firmly Willi figured they'd need a crowbar to get out. The walkie-talkie blurted, "Pizza's here. Come pay your part."

When the outer door shushed close, Willi asked, "What now?"

"Perfect."

"Perfect?"

"It'll take a few minutes to sort out money. She'll go ahead and eat while it's hot. Then she'll get the hypo."

"Maybe."

Elba sighed. "Maybe. We'll give her two minutes before leaving here."

Room forty-five had no ambiance, no knickknacks, nothing personal or of permanence. This was the first time Willi understood that the two sisters might have the right of things. Elba lifted the blankets. A rather florid-faced, round woman of the generous proportions assigned to extra-extra-extra-large sizes, rose up and grabbed Elba's arm.

"And blessing the angels will be giving you. Elba, you're gooder than the leprechauns' own gold." Tears flowed down her cheeks. She pushed a curly bush of salt-and-pepper hair back. "You came for these old bones."

"Viola Fiona McPherson Ventnor, of course I come for you. Now, stop blubbering about being sixty. Old! Good grief, I'm just starting on my second childhood, and I'm sure as hell not old, so you can't be neither."

"I'll be needing my glasses, that I will. Agatha looks like she's shrunk to five feet, and I could-a sworn by the green she was a six-footer."

"Here's your spectacles. This here ain't Agatha. It's Willi."

"Willi is it? And I've heard so much to the good about you, child, yes I have."

Child? "Nice to meet you, too, Viola."

"That's Viola Fiona, that it is, if you please. If you've come to help, then I'm doubly glad to make your acquaintance. But it's a bit of downer I have for you now."

"Girlfriend, we're going to have to chat later. We got to get our booties in high gear. That damned Nurse Rufflestone is coming this way soon with a hypodermic to put you into a stupor. Your husband asked for that. Then your sorry piece of excuse for even an ass is hiding you elsewheres."

"Elba!"

"No, Willi, she's right, she is. He's a fartleberry if ever there was one, and there was many." Viola Fiona guffawed and covered her mouth. "A fartleberry being, don't you know, the dried bits of dung back o' the sheep or cow."

"Well, wasn't that what I said, a piece of shit?"

"Ladies, ladies, ladies. We have to go. Where is the wheelchair?" Willi glanced at her watch. "Agatha has already driven by once. We have about ten minutes to get to the front and meet her on her second trip around."

"That's part of the downer, don't you know."

"What?"

"The blasted nurse already come in. A pill I could have hidden until me first love O'Flannery afore Ventnor, don't you know, rode me bones again—and a good job he did of it—but what could I but do? I'm in an awful state of sleepy, that I am." To prove her point, she yawned.

Willi yelped. "No, no, no. We need you awake. Carrying you out of here would be like . . . like—"

"Like hauling the cow before the wagon? Oh, child, don't I know it. The wheelchair is inside the closet there."

With trembling hands, Willi grabbed the contraption, opened it up, and turned around to help Viola Fiona out of the bed. The woman's eyes fluttered shut, and her mouth opened in a peaceful snore. A great clatter behind Willi alerted her to the chair collapsing in on itself. Willi's heartbeat, revving somewhere near 800 rpm's, would have her in collapse if she didn't calm down. Elba grabbed the chair to lock the mechanisms open. Between them, they managed to heft the totally relaxed poundage of Viola Fiona into the chair. One of her very white legs, freckled profusely, hung over a metal arm.

Willi said, "That doesn't look right." Try as she might,

she couldn't shove the great heft of the woman into a more pliable or more ladylike position. "We have five minutes. Five minutes, Elba. That's all we have left. Five!"

Elba stood tall as her four-foot-eleven frame would allow. "Don't go mental again on me, Willi. Five is plenty. We'll just cover her snoring ass with this blanket and wheel our way to the front. The doors don't automatically lock until nine-thirty P.M. Everything is dangnabbed fine. No reason to panic. Here we go."

Willi's legs shook so badly she wanted to jump on top of the chair, too. Somehow, she managed to shuffle her way through the long Hansen Hall. At the hub, Nurse Inga and another aide rounded the corner from Lattimer Lane. Deftly, Elba turned to the right into the next of the six wings, Wilde Way. Willi could no longer feel her legs and wondered how in Hades she was managing to move without them. This wing, next to the outside windows, offered a view of the portico. Agatha and vehicle seemed to approach in slow motion.

Willi, too cotton-mouthed to speak, tried to swallow and pulled at Elba's sleeve. She pointed out the window. Elba nodded. "Here's a side French door. Maybe we can go out it." Just as Nurse Inga from around the corner announced "Lockdown in one minute," Elba, with her back to the glass, shoved with her rear. The door opened. Willi came through. The door slammed shut. A resounding click said the automatic lock did its job. Elba and Willi met Agatha in the darkest curve of the drive. Nothing could stop them now. Laying rubber, Agatha took off and sped up to a police cruiser.

"Who in thunderation is that?" Elba asked.

Willi yelled, "Brake, Agatha!"

Elba said, "Stomp on it. Swerve around. We ain't stopping for sirens, lights, or policemen."

The patrolman, flashing lights swirling out into the night, had other ideas. As they passed FM314, he gave chase.

Elba, from the backseat beside Viola Fiona, peered over the seat and shook Willi's shoulder. "Your eyes are big as tortillas. Calm down."

With a frown that would have melted every misfit in her seventh-period class, Willi said, "If either of you say one word, one syllable, I will . . . I will, so help me God, hurt you. Let me handle this."

Officer Jon Piedra knocked on Agatha's window. She didn't say a word after lowering it. Willi leaned over. "Officer Piedra, evening."

"Ms. Gallagher."

"What seems to be the problem?"

"May I see your license and registration, please?" he said to Agatha, who looked pointedly at Willi. She nodded curtly.

"Yes, ma'am, thank you." Jon Piedra wrote out a ticket. "This is for going seventy in a forty. You ladies been to a party, maybe drinking a little?"

Agatha, a teetotaler, gasped. Willi said, "No, Officer Piedra, not at all."

He leaned his head farther inside the car. "That lady isn't sleeping one off?"

Willi swallowed and tried three times before she could pass words over her dry tongue. "She's just getting out of nursing care. Medications make her sleepy. We were trying to get her home before she completely went off to La La Land, but—"

She took a couple of deep breaths and tried to smile through the glare of his flashlight. "Her wheelchair is in the back, if you'd like to check it out. We want to cooperate any way we can."

"Not necessary, Ms. Gallagher. And you, Mrs. Agatha Carstairs, slow down the rest of the way home. I don't think it's going to make any difference to the lady."

Agatha opened her mouth, but Willi quickly said, "She reverted to her maiden name, remember, Kachelhoffer."

He nodded. "Need to get it officially changed on your license, too, ma'am." His shoulder microphone blared to life. He leaned his head and listened to what seemed to be unintelligible pig Latin to Willi. "Got to run. Accident out west of town. At least, they're close to the hospital. Be careful, ladies."

Willi said, "Of course," to his retreating back. She leaned against the headrest. After a full minute she said, "Agatha, you may start the car and move off at a sedate—very slow and sedate speed. You both did very well. You get to live."

Agatha gunned the motor, peeled out, plastering Willi's head to her seat.

"What in hell?"

Agatha, with polka-dotted scarf flapping out the open window, said, "Willi, he's miles away by now."

"And besides," Elba said, "we got to get home and plan. Jarnagin Ventnor will find out in about an hour and a half that Viola Fiona did a bunk."

Willi muttered under her breath the rest of the way. ". . . going to be in jail . . . deserve to be incarcerated . . . less than model citizen . . . Quannah will never speak to me again." She sighed all the way down to her toenails.

Willi agreed to put Viola Fiona in one of the six upstairs guest rooms as long as the Kachelhoffer sisters stayed, too. "It will make it so much easier for Sheriff Tucker to have us all in one place," she said, "when he comes to arrest us." After a quick shower, she climbed under fresh sheets and listened to her messages.

One from Hortense Horsenettle to remind her about the Monday evening dinner the faculty and church was to bring for India Lou. She also said the body had been released and the service set for Tuesday afternoon. The message would have been much shorter if Hortense hadn't tried to work in the old slang word *piccolo,* referring to a jukebox, three times.

The second electronic touch came from Sheriff Tucker.

His gravelly voice said, "You clear up that Oxhandler Barbecue loose end tomorrow, would you now? Don't forget to check out the Tyler, Texas, connections. Kind of dull stuff, but safe paperwork for you, Miss Willi."

While she waited for what she was sure was going to be a sweet good night from Quannah, she mentally ticked off items. One: Get Viola Fiona's lawyer here. Two: Talk her way out of an accessory to kidnapping charge. Viola Fiona never did say she wanted the lawyers. Three: Ozzie Oxhandler. Four: Yes, see if she could find out what was missing from the high school library.

The sisters said things happened in threes, and Quannah sort of agreed. Frankly, after three break-ins on her private property, she was inclined to agree. Certainly their tale of the peacock made her take more notice of the constant spirit contacts or whatever one wanted to call them. As long as the old Celtic ghost, the banshee, didn't rise up, she'd manage everything else. Maybe she ought to find out now. Waking up Hortense at this time of night might be satisfactory retaliation for the *piccolo* word. As the tape wound down and clicked off, she lost all heart in that pursuit or anything else.

Quannah had left no message. She knew sometimes he couldn't, but she peered at the phone a good five minutes before pulling a light blanket over the sheets. Just to be sure she wouldn't fumble for the phone when it did ring with his call, she left her bedside light on until she became so drowsy the clock hands were blurry. She flicked the light off, turned over, and covered her head.

Monday dawned with the balminess of a spring day rather than the usual heat of August. Classes would begin next Monday, and she hadn't been into her own classroom once to set things in order. As a salve to her conscience, she grabbed a box of posters and a bust of Shakespeare she always set on her desk. She would find time to do some planning today. Might be the whole NISD personnel would be in for some surprises about their new superintendent. She vowed not to say a word until matters were settled.

Viola Fiona's lawyers had arrived and called Sheriff Tucker's office to let them know she was of sound mind. She had not signed anything to give her husband the right to place her in the Meadowbrook Home, and Sheriff Tucker was to locate Mr. Jarnagin Ventnor for questioning as soon as possible.

"Okay, ladies and gentlemen," she said to the group in

her living room, "Sheriff Tucker is on his way. I'm out of here on an errand for him if he asks."

"Don't forget tonight—the supper for India Lou," Agatha said.

"I'll be there."

"And, thanking you, I am," said Viola Fiona, grabbing her arm. "Not since I left the lochs of Ireland again last year have I met up with such kindness. Aye, he left me years ago, but without benefit of divorce. Never asked for one, 'cause he loved the money, don't you know, and I wasn't into another marriage, not by a long shot, no. Guess he was thinking he could hide the old bag away and go on his merry way. Now, I'm wondering if I hadn't shown up, how'd he have managed to put me under. Don't know what set him on this path, but by all the green of Ireland, we'll be finding out. Thank you, Willi Gallagher, and the Irish who begat you."

"Elba told her," Agatha offered, "about your American Indian ties on your mother's side and your Scotch-Irish on your father's."

"Aye, look-a-here, Agatha, would that be your feller a-driving in now?"

Willi scooted out the back, peeked around the corner of the garage to make sure Sheriff Tucker went inside, then she opened the garage and took her and her car down the road to Ozzie Oxhandler's Barbecue and Emporium.

Monday, never her favorite day, might just take a turn for the better if the weather stayed this way. She drove onto the tarmac parking lot of Oxhandler's Barbecue and Emporium. From childhood she always patted the feather of the wooden Indian statue beside the door. In her mind, he was Kawliga, keeping watch over Nickleberry's near east side. The restaurant was just on the edge of an area of run-down homes and streets full of chuckholes. The rough-hewn wood of the restaurant, outside and inside, smelled fresh. Maybe it had to do with the sawdust on the floor. Both hands aside of her face, she peeked in the window. Margarita Uriegas, cleaning tables, recognized her and opened the door. From the green, red, and yellow jukebox, Garth sang about how he just wanted to dance.

"Ms. Gallagher, you know we don't open until quarter of noon." Her strong features, especially the thick brows, knit in disapproval. Her tight red jeans attested to the fact that she shouldn't wear them, she being of more generous portions than they seemed able to hold without strain. Her red and white striped shirt, also tight across forty-two double D's, was crisp as her white-toothed smile. That sunny disposition won and kept the job for her.

"I called Ozzie earlier. He said he'd be here."

"Why didn't you say so? Have a sit down. You want an orange juice, a Dr Pepper, something?"

"You bet. How about a tomato juice. " She sauntered around the wagon-wheel divider, chose a bench, and sat at the end of one of the long tables. "You got a few minutes to chat?"

"Thought you'd never ask. That girl of mine is looking forward to your class this year."

"I've heard from her previous teachers. Dorotea is a jewel in class. Such a stickler for details and always turns in work on time. She seems to have fun with whatever is going on. I'm looking forward to having her in class, too."

Margarita set the drinks on the table. "That would be Shakespeare's *Romeo and Juliet* right now. Yeah, she's checked out a copy for the summer and has been reading it aloud. It's a wonder the fajitas last night didn't turn out to be Italian spaghetti, the way we were smack-dab in the middle of Verona."

"You were a good student, too, and under difficult circumstances."

"Yeah, Dorotea was almost five when I graduated ten years ago. You do what you have to do." She pushed the pitcher of tomato juice toward Willi. She grinned, and her beautiful teeth filled most of her broad face. "I was surprised to recall as much of the story line as I did last night."

"You always had a good memory. Speaking of which—"

"Yeah?" She leaned across the table in response to Willi's bending closer.

"It's about . . . the Friday Special."

Margarita leaned back. "Darn, and I thought you were going to ask me about ten years ago and Tessa Aiken."

"Should I?" Now it was Willi's turn to lean across the table. She refilled her tomato glass from the pitcher.

"Naw, not really. Just gossip, I guess."

"Give it up, girl. You can't leave me hanging with that tidbit."

"Ms. Gallagher, you'll never change. One of these days that curiosity of yours is going to land you in big trouble. This is nothing but gossip, like I said. Dan Oxhandler is involved. You really want to hear? I know you and he went out for awhile."

Willi sighed. She'd be living those couple of dates with a younger man down for the rest of her life. "We were just going out as colleagues."

Okay, not quite true, but it's nobody's business, and it was certainly not a long-running scene.

"I think," Margarita said, spreading her hands across her red-and-white-striped bosom, "the lady doth protest too much." She flashed that winning smile again. "Just teasing, Ms. Gallagher. Everyone knows you and that special investigator are an item. Whoo-hoo!" She took a sip of juice. "Word has it that Dan Oxhandler is having some problems. Maybe the same kind Tessa Aiken had."

"Which was?"

"This is going to sound like poor hometown girl sour grapes. Me telling you about two of my classmates who were college grads while I was the one into motherhood in junior high."

"I know your intelligence, Margarita. Don't pull that with me. Life just dealt you a different deal. I'm proud of you."

"Thanks, Ms. Gallagher. Well, the word is Tessa was into the drug scene. You know, like with her lawyer friends and uptown and all. Started in Austin. Maybe the pressure of corporate law was more than she planned for, but whatever, she was needling and sniffing. Some folks say Dan is, too, and that's why he and Vic Ramirez have been at each other's throats."

The telltale blush upon Margarita's cheeks at mention of the fireman gave Willi pause for a moment. Vic Ramirez could do a lot worse than this fine young lady.

"This sounds really disloyal, considering the Oxhandlers are the ones who have hired me all these years, but I'm just repeating what others have said, Ms. Gallagher."

"No problem. And this won't go farther if it doesn't need to."

"The town jive is Tessa was into using and Oxhandler maybe worse."

"Worse?"

"Yeah, selling. Dealing off that boat of his cousin's."

Willi could believe Dan could be a womanizer, culturally an idiot of a bubba, but not just out-and-out stupid enough to traffic drugs. The disbelief must have shown on her face.

"Hey, Ms. Gallagher, remember the minister over to the Grandfeldon church?"

"Yes, no one could picture his wife and him as part of a swingers' group, and their photos and advertisements were in one of those lewd magazines you can't even find in this county."

"Yeah, they definitely made the *Playboy* magazine seem more like a *Jack and Jill*."

"Uh, well, no, but I see what you're saying. Although Dan is a friend and a coworker, doesn't mean he couldn't lead a second life."

"Exactly. All this could be horrible gossip, too. Folks in Nickleberry have been known to lie right in the pews on Sundays."

Willi said, "That sounded bitter."

"Yeah. Yeah, it was. Hey, I better get my butt back to work before Ozzie comes in." She strode off in her red jeans. "Oh," she said over her shoulder, "you bringing something for the meal tonight for India Lou over at the high school cafeteria?"

"Yes. *Food*. Uh, yes. What was you all's special on Friday?"

"Oh, you heard about it. Yeah, it was good enough you might want us to cater it to your place sometime for one of your outdoor picnics, right?"

"Okay. There's an idea. What all was it?"

"Sweet ribs with jalapeño sauce on the side, fresh thin-sliced potatoes with fried onions, avocado mandarin orange salad on greens, and flour tortillas. We sold out long before closing time."

"What about—?" Willi shook her head. "Uh . . . do you remember seeing Neeper Oxhandler that afternoon?"

"No. I had to leave early to pick up Dorotea from the TCU Cheerleader Camp. But, here's Ozzie. He can tell you."

After a few minutes of amenities, Ozzie cleared his throat and boomed out, "Oh, you bet. That big galoot of a nephew. Yep, he sat right over there at one of them booths, them there surrounded by cactus plants and fishbowls of beans and colorful pasta. Mostly families choose these long tables, of course."

"Ozzie, Margarita said you all ran out of the first special. I guess that's when you started serving fried venison and quail pie."

"Never did no such thing. Ain't never been venison in this here building. Don't like it, never have and never will. You want venison, you go on over to the Dugger Brothers Restaurant near a mile this side of Stephenville."

"My mistake," Willi said. She tried to smile and look confused. "I could have sworn that's what Neeper said he ate and that it was here."

"Probably not your error, Ms. Willi. More than likely, his'n. He didn't know what he was a-eating."

"Why?"

"Looking into them pretty eyes, I guess. I remember them days." Ozzie blared out the words so loudly they seemed to bounce off the old sterling ware on the table. "Well, sorta, I remember them days."

"Pretty eyes?" Willi snapped her fingers. "Yes, he was with—?"

Ozzie asked, "You know her name, do you? I'll be horn-swaggled, I sure don't. What was it?"

The tables having turned deftly upon her, Willi coughed. "I can't for the life of me recall either." At least, she didn't have to revert to a falsehood.

"Ain't that the way of it. I'll describe her, and you see if something strikes up the band for you. Of course, I didn't pay a lot of attention to details."

"Sure," Willi said. This was working out well. "Go ahead. What did she look like?"

"She looked somehow familiar, like kids I see coming in here until their teens. Then they ups and leaves for a couple years of college, some work elsewheres. Then they come back and plop into the town life. Now where was I?"

"Describing her," Willi prompted.

"Redheaded. We Oxhandlers was always partial to them redheads, yep-yep. Wore way too much makeup to my way of thinking. She swung that hair to and fro. Long nails. Pretty hands."

"Of course, you weren't paying attention to details."

Ozzie guffawed. "You got me, you did. Might as well tell you, she had the prettiest blue eyes, too."

"Might have been Melanie Knowles or Peggy Leander or—"

"Or half a dozen others in this town. We Oxhandlers got our share of redheads in the family, and you know—"

"Uh . . . I appreciate you telling me this, and—"

"The Driver family," he said, holding up a finger, "has a couple pretty good-looking young ladies, too. They's all redheads."

"That's great, Ozzie, and I thank you for sharing, but now I have to—"

"Course, if you're smart, you don't get on their wrong side. Been known to have smarts and a feisty temper, those

Drivers. Still, it could have been a Driver girl. Might have been a McDaniel lady. Naw, naw, on second thought. Sondra and Iravel McDaniel got blond red, but this woman was younger than them, and I imagine—"

"Ozzie!"

"Yes ma'am?"

Willi tapped her watch. "I have to run."

"Now hold your horses a spell. I recall those lovely blue eyes, I do, and she also wore a bracelet and ring contraption. That bring any names to mind?"

"As a matter of fact, yes. Thanks, and I really do have to run, now."

"Well, you do that then, and stop by again when you got longer to stay."

In the sunshine Willi paused. Her first thought had been the new English teacher, but Saralee had brown eyes, not blue. Everyone had been buying up that Celtic jewelry at the festival. Oh well, at least one question was answered. Neeper had been here. He hadn't lied about that. He was just so besotted with a pretty face he didn't know what he had eaten. Men.

CHAPTER
9

Willi spent the next half hour wondering which way to run. Home would mean having to come clean to Sheriff Tucker about her activities the last two nights. Going to do the second errand Sheriff Tucker had asked—check on backgrounds of folks who had also taught in Tyler, Texas—held no appeal. With one hand managing the car steering wheel, she used the other to pull at her hair from the scalp out. Her thoughts of the demise of Chaucer and Beowulf left an emptiness. The death of Tessa opened up a horrible sadness.

Now she worried because of the unanswered questions about whom Neeper had eaten with, but he hadn't lied to her and to Sheriff Tucker. Along with that, the info from Margarita Uriegas, whom she considered an honest and conscientious source, about Dan Oxhandler's possible involvement with drug trafficking rankled. Realizing she'd driven around the Nickleberry Square two times, and folks from The Apothecary Shoppe were studying her, she sighed. Home or . . . where? Home or . . . of course, the next best thing to home. Aunt Minnie managed to heal all wounds, even those the human eye couldn't see.

Aunt Minnie hugged her, and Willi grinned. Sometimes embracing her aunt was like holding a perfumed and over-stuffed bear. Her aunt's white curls, bouncing with every turn of her head, looked like cotton balls kids glue on pictures of Santa Claus. From her metal-rimmed glasses resting on her button nose, down to her rosy cheeks and cherry mouth, she represented a cherub. In height, she was more like the elves, and her eyes shone with that mischievousness associated with boys who pull pigtails and throw baseballs through windows.

There ended the childlike caricature. When Aunt Minnie opened her mouth, her words were well modulated and carefully chosen as befitted a retired teacher, but in that well modulated voice she was likely to say anything. Her sister, Willi's mama, had said when of a mind to, Minnie could cuss the paint off the side of the house. She flavored her speech with a deep Texas drawl so that at first this discrepancy seemed to flow over one and take a person by surprise after she uttered one of her diatribes.

"Damn and Hell's bells, if you aren't a sight for sore old eyes, hon. Sit down right here." She led Willi to a wing chair in hot-pink velvet.

"Wasn't this chair in a cotton plaid last time I visited?"

"I celebrated my seventy-third by redoing all the furniture. Sensual, isn't it? Black wood for sexy, hot pinks for passion, lots of textures. My El Cid loves it, too."

"Rodrigo loves you, you ninny. He'd be wherever you were, even if you lived in a grass hut with rocks for chairs."

Aunt Minnie grinned. "You're right. He's definitely special. In every way, and he doesn't need a dose of Viagra in any department. I bet you anything that handsome Quannah Lassiter of yours doesn't—"

"Auntie, sometimes you're as bad as Elba. My love life or . . . or lack of it is no one's concern."

"Better remind Elba, because when I stopped by to get coffee at David's Grocery the other day, she was hobnobbing with the church choral director."

"About me?"

"Hon, you are fair bait, being beautiful, single, and with someone eligible in the wings."

Willi shook her head and held up her hands. "I give up."

"Small town life, hon, just the way it is." Aunt Minnie picked up a porcelain bell and jangled it. She frowned. "India Lou isn't here, of course. I made her take a month or so to handle matters. I got someone meanwhile." She rang again. A young woman, maybe all of eighteen or so, waddled into the room. Weighing in around 300 pounds and with only about four-feet-seven-inches' length to disperse it, she had no choice but waddling.

"Yes ma'am?" Legs splayed out from the knees down, arms winged out like a penguin, she put Willi in mind of one of those Northern birds as she was dressed in black and white. Adding to this persona, was a beakish nose and dyed ebony hair pulled back tightly in a ponytail caught with a black and white scrunchie band.

"Nicoletta Leesha Horsenettle, this is my niece, Willi. She works with your cousin, Hortense, at the high school."

Willi blinked. There was absolutely no resemblance to Hortense's buxom but svelte figure, her frosted shag. Well, yes, the nose was definitely a Horsenettle appendage.

"Nice to meet you, Ms. Gallagher. I've heard so much about you. I'm majoring in English lit at Nickleberry College."

"Ah, yes, I think I did see you at one of the committee meetings for the Irish Fling Festival. I didn't know Hortense had relatives in the area."

"Just me and my twin sister, Tabithia Meesha. We moved because Cousin Hortense got us scholarships to Nickleberry College."

"Would you bring the iced tea and the sausage rolls?" Aunt Minnie asked, and Nicoletta Leesha left. After she got out of earshot, Aunt Minnie said, "Unfortunate."

"The nose, you mean, and the Horsenettle snorting?"

"Yes, poor girl. Of all the things to pass down from the past generation, seems those would be the worst. Not—"

Aunt Minnie added with a twinkle in her eye, "—like what I've passed on to you."

"And that is?"

"Insatiable curiosity about folks and a bent for getting into trouble because of it."

"No argument there. How about exercising that ability this afternoon. I don't think it's anything that could get us into trouble. And since Rodrigo used to work in Tyler School District, I thought he might pave the way with a couple of phone calls."

"I'm game. He's down at The Apothecary Shoppe holding down a chair and having a coffee with his cronies. We'll have this snack and be off." Aunt Minnie made the call from her living room and came back to the sunroom. "Easy as pie dough. My El Cid will make a couple of calls to his old district for us, so someone will be in the offices and expecting us. He'll have to do it from one of The Apothecary Shoppe's phone booths and hopefully in a low enough voice all the Nickleberry nosy bones won't listen in. Anyway, like I said, hon, easy as pie."

"In my case that was never easy. Shame you don't have a phone out here or a cell phone."

"I hate those intrusive things. People always have them glued to their heads at restaurants. Act like they are so in touch with people, and yet they're ignoring all those around them. You finally got one up in your bedroom, right?"

"Just an extension to the regular phone. Quannah insisted. To ease the worry from his cop's mind, I put one in. Haven't replaced my cell phone since the horrible trip to Austin, so you won't have to worry about it being stuck to my ear."

"Oh, yes, when you all's train was stopped in that blizzard, and you had that killer loose in that old run-down hotel. Oh, goodness."

"It wasn't a relaxing trip what with the case being touted as *Death Medicine* Express."

"So glad you're on the safe end of things this time

around, Willi." They finished the midmorning snack and were looking at the map before heading out.

The doorbell rang. Nicoletta Leesha answered it. She puffed her way in, telling the visitor behind her. "Wait just a moment, sir." To Aunt Minnie she announced, "A Mr. Oxhandler is here."

"Ozzie?" asked Aunt Minnie.

"Neeper or Dan?" Willi asked.

In her penguin stance, Nicoletta Leesha turned her head sideways. "Hmm. He's in his early thirties."

"Neeper or Dan, then," Willi said.

"Wears his cap backwards," Nicoletta Leesha added.

"Dan."

Aunt Minnie said, "Show him back here."

Dan Oxhandler boomed out as he came in, "Ladies, ladies, how you doing?"

"Fine. What brings you around?" Willi asked, "I thought you were practicing your Irish jig dance this morning."

He adjusted his hat. "Be getting to that. Heard down at The Apothecary Shoppe, you all were heading out for Tyler, Texas, this morning."

"Not fifteen minutes since your call, Aunt Minnie, and the whole of Nickleberry knows our business."

"Not everybody." Dan's voice ricocheted off the sunroom's walls. "Just those sitting up to the Coke counter for the late breakfast. Me and Neeper and Ms. York, Officer Piedra, Vic . . . uh . . . couple others. Hardly the whole town. Don't get your panties in a wad, Willi. We just heard Mr. Vivar talking to someone on the phone. Knowing he used to be super there, we thought maybe it was something for in-service. Just thought it best one of us check."

Aunt Minnie said, "Superintendent of special services, not super of the school district."

Willi glared at him. "And by Ms. York, you mean Saralee?"

"Yeah, her. She's sort of standoffish. Doesn't seem right to use her given name, yet."

"You all being the same age, I don't think she'd mind.

And seemed like Neeper had no problem with using her name at the lake on Fling opening night. Was she the reason you gave him a shiner?"

Dan waved the question aside and Willi said, "To calm your dedicated hearts, this trip has nothing to do with in-service. And for your information, Dan Oxhandler, I know bunk when I hear it. You'd be running backwards six ways from last Sunday to get out of any extra in-service duty."

He solemnly took off his cap and placed it over his heart. "You wound me. I'm just the messenger, anyhow. Inquiring minds want to know."

Willi could have told him, but something—that inner warning bell—sounded, and she wondered how to hedge.

Aunt Minnie saved her the trouble. She said, "Oh, it's just an old lady's bent to renew some acquaintances out that way, Dan, and I wanted company. Rodrigo was merely calling past friends from the district and checking to see that we wouldn't be a bother. Their classes start a week earlier there, you know."

Dan slapped his cap back on and twisted it so the bill lay over his neck. "Makes sense. Well, don't guess you need us for help with a conference or anything, Willi, so I'll be off. Guess we should have just asked Mr. Vivar. Would've saved me a trip out."

When he left, Nicoletta Leesha peeked out the window. "He's with a real pretty lady. A redhead."

Willi scrambled to the window. Aunt Minnie, at a height to reach her shoulder, peered outside, too. Willi said, "Nope, he's with two redheads. Saralee and one of the Driver girls."

"They should have come in, too. They would have been welcome in my home."

"Maybe . . . maybe for some reason . . . he didn't want them to. Why is he concerned about us making a day trip to Tyler?"

"Didn't he once work there?"

"Sheriff Tucker only said Dan had a connection there. We're to find out what that connection is."

·

"Strange," added Nicolette Leesha. "Lame excuse he used to ask, too. Real lame, not that it's any of my business."

Willi considered the girl in black and white, balancing on her small feet. "Nothing wrong with your thought processes. It *was* a lame reason. Thanks for the save, Aunt Minnie. Let's go find out why neither of us felt like telling Dan the truth about our purpose in going. And perhaps a few more things I should catch you up on." And a few things, she wouldn't mention to her Aunt Minnie. *Like an illegal entry onto a boat on Nickleberry Lake, an abduction of a senior citizen. Couple of tiny little things. Nothing worth breaking a Texas sweat over.*

While driving I-20 northeasterly out of Nickleberry, she had plenty of time to regale her aunt with the details gleaned the last few days. Heat beat down relentlessly, seeming to bypass the AC's efforts with ease. Shimmering waves rose off the highway. The parched fields farther to the east of Nickleberry gave little scenic relief until they reached areas where pine trees sprouted.

Within the administration building, Rodrigo's contact, Lois Aaron, didn't seem like she wanted to help at all. She was approaching a hard sixties, as Elba would have said. Lois's cream manicured nails clicked on the phone receiver.

"I'll just check this with Dr. Smythe."

Her voice held enough frigidness Willi figured the person who gave her the diamond ring on her left hand got very little warmth with his evening meal. In fact, Lois was covered in diamonds. Bracelet, watch, earrings—six earrings—thumb rings, pinkie rings. She even had an upper-arm slave bracelet.

"Shame," whispered Aunt Minnie.

"What?"

"There isn't any sparkle in her eyes to match the gems."

Willi tapped her aunt's arm. "You know, we *are* a lot alike."

Lois glared at them, set the phone on the cradle, and sighed. "Investigation?" Lois asked. Obviously, she was not happy to be forced to comply and help them.

Willi smiled. "This may take a little time. Could I get a chair for my aunt?" Lois pointed to a hard wooden chair in the corner. Willi drew it forth and nodded for Aunt Minnie to sit. "Perhaps we could locate one more. I have to take a few notes, and—"

"Oh, for heaven's sake." She buzzed an intercom. "Greg, bring an extra chair in."

An answering buzz and a voice asked, "Would you like me to bring a couple of coff—"

"No."

Seated at last, Willi wondered how to soften this gem-encrusted creature. "It's such a lovely day out, so we'll try not to keep you long. Whatever you can share will be so appreciated."

"Yes, yes, yes. What is it you need to know?"

"Well, first off, Jarnagin Ventnor—"

"A past assistant superintendent here. He's employed as super now in the Nickleberry District."

"Exactly. Sheriff Tucker just wanted to know anything—"

"Oh, Ventnor had rumors going on all the time. Nothing was proven, and I'll call you both liars if this is repeated with my name attached." Lois polished one of her earrings. "Agreed?"

"Whatever," Willi assented. Oh, good. A gossip. Thank you, Great Spirit. Now, if nitpicky Lois had a good memory to go with that gossipy tongue, they might get something valuable.

"He had something to do with the school coffers being emptied. He survived one more year after all that problem was hushed up."

Willi frowned. "He has a rich wife. Why would he have need of money from other sourc—?"

"Wife? I think not. He and I were quite close." She tapped the gem-studded pinkie ring. "This was a gift from him." She sighed. "Years ago."

Willi didn't want to antagonize her. "I must have had wrong info. I'm glad you knew the right of that."

"You want the straight stuff, I'll tell you."

Willi exchanged a look with Aunt Minnie. *Full of herself, isn't she?*

Lois said, "Bernie Burkhalter, your retiring superintendent, worked here years ago, too." She tapped her right wrist with the tennis bracelet. "When they were both here, there were questions concerning mislaid funds, also. Both of them were slick."

"Is there any reason you believe so strongly they are guilty of fund finagling?"

Lois rolled her eyes. "I knew them, you understand? Someone gives you diamonds, you *know them,* and know what makes them tick." She gave a self-satisfied little smirk.

Yeah, boy, and we know what makes little Lois tick. Willi asked, "Did you ever know Tessa Aiken by any chance?"

Lois leaned over her desk. "Yes, yes, yes. When I read about her death in the paper, I remembered."

"But," Aunt Minnie said, "she wasn't a teacher here or in Nickleberry. She was a lawyer in Austin. She only graduated some ten years ago, right, Willi?"

Willi said, "Yes, and—"

"Hey, you want to know or not?" She wasn't looking at her monitor. Obviously, she did have a long memory.

Willi pursed her lips and thought about the black and white wolves. She'd bet her last dime which one Lois represented *all* the time. Willi managed to bite back a retort. Quannah would be so proud of her. She opened one hand in a gesture that said, *Please continue.*

"Bernie was on the local junior college board of trustees even while serving in an administrative position here." Lois tapped her nails on the desk. "He almost had Tessa Aiken thrown out. Not just once, a couple of times. Had her begging."

"What? I mean what for?"

"On the surface the charges were to do with too many classes missed, some cheating on a test, pilfering from others in the gym class."

"I don't believe—"

"Oh, you're one of *those* teachers. You don't think any of your darlings change from high school on? I bet you always say, 'Once one of mine, always one of mine.'"

Aunt Minnie piped up, "Willi is always saying that, and it's commendable. She has an emotional investment in her students. They aren't just numbers and—"

"Oh, *please*." Lois bent her head down, raised her eyebrows, and peered upward from under her lids in that give-me-a-break look.

Willi patted Auntie's hand. "You were the same type of teacher." She took a deep breath. "You said, *on the surface* those were the charges. What did you mean by—?"

"I meant," Lois said, interrupting for the jillionth time, "Bernie told me it really had to do with drugs. Tessa was into abusing. Don't know if it was over-the-counter or hard stuff."

"Why then didn't the trustees shift her off the college campus?"

"Proof, according to them. They said Tessa Aiken was smart. She either hid her tracks or had something on Bernie, something to make him drop the charges." Now Willi raised her eyebrows and held both hands, palms up.

Lois smirked. "But I know Bernie. Bernie Burkhalter uses people. He never tells the whole truth." She paused and pursed her lined lips together. "You didn't hear this from me. I think Bernie dropped the charges after convincing Tessa Aiken to help him run drugs onto the college campus. That's what I think, simply because I know the smarmy man. But he did know how to pick out a gift, didn't he?" She waved her right wrist to let the sunlight glint off the stones.

To avoid answering that sick question, Willi said, "Kassal, Bernie's daughter, is the same age as Tessa. I had both girls in my high school lit class ten years ago, but lost touch with all of them during their college years and some few years afterwards. When Mr. Burkhalter came here, I know his daughter attended the local junior college. Wonder why he didn't have her attend the more prestigious four-year university right off?"

Lois twirled the bracelet around and raised one eyebrow in question. "He had better places to spend his money?"

Only by grabbing the sides of her chair did Willi manage not to pull the woman's coiffed hair.

Aunt Minnie rose. "These old bones can't sit long. I'm going to find a water fountain, hon."

Lois peered pointedly at her gem-covered watch. When the sun glinted off it, a myriad burst of color swirled around the room as if a peacock had just fanned its tail feathers.

Willi gasped. "Peacock."

"What?"

"Uh . . . nothing, just a warning of where to tread and not to tread." Willi shook her head. "I mean, we've tread upon your time. One or two others I need to ask about here." Willi really didn't want to put the next name out on the table, but squared her shoulders and did so. "Dan Oxhandler taught in this district right after he graduated college, right?"

Lois turned to the pencil-thin monitor on her desk, tapped a few commands in, scrolled for three minutes, and finally said, "Humph."

"Yes?"

Lois flicked a diamond stud on her right ear back and forth. "Lists his hometown as Nickleberry, so he was one of your boys, too."

"Right."

"All the miscreants have come home to roost again, huh?"

"Dan has taught science and coached baseball for five years in Nickleberry High. He's a fine instructor, and his team adores him." Willi was not going to let this cold harridan corrupt her against a friend. She knew Dan had his faults, one of them being a typical tobacco-chewing bubba, but he was not a bad person. "Why do you call him a miscreant?"

"Seems you folks from Nickleberry have a way of slipping out of the noose just in time."

"Meaning?"

Lois lifted the sparkling cross from her neck and twirled it between her fingers. Obviously noticing Willi's glance, she said, "A gift from husband number two. Wish it had

been just a simple drop, but one takes what one can get."
Considering the number around Lois's neck, Willi figured
the woman had had seven husbands, give or take a strand
or two. She asked, "Dan Oxhandler?"

"Oh, well, nothing was ever proved one way or another.
Just like with Tessa Aiken."

"There was a question of drugs?"

"No, no . . ." She consulted the monitor. "He worked at the
high school, but a rather buxom eighth-grade girl claimed
he'd made advances. He was *volunteered,* as all instructors
were back then, to work the varsity football ticket booth for
home games. He met her there. The girl claimed he made
dates to meet secretly after games. Thrilled with attentions
from an older man—all of twenty-one probably—she
accepted."

"And his version, I'm sure, is quite different."

"Of course. He claimed she sought him out." Lois
seemed to be glancing now and again at info on the monitor as confirmation of her memory. "Said he tried to pleasantly discourage her and never went anywhere with her.
Hey, would you looky here. There *was* a drug connection."
Lois clicked her nails together. "This girl was tested for
drugs. So happens she was using and claimed Oxhandler
was supplying her. But, like I said, there was no proof.
That's when he went back to his hometown of Nickleberry.
Had any problems there with complaints?"

"None. Absolutely none." Willi's cheeks turned red at
the thought of her going out with him. Talk about tables
turned. But despite him being a former student ten years
her junior, they were both adults when they had had their
few dates . . . evening dinners out.

Lois didn't miss the telltale blush. "Ahhhhh. So that's
how it is."

Willi chose to ignore the riposte. "Just this year we'll be
having in the classroom another of your teachers, Saralee
York. I know she has no connection to this situation at
Nickleberry and Tessa's murder, but she is on Sheriff
Tucker's list, so could you—"

"You're more than welcome to her. I remember her from last year." Lois clicked off her computer, started clearing her desk debris, making it obvious the interview was about to be terminated. "Dull as dishwater. Spoke in a monotone or didn't speak. How she functioned in a class, I don't know. Oh, to give her her due, she got commendable evaluations from her principal and secondary evaluator. Had looks with that gorgeous red hair, even if it was out of a bottle, and those blue eyes drew men to her like salmon spawning. Fool that she was, she rebuffed all of them. She could have been covered in jewels."

"Imagine giving up that worthy goal," Willi said, her eyes shooting out arrows in Lois's direction. "But she's not blue-eyed. Guess your memory failed you on one tiny detail."

"Not according to what she filled out on the forms. Figure of a model she kept covered up all the time. It was like she was a holy nun on some undercover mission requiring her to wear secular clothes, but she was totally uncomfortable in them. Good luck with her on staff."

Lois pulled a neat clutch purse out of an otherwise empty drawer. The clasp was a seashell shaped in diamonds with one tiny ruby on top. With a smile, she shined it up before placing it underneath her arm. "It seems we are through here."

Willi stood also. "I could have sworn Dan and Saralee had never met until she came this year to Nickleberry."

"Oxhandler worked at the high school. She worked at the junior high. No reason for them to meet, really. So . . . you needn't worry," she needled, "that your boy toy played around with her here."

"Dan and I are colleagues, nothing more. My fellow is Special Investigator Quannah Lassiter."

"Nonsense." Lois grabbed Willi's left hand and glanced at her bare fingers. "Darling, until they've placed a ring somewhere on you, they aren't really claiming you as their one and only." With that, Lois handed her a slip of paper, walked out the door, and said, "That will get you and your aunt into the old files room across the street if you need more information. I've an early supper date. I believe this is going to be the one where I am gifted with a tiny memento, perhaps the ankle bracelet I suggested. I don't have an ankle bracelet with Lois engraved and surrounded by diamonds."

Willi glared at the woman. If Great Spirit humbled souls, Willi knew one she'd like to grasp, chew up, and spit out for him to work with. Talk about the Black Wolf being alive and well in her. She rubbed her temples, peered at the paper, and sighed. Now where had Aunt Minnie gotten off to? A little niggle of worry settled around her. It couldn't have taken this long to find a water fountain. Willi rushed down the hallway.

She yelled, "Aunt Minnie! Auntie!"

CHAPTER
10

Aunt Minnie sat in an enclosed courtyard. A cardinal twittered on a branch above her. Willi halted at the scene to give her cantering heart, not to mention her imagination, a moment to settle down. Aunt Minnie peered up at her. "Saw Lois Aaron head out, so thought you'd be coming, too. Hope I didn't worry you by popping out here. Couldn't abide that gold—rather, diamond—digging woman another minute."

"No problem." Willi didn't confide that ever since Aunt Minnie had had a near heart attack during an earlier investigation, Willi had been extra watchful. "In fact, why don't you linger here while I run across the street to check the files?"

"No argument from these bones." She opened a nature magazine. "I'll finish this article on the Australian dingo. Quick learner like our Texas coyote but much more cautious about approaching humans than the coyotes are. So, you run along. I'll be fine."

Willi was glad she'd insisted Auntie stay under the cool trees when she found she was inside a windowless room with no AC vented into the vault. From an old-fashioned bank of steel cabinets full of gray files, she copied pertinent material about Saralee York, Dan Oxhandler, and Bernie Burkhalter. Bernie had been assistant head of transportation and maintenance. Lois had made him sound like an administrator while he was only directly under the administrators.

Willi sighed and wiped perspiration from her brow. Of course, he'd been headed up that ladder, hence his last eight years or so as superintendent at the Nickleberry District. About to close the old steel file cabinet, she peered far to the back, and a bright red folder caught her eye. Odd among all the gray ones. In the Vs, the folder was stuck so hard she had to wrestle it out.

"Well, I'll be darn. Jarnagin Ventnor." She glanced at the clock. "Maybe there's an unstated trail all administrators have to follow, Tyler being just before heading toward Nickleberry. I'll just copy it to peruse later, or we'll be late for India Lou's meal." She gathered the rather hefty pile of copied sheets, turned the handle on the door, and moaned. The dang thing wouldn't open.

"One of those thingamajigs and whatchamacallits in life that never want to work for me. Hell's bells! Why does this always happen to me?" She set the folders down and jiggled the handle again. Her heart cha-cha-chaed for a millisecond. "Now, I will not let my imagination get the better of me, here. Just stay calm. Why didn't I bring my *Tunkasila* stone?"

Despite her calm intentions, scenes flashed before her eyes. *Tessa's crenellated welts. An Irish quilt square tucked between the Oxhandlers' cushions. Chaucer's and Beowulf's remains skewered to the bottom of the moat. A Celtic playing card with a dark tree upon it.*

The cha-cha picked up tempo for a full measure. She licked her lips and tried the door again. Someone had murdered Tessa; someone had broken into Willi's personal space—twice—and the cottage equaled three. Now, that dang rule of three might backfire on her to bring her some horrible bad luck or something. She'd broken into the

Comanche Raider, the Meadowbrook Senior Citizens'
Home, and now the Tyler District's files. Well, she sort of
had permission for the last, but maybe she should have used
that Australian Dingo Medicine and been more cautious.

So many knew she was doing legwork for Sheriff
Tucker. Maybe that's the real reason Tucker had sent her
out of town, to get her out of harm's way. Be just like
something he and Quannah would cook up between them.
But . . . what if someone had *followed* her and . . . and . . .
Aunt Minnie? After the phone call Rodrigo made from The
Apothecary Shoppe, everyone in Nickleberry had known
the destination in a matter of minutes. They might have
even gotten here before she and Aunt Minnie arrived. Oh
my gosh, Aunt Minnie, unaware and sitting underneath the
trees, listening only for the cardinal's twittering, would be
so vulnerable.

Willi scrabbled again at the handle. She leaned against
the door. Above the thrum of blood in her eardrums, the
sound of heavy footsteps approached. Lights flickered on
and off. Willi yelped, the door swung outward.

A gnome of a man, not over four feet four, studied her.
He touched the brim of his janitor's hat before he scratched
at his five o'clock shadow of some three days' growth.
"Sorry about the lights. Thought everyone was out of the
building, ma'am."

Willi managed to stop her cha-chaing heart and even
laugh about the incident by the time she and Aunt Minnie
got in the car. Willi did drive around the Tyler Junior College but didn't have time to stop. She'd review with Tucker
the info she'd gathered today and try the college later on if
needed. After rushing Aunt Minnie back to the Bluebonnet
Apartments, Willi only had time for a quick shower before
gathering her contribution for India Lou's dinner at the
high school cafeteria. The third night of the Irish Fling
Festival was under way out at the lake. Willi admired the
glitter of the lights even from the high school parking lot.

A distant rumble of thunder reverberated, but stars
shone above. She hoped any storms would hold off for

a couple more nights. Still, she carried a light jacket and a fold-up umbrella. In Texas one prepared for anything during spring and summer. She glanced again toward the lake and strained to hear a few notes of the Irish favorite, "Granny, Will Your Dog Bite?" Tonight booths of all types were set up and would stay up for the rest of the week. Irish vests, jewelry displays including Claddagh rings, Irish lace, leatherwork, Irish hand drums. Willi paused before going inside the cafeteria. Perhaps she could find a booth with those Celtic cards or locate the Landises' cousin. There had to be a reason Chaucer and Beowulf had one left outside their fish tank.

Now, if she could just get through the meal for India Lou and the faculty meeting following it without encountering the sheriff, she'd be grateful. She wanted time to go over the Tyler notes and digest what she'd learned at Oxhandler's Barbecue and Emporium.

Inside the door, India Lou engulfed her in a warm hug. "Thank you for coming. Whole town turned out for this. Everybody so kind." She wore a long caftan and matching black turban with gold prints of lions and tigers and some sort of lanky dog.

Willi said, "You look very African and very regal."

"Thank you, Miss Willi." She leaned closer to whisper. "I thought it was an African print, too. Turns out these here is Australian animals." She pointed to the dog. "I guess that's a greyhound."

"I believe dingo. Auntie would know; she read an article about them today."

"Whatever they is, they's pretty, though, and my church friends say the dress suits the occasion, so that's fine 'nuff for me."

"You bet it is. Everybody loves you and loved Tessa. I'm just sorry Terrance can't be here for you."

The next two hours were spent in meeting and greeting, eating and grazing. Across the huge cafeteria that seated 600, she glimpsed Sheriff Tucker. He signaled to her once, but she deftly pulled Elba in front of her to block the view.

Table switching with each course was a matter of form at such gatherings. With a sliver of lemon icebox pie in hand, she sat between Elba and Agatha. Viola Fiona Ventnor sat across from her.

"So?" Willi said. "What happened this morning after I had to leave?"

"*Had* to leave?" Elba and Agatha said in unison.

Elba continued, "More like *escaped*, wasn't it?"

"Now, don't be chiding the girl unduly," Viola Fiona said, shaking the business end of her fork at them. "Brought me out of the very jaws of death, I've no doubt, no doubt a'tall, and it's thankful I am. To tell you true, Willi, was a mite touch and go for a bit with Aggie's darling sheriff, it was. A tad angry he was and not a'tall inclined to give us a listen. Intimated we'd not used the caution God would be giving to a goose, much less a gander. Said some right unkind things about a certain deputized young lady. Would that be you, now?"

"Probably. Didn't your lawyers convince him?" Willi peered over her shoulder. Sheriff Tucker had been keyholed by the Horsenettle cousins. Bless them, snorts and all. She repeated, "Didn't the lawyers convince him?"

"Aye, that they finally did. Still, he was angry at the way we went about the escape for some reason. Men." She waved her fork overhead.

Elba said, "After all is said and done, that dang-nabbed, knuckle-dragging lowlife of a varmint she's tied to lawfully can't be touched for what he tried to do."

"What do you mean?" Willi pushed her half-eaten pie aside. "You all told about him putting her in the care facility against her will and having her drugged?"

"Of course, Willi," Agatha said, wringing the end of her blue-sequined scarf. Her earrings of large coins tinkled in agitation. "Of course, we explained. The lawyers told us it was his word against hers. That he was a respected person in the community. He claimed he was just seeing she got the best of care after her gallbladder operation. Can you believe? They did say they'd talk to Nurse Inga Rufflestone, but didn't hold out any great hope that she would incriminate herself."

"He's got the silver tongue of a fox on the run, yes, that he has," Viola Fiona said. "I told them about when he tried in Ireland long ago to do the same right after a hysterectomy, don't you know, oh yes. Had me signing papers right and left, but praise be to God, they were destroyed in a fluke of a fire. Ought to have been a sign right there. Only them ruined, nothing else. Well, to make a bit of a wandering tale short, there, on the home green, I had relatives, praise be to the saints, who protected me by coming to check on me, so he couldn't do away with me then and there. That's when he up and left and stayed away all these years, coming round on holidays only. Well, there's nothing to be done now but go against me very vows and divorce the scoundrel. And to that end, I've set me barristers. Happy he wasn't about that, I can tell you. Froze all his assets, you see."

"Good for you, Viola Fiona. And what will you do then?"

"As you know, Elba and Aggie and I were friends—close friends—the one year I was here years ago in Nickleberry. Moved to Kansas, went to college, met Jarnagin and off we went back to Ireland for awhile. This is a pleasant little place, it is, but has an inordinate amount of murders from what I hear. Ah, well, that aside, I've no closer kin than cousins in Ireland, so I'm thinking about staying. Perhaps something will come to mind for me to turn my hand to."

"You got more money than a bank, more loot than a Fort Knox, probably more than the Pope spends on gold leaf at the Vatican," Elba said, "so why turn your hand to anything?"

"Hands not turned to the good will play havoc with the bad, don't you know, my friend. Something will show itself by and by. I'm just hoping your little town will welcome me, that I do. Well, I tell you, let's look into me teacup and see what the leavings will tell us." All three—Elba, Agatha, and Viola Fiona—bent over the cup.

Willi laughed. "Maybe you three ought to open a tea

shop on Nickleberry Square? Call it The Merry Witches' Berry Brew."

The three studied the leaves, blinked, and stared at Willi. "What?" she asked.

"The leaves—" Agatha said.

"Say endeavor—" Elba added.

"Together," finished Viola Fiona, "but that you already knew, did you not? Merry Witches' Berry Brew, huh?"

Willi's scalp crawled, a not uncommon phenomenon when around her Kachelhoffer neighbors. "I have to go into the library now. Principal Wiginton called a meeting tonight, since the investigation proceedings took so much of our time the other day."

On her list of things she disliked were faculty meetings— not her principal, not her fellow workers—just the meetings. They rated somewhere down there with disposing of toe clippings. They became especially irritating when she had other matters calling to her: notes from Tyler, Texas, to go through, a promised call from Quannah, a necessary talk with Sheriff Tucker, and she really did need to shampoo her hair and take time to give herself a French manicure.

Willi crossed underneath the covered walkway between the two sections of high school, bypassed the stairway, and entered the first door on her left. Ah, at least she'd not likely have to report to Sheriff Tucker tonight. Outside the floor-to-ceiling windows she glimpsed a frightening vision: the moon, round and full, drifting ominously through an angry bank of clouds. Glancing to her right, she spotted a lone coyote slink into the underbrush. Such a thin specimen, he put her in mind of the outback animal.

Hortense sat beside her, cleared her nasal passages with her usual snorting, and said, "No need to worry. We are in a *bastion* of strength, even if this weather turns into a tornado. Oh, and we have a knight to guard our *bastion*. Isn't that Officer Piedra just outside the lighted area at the corner of the school?"

"Yes, you're right." Willi immediately thought of the folks enjoying the outdoor amenities of the Irish Fling. Many had just left the supper and headed in that direction. "Let's not call bad weather to us or them." She glanced toward the lake's lights, then back to the spot where Officer Piedra stood. Saralee stood talking to him, then finally turned and came into the library. She sat between Neeper and Dan, who were across from the secretary, Sammie Yannich.

Hortense snorted and said, "Oh, if the bow-tied fellow on TV is right, we're in for intermittent light showers. Folks out at the lake have their own *bastion,* you know— the clubhouse." Warming to her word of the day, Hortense shoved her red-rimmed glasses up her sloped nose—the one that made kids call her Horsy behind her back. Willi sighed. Hortense's unfortunate nasalization didn't help dispel that comparison. Willi put a hand on her friend's shoulder. Kids could be so cruel to those who only had their interests at heart.

"You're probably right, Hortense. A light shower won't hurt anyone."

Hortense slapped the top of a *National Geographic* with a picture of a pack of dogs approaching a barren rock outcropping. Willi gasped. Among the subtitles listed on the front was "Caution in Dingo Lands." Her scalp crawled. She frowned, wondering why that subject kept slapping her in the face today. Recalling the Kachelhoffers' Peacock story, she raised an eyebrow. Hmm. Was there some message in all these dingo encounters? Something about *caution*. Why in Hades did that message need attention from her? She was always careful and cautious, no matter what Lassiter and his uncle thought.

Despite Principal Wiginton's laid-back manner and pleasant voice, the meeting dragged slower than a hearse through mud. Typically, people wandered off the subject time and again. During one interval when Principal Wiginton was trying to field questions about the new superintendent and the expected changes, Willi went upstairs. She couldn't add her two cents' worth, anyway, while she was officially wearing a deputized hat. She'd just take a quick attitude-adjusting break in the teaching lounge upstairs.

Always, she encountered a cockroach there, one she named Titanic because of his huge size. Her mind told her this was an impossible encounter each time, since the school periodically sprayed for such critters. She was about to click on the light and greet the beastie when a muted flicker from one of the classrooms down the hall beckoned her.

What would anyone be doing in the lab at this time of night? All those with classes were downstairs: Dan and Neeper, Saralee, and the rest of the instructors on this floor. In fact, they had all been clustered at the same library table.

Hmm.

She shoved on the door. Unlocked, it swung quietly open. The light came from beneath the supply room door in back of the science lab. Flickering escaped as if the source of light were moving, not stable. She swallowed and peered back toward the darkened hallway. She approached the supply room door, one she always thought of as a portal hiding all sorts of mysterious and magical potions. The beam of light settled, and Willi stopped.

A nervous flutter made her shiver. She needed to cross that room filled with lab tables about as much as she needed a lobotomy. But obviously someone was in there who shouldn't be, hence the flashlight or candle, and this was a room from which a possible source of acid could have been taken. Acid that had cruelly and horribly been forced down the victim's throat and ended a beautiful life.

She stepped around the end of a table. Light glinted off a nameplate: Oxhandler, N.

She felt her way with trembling fingers across the cold edge. When her hand struck a bottle, her heart cantered and stopped for a moment. Warmth of blood rushed away from her head. She trembled and held her breath for the inevitable crash. With one finger, she caught the glass and tilted the container in place among the myriad tubes and canisters only her imagination could project within the darkness. A glint here and there told her this room was a computer lab on one side and science lab on this half, which one of the other teachers used during Neeper's conference hours.

To her left the ribbon of light wavered. She strained to hear. Sounded like some large bottle pulled across one of the metal shelves. Willi gulped. Perhaps that bottle might contain . . . the same type of . . . acid.

Ohmygosh, yes, and then the person will come out here and throw it in my face and the pain would be excruciating and I'll be blinded and Quannah isn't here and will leave me forever because he couldn't stand to see me in such pain and I'll—

Willi bit down hard on her bottom lip. Get a grip! Yes, she'd been a fool to leave the security of the boring meeting. Yes, she'd been two times a fool, and shame on her for checking the light out by herself. She sighed all the way down to her pink toenails and knew now exactly why the cautious dingo kept showing up. Why could she not listen and learn from the messages the universe offered? Quannah would certainly have an answer, but he wasn't here right now.

Okay, she had thrown caution to the four winds by coming in here by herself, but she did not have to ignore the clearly offered caution signals from this point on. She needed to get out of the room without alerting the intruder. Then she'd get help and return. That would be the sensible thing to do, and she had every intention of carrying that out as soon as she overcame the trembling bout and the pressure on her bladder.

In the middle of Neeper's lab room, she took a slow and steadying breath. The person wasn't him. She'd seen him in the library. Even if he'd gone up the other stairway and gotten up here first, he'd have turned on the lights in his own classroom as well as the storeroom. Wouldn't he?

Wait a just a cotton-pickin', snuff-chewin' minute. Think.

The supply room ran behind all the science and computer labs. The next room down was Dan Oxhandler's. *Oxhandler's.* "The Stripper" played through her head, and she pictured an Irish double-chain quilt square aboard the *Comanche Raider.* A scarf that others had seen around Tessa Aiken's head only hours before her death.

The glimmer of light went out. Willi clutched at her throat. Dan or Neeper or whoever could not find her here. At last, trying to use Dingo Medicine and move *cautiously*, Willi inched toward the door. Confused now, she stopped. Was she moving toward the door or the storage area?

A scraping noise brought her on point, head in the air, body frozen. She could see the viscous welts on Tessa's face. Oh, pleaseohpleaseohplease. Just let her get out in one piece without a confrontation, without scars. Why hadn't she had the forethought to turn the hall lights on? A welcome beacon would now be showing around the correct door to lead her to safety. She licked her lips. She urged her trembling knees to support her, and she touched the edge of another table. Damned if she recalled how many there were.

Hinges squeaked. Light from the storage area flickered and widened. She did a deep knee bend behind one of the black lab tables. A beam of light, searching outward, jittered from corner to corner. Blood pounded so heavily in her ears, she couldn't hear anything above the roar. An air draft from the supply area chilled her neck as the frigid breeze hit her flushed skin.

She knelt lower, willing herself to blend with the surroundings: the tables, the hazy design of vinyl flooring. Three warning beeps burped from the overhead intercom. The approaching footsteps faltered.

Mr. Wiginton's voice burbled through the address system. "Teachers—all of you—come to the front foyer now and pick up these pamphlets as you leave."

Willi peered up at the edge of the table. A black-gloved hand tapped on the countertop. She shut her eyes, prayed the flashlight's rays wouldn't bounce in her direction, wouldn't locate her, a ready victim, crouched below. *Damn. Damn, damn, damn. Go away, just go away.* The intruder moved across the lab, stood a moment in the storage doorway, and finally disappeared into the abyss of petrie dishes and acids. A metal door slammed. Willi jumped to her feet and scrambled to the wooden classroom door leading to the corridor.

Her thigh hit the edge of a sharp chair. She caught the back rungs before it slid across the floor. She kept moving. The flashlight beam had shown where that door was, and she had to reach it before the darkness confused her again.

Through the beveled window, corridor lights blinked on. She reached for the doorknob. Hell's bells, he'd gone through the narrow storage area and into another classroom before exiting into the hallway. Footsteps passed by the window. Willi clutched but did not turn the doorknob. A shadowy figure materialized in front of the window again. If she turned loose, there'd be a click. Her throat, a roughened concrete corridor of dry phlegm, wouldn't let her swallow.

Trapped.

No friendly gnome of a janitor was going to rescue her this time. Willi shut her eyes. When she opened them, the shadow had disappeared, and footsteps rang out on the right-hand stairway.

Willi edged out the door, took off her pumps, and in stocking feet pattered down the left hall and stairs. She stopped by the water fountain to put on her shoes and calm her breathing. She rounded the corner and strode into the foyer. Dan made way for her in the crush between himself and Saralee. Willi managed a thankful smile as she tried to scrutinize everyone's hands when papers were handed out.

She spied a pair of gloves sticking out of Saralee's coat, but they were soft brown leather and certainly not as large as the ones she'd seen. Or maybe her mind had created a larger-than-life monster looming in the shadowy room. Brown or black would look the same in the darkness. It would also do no good to cause a general alarm by insisting someone come and check the lab, since the culprit was downstairs. She would use *caution,* however, and report the unusual circumstances to Sheriff Tucker. Tomorrow. Along with the rest of her report.

Most of the teachers carried sweaters, overcoats, or raincoats, many obviously with gloves. Those who hadn't stuffed them in pockets could have stashed them quickly in a briefcase such as Neeper Oxhandler carried. She sighed and actually listened to Principal Wiginton's last instructions. "Come in late tomorrow. You'll just be working in your rooms. The authorities will be visiting with some of you."

Through the crowd milling toward the doors, Willi nodded at Superintendent Jarnagin Ventnor and two school board members. She had no idea if he knew of her part in the escape of Viola Fiona, but she'd not find out by ignoring the situation. She also admitted to wanting to know if others knew about the sudden materialization of his wife on the scene and how he was going to explain his previous claims of bachelorhood. She'd felt like a wimp in the lab at the way she stayed hidden, but she *could* approach him. After all, what could he do in this crowd? She would play it very professional.

She squared her shoulders and got between him and the board members as they went down the outside steps. "How are you liking your new job, Superintendent Ventnor? Despite this murder upheaval, I hope you're finding Nickleberry friendly and supportive." She almost gagged on that last sentence, but she smiled.

"Yes, indeed. Indeed."

Oh, great. One of those. Mouther of inanities without any meaning whatsoever. Okay, fine.

"How is your wife taking the move to a new town? Guess you all are used to changes after all these years on the administrative ladder. I'd be glad to show her around anytime."

One board member, Eldritch Bower, elbowed her aside. "Sir, I believe the coaches are waiting for that quick fifteen minutes you promised them in the field house."

Frowning, Willi elbowed right back into place and offered the pockmarked Eldritch her best English teacher glare. "No problem, I'm heading that direction. I had to park over there since I arrived a little late."

With no booming warning of thunder or glare of lightning flash, the heavens opened up. All three ran underneath the canopy connecting the two parts of the high school. Willi grinned and peered upward. *Thank you, Father Sky. Your timing is most helpful.* To Jarnagin, she said, "I could introduce her to the quilting group if she's interested in such things."

"I've no idea what the woman is inter—" He wiped his forehead with a monogrammed handkerchief. "We've been separated for some time. In fact, Ms. Gallagher, you may as well know, as I will be making an announcement to the school board soon. Viola Fiona and I will be divorcing."

"Oh?"

"Irreconcilable differences."

"Such a shame. Such a shame, too, that so few of us have met her before now. I would have thought the school board members would have wanted to meet your family before hiring."

"Look," Eldritch said, "That's none of—"

Ventnor said, "It's okay. Others will be curious, too. This is a small town."

Willi wanted to see how the smarmy man would wheedle his way out of the fact he had tried to incarcerate a wife so he wouldn't have to claim her, much less introduce her to the community. "So, why didn't the board get to meet Mrs. Ventnor?"

"Well, she was, in fact, having mental problems. Late menopausal complications, hormone imbalances, and recovering from gallbladder surgery. I was doing my very best to get her proper treatment, as I explained to the board members. They and I thought she would be brought under—that is, that her condition would be under control in a short time. But as that is not the case, I have no recourse but to dissolve our long-standing marriage. I've tried and failed to help her. She has turned absolutely delusional. Claims she's been incarcerated, robbed of thousands." He waved his handkerchief in a dismissive manner. "Even told a ridiculous tale of having to be saved by some local ninja nurses."

"Yes," Eldritch backed up his head honcho. "The media

will love that." He wiped his thick-lensed glasses on his coat and stared at Willi. "That's our story, and we're sticking to it. Sir, this is getting worse. Let's make a run for it."

"Yes, perhaps you two should make a *run* for it."

She raised her umbrella and purposefully strode toward her car. Happily, she noted both men resembled the drowned rats they were by the time they reached the field house. Inside her car, she flipped on the radio to one of her favorite country western stations from a nearby little town of Cleburne. KCLE on frequency 1140AM offered the golden oldies of country western music. After Quannah had introduced her to the world of C and W music, she loved it as much as her rock 'n' roll oldies. "Near You" sung by Porter and Dolly came on.

Willi sighed. Right now, she wanted to be near a certain Lakota-speaking special investigator for the Texas Rangers. *Please.* Please let there be a phone message when she got home. Tomorrow night he'd be home to dance the jig in the contest, but that seemed ages away. Porter and Dolly drifted off the airwaves to be replaced by "Slowly" sung in the hungry tones of Webb Pierce. He sang to Willi's heart and only hers tonight with ". . . slowly I'm falling . . . more in love with you." A blush spread over her from head to foot. Was that what was happening to her? Slowly? But so completely?

She smiled.

"Yes, slowly."

CHAPTER

11

When she rushed inside, the phone rang. she slammed
her books and umbrella down and grabbed at the kitchen's
phone receiver. "Lassiter?"

"No, it ain't that handsome feller of yours. We three,"
Elba said, "have some good Wicca messages to give you.
That dang meeting of yours took forever. We're bringing
leftovers. I'll brew the tea when I get there."

"But I'm really tired, and—"

"We all keep getting messages for you, and they're
important. Got one from a Mr. Special Investigator—that
Indian bu—"

"Elba, I've told you, don't use that derogatory word, nor
the word *squaw*. Quannah has explained that both those are
offensive and ignorant. The latter refer to a female's nether
regions in a rather nasty way, and—"

"You're right, and I ask pardon. You know, you are sure
quick lately to defend that feller. Wonder why that is,
hmmm?"

Willi ignored the question and said, "I'll leave the back

door unlocked. I'm heading up for a quick shower before you all get here."

"We'll make ourselves to home."

"Kind of thought you whould. *Mi casa es su casa,* you know."

Upstairs, she glanced at the answering machine light. "Oh, how did I do that?" It was turned off. She clicked the button and peered at the last calls on the ID. "He did call. Damn, and I had the machine off. He couldn't leave a message." She threw her clothes into the hamper and climbed into the shower. For a moment her world became a comforting steam bath of Irish Spring soap. She rubbed off with a nubby towel and wrapped one around her head. With clean undies, jeans, a black pullover, and leather pumps, she could face the world . . . even what were becoming her three, not two, but *three* neighbor-sisters. Scents of honey and meat-stuffed cabbage rolls drifted up the stairway. She ran down.

"Guess when you eat supper at five-thirty, by ten you are famished again," she said but refused a proffered plate until she asked, "What message?"

"Oh, and which of them would you be a-wanting first, child?" asked Viola Fiona with a twinkle in her eye. "Probably that long-winded version of Elba's dream. Yes, would that be the one?"

"How about the one from Lassiter?"

"In my day, we'd not be cutting off the message machine if we'd a-had them, no we would not. Isn't that the right of it, Agatha?"

Willi put her hands on her hips. "What did—?"

"Yes, indeed. He wouldn't have to call and tell all his business to us if he had a way of reaching you."

"So, just what was this all-important—?"

"Hmmm," Elba said. "You mean my dream?"

"Elba!"

Elba patted Willi's shoulder. "Sit. Sit down. You'll be glad to know he was worried as a man with a three-day itch, as concerned as a groom without no one at the altar, as near worried as a—"

"Elba!"

"Well, he was. Put yourself in his shoes. Last time he couldn't reach you, the phone had been cut, and the place had been broken into. By the by, here's the new keys. Dang locksmith finally got here. Just don't forget to lock up when you leave."

"So, he was worried about me?"

"That's what I was trying to tell you. Said he'd be home on tomorrow's—Tuesday's—afternoon flight, but you may not have to fetch him. Said he'd get word to you somehow. After he books the prisoner he's flying in, he's transporting another one down to San Antonio. He'll be in time for the Jig Contest . . . and yes, he's been practicing with the tape you gave him. That about cover it all, Agatha?"

"Well, Sister, he did say something about the stars and looking up . . . oh, I can't remember how he put that."

Willi pulled the towel off her head and ran her fingers through her hair. *"See those stars twinkling up there? The one winking, that's me."*

"I believe you're right, Willi, yes." Agatha swished her silken skirt to one side and sat down. "Willi, Elba had a nap when we got home and had a horrible dream. Another dream about the white wolf and the black wolf with you in between the two. Could you give us any clue as to what it means?"

"How would I—?"

"Because," Elba said, "it were one clearly to warn you. You said Quannah told you a tale about them two wolves. Now, do you have any idea?"

Willi shrugged her shoulders. "Could be simply that I've thought about how I'm battling the two inside myself. You know, the good feelings about helping with the investigation and doing something for India Lou's sake, and then there's the other side—"

"And what would that be, child?" Viola Fiona asked.

"The anger—worse, the rage—that overcomes me now and again until I want to see the same thing happen to the damned perp who did that to Tessa."

"Could be," Agatha said, "but somehow that doesn't feel like the total we're to get from the dream."

"Sister, I agree." Elba shook a gnarled finger in the air.

"As do I, child, as do I." Viola Fiona piped in.

"If that's all there is," Willi said, "then I'm going to tuck into this food and then tuck myself into—"

"Not by a long shot," Elba said, frowning. "We're a-going to read the tarot to get clearer meanings here."

Willi knew better than to try to sway all three headstrong women, and they were, after all, concerned for her welfare. She cut the cards.

Elba laid them out. "Three queens again. Fourth time we've done this read for your benefit in the last couple days, and we keep getting those three queens."

"And that means?" asked Willi after taking a sip of tea.

"You're being dang-blamed deceived by many women."

Willi grinned, tapped the three cards, and looked at each of those surrounding her.

Agatha pulled at her many necklaces. "No, they don't represent us."

Elba continued. "This, Willi, is the significator card, which means—"

"Which means that it's me. You have done a few of these reads before."

"Don't," Elba said, "be interrupting the flow. Yes, this is you. This queen laying across you is one of the obstacles in store." Elba's gnarled fingers shook, and she wrung her hands together. "All these to this side indicate problems. The one above tells us the best you can hope for, and this read says that happens to be lies and deceit from women."

"It's just like the read you did at Frogs' Feet."

Elba intoned, "Yes: Black wolf in white. Eyes hidden. Passion wrought the nemesis unbidden."

"Okay, so what am I supposed to do about that?" Willi asked.

Viola Fiona set her teacup aside. "Child, you put your head to work, is what you do. Ask yourself what women you've been with lately concerning the murder, consider carefully what each has told you . . . or not been telling you. The blessed saints know, not all will be telling you the right of things. Could be they simply told what they might consider a little white lie, what they think has nothing to do with the horrible mutilation and killing of that poor girl. But you'll have to be sifting the true from the lie, the insignificant from the important. The cards are merely saying you are to be heightening your awareness right now."

Agatha rubbed the silk sash at her waist, while Elba continued her hand wringing.

Willi frowned. "Ladies, give it up. What else is bothering you?"

Elba crossed her arms underneath her ample bosom, the better to shift it to a more comfortable position. "You never did have no holes in your screen door, never lost no oars, and your dang elevator most times goes right to the top."

"Thanks, I think."

"Best we can tell is these are mostly redheads, maybe a blond among them, none up to no good."

"Yes, Sister," Agatha said, "true. Considering the dream of being caught between the wolves, it might be serious enough that they mean you physical harm."

"So, now she's in the know, Miss Willi will be more careful and more aware."

Elba snorted. "Begging Viola Fiona's pardon, but she don't know you like we two do. You, Willi, got to be more than aware. You got to think and not go out looking for trouble and—"

"When have I ever—?"

"Like when you went snooping today in Tyler and—"

"Not so. Aunt Minnie wanted to visit old friends."

Elba sniffed. "The Apothecary Shoppe grapevine is trustworthy, and your auntie went only to cover up your real intent."

"Be that as it may, even if that were true, and I'm not saying it is—"

"Kind of teetering all over that fence before you jump, aren't you?"

Willi took a deep breath. "I mean that Sheriff Tucker asked me to look into a few things. That's not something I did without his knowledge."

"So, you're telling us you haven't done anything since the murder that Sheriff Tucker hasn't told you to do?"

Willi looked up at the ceiling and held her hands and waved them at Viola Fiona. "Well, one little abduction."

"Aside from that, which was an ethical need, have you?"

"Would you rephrase that question?"

Elba slapped the cards together. "I knew it. Now where have you been, who you seen, what did they say, and—?"

"Ladies, ladies, ladies. Really, nothing to enlighten us tonight." She wasn't about to fess up that she went to Nickleberry Lake and boarded the *Comanche Raider* without permission.

"Of course, they'd be worrying about you, child," Viola Fiona offered. "After all, your very home was broken into, don't you know. Then there's your two fish, and that's a crying shame that is. Have you no idea what the thief wanted? You keep great valuables or expensive first editions there in your little book nookery?"

Willi smiled what she hoped was a smile of reassurance. "No valuables, no books signed by Mark Twain or Hemingway or Steinbeck, not even Erma Bombeck, although I do have one of her articles framed to remind me to enjoy each day. Forget about dusting, things like that."

Agatha laughed. "That's why you hired us. For the housework. And we love doing it, but you're not going to so easily get us off the subject. We have reason to worry, considering the tarot reads, the fish deaths, and the calling card left as some kind of warning. The phone line was cut, too." Agatha took out Willi's favorite cards, the Native American Animal Totem deck.

Now, Willi sat up, sort of hoping Agatha would do a read with those very gentle teaching guides. "Okay, friends, you're right. I will be careful. I won't go looking into things without Sheriff Tucker's okay." She kept her fingers crossed behind her back for a moment. No sense worrying the Kachelhoffers if she needed to just talk to folks without informing the sheriff of every little conversation.

Elba said, "Glad you understand, Willi, because I was as nervous as a Easter bunny without no basket, as skittered as a frog without no hopper on a freeway, as crazy as—"

"I get the idea, Elba."

Agatha shuffled the Animal Totem cards, lifting and flipping them in a way perfected through much practice with the reads. Suddenly one card popped out of the deck to land straight up against the sugar caddy. All four managed a universal gasp. Agatha, Elba, Viola Fiona, and Willi all leaned in nose-to-nose to see it better.

"It's the Mouse Medicine card," whispered Willi. "Shouldn't you put it back and reshuffle?"

Agatha gently touched the card. "No. That happens now and again, a card practically flying out of the deck. There's always a reason. We were just talking about being aware and how Willi can do that."

The three *sisters* nodded in unison. Willi raised her shoulders and opened her hands, palms up. "You lost me."

"You asked a question a few moments ago, and the cards have provided the answer. Are you open to hearing it?"

"Well, it can't hurt. Just so we're on the same page here . . . what question did I ask?"

"How to handle these warnings received," Agatha said, smoothing her many beads against her silken blouse.

"Mouse . . . Mouse Medicine doesn't sound too powerful. Shouldn't we try for something big and awesome, maybe lion or tiger or bear?"

Elba flapped her on the head with a hot pad. "Just listen. Go ahead, Agatha."

"Mouse tells you to pay attention to details."

"Which we already knew," Willi said.

"Yes, and Mouse also indicates organization. You said, Willi, you felt pulled and twisted and confused. The opposing strong forces of the black and the white wolf inside you were battering you around emotionally."

Willi frowned in concentration. "So?"

"Remember?" Agatha gently reminded her of the lesson at Frogs' Feet. "Confusion is the way to self-discovery. So Mouse also says to get down to organizing what you know to remove some of the confusion. A place for everything, and everything in its place."

Willi sighed. "How many times have I given that advice to my students? Of course, you're right, Agatha." Willi jumped up, got a Wally World notepad and her favorite Pilot Precise pen—red, of course. "Normally, I'm a list-maker, but what with all the organizational details of getting the Irish Fling together, lists for the first day of school, reminders sent this way and that, gathering the recipes and the judges and . . . oh, all of that and more, I hadn't taken time to do anything but react to events since the murder."

Her three friends sipped tea quietly for a few minutes, talking in whispered tones so as to give her a few moments to gather her thoughts on paper. At last, Willi grinned and set aside the spiral notebook. "Now, if one of you wanted to renuke that for me, I think I do have an appetite, and thanks to all three of you, a plan. Now that I've calmed and got my thoughts in order, there are things I need to share and get some feedback."

"The blessed saints have inspired you." Viola Fiona clasped her hands together.

"The Medicine Totems have offered assistance," Agatha said.

Elba set the heated food before Willi. "The angels—in many forms and guises—are always there for us. Now, eat quick like and tell us what you're going to do."

When she finished the cabbage rolls, she said, "Now I should catch you all up on a few things that I'd been holding back but now realize you all could help if you knew the whole picture. However, if I hear one snide remark, you're all three out of here until next summer, hear?"

"Just as I dangnab knew, you been into things you shouldn't ought, but okay, go ahead." Elba settled her ample frame more comfortably.

Willi told the three friends about the *Comanche Raider*

and her findings there. She flipped up a corner on her page of notes. "There was, like I said, the Irish double-chain quilt square."

"That would be," Viola Fiona said, "the one the dearly departed was wearing at the lake earlier in the day, if I've the straight of your story."

"Yes. So I need to figure some way to ask Neeper and Dan Oxhandler about that 'scarf' and just why it was on their boat when they claimed they last saw Tessa at the lake earlier in the day."

"Secondly," Agatha added while clearing the table, "you should also ask why one of their magazines ended up in your cottage."

Willi made crimson swirls around the number two on her pad. "Right. Then there's the matter of Neeper's quail pie story. That, at least, is solved."

"Out-and-out lie, you mean? You call that solved?" Elba said, pouring everyone a steaming cup of tea. "Definitely two birds can be brought down with the one stone in this case."

Willi blinked. "Meaning?"

"Meaning he's got to explain the lie about the meal and the redhead who was with him."

"Hmm, yes, I suppose." Willi drew a scarlet curlicue around number three and four. "And the last two items." She chewed on the end of her pen. "Agatha, bet you could help here."

Agatha swirled her skirt beneath her as she sat and leaned forward. Her eyes twinkled. "Yes, Willi?"

"You and Sheriff Tucker being an item might make this one easy."

"Now I won't use him in any way. That would not be right."

"Agatha, Agatha, Agatha. Was it not you and Sister here who talked me into not talking to Sheriff Tucker ahead of time about a certain visit to Meadowbrook Senior Citizens' Home? Hmmm?"

Agatha played with the fifteen bead necklaces around her neck.

"You said you saw a plastic evidence baggie with one of those strange Celtic cards sitting on his desk. It would be perfectly natural for you to ask about and wonder what case it was linked with. You know the type of questions. We need to know, too, if you can finagle him around to show you, if it had any markings other than the norm. Then, when I do find this cousin of the Landises' who's a Celtic historian, I'll have more details to give."

Agatha pursed her lips. "I am curious, and yes, he might very well expect me to ask."

Willi put a square with spikes beside number five. "Fair enough?"

"I believe I can handle that assignment, Willi, yes, I do."

"This last one, perhaps Viola Fiona can help with." Willi etched little red fish swimming around number six. She got up, scrabbled in her purse, and shoved onto the table the Celtic card with the heavy knot-work design around its edge. "Didn't you say you were a practitioner with the Celtic cards?"

"Oh, girl, no. If I did, I must've been under the influence of the blasted drugs they stuffed me body with at the home. It's sorry I am, but no help can I be giving you. The reading of the tea leaves and the runic stones, yes, those I have a most profound affinity and insight with, but these, no."

"Oh." Willi sighed. She must have expressed her feelings in a woebegone look. All three ladies reached out a hand to pat her arm. "Wonder how I got that idea? I could have sworn I saw a wooden box in your belongings we brought back. On the front was something about the Celtic Tree Oracle. My mind must be going."

"Don't go there for a minute." Elba shoved Willi's cup closer. "Drink up. Might be you just have two encounters mixed up. That happens to me when events pile up faster than cut kernels off a corncob. Sort of like a kaleidoscope twirling around in my dangblame head, colors switching into more patterns than a body can keep up with, more colors than Sherwin-Williams can make, more brightness than a dozen meteors coming through space."

"Space being your gray cells up there?"

That earned her another thwap with the potholders. "Ouch."

"You get the point?"

"Yes, Elba, it scares me to say this, but I did understand all that rambling. Elba, see if you can find the Landises' number and make an appointment with the cousin, whoever that is. I might have seen the box of cards at one of the booths at the Irish Fling fair or maybe at school."

"Oh, and wouldn't that be a good place to be starting your investigations on the morrow? As me old bones are creaking, I need to be seeking the downy covers and sleep." Viola Fiona rose.

"Viola," Elba said, "you been back in Texas long enough you know *downy* ain't gonna work for you here, but we got some right soft Dacron. Yep, let's finish the cleaning and get back to Frogs' Feet."

Willi said, "You're all welcome to stay here."

"Oh, we know," Elba said, "but now we know you're safe, and we got Viola Fiona's lawyers a-working, we'll be going along home."

"And," Viola Fiona added, "the corner room at Frogs' Feet is just fine for now while we're planning the tearoom."

Elba shook her sister's shoulder. "Agatha, what you sitting so still for? Let's get going."

Agatha smiled sweetly and tucked a gray hair in her bun. "Gnawing thoughts need to be set out in the universe for consideration. Willi, could the black and white wolves be trying to communicate on many levels? Questions keep coming to mind. Mull them over. Is something or someone *not black or white?* Is there a reversed disguise? White is not always good like the white cowboy hats. Sometimes a bolt of white lightning can kill. Therefore, I keep getting this idea flashing by that something white is coming ferociously out of the black abyss of time."

Willi raised an eyebrow. "Black abyss of time?"

Agatha nodded. "Everything concerned with this is rooted in the darkness of a past age." She sighed. "Wish I could be clearer."

With red pen in hand, Willi drew an open book and wrote number seven and eight upon the pages. Elba peered over her shoulder. "Messages coming at us fast tonight. What does that mean?"

"I'd forgotten, but now that I've started writing things down, items just keep clicking. Someone had riffled through my collection of the high school yearbooks two times. The first time I took a couple of them upstairs to go through later."

"Two?" Elba asked, folding her apron away into a drawer.

"Actually, three. One the night Rose Pig came upstairs and the phone line was cut. A second when Beowulf and Chaucer were killed in the moat. But they didn't take any of them."

"Perhaps you'd taken upstairs the ones they wanted," Agatha said.

"And the third?" Elba insisted.

"At the Nickleberry High School library the day of the murder."

"Well, they be saying," Viola Fiona said, with a hand on the doorknob, "trouble, he comes in threes, he does."

"Perhaps fours," Willi said. She was as surprised as the three pairs of eyes staring back at her. "Just then I heard Quannah's voice clear as if he stood here with us. *The Sacred number is four. Look for four.*" Willi shrugged. "You all scare me sometimes."

"Us?" they all three said.

Elba added, "That came to your head, not ours."

"Well, I have no idea what it means, so it's just a useless, random thought."

"Oh and it seems so easy to me," Viola Fiona said. "Easier than McFinnian getting a piece of what's under Mrs. McFinnian's skirts, it is, and nothing's easier than that, just ask their mailman, paperboy, and neighbor."

Willi shook her head.

"I'm simply saying—"

"Simply?" asked Willi.

"I'm simply saying there may be four libraries or four books. I can't recall if Nickelberry has a city library? If so, wouldn't it be worth checking out, now?"

"Great idea," Elba said, as the three traipsed outdoors. "And Willi loves the Hall of Horrors there. They started it in Depression times and have added something new to it each year. We'll have to take you there after all this Irish Fling fair is finished."

"Love isn't exactly the word I'd have used." Willi shivered at the thought of walking through that hallway again but agreed it would be worth checking out.

Agatha said, "Willi, the stars are twinkling. Come see. So beautiful. Is he winking?"

Willi walked out on the porch and stared up. She pointed at one of the brightest. "Yes, he's winking. Night all."

"He'll be home tomorrow," Agatha added.

Willi smiled. "Yes, tomorrow."

CHAPTER
12

The next morning played weather games, tripping back and forth between sunshine and lowering clouds. She mentally kicked herself from here to the Rio Grande. Dang if she hadn't fallen asleep without perusing the Tyler files, so she wasn't ready with a report for the sheriff. But after two summonses from Sheriff Tucker, Willi joined him in front of number 225 of the Bluebonnet Apartments. From the second-floor doorway belonging to Saralee York, Willi peered at the high school a couple of empty lots away. Water sprinklers were twirling on the football field.

She'd at least used what Sheriff Tucker called her *integrity*—honesty with herself—and understood her reluctance to share info right now. The facts so far proved her coworker at school, Neeper Oxhandler, as a possible liar and his cousin Dan as a possible drug abuser. She just knew there was a piece of the kaleidoscope missing that would bring everything together into a beautiful pattern with explanations for everything.

Sheriff Tucker said, "Got a call just afore leaving. Quannah said to pick him up at the airport, please." She nodded at

the particulars, wishing she'd brought her purse with pen
and paper upstairs with her.

"Ain't this," Sheriff Tucker asked, "where your aunt
lives?"

"Yes, but downstairs within an inner court and close to
the pool and spa." After Willi pushed the bell button for the
fifth time, Saralee graciously ushered them into an airy living room.

"Please make yourselves comfortable," she said in such
a monotone Willi wondered if she were on Valium. "I've
squeezed fresh orange juice for us. Be right back."

In a stage whisper, Sheriff Tucker said, "Now, do your
thing, Miss Willi. You said you learn a lot from a person's
surroundings and just talking to them. I do, too, but this is
a lady's domicile, so that's what we—meaning *you*—are
going to do today. Take a gander, girl." He tried to get comfortable in a white plastic modular chair and finally managed to cross one ankle over his other leg.

"Certainly, I told you that was my goal today, to clear Saralee York from the picture."

"Shouldn't be hard to do, being as how there's only the
one connection to the Tyler school system. Do it right fast,
and let's get on to others."

Willi considered the shelves of books. Saralee's reading
material was sparse by Willi's terms. No magazines, not
even on the occasional tables. Well, this young woman would
be easy to clear from any suspicion just on the grounds of
dullness. *Bless her.* Surely, she had more in life than this
cold apartment and work. Willi shook her head. That was
harsh. She was new in town. She'd get involved with special groups eventually. Willi touched college texts ranging
from English literature to geology up through upper-level
chemistry perched neatly beside reference books on building decks, fingerprinting, lightning, amateur investigation,
dinosaurs, cooking for one, face-lifts, chemicals and the
brain, robotics . . . and scores of other subjects.

"Whew." She looked upward at the top shelf and
squinted. "Harlequin romances?" She stood tippy-toe to

touch the spines. No knickknacks perched between sections of books to add definition, spacing, or texture. Like
Saralee's voice, her books were arranged in a monotonous
manner. "Good grief and Mother's molasses."

"Mayhap you want to translate?"

In her own stage whisper, she said, "Something about
the situation is sticky and hard to see through. A person
that reads Harlequin romances for fun usually doesn't
alphabetize them by the author's last name. See? Even the
modern mainstream novels in hardback are perfectly
filed." She grimaced. "I'm an English teacher and considered very organized. On top of that, I have hundreds of
books, and none are alphabetized like this."

Saralee, in her cool lime pants suit, entered with a tray.
The lace-edged blouse was long-sleeved but was an almost-
but-not-quite see through. With her red hair, the outfit made
her a knockout. "Here we are." She served the orange juice
over finely crushed ice with a lime twist. "Help yourselves
to the miniature croissants."

After a few appreciative bites and two glasses of juice,
Sheriff Tucker said, "You shouldn't have gone to all this
trouble, but I'm glad you did." He grabbed a stub of pencil
and his three-by-five-inch spiral notebook. "We still have a
few loose ends to account for here and there, like I told you
on the phone."

"I thought that was what we did a couple of nights ago
in the teacher's lounge."

"Just a repeat, now and again, helps this old feller keep
in the know." With that, he proceeded to ask the same dis-
mal questions. Finally, he put his notebook away as if finished and said to Saralee, "Miss Willi went to visit your
old stomping ground yesterday."

"Oh?" Saralee scooted to the edge of her white plastic,
shuffling her green flats along the beige carpeting. Two
minute spots of color came to her cheeks but faded as she
took a deep breath and repeated, "Oh?"

"Might have been by accident she mentioned you to one
of her auntie's friends."

Willi raised a brow. He wasn't fibbing, but he was sure getting a lot out of the truth in that confusing statement. Jeeze. "My aunt taught many years ago in Tyler."

"Yes, I've heard of her. She is one of those with her name and picture on a plaque in the superintendent's office there. I believe she got it for being a master teacher."

"That's Aunt Minnie. How she could manage thirty years of corralling third graders much less teaching the pointed-headed little monsters anything, is beyond me, but she did. Give me high school any day."

"Absolutely."

Sheriff Tucker got up and pulled at his earlobe. "Could I use your—?"

"Of course, right down the hallway to the left."

Willi continued, drawing Saralee's attention back to the Tyler connection. "Lois Aaron in the super's office is the one we talked with."

"Lois Aaron is an old friend of your aunt's?"

This time Willi's cheeks heated up. *Dangblame you, Sheriff.* She grinned and simply said, "No accounting for camaraderie across lines of age and creed, as they say."

"I suppose."

"She thought you were a most efficient teacher. Even when I—" Willi cleared her throat. Good heavens, she almost said, *When I checked the files.* Obviously, that would go beyond the cover of a simple sentimental visit. "Even when I asked her point-blank what the superintendent thought, she offered only glowing terms." *Maybe that was pouring it on too thickly.*

"They are kind."

"I can't imagine what would make you leave the district."

"One sometimes just needs a change. I wanted to come back to—"

"Come back? You've lived in Nickleberry before?"

"No, Willi, I wanted to come back to a more simple life, but close to big city amenities. Nickleberry County being near Tarrant County and the DFW Metroplex offers me that."

Sheriff Tucker chose that moment to return. "Miss Willi, I know you love artwork and such."

"Huh?"

Sheriff Tucker frowned and waved one of his blue polka-dotted bandannas toward the hallway. "Miss York has some right colorful prints. Couldn't help noticing down the hall there, ma'am."

Shocked that Saralee had anything *colorful* in this arctic environment, she almost said *huh* again, but swallowed and tried, "Really? I'd love to see."

Saralee hesitated, rose slowly, and waved a permissive hand. "This way." Two thirty-by-sixty-inch prints in golds and bright greens mixed with umbers and reds resided within polished wooden frames on the pristine white walls.

Willi took a deep breath. "These . . . these are Celtic? I recognize the ornate knot work around the edging."

"Yes, this is a warrior male, and here is the female warrioress. They are such strong and vengeful characters, resonating the fierceness it took to survive in the Old World, yet representing the hope that after horrible wars, ease and love and laughter will come back into their lives."

"They are breathtakingly beautiful. In the background there, are those—?"

"Wolves. A white one walks behind her, a black one trails after him."

"Wolves?"

"Yes, let me turn the spotlights on over them. See?"

Willi's heartbeat loped as fast as any wolf's would on the hunt. "Yes, oh, yes, I see." Questions hurtled through her mind, but she couldn't seem to get her breath under control. Maybe she wouldn't be able to clear Saralee totally, not with this touch of the Irish artwork. Not that having it made her a killer; it just simply raised questions.

Saralee led her into a bedroom, also beige on white with the exception of a framed set of Celtic fairies, much lighter in emotional depiction, but still surrounded on the perimeter by a twisting band of golden, braided knots. The room was beautiful and obviously a comfort zone. Saralee had even gone wild with a couple of gold and rose-colored throw pillows. Two chairs in matching hues made a picturesque seating area. Peeking out from behind the golden chair was a Stetson cowboy hat. Saralee drew her attention to the jewel box of silver also entwined with the work of the angels. When Willi glanced back at the chairs, the Stetson was gone. Saralee led her into the living room just in time to hear the lilt of her phone—an ivory and gold Victorian style. "Yes," she said into the receiver, "he's here."

Sheriff Tucker wrapped his meaty paw around the dainty instrument. "Why didn't you call me on my radio or my cell phone?" He hung his head down. "Oh?" Setting the receiver in the cradle with one hand, he drew his cell phone out of his pocket. "Yep, dispatcher was right. It's dead. Might be somebody else will be if we don't hurry."

"Oh, my." Saralee walked them to the door. "Another murder?"

"Don't know yet. Let's go, Miss Willi, to the high school."

As they headed down the steps, Officer Jon Piedra, in white shirt and jeans, headed up them. Obviously, it was his day off. Sheriff Tucker said, "Keep your phone nearby . . . uh, and the battery up and going. Might need your help. Maybe another murder over to the high school."

"I just came from there. That Mrs. Horsenettle is damned determined something be done about the vandalism at the high school library, so I gave her fifteen minutes of my day off to write out that report. Maybe that'll make her happy."

The sheriff scratched his head. "Didn't know you lived here—"

"Don't, sir. Just left something at a friend's place and was picking it up. I'll get it later. Let's go." He turned and walked down behind Willi.

They were in the sheriff's cruiser with Officer Piedra following them in a huge black Chevy pickup, before Willi thought to squeak out, "Who?"

As he maneuvered into the parking lot at breakneck speed, the question of "who" hung in the air, unanswered.

She raced in after the two men. Their long strides kept her own steps at double tempo. Moans came from the right. Willi stopped on the proverbial dime, changed direction, and rounded the corner to the water fountain. India Lou pushed the button on the water fountain to send a cascade over Vic Ramirez's arm.

Willi grimaced. An ugly welt rose on his forearm. Her knees developed that sickly feel of an elevator moving too fast beneath them. To combat an overpowering feeling of déjà vu, she put her fingers to both temples. Ohmygoshmy-goshmyGod, she'd been in this same hallway witnessing this same scene before. She closed her eyes. When she opened them, the fleeting sensation disappeared.

Vic Ramirez ground out his words. "If I ever get my hands on the damned prankster. Details about Tessa must have gotten out, and one of those sicko kids who get their kicks in the most stupid—"

India Lou said, "Never you mind about that right now. I done called the ambulance. Bottom line, that got to be seen to." India Lou offered to cover the wound with gauze.

"*Gracias,* no, Ms. Aiken. Best to leave it open to the air for now. Best thing for this acid burn at the moment is clear running water."

Officer Piedra stepped away, got on his cell phone, and confirmed the ambulance. Vic twisted the injured arm underneath the water. Willi took a deep breath. The raw wound wasn't as horrible as she first imagined. Maybe three inches long and only the first layer of skin deep. The weakness left her knees, and she stood straighter.

The sheriff said, "Dispatcher said you had found another body, India Lou."

"Sorry, I am, so sorry. Guess I overreacted, yes, sir, I did."

Willi patted India Lou's arm and took over the job of pushing the water button for her. "Why are you at the high school, anyway, India Lou?"

"That be your auntie's fault. She give me all these weeks off, but a body has to be a-doing something, so Mr. Wigin-ton, he needed extra hands to get this old building ready for school next week, and so I sorta got my old job back for a little bit, you see?"

Sheriff Tucker sneezed, caught it with the flash of a purple and orange bandanna, and said, "And wouldn't this just be a darn convenient job to do some snooping, some trying to find answers out about your niece? Now, India Lou, you got to let us—"

"I don't need to do no snooping. I got Miss Willi for that."

Sheriff Tucker raised his gray red-banty-tipped eyebrows. *"Ooooooooh?"*

Willi smiled. "I bet I can clear that up for you later. What happened here, Vic?"

Shaking his leonine head, Sheriff Tucker worked his little finger around his earlobe. Obviously, the possible tick bothering him right now was his deputized helper.

She got very businesslike and repeated, "Vic?"

India Lou instead took up the tale. "I went looking for the cleansers, yes ma'am, I did. Opened up that storage closet. He were just a body on the floor. I runs and calls the police. I did, so helps me Jesus, I did think he was dead."

Vic said, "With reason. But when she got back, I was up and moaning."

"How," asked Sheriff Tucker, "did the arm get burned?"

"I came today to finish the inspection before school next week. I'd started the other day, remember, when Tessa . . . well, anyway, I came back to finish the job. I have my clipboard with each area listed, which I check off as I go through the building."

"So," Willi asked, "this storage is one on your list?"

"Yep." He pointed a finger at item fifty-seven. "Have to make sure these flammable items are stored properly, no fuse boxes with loose wires. That sort of thing. I'd just passed a few words with Jon Piedra as he was leaving."

"I heard them slapping that Spanish back and forth, so he's remembering that right," India Lou added.

"Someone surprised you and threw acid on your arm while you were inspecting this?"

"No, Ms. Gallagher. The sorry damned *perro de puta*

rigged a bottle of acid to tip and fall when I opened the door. Typical kids' type of prank if done with water or even paint, but acid? Some little jerk knew I was doing the rounds today, had read the gruesome details of the murder, and thought it'd be cool."

Willi shook her head. "No, no. That doesn't fit. None of the kids are around right now. Only the office aides, and they were sent home for a couple days." Willi swallowed and met India Lou's stern visage. "Only office and janitorial staff are here."

Sheriff Tucker called Deputy Piedra over. "You see anyone around this area as you were leaving the premises a while ago?"

"No, Sheriff. I talked with Mrs. Horsenettle, came out through the hall, saw Vic. We spoke. I left. No kids in the hallway. None outside."

Sheriff Tucker said, "Mayhap we'll get prints, Vic, if you didn't touch the bottle and doorframe."

"No, I had sense enough not to do that. India Lou?"

"Naw, sir, I didn't touch nothing but you, trying to get you up and out to this here water fountain."

Ambulance attendants rushed in to take care of Vic's injured arm. Two deputy sheriffs arrived with a crime scene kit to put tape around the storage closet and the fountain. Willi walked over to a group collected underneath a stampeding herd of the yellow paints—the Nickleberry horses with royal blue markings—on the marquee in the front hallway. Sheriff Tucker wrote their names in his spiral notepad. Dan Oxhandler, Sammie Yannich, and Neeper stood like a cluster of green grapes, their complexions at the moment giving credence to that comparison.

Willi imagined her face the same color as a second wave of déjà vu hit. No, hardly that. Simply all the excitement, too many late nights, too many things happening far too fast. Who wouldn't feel light-headed after a murder, a horrible dip in Nickelberry Lake, the monster vehicles—yellow Caddy and black pickup—giving her the heebie-jeebies, a freewheeling abduction on the wrong side of the law, and the discovery that friends told her lies. Neeper's fib about a meal rated just as strongly with her as Dan Oxhandler's possible involvement with drugs.

Sheriff Tucker put a hand on her elbow. "You okay, Miss Willi?"

She placed her fingers over her eyes. "Yes, just tired."

"That wandering nephew of mine returns, you'll perk right up."

Willi grinned.

"See? What'd I tell you? Already smiling. You need a break, you take it, now hear?"

"I'm fine. Wouldn't miss one bit of this."

Sheriff Tucker offered her a Luden's cherry drop. "Good for what ails you and besides—"

"It tastes good," she finished the longtime ditty she and he had used since she was a kid. "Thanks. Hey, someone just snuck around and up the stairs."

Sheriff Tucker moved as ponderously and as fast as a bison. "Right down here, folks, with the rest, if you don't mind."

Jarnagin Ventnor walked over. Bernie Burkhalter stepped down the stairs and beneath the marquee of mustangs. Ventnor sniffed and straightened his jacket, unbuttoned and buttoned it at the midriff. "What's going on, sir, and how can we help?"

"Looked to me like you all were making like cattle rustlers and sneaking away."

Bernie rolled his eyes. "Whatever was going on wasn't our business. We figured to let the law take care of this. I was just showing Ventnor a few details about the different school campuses. Passing the reins in such a way as to make things go smoothly."

Jarnagin Ventnor said, "Right you are, right you are. What is going on, Sheriff Tucker? Or perhaps we should ask our campus sleuth, our own Ms. Gallagher, is it?"

Willi nodded, but said nothing.

Hortense Horsenettle approached with an armload of books. "Here you go." She proffered these to Burkhalter.

"Took me a moment to locate them in the archives. Sorry you had to wait for so long." She glanced over at the spewing water fountain. "Ah, we've a group of *hydropots*. Wonderful."

In unison all said, "Huh?"

"Hydropots. Aqua quaffers."

This received a group groan.

Willi turned loose of the water fountain's button and hazarded a guess. "Ah, someone who likes to drink water."

Hortense beamed. "Yes. I'm a *hydropot*."

Burkhalter muttered, "*Pot* is about right." He took the books.

Willi frowned. Those looked like the high school yearbooks.

Hortense said, "I wouldn't let just anyone check them out, but seeing as you are our outgoing superintendent, I see no reason not to let you have them for a few—a *few* days. Couple of them are missing, by the by. If I locate them, I'll let you know."

Bernie quickly grabbed the books and shoved them into his black leather shoulder satchel. Officer Piedra walked almost everyone to the cafeteria. Sheriff Tucker said, "I'll be with you all directly." He flipped his spiral closed, shoved it in his shirt pocket, and nodded toward Vic Ramirez to follow. "Where might a body sit quiet like to chat?"

"Little janitorial closet right down this-a-way."

Willi excused herself and followed Hortense around the corner. "How did the final info session go with Deputy Piedra?" Willi asked.

"You know. He gets his silver clipboard out, fills in the blanks on a statement, and then nothing will be done."

"High school vandalism is hard to pinpoint, Hortense, unless our surveillance tapes caught them."

"That was odd, too."

"Excuse me?"

Hortense fumbled with her red-rimmed glasses. "The tapes, well, no . . . the camera . . . was turned toward the wall, not out into the library."

"That is odd. Then the camera must have caught a glimpse of something as it was being turned."

"No." Hortense brayed in a way only those with horrible sinus problems can.

"No?"

Tears came to Hortense's eyes. "They blame me."

"What?" Willi blinked. "For what?"

Hortense sniffled—a mistake—as it seemed to have cleared her entire nasal passage in one great honk and snort. "Sorry. Uh . . . Officer Piedra said I must have accidentally turned the camera when I cleaned those shelves right beside it. I'd like to say I didn't, but . . . what with training the new assistant, processing the incoming books, and shelving them along with all the Irish Fling Festival's activities, I've been rushing to meet myself. I could have, but . . ."

"Nonsense." Willi closed her eyes a moment and tapped her nose. "Kids are wise to such surveillance and certainly could turn those mechanical thingamajigs around easier than you or I. You have never been lackadaisical in your work, Hortense, and don't let anyone tell you otherwise."

Hortense wiped beneath her glasses. "Wish Principal Wiginton believed the same."

"He does. Just has a harder time saying it. Now, what exactly did the kids take?"

"Why?"

"Hortense!"

"Willi, you're helping Sheriff Tucker on something important, for Heaven's sake. Why do you care about our little high school library?" Hortense gasped and placed her hands—long nails manicured in bright red—over her mouth. "It has something to do with the murder on the school grounds? Oh my gosh, I would never have—"

"Stop. No, no no." Good Lord, she didn't need to let Hortense know that there was even an inkling of that possibility. She'd have it on the gossip trail faster than a Texas jackalope could drink a Budweiser, and that was damned fast. "Not at all," Willi emphasized. "I mean, how much farther apart could a mutilation in a yellow Cadillac and a snitched high school trophy be?"

Hortense laughed, which did unpleasant sounding things to her adenoids. "Sure, you're right. A couple of trophies were stolen. Just a few yearbooks, can you believe that? Odd. They threw the trophies in the trash bin behind the Ag building, but not the yearbooks. And they might not be important to you or anyone else, but I'm responsible for everything in that library and—"

"Whoa. Hold the Nickleberry paint! Whew! Of course, the library and all that you do there is important to the school, Hortense. That is a strange thing to pick up, though, a school annual. How did you even know it was missing?"

"They were in a glass-fronted old case, the one Mr. Dandridge made and gave the school so many years ago. Has those beautifully carved vines all around the edges. Anyway, I suppose that's the true loss. Glass was crushed in, books pulled out. Luckily, we can replace the glass. I'm glad they didn't hurt the wood."

"What did Officer Piedra say after seeing the case?"

"That the kids had just started a wild spree of vandalism, tearing into everything, probably got interrupted and scared off before doing more damage."

"So they tore up a couple of yearbooks, broke the glass. Guess we're lucky, like Piedra says."

"I suppose. He's certainly a churlish man, word wise. That was the other odd thing."

"What?"

"They didn't destroy the books, at least, not on the premises."

"They took them?"

Hortense chewed and nodded. "Uh-humm. Some of them. The rest of the yearbooks were checked out this morning by Mr. Burkhalter."

Okay, do a double take. Maybe there was a thread linking the murder, the annuals, and the killer. Willi pursed her lips. Books had been pulled out of her nookery. She'd thought them interesting enough to take upstairs to read but had shoved them underneath the bed. Those were year-books, too, weren't they?

"Hortense, what years were those books?"

"About ten years ago and a couple before that."

Willi nodded. *Maybe so, maybe no.* She changed tack. "Why did Bernie Burkhalter want them?"

"Oh, how forgetful of me not to share the latest about Sammie. She's in the Nickleberry Hospital."

"How could you not tell me that right away? Did the murderer try—"

"No, Willi, she's simply had some sort of collapse." Hortense looked over her shoulder and lowered her voice. "You know she drinks—not as a *hydropot,* unfortu-nately—and that sorry excuse for an ex-superintendent encourages her."

"Burkhalter?"

"Right. Anyway, she wanted the yearbooks. I told him I'd send some nice magazines along, but he said that's all she wanted and in his words, 'Whatever Baby wants, Baby gets.' "

"What happened to Sammie?"

"She's just been so weird the last few days. Jumps at everything around her. The coffee machine broke the other day, and from her reaction, you'd have thought Osama had sent a suicide bomber through the building. The phone rings, for heaven's sake, and she's a twittering case of nerves."

"Not good for a secretary, no. What brought this on?"

Hortense cleared her sinuses before pushing her red glasses frames up her nose. "No one knows. How could someone go so mental in two or three days? Willi, you won't believe this part."

Willi leaned in as Hortense did. "She inspects her food. Mrs. Wiginton brought a coffee cake for us the other day, and Sammie wouldn't let anyone touch it because it had powdered sugar. She was about to throw it in the trash when Mrs. Wiginton grabbed it. The rest of us took a slice.

Sammie waited until the afternoon, I guess to see if we keeled over, before she'd take a bite."

"Oh my gosh."

"That's not all."

"There's more?"

"She won't drink coffee made in the office or the lounge. She brings her own from home now."

"Poor Sammie. She's not only taken her paddle out of the water, she's thrown it across the waterfall."

"And she won't talk. Sammie always gossiped, talked about everything, everybody."

"And now she's quiet?" Willi asked.

"Weird, huh?"

"I think that's the most frightening thing of all. Sammie? Silent? I'll go by and visit her later."

Willi hurried back around the school corridor to the janitorial closet. She stood between Officer Piedra and Vic Ramirez while Sheriff Tucker sat on a small stool across from India Lou's chair. He peered up at Ramirez. "Getting in here as if I was going to yap my jaws at India Lou was just to put them off. Mayhap you had more to say, Vic, but all them other firemen showed, and you clammed up."

"*Sí, tienes razón.* Yeah, you're right. About the time I remembered, the attendants were putting salve on this arm."

"Spit it out, son."

"I wasn't planning on coming back until next week to finish the inspection, but I got a call at the station this morning."

Willi tilted her head. "From the school? About the school?"

"I don't know. Dispatcher gave me the message that some busybody wanted the inspection done this morning and wanted only me. To tell you the truth, I thought it might have been Mrs. Horsenettle."

"Thought?" asked the sheriff. "You reason to think otherwise now?"

"Dispatcher said she knew Mrs. Horsenettle's voice. It wasn't her. In fact, she didn't know if it was male or female. They said the high school was in violation of the fire code, especially within the storage areas. So, for the sake of community relations and all, I figured I'd better come on and finish the job."

Jon Piedra clapped him on the shoulder. "Man, you were lucky. I looked at how they rigged that bottle. By all rights, it should have hit you square in the face. Might have blinded you."

Vic shivered and scratched the back of his head. "Yeah, funny the things you do for no reason."

"What do you mean?" Willi asked.

"When I got out of the truck, I reached in and exchanged my hat for a helmet. No reason to do that with such a simple walk-through. That's what saved me . . . my eyes. *Gracias a Dios.*" He rubbed his neck again and cleared his throat. "Can't believe I exchanged that hat."

Willi patted his good arm. "We all do things like that, Vic. We don't have to understand why. Some call it angels watching over us or spirit helpers guiding us. Just be thankful that sometimes we don't act with so-called reason. How exactly did the helmet save you?"

"Soon as I opened the door, the acid splashed down. The paint job on that helmet is shot to hell, but anyway, the hat directed the splatter away from my face onto my arm. If I'd been dressed for a full-fledged inspection, I'd have had protective wear for my arms, too. Who knew? *¿Quién sabe,* huh?"

Sheriff Tucker worried his left earlobe as if a pesky tick was in residence. "Sounds purpose-like to me, son, sure does."

"Preaching to the choir, Sheriff. The question is why?"

"Got any enemies? Had any problems with anyone lately?"

Vic studied his boots. "Naw, sir, naw."

Willi put both hands on her hips. "Excuse me, Vic Ramirez, but I happen to know you and Dan Oxhandler had a few words the other day at the Irish Fling Sourdough Baking Contest."

"Aww, Ms. Gallagher, that didn't amount to anything."

"A fistfight that spilled lime punch on a half dozen people and left you with a bruise or two and Dan Oxhandler with a couple of scrapes wasn't something to sneeze at."

"Must've been too much *tequila* in the punch. We just got carried away."

"I beg your ever-loving pardon. There wasn't any—"

"Just teasing you, Ms. Gallagher. Just a little *broma*."

Willi gave him one of her best evil-eyed teacher glares. Fisticuffs at their age was not normal, certainly not for a high school teacher and a fireman, both respected in the community. Maybe there was something to the rumors about Dan Oxhandler and drugs. No, no, she just wouldn't believe that of Dan. She had to have proof. Might be he was getting grilled over the fires of gossip when the blame really belonged to Vic Ramirez. She shook her head. Hell's bells, that was as hard to believe as Dan being involved. Willi glanced at India Lou's reddened eyes. She was holding up well, but the swollen lids, the sagging shoulders attested to her grief. Willi straightened her back. She'd made a promise to help bring Tessa's mutilator to justice, and no matter how hard the questions, how difficult the truths were to face, she'd by blazes keep her word. The overhead intercom blared into action. India Lou was instructed to mop up an iced tea spilled in the cafeteria.

When the door shut behind her, Sheriff Tucker asked Vic, "You know anything about Tessa Aiken using drugs?"

"*Caramba*. Sheriff, not any drugs in this town to worry about. Better get relocated in Dallas or Fort Worth if you hanker after drug busting, Sheriff, and don't look at me. *Drogas* aren't my style. I give programs to the grade-school kids about saying 'No.'"

Willi chimed in. "The day she died, you all—the Oxhandlers, Tessa, and you—were out at the lake. If she wasn't using drugs, maybe she was drinking heavily that day."

"We all had a couple of beers. Everyone except Saralee—you know, your new English teacher. Said she didn't do beer or beans. How can you call yourself a Texan and not do one of them, at least? Now, I'm not sitting around for this third-degree stuff when I'm the victim." He jumped up, dumping over his chair.

Tucker grabbed his shoulder. "Hold up, son, hold up. *We* are trying to help *you*. Seems mighty coincidental that Tessa died on the high school grounds and now you was attacked here with the same instrument, so to speak."

Vic picked up the chair. His faced drained of color. "Naw. No way are these two things connected. I mean . . . no, no." He straddled the chair with his good arm across the backrest. "Naw . . . why would—?"

While the wind was obviously knocked out of him, Willi pushed. "Vic, what do you think of Bernie Burkhalter's story?"

"Huh?" He licked his lips and took a cherry cough drop Sheriff Tucker held out. "Huh?"

Willi leaned down closer to him. "According to Burkhalter, he was in the habit of leaving his Cadillac unlocked. Then he claims Tessa stole the car. Does that sound like Tessa?"

A bit of color returned to his normally dark skin. He nodded. "It's possible. Tessa was smart. If someone was chasing her, she might have tried to get in a lot of cars, found his open with the keys, and took off to escape." He stood up and took a deep breath. "She had a quick, sharp mind. Hey, she was a lawyer. Sure, she'd do whatever to survive." He opened the door and gulped in more fresh air. "I've got to get going. If you need me for more questions about today, Sheriff, you know where to reach me." He pointedly ignored Willi's finger raised as if to ask another question.

Sheriff Tucker was no slouch, and he backed his sworn-in helpers. "Appreciate it, Vic, I do. Willi might think of some questions later, too. I'm sure, seeing as how she's a sorta sworn-in liaison, you'll cooperate with her if needed."

Vic shrugged his shoulders. "Sure. You or Ms. Gallagher. Sure." He rushed down the hallway.

Sheriff Tucker stood and winked. The action reminded her of Quannah, and her heart did an instant meltdown. Oh God, how she missed him. This afternoon, he'd be back, though. Yes, yes, yes.

Sheriff Tucker snapped his fingers in front of her face. "Miss Willi? You off daydreaming?"

"Huh? What? I . . . uh . . . do not daydream."

This time he exchanged one of those superior-gender looks with Officer Piedra. "Mayhap," he said, "you had another question right then for Vic Ramirez?"

"No . . . well, sort of. An observation, I guess."

"And that would be?"

"Tessa was running from a pursuer, right?"

"Could be?"

"It's an older Cadillac."

Sheriff Tucker worried his ear like that troublesome tick was in residence. "You just might have lost me there, Miss Willi. Piedra?"

Jon Piedra shook his head. *"No comprendo, Jefe."*

"For heaven's sake and Granny's garters. She's running, jumps in an unfamiliar car, and manages to start the thing. Probably her heart is pounding ninety to nothing, her hands are shaking. Mine would be. The Caddy isn't one with automatic seat belts. If you're running for your life, are you going to gun the motor and get the hell away or take time to figure out the damned seat belt contraption in a strange car?"

CHAPTER

13

Okay. Time to slow the kaleidoscope down, but her mind would not stop twisting and turning facts and folks, dates and schedules, scenes and feelings around and around and—

Relax. Stop it.

Willi headed out on I-35 north toward Airport Freeway to pick up Quannah. She turned on the AC and the radio. *"Sí tu amor pusa una canción en mi corazón"* wove into the tapestry of her mind as a male voice sang the last lines of the song: *" . . . Yes, your love put a song, put a song, put a song in my heart, a beautiful song of two people in love ever more."* His Mex-Tex segued into Ferlin's "The Waltz of the Angels."

She banged her head with an open palm. Great. That brought to mind the work—the knots—of the angels, the unusual Celtic designs on the cards. She hoped Agatha would be successful in getting hold of that card she'd seen in the sheriff's office. If she couldn't, no one could. As Quannah would be the first to tell her, seconded quickly by the Kachelhoffer sisters, when things kept showing up over and over, the universe was trying to get your attention focused on that for some reason. She was certainly aware of the possible importance of the artistic knots, but focused wasn't something her mind could do.

She glanced down at the clock. "Drat and damn. Where is my head today? His plane isn't due for another hour and a half."

She screeched to a stop on I-35, swerved to the shoulder and onto an off ramp. Brakes on the cars behind squealed and horns blared. "People are so inconsiderate sometimes. What in Hades am I going to do for that time? I'm too far from Nickleberry to make a return trip and back, but there's so many things I need to do and so many people I need to—"

You can only do what you can do. The only control you have over a situation is how you react to it.

She shut her eyes for a moment, listened to the tail end of Patsy Cline's "Honky Tonk Merry-Go-Round," and sighed. A police cruiser passed her but put on his brakes as if he were going to turn and check on her. Quickly, she pulled back onto the ramp, drove down a couple of intersections until she came to one that said Goober Joe's Lake.

"Why not?"

At the small entryway was the obligatory minnow shop with minimum groceries, mostly of the liquid kind labeled with Dos Equis and Budweiser. She grabbed a bottled iced tea before driving around the curving laguna of swimmers and past the majority of the occupied campers. Finally, she spotted a clean, grassy area with a small concrete table and benches. A beautiful oak shaded her car and the picnic spot. She grabbed a yellow blanket she kept in the back along with bottled water and tools and such. Why there were tools she had no idea how to use was beyond her. She was pretty sure it was one of those long-ago parent-ingrained teachings you truly did do because *they said so*.

A red cardinal swooped in front of her and back into the branches. "How beautiful!" She downed the iced tea while sitting on the tabletop, the better to use the bench as a foot prop. The noise from the swimmers drifted toward her in an occasional giggle or a surprised yelp as someone was pulled underwater by a sibling. Three sailboats tacked back and forth lazily.

She saluted them with her empty bottle. "The *Niña,* the *Pinta* and, no doubt, the *Santa María.* Ahhhhh. This is nice, very nice." And she desperately needed a mental break, a pause in the rush of events and information. Heat shimmered off the water as a fish splashed nearby.

Within the heat shimmers two people frolicked in the water. A strong muscle-hardened warrior, browned torso glistening, carried within his arms a maiden, dark tendrils clinging to her breasts as her arms encircled his neck. Cardinals danced in the air around them. From a floating log, a half dozen turtles blinked at the lovers. A rabbit scuttled to the bank to twitch his nose.

"Winyan, when did it all begin?"

She clung to him tightly, reached over, and leaned in for his kiss. He nuzzled behind her ear. With this action her hair seemed to grow thicker as did his and long, very long, down to their feet. It twisted and twirled around their torsos in an erotic hide and seek. "It's beginning now," she whispered, while her heart fishtailed.

He sat her down. They clung to each other. He caressed the curve of her waist, laid a trail of kisses across her hairline. "When did it all begin?"

She pushed away to look up into his eyes. Her own mirrored some of his confusion.

He growled. "When? Go back, retrace the path. When? It must be answered."

As she pushed back in thought, their hair caught them up like wild vines, intermingling them. She couldn't breathe, nor could he. Suddenly they were covered in the horrible knots and shape-shifted. As they parted, one became the black wolf, one the white. They nuzzled and yipped at each other. Scrambling one after the other, they mingled beneath the branches of two distinctly different trees. Yet even as they growled and snarled in their lovemaking, the trees above them became entwined with vines. There was no beginning

*or end to the muskiness, the trees, the wild abandon that
now could only be heard, not seen.*

The crash of broken glass against concrete made Willi
jump. She peered at the lone oak tree sheltering her before
glancing down at the broken bottle of tea. She scrabbled in
her backseat and found a file folder that she tore in half to
sweep and scoop the glass into the picnic area trash can.

The cardinal sat at one end of the concrete table. "Well,
at least," Willi said, "you won't be able to tell anyone I was
daydreaming. If I can stop shaking, I'll get out of your
territory."

The scarlet bird tilted his head as if to say, "No problem.
You're welcome to stay longer."

"Thanks. But I've got to pick up Quannah and . . . and
find out when . . . uh . . . *when it all began.*"

At home alone with Quannah holding her in a long
embrace, Willi relaxed. "I've . . . I've missed you."

"Is that so hard to admit, *Winyan?*"

Men. He hadn't admitted to missing her, she had said the
words that made her vulnerable, and now he teased her
about it? She pushed away from him. "I meant, I'd
missed . . . uh . . . being able to talk to you about the murder case. That sort of missed."

With one strong finger he traced the gentle curve of her
jawline, tilted her head up, and winked at her. "Right."

Infuriating man. She pointed to a big package on the living
room coffee table. "The dance master left that here for you.
Next time, I'll have them send it around to your apartment."

"There's that Porcupine Medicine coming out in you,
Gallagher. Little prickly today, are we?"

"Oh, Hell's bells, just open the damned box without any
lessons in Native American lore. I've had Celtic and Indian
motifs, fife and Indian flute music, Irish paintings, and
dreams of American Indian wolves mixed in my head all
week. No more!"

Quannah stared at her and frowned. His broad shoulders
slumped. She reached out to him just as he turned away.

She lowered her outstretched hand. Oh no, she hadn't meant to hurt him.

He opened the package. It contained emerald green and gold socks, black pants—sort of like toreador pants in that they were cut tightly to just below the knee and there would meet up with the bright socks. A red fluffy bow tie fell out of the folds of a gold shirt with ruffles edged in green Gaelic designs. A bit of an Irish hat completed the outfit. Quannah lowered his head and his bottom lip protruded. "Going to look like a *Heyoka* clown in this."

"I thought *Heyoka* was another word for Coyote."

He peered up at her without lifting his head and sighed. "You want to know?"

She matched his sigh, edged her way into the circle of his arms, and laid her head on his chest. "Forgive me for my behavior? Yes, I want to know. What is a *Heyoka clown* as compared to *Heyoka the Coyote?*"

"Coyote is a clown in that he's the Great Trickster, usually teaching us lessons through the goofy things he does. A *Heyoka clown* is one of the tribe who dresses like him and performs everything backasswards to symbolize how Coyote *Heyoka* teaches through opposites. Sometimes they'll put their clothes on backwards or dress in wild, unmatched colors or—"

"Or in another ethnic type of costume?"

"Uh . . . well, I'm not saying that—"

"What? That if you're not in feathers and beads of the tribe, you're not as good, therefore saying this costume and the culture it represents isn't equal? Hmmm?"

Quannah pushed her away this time, but with a smile on his lips. He crossed his arms across his chest. "Gallagher, Gallagher, Gallagher, you may have a point—a very tiny point."

"Yes, if I recall correctly, it has something to do with *Mitakuye Oyasin.*"

"All Our Relations."

"Ah."

"Ah-ho." Quannah shoved his bottom lip out again and

shut his eyes. After a moment, he rubbed his hand down
across his face. "I suppose that all clans—all tribes have
their worth and their traditions—"

"*Suppose?*"

"I *know* that all have worth, and their traditions are
valuable, and all come from the same Great Spirit within
the Great Mystery." He grinned. "For that part of you that
is Irish, Willi Gallagher, I will dress up in this—*Heyoka*
costume—and do my stomping best to win the Irish Jig
Contest. I'm also going to pray to Great Spirit and my
Medicine Helpers since the contest is outside to let those
dark clouds open up."

"Bad boy, bad boy. What you gonna do when they come
for you?"

He drew her to him, laid butterfly kisses across her forehead, and whispered, "You are the only woman who, within
a sixty second interval, can irritate and distract, sooth and
cajole, challenge and honor me. I sort of hate to say it, but
maybe that bit of Porcupine Medicine in you is something I
might have . . . uh . . ."

"Missed?"

"Missed? Naw . . . uh . . . is something I might have to
do something about, that's what I was going to say."

"Right."

"Damned right. Give me that stupid little bow tie,
Winyan, and let me get into this contraption. While I'm
doing that, you can tell me about all these wolf visions and
Celtic paintings you've encountered. By the by, in our last
phone conversation Uncle Brigham told about you and the
Kachelhoffer sisters impersonating nurses. Were you all
trying to teach something through opposites?"

While he put on the outfit, she gave him high spots about
the last two days. She did leave out her swim around the
Comanche Raider.

"So," he said while braiding his hair and tucking it underneath itself, "you got the message at the lake to *find out
where it all began.* What in particular do you think that
means, *Winyan?*"

"I was sort of hoping you'd tell me."

"Nope. Seems like you're winging this one mostly on your own. Must be lessons here for both of us, because that makes me nervous, very nervous. I'm sure Uncle Brigham has told you not to do anything without telling him, right? And you know not to go out at night snooping—"

"I do not snoop."

He raised an eyebrow and looked at her in the mirror as she stood behind him. "Of course not. You are helping by—"

"By . . . by investigating, by talking to folks, nothing more."

He turned around to let her help with the red bow. She reached up to do so. "In fact, while you're doing the dress rehearsal for the Jig Contest, I'm going to go visit Sammie."

"Mrs. Yannich? The secretary who's making like a *Heyoka* clown?"

"What?"

"You said, Gallgaher—whoa, that's tight enough—that she's completely opposite of what she was a few days ago. Therefore, she offers some message, some important message. *Heyoka* may dress like a clown, may dance backwards, may make jokes at his own expense, but his lessons for the ceremony's participants are very serious."

He patted the bow, groaned, and rolled his eyes. "All right, Gallagher, I'm sure you've mentioned your intentions to see her to Uncle Brigham as part of your liaison work, so you're bound to be safe on a simple hospital visitation." He straightened, twirled, and tapped his wee hat on with a jaunty flip of his hand.

Willi grinned and in her best Irish attempt, said, "Ah, and if you're not such a handsome figure of a man to tempt the very angels to bed you."

"*Winyan,* it wasn't the angels I had in mind, but I like the way your mind works." He gave her a quick peck on the lips. "Don't forget. Sometime soon, you're going to have to slow down and figure out *where it all began.* Lots of knots to unravel, lots of knots to unravel, lady."

CHAPTER
14

At the Nickleberry Hospital, Willi grabbed herself a bottled iced tea. A few steps down the corridor, she went back and got what she knew to be Sammie's favorite, a lime and lemon mix. The can was ice cold, so she ought to like that, too. Best go in with gifts if she was to find out what important message Samantha Yannich had to offer about the murder of Tessa Aiken.

After very quiet greetings, Willi poured Sammie's drink over crushed ice and got a straw from a passing nurse's aide.

"Thanks, Willi. Ah, that's so good."

"Glad it hit the spot. So what's going on here, Sammie?"

For a split nanosecond, Samantha Yannich grabbed the sheet so tightly, her knuckles whitened. "For one thing, they won't let me smoke in here. Can you imagine? Pieces of sorry damned—"

Uh-oh. She'd been through this one jillion quadrillion times with smokers before. She commiserated with them, but that's about all the help she could offer. And certainly none wanted to be told they had made the choice to smoke and must accept the consequences of that action. Those consequences, she had to admit, bordered on cruelty within the confines of a hospital. She sighed. Okay, she wanted info from Sammie, but she knew the only thing on the secretary's mind would be the horrible need for nicotine. The question was how to satisfy that need, relax her, and get her to talking.

"Maybe I could help."

"You guard the door, and—"

"No, Sammie, no way. But don't they have a smoking area somewhere outside?"

"Sure, under the pecan trees where those picnic tables are, but—"

"Let's walk out there."

Tears welled in Sammie's eyes. "You'd do that . . . that . . . for . . . for me?"

"Certainly, let's—"

"What do you think you're doing? Get back in that bed." A familiar figure darkened the doorway, and a booming voice, one belonging to Inga Rufflestone, broke the sound barrier.

"You're supposed to be at the nursing home," Willi said. "What are you doing here?"

"Last I checked it was legal to have two jobs. Guess you wouldn't know much about legalities, huh? You trying to abduct another patient?" The warts on Rufflestone's face took on a life of their own, bouncing and fluttering as her jaws worked.

Willi stood tall as her five-foot five frame allowed and managed her steely eyed English teacher's glare. "I believe Sheriff Tucker explained that . . . undercover tactic to you."

"Not to my satisfaction, and—"

"We who are concerned with the true legalities of the situation know the facts, and you've been told all you need to know. Now, if you are the nurse on this floor, I have a reasonable request, or rather Mrs. Yannich does. She wishes to go out and have a smoke."

"Smoking isn't good for you. It'll kill you. Besides those clouds could break loose any moment with a downpour."

Sammie quivered under the covers and dropped her cigarette case on the bed. Not good. A nicotine fit was one thing. Trying to get her to talk through despondency would be horrific if not impossible.

With both hands on her hips, Willi said, "I neither asked for your opinion of smoking nor your meteorological interpretation of the weather. Being as they're in Texas, those clouds could take until next week to make up their mind. I believe this patient is an adult and should be treated as such. If you cannot do that, then perhaps you'll provide the name of your immediate supervisor. *Now.*"

Inga crossed both her massive arms in front of her chest. Her great orbs seemed to swell farther out of their sockets. "We do not allow patients to walk outside."

"Then please bring us a wheelchair, and I'll wheel her out."

Inga smirked. "You've certainly had practice at that."

Willi's face flamed hotter than coals under a brisket, but she held her ground. At that moment, the nurse's aide who'd provided the drinking straw, brought in a chair.

Inga swelled to the size of an enraged dinosaur. "Eavesdropping again?"

The young woman smiled. "Not really. The door was open, the voices loud. Thought I'd help you out, Nurse Rufflestone." To Willi and Sammie, she said, "The hospital only allows fifteen-minute smoke time every two hours. I don't think Mrs. Yannich has had any, so guess she's due about an hour outside, if you're willing to stay with her. She has to have an aide, nurse, or family."

In unison, Willi and Sammie said, "We're family." Willi added, "Could I grab us something in the cafeteria on the way out?"

"That'll be okay, won't it, Nurse Rufflestone?"

Inga glared at all three, turned her linebacker rear toward them, and stalked out. "One hour."

Willi got Sammie a lasagna plate and another lime drink over ice before settling her in the shade of a spreading oak. Okay, now surely, they could get down to business. Sammie shut her eyes and inhaled deeply. She had two cigarettes before she dug into the food. "You not eating?"

"No, Hortense and I had a feast at The Outback earlier. I won't be hungry for hours. Maybe now you feel more like talking?"

"Oh, this is Heaven. Thank you, thank you so much for standing up for me. I just . . . just didn't have the strength . . . of spirit today."

"Did you have food poisoning or something?"

"No. I . . . I'm not sure what it was. Panic attack maybe. The murder on the school grounds. We've never had a person killed right under our noses, almost at the front door. Yes, I think I suffered a severe panic attack, that's all." With fork in midair, she grew quiet.

Willi encouraged her. "Blue blazes right. Horrible situation like that would give anyone the heebie-jeebies."

"And the way . . . the way she died." Sammie's hand trembled, and she dropped the fork. "The way she died. The acid, you know."

"An absolutely evil-minded monster's work. You're right."

Sammie lit up another smoke. She used her little finger to wipe a bit of tobacco away from her bottom lip. "Nobody with any sense in that school."

Ah, now this was more like the old Sammie. Willi wanted her to keep talking.

"Isn't that the truth?"

Sammie blew a plume of smoke into the treetops. The Standing Person seemed to embrace it, dissipate it, and send back blessings on the very one who had thoughtlessly sent more toxins into its space. "They don't remember."

"Who?"

"Don't know what they've got themselves into."

"What?"

Sammie ignored her questions while her words tumbled over each other. "I'll tell you something else. That Dan Oxhandler is a strange bedbug, you mark my words. Ever seen that place of his and his cousin's?"

Willi scratched her head. "Uh, have you?"

"Been there many times. The boys have had me over to
dinner now and again, bless 'um for that, but Lordy mercy.
It's a den of iniquity, that's what it is."

"Well, they're young." Willi sighed. They might be
young, but more thoughtful than she. Sammie was her colleague, too, yet she'd never had her over for a meal or
asked her on an outing.

"Twenty-seven, twenty-eight years old, Willi. Yes, young
but tasteless, too. Maybe I'm just getting old and tired of
dealing with knuckleheads. They aren't the only ones."

Figuring she ought to give the conversation more focus
before it meandered all the way down the Rio Grande,
Willi asked, "Where were you and the others when Tessa's
body was found?"

"Just like I told you and the sheriff already, in The Mall
drinking a Coke and eating stale cookies from the vending
machines."

"Yes, I remember, Saralee was with you, too, along with
Dan Oxhandler, maybe Neeper."

"I don't remember them being there, but it was confusing
afterwards. My head is hurting. Weather like this makes my
head hurt. Wish it'd go ahead and rain. That'd feel good."

"You get wet, and Nurse Rufflestone will have a few
nasty words to impart. Back to the day of the murder for a
moment. Why not go upstairs to the teachers' lounge?
Machines are better stocked there."

"The students aren't allowed in there with us, and I didn't
want to leave the office aides—new trainees—alone. Those
ceiling fans whizzing around give me a headache, too." Sammie rubbed her temples. "I have to get out of here tonight.
Records have to be up to date before the first Monday of
classes. Yes, maybe . . . I can find out for sure . . . from
the . . . records."

"Find out what from the school records?" Willi asked.

"What? Oh, nothing . . . my CRS acting up again . . . you
know, can't remember stuff?"

"Seems to be a lot of that going around. Sammie, don't

worry about leaving the hospital until you're okay. Paper-work will wait."

"Maybe in the classroom; not in the office."

Willi shoved the cigarette case closer. Obviously, the nicotine opened up a flow of words in Sammie. "You were telling me about the folks at the high school."

Sammie waved her smoke in the air. "All of them—they're why I'm here and a nervous wreck."

Willi leaned forward. Maybe Sammie Yannich was like a lot of folks who'd blame anyone and everything but themselves for life not being the way they wanted. That was a lot easier than getting up off one's duff and getting into action. "We make you a nervous wreck?"

"Oh, not all, but like Hortense Horsenettle. She brays, for God's sake. The woman brays, and that word of the day drives me crazy sometimes. Pants-chasing shaggy-haired thing. Anytime there's a UPS man delivering, you can bet she'll be in that office. And that new teacher, Saralee. She might have fiery hair, kind of like my cousin, Amanda, but Saralee—she's frozen around me. Can't get her to speak up, and when she does, she might use two or three words. Just the opposite of Hortense. See? I guess I am the crazy one, 'cause I can't stand either one of them right now. I'm afraid."

"Afraid? Of Hortense? Of Saralee?"

Sammy just blew smoke and coughed.

Willi said, "You've been through a lot lately. You've probably needed to talk to someone." *Like me. Keep talking.*

"Little things getting on my nerves, and I don't know why. She flirts with the Oxhandlers and with Vic Ramirez, the fireman, and with Jon Piedra. He's one of the sheriff's deputies, you know."

"Hortense flirts with everyone."

"Not her."

"Oh, well, Saralee, of course. She's going to feel out the waters, so to speak."

Sammie pointed the cigarette in Willi's face, stubbed it out on the ground, and returned to eating her lasagna.

"Four men after a cold-hearted one like that? Something is wrong with that picture. They were four good friends, and since she's come into the picture, I don't think any of them are speaking to each other."

Sammie brushed a nervous hand through her dusky locks—more gray than auburn under the unforgiving sunlight. "She's got blue eyes, or she'd be the spitting image of my cousin when she was about seventeen years old. Yeah, the . . . spitting . . . image. I wonder—" Again, the fork dropped from her hand. In her beige hospital gown, she resembled a deflated soufflé.

"Sammie?"

"My heart's just a-fluttering. I don't want to talk anymore. Take me back; take me back. No, wait a minute." She grabbed one last cigarette. Despite numerous attempts, Willi couldn't engage her in small talk again. Just as the first few drops fell from the sky, she wheeled Sammie back inside where Nurse Rufflestone waited at the door.

"I was about to send the orderlies."

"Nonsense. We had another good ten minutes to go."

Rufflestone peered at the rain now slashing across the windows.

Willi shrugged her shoulders and said, "See? We do have sense enough to come in out of the rain." She helped a subdued Sammie into bed. As she left, she told Nurse Rufflestone, "I hope it's on her chart for an aide to take her out every two hours. I'll call and check tomorrow."

"No need. Her doctor's releasing her in the morning. Perhaps even this evening."

As so typical in Texas storms, by the time Willi got out of the hospital parking lot, the cloudburst was over and the air was muggy and hot. She grinned. "Aha. Quannah Lassiter, you will be jig-jig-jigging tonight."

Willi headed toward Nickleberry Lake. The lights glowed and music escalated. There were team and individual dance contests. Willi scrunched into a row with Viola Fiona and the Kachelhoffer sisters. Elba said, "Your feller is getting hisself ready. Been nigh on a dozen young college girls chasing round his hide."

"Oh, really?"

"Got to hand it to him, though."

Willi touched the back of her hand to her hot cheeks. "Why's that?"

"Heard him ourselves didn't we, girls, telling them coeds to hightail it elsewheres."

"That he did. Said he's a one-woman man. The wearing of the green becomes him, it does," Viola Fiona said. "That handsome he is the very saints would enjoy a kiss upon his lips."

"But . . . but he ran them off?" Willi wanted to get this straight.

Agatha, purple silk scarf fluttering in the evening breeze, added, "That's not all he said."

Viola Fiona guffawed. "You've a right lusty man there, you have, and he thinks the same of you."

Hell's bells. "What exactly did he say, Viola Fiona?"

"Told them frilly sillies he wanted a mature woman, had him such a woman, and wasn't about to do anything to mess up the sweet winds dancing between the two. A bit of a poetic bent, he has, Willi, when it comes to you."

Willi's heart fishtailed in warm waters. The mellow glow lasted through the first two teams, mostly made up of college boys. Then the group consisting of Neeper, Dan, Quannah, and Vic strode onstage. Willi sat up proudly. "They do make a nice showing."

Elba snorted. "Yep, for a couple of country yokels, a hot pepper eater and a brave, they clean up nice."

"Elba, about that phrase *hot pepper eat—*"

"All right, all right. We're gonna get us so politically right one of these days we can't even make distinctions between skin no way, no how, no where without getting a ticket."

The song "Duffy the Dancer" began, the four, in unison, neatly executed a step, and when the tempo changed, each did an individual pattern before coming back together. The music increased in speed with the "Fisher's Hornpipe" until the audience was breathless, much less the four men. Flushed and pleased with their efforts, they took a dramatic double bow before exiting stage left. Willi applauded so hard for their standing ovation, her hands tingled when she sat back down.

She caught Quannah's eye on his last return to the stage. He touched his hat and winked at her. It was one of those moments she wanted to freeze and savor over and over again. She was so glad Agatha was snapping pictures along with Vic Ramirez's folks. She'd beg some good copies from them later. At the end of the evening's festivities, she strolled arm in arm with Quannah.

"Proud of you," she said for the third time.

"*Pilamaya yelo, Winyan.* Wish it could have been first place instead of third, but it was for a good cause, and folks really enjoyed it, didn't they?"

"Oh, yes, your group was definitely a hit. Now, aren't you glad your Medicine Helpers didn't come through with that rain?"

"To be honest, I didn't ask them to, anyway. Guess I wanted to see how I'd do alongside those younger guys."

"Ah, that *Peacock* Medicine coming out in you again, Lassiter?"

"Well . . . uh . . . yeah."

They stopped at one of the food booths, and he offered to share a shepherd's pie and a glass of ale. "I'm not hungry, but I know you are," she said, wiping a few crumbs off his chin. That, too, seemed like a Hallmark moment, a turning point in their relationship. Funny, she always thought those great moments of change would be marked by a more hot and lusty roll or by tears or . . . or something other than pride in his accomplishment and dabbing a morsel from his chin.

His eyes bored into hers. "The world turns on the proverbial dime, the smallest flicker of a candle, the whisper touch of a butterfly's wings, the commonplace and everyday happenings."

Her breath caught. This time she didn't think, *Get out of my mind, Lassiter.* "Yes, there is a sweetness in the mundane when . . ." She swallowed, not willing to say things he'd make fun of or ignore.

"Yes, *Winyan,* when it is with the right person, the tiniest of things gain import and wonder."

They stood quietly, she in front of him with his arms surrounding her. They listened to the lapping of the lake against its banks. He sighed. "Sometimes we have to take great leaps of faith to get to the next step in life."

"What do you mean?"

"I mean, Woman-with-Hummingbird-Medicine, I love you. We could become sometimes lovers, meeting between my job and yours and seeing each other only when hunger lust struck, but there is a true sweetness, a respect, lots of things between us."

She stiffened. "I don't know—"

"Or we could show honor one to the other and trust the winds—"

"The winds that dance between us?"

He nuzzled her hair. "Yes, *T'ate,* the wind that dances between us and around us, drawing us constantly together. I . . . I am going to make a suggestion—notice how I didn't use the phrase, *make a proposition*—here and now."

Her heartbeat escalated to a Latin beat that would have rivaled any Cuban version. Panic set in. She twirled around to face him. "Oh, I'm not sure I'm ready for wedding bells and such. I . . . I . . . I just—oh my God, I can't breathe."

"Nor am I, Gallagher, but we are ready for another level of commitment, yes?"

"Oh, yes, but—"

"You're afraid."

"Well, yeah."

He laughed softly. "As I am."

Something brushed against Willi's foot; she yelped and hopped to the side. "What in the world?"

"Good Medicine, Gallagher. A message needed by both of us."

She eyed the flash of the rabbit's tail and said, "From that little critter?"

"Rabbit Medicine has many facets, but the foremost is a message to drop any fears. What do you say, *Winyan,* to us committing to each other, living together?"

Beneath her hand, his heartbeat had escalated and told her what an effort his offer cost him. He truly was afraid, too, but brave enough to move ahead to the next step. She would do no less. "Yes, Quannah Lassiter, you ornery, wonderfully irritating man, I love you, too. Let's try, please."

He laughed at her declaration. His embrace and kiss left her gasping, and happy tears welled in her eyelids. In the background the lilt of a soft and slow Irish tune wafted toward them. Not another word was spoken until they reached the parking lot. He kissed her again after she closed her door. He jangled the keys to his Rover in his hand.

Suddenly shy, she asked, "Since you live in an apartment, would you consider us having a mutual domicile out at the farm?" *Please, Great Spirit, don't let him say no. Please let us start there together.* At the stretched-out silence, her heart skipped a beat and then another.

He leaned in the window. "That sounds perfect. I was hoping you'd say so. I need a place that needs fixing here and there on a weekend, that is if—"

"Guess everything will be a little strained until we work out particulars, but please, let's decide now, wherever we are—it's *ours,* not yours or mine—it's *ours.*"

"*Ours.* There's a nice ring to that, Gallagher. How about next weekend for the big move?"

"Wonderful. And in the meantime I'll try to work on Rabbit's message."

"Drop the fear."

"Right, drop the fear."

He gave her a last lingering kiss. "You're doing fine, *Winyan,* just fine." He walked away and then came back. "Uncle Brigham and I are going to check out a spot having to do with possible drug trafficking. I'm not allowed to tell you more . . . but—"

"You wanted me to know you were learning to share and trust?"

"Gallagher, Gallagher, Gallagher, of course, I trust you . . . but you've got to realize, even when I'm helping out Uncle Brigham, and certainly when on duty, I can't always tell you everything. I wanted to let you know as much as I could because if you tried to reach my cell phone, you might not be able to get through where we're on stakeout."

"I . . . I don't believe you've ever shared your cell phone number with me."

"Oh."

"Hmmm."

"Here. I meant to. . . . I thought you had it . . . so, now you do."

"Hmmm." Maybe she could get just a tad bit more info from him. "I've heard lots say when they're out at the lake, they can't call in or out."

"Gallagher."

"Would it hurt just to know the general direction?"

"The marina, if you must know. Some break-in out there the other night. There's one tennis shoe as evidence, can you believe that?"

"One tennis shoe?" *Uh-oh.* "And this has something to do with drug trafficking?"

"The tennis shoe? Who knows? But there have been rumors about the place, and considering there's a tie to the Aiken murder, Uncle Brigham wants to check it out quietly on the QT."

"Ties to anyone I know?" She tried to look wide-eyed innocent. Right, as if she didn't realize they were going to stake out the Oxhandlers' *Comanche Raider.* What if they found her fingerprints there, *her* shoe?

"And we've got to get you another one. Soon."

"Another shoe? Why? What? I . . . I was—"

"Daydreaming?"

She tilted her nose in the air.

"I said we've got to get you another *cell phone.*"

"Not a shoe, of course not. A cell phone. Okay. No hurry. I'm seldom anywhere I really need one."

"*Winyan,* don't say things like that. See you later, alligator."

"After a while, crocodile."

Willi channel surfed between her country western station and a golden oldies spot. Ricky Nelson's "BeBop Baby" finished, and she pushed the button to hear, "I'm singing love's old song . . . the one that tells how, darling, there'll never be anyone above you. . . . I'm singing . . ." Some lucky listener who identified the music as Jerry Crutchfield's won tickets, according to the disk jockey, "to a Tarrant County, Fort Worth, honky-tonk show at Billy Bob's, yes-sir-ree." The clouds opened their underbellies in a soft rain without lightning or thunder, what folks called a soaking rain.

Willi peered behind her. Her heart made a calypso dip. The black pickup. She was sure, even through the downpour, it was the same one with those lamps on the top of the cab, blinding her. She swerved into her gravel drive and screeched to a halt behind Elba's disreputable excuse for a truck blocking the garage entry. A pink snout hung over the back, and Rose Pig oinked. The smoking dragon behind her must have seen her company, too. He squealed to a stop, took a nanosecond to step on the gas, and burned rubber getting away on the asphalt road.

"Who in dangnab tarnation was that?" Elba asked, huffing around to the truck bed. She held a yellow slicker over her head and covered Willi as well.

"I don't know. That same truck followed me home the other night."

"What was you up to?"

"Up to?"

"Well, folks don't go chasing others down the road for no reason."

Agatha swooped around the other side of the pickup. Her purple skirt swirled around her thin ankles. She held and stroked her cat, Clyde, before racing to the covered porch.

Willi rubbed her temples. "Why are you all here at this time of night?"

"Well, now, it's three hours short of the devil's own hour, now isn't it?" Viola Fiona's voice rose eerily from behind the azaleas protecting Willi's porch. "The wee folk are the ones about right now. If you watch most carefully, you'll be seeing the little creatures. And they do love the very rain from the skies, they do, seeing as how it brings the greening to everything. Blessings the sight of one of the little creatures would be bringing to you, don't you know?"

Charlie Brown yipped around Willi's ankles until she patted his ears. Then he ran onto the porch and growled.

"I'd get more blessings from seeing the inside of my eyelids for eight hours straight," Willi said, sitting down in a chair. "And Charlie Brown is the only little critter I want to see tonight." Willi reached inside the door and flicked one of the many porch lights on. An old rocker creaked as Elba lowered her bulk. Agatha's metal chair screeched on the concrete as she moved it nearer.

"Okay, ladies, spill it and let's grill it. It may only be nine o'clock, but my peepers say it's hours later."

"Oh, you've a way with that Texas banter, you have, and that's the Gallagher clan blood showing there, you know." Viola Fiona held and patted Charlie Brown. He settled contentedly in her lap, head on his paws. As a miniature dachshund, he made a comfortable lap rug. "A wee bit of silky fur this one is, and that's the God's truth. Now isn't he the softest thing? And isn't this the most pleasant of moments, the rain softly falling and all?"

Elba blurted out finally, "We want confirmation."

"What?" Willi asked.

"You have had," Agatha said, "an entire day to remember and to find out."

She repeated, "What?"

Elba creaked forward and backward. "The read we gave you could have covered two, maybe three days' time. We're talking about the three furies that have been lying to you, the nasty witches—that's bad witches—who ain't been honest, the felines who've dealt out fibs. Who are they?"

"Aha." She rocked a moment. "I saw Saralee York, Hortense, Samantha, and Nurse Inga Rufflestone."

"The Rufflestone woman?" Viola Fiona shook her hands in front of her as if to ward off the devil. "Oh, and the very thought of her and her needles and pills sends the shivers through me bones and curdles me blood. What were you going to see her about?"

"Nothing. She happens to do two jobs, one at the Nickleberry Hospital." Willi sighed. "I don't know of any lies told by any of them."

"Those you saw today," Agatha said. "What about the day before?"

"Guess I'd have to add Lois Aaron, that diamond-covered woman. Oh yeah, Margarita Uriegas down at Oxhandler's Barbecue and Emporium. Nicoletta Leesha Horsenettle."

"Another Horsenettle?" the Kachelhoffer sisters asked.

"Two more. Nicoletta Leesha has a twin, Tabithia Meesha."

"Oh my." Elba closed her eyes.

Willi leaned toward her. "That's all? 'Oh, my'?"

"Words fail me."

"Ah," Willi said, "there are small blessings. I'm off to bed, ladies. When I know who are the fibbing damsels, I will tell all."

"Oh, there be one more little matter we would be discussing with you. Not a moment more than a minute would it take," Viola Fiona said.

Agatha played with the numerous strands of bright beads around her neck. "Yes, Viola Fiona's wanting a green one. For the Irish in her."

Willi sighed. "Green one?"

"Seems reasonable," Elba said, coming out of her Horsenettle-induced stupor. "Green for Irish. Green for where she's living now at Frogs' Feet, and green for that great big ol' bullfrog."

"Reasonable? Bullfrog?" Willi stood up. "You've thirty seconds to clarify."

"You and Agatha and them big words. I just did *clarify.* A familiar has to come to you or be gifted to you. We want that cantankerous ol' bullfrog that lives beside your back-yard duck pond for Viola Fiona's familiar. She's been hear-ing him in her sleep, dreaming about him. Bound to be they's to be together."

"Aha. You want my fly-zapper friend? He's been there for years. I think he keeps mosquitoes at bay, too."

"Well, now, if you've a soft spot in your heart and can't see your way to parting with the verdant creature, I don't want you to fret on it another minute. Of course, we'll find another. I've not even seen this critter. I've only dreamed of a huge bullfrog with a yellow circle around one eye. There's bound to be dozens just like him, isn't that so?"

"You all," Willi said to the sisters, "didn't tell her about his yellow eyelid?"

"Wouldn't do that," Elba said. "Picking a familiar is a serious thing. Now, how many do you think there are around here with that strange marking?"

"None. Okay, with my *blessings,* he's yours."

All three friends scrambled up to head to the backyard.

"Whoa-ho," Willi said. "You all may collect him *mañana,* not in this downpour. I'm not going to get any sleep with the three of you clogging and slipping around in the pond and making a muddy mess of the yard. Go, and come again another day."

"Oh, be thanking you, I am, sincerely, most sincerely. You're a most giving person, Wilhelmina Gallagher, you are."

Willi gasped and glared at the Kachelhoffer sisters. "I know who told you my full moniker, but if you want me to stay most giving, you'll never use that form of my name again."

"Willi, I meant only to say Willi, of course, and blessings on you for your kindness. Godspeed and good night to you."

"Speed to you three, also."

CHAPTER
15

The distinct sound of Elba's old truck revving made her smile and shake her head while locking up the house. She might as well take the reports from Tyler, Texas, upstairs and see if any interesting tidbits could be gleaned. She should have given them to the sheriff earlier, but in all the excitement of Quannah's performance, she completely forgot. Maybe purposely, since she'd not read them all yet. Reading might keep her from worrying about one special investigator for the Texas Rangers, his uncle Sheriff Brigham Tucker, and one lost tennis shoe. Yeah, right. When jalapeños stopped burning Texas tongues.

In her nookery, she clicked the briefcase snaps. What in Hades? No folders, no photocopies. Even her new grade book was gone. She hadn't left any doors unlocked. Damn. Her heartbeat picked up tempo. She glanced over her shoulder, ran through the house to check all the doors, and returned breathless. Everything was fine. *Think. Think; don't just react. Okay.* She'd also had the briefcase when she went the other night to the teachers' meeting. When she went snoop—uh—investigated in the lab, someone could have opened it and cleared everything out.

What in blue blazes is that? Tucked into one of the side pockets were two items. She pulled the first out. Another Celtic Tree card, one titled Ohn at the top and Furze at the bottom. A honeycomb with bees swirling around, gathering in a wild frenzy, was depicted at the bottom of a bush with bright yellow blossoms. *Bees. Gathering.* Gathering information like Willi did. Someone who knew she was bound for Tyler found *her gatherings* and was letting her know. Might be more to the card's meaning, but she'd need to check with Elba about the appointment with the Landises' relative.

The other item had to be tugged out of the pocket. Willi dropped it in the middle of her briefcase. One of the Irish double-chain quilt blocks. A tiny sliver of paper stuck out of the folds. She reached for a magnifying glass on her desk. The message left no doubt in her mind this was planted by Tessa's killer. It read: "Stop. Stop now. I don't want to hurt *you.*"

Charlie Brown, sensing her distress, rubbed against her ankle. The warmth of his small body did help slow her cantering heartbeat.

"I'm okay. We're okay, Charlie Brown. Just have to catch my breath. No one is here. This was done carefully and slowly, with purpose, at the high school." She grabbed for the phone, remembered neither Quannah nor the sheriff could be reached, and sighed. Maybe whimpered. She teared up and bent down to grab Charlie Brown to her chest. His soft velvety fur, his warmth comforted her. He licked her face until she made one last big sniffle and grinned. "Makes no difference. They couldn't do anything tonight, anyway." The phone jangled; she yelped and picked up.

"I'm sorry. You'll have to speak up."

From the receiver a voice, obviously disguised, said, "Ms. Gallagher, you should be at your *cabin*—yes, that's right, your cottage. *Tonight.*"

"What? Who is this?" Willi felt sure she'd recognize the feminine voice if she could get her to talk a moment longer. "What's going to happen at the cottage?"

"I don't know why I'm telling you this much. I don't want to be involved. It's something illegal, and they should be stopped." The phone line went dead, and Willi set the receiver down. She nuzzled Charlie Brown as she walked upstairs. "There was no Spanish lilt to the words, so that left out Margarita Uriegas and three thousand other inhabitants of Nickleberry. A woman's voice, definitely, but masculine, too." She sighed. The locksmith had called to tell her he'd replaced the front door lock and told her where to find the new key. She held it now and said, "Hmmm."

Charlie Brown jumped from her arms at the top of the stairs and ran to the window seat that looked out toward the cottage. Suddenly losing interest, he ran under the bed and growled.

"Charlie Brown, don't disturb my dust bunnies, you little fur ball."

He was tearing into a veritable tiger, if his growls and snorts were any indication. He nosed out a dusty book from under the bed. "Bad dog. Now, go lay on the rug." She bent to retrieve the book, one of three she'd stuffed under the bed—what, two nights ago—oh, well, she couldn't remember.

She snapped her fingers. "Oh, yeah. After Rose Pig's trip upstairs, after that break-in, I brought these up to put me to sleep. What the heck were—?" She dusted off one of the covers. One of the Nickleberry paint horses—yellow with blue spots—careened across the cover of the Nickleberry High School's *Coup Counting* yearbook, one of ten years ago. Hairs on her arms quivered. Charlie Brown sneezed and peered up at her with his tail wagging. "Yes, I owe you an apology. Good baby. I'd forgotten about these, and . . . and I think now . . . they *are* important. That night of the first break-in . . . that's . . . that's *when it all began*."

A coyote howled from the nearby woods, another joined in, and soon a whole chorus sprang up. Charlie Brown had used up his reserve of bravery. He ran to the warm rug in front of the window seat and curled into a ball beside one of his many baby blankets. Willi grinned and pulled it around him so he'd feel cozy and safe.

"One of us might as well feel that way, and it's not going to be me if I have to do my own . . . *stakeout.*"

Dressed in black jeans and turtleneck, black driver's gloves and a ski mask showing only her eyes, she figured she had everything covered she could cover so as not to be easily seen. Black tennis shoes, she tied extra tightly. A small niggle of worry attacked her. Perhaps she shouldn't go by herself? Maybe she should have waited until she could reach Quannah and Sheriff Tucker. Of course, this thing with the cottage wasn't part of the murder investigation. She didn't really have any reason to tell them.

"It's something illegal, and they should be stopped."

Well, blue blazes, she wasn't going to let some hooligans tear up her property again. She had a right to protect it. To appease the last little niggle of conscience, she left a message with the Sheriff's Department's dispatcher.

Outside, the rain became a drizzle that nuzzled the lawn and rosebushes while teasing the tree limbs. Come high water or hell, she would find out who used her property for clandestine meetings. If it were one of the Oxhandlers, so be it. Either way the night turned out, seemed like they'd be in some kind of sump water. She strode purposefully toward the woods and the cabin. The ululation of the coyote clan rose loudly but then diminished as they chased their nocturnal prey. She had prey of a different kind she wished to trap.

She chose a hiding place behind a huge bush with a convenient rock for a seat. From the leaves above her, water occasionally fell. Her luminous watch indicated 11:30. She had been on point for two hours. By blue blazes and hades, she would not stay past midnight. Her thoughts dripped as intermittently as the cold droplets. Good Lord, this stakeout stuff was boring. At least Lassiter had his uncle for company. Only thing she'd had was a damned spider that had snuck up her sleeve to leave her an itchy bite. With her tiny flashlight, she'd checked to make sure it wasn't of a deadly variety. It wasn't, but she was due for a dose of Benedryl antihistamine when she got home. Until then, she had plenty of time to think about *when it all began.*

Well, of course, it began with Tessa's death on the high school parking lot. Sure. Where else? Of course, Tessa drove there, so that scene might have begun at the lake either at the swimming beach or around the far end at the marina. At least, her death happened in Bernie Burkhalter's yellow Caddy. Bernie Burkhalter, principal during Tessa's high school years, member of the reviewing committee for her junior college, perhaps held some threat over her. Or vice versa. Hmm.

So maybe the tenuous thread holding all the suspects and the victim entwined was an old one from a decade in the past.

On the same afternoon as the killing, Hortense had discovered the ransacked high school library. That Friday evening Willi's own nookery had been broken into.

A cold raindrop hit her in the eye, and she jerked, rustling the leaves and shedding water all around her. She tried to snap her fingers, but the gloves merely made a whisper. Oh, darn, the Nickleberry City Library hadn't been checked out for missing yearbooks yet. She added that to her mental to-do list. She yawned before continuing her stumbling attempts to figure out *when.*

She'd found out through the *Comanche Raider* either Dan or Neeper or both had some involvement. Either Tessa had been to their boat the day she died, they had taken her quilt square . . . or someone else had and planted it. Possible, since some woman in high heels had visited them that night. Willi blinked water from her eyelids. With the Oxhandlers, that feminine list could go from here to El Paso. Yeah, and a confrontation between longtime friends, Vic and Dan Oxhandler, and others might play a part. She tapped her watch and peered down at the cottage from the vantage point where she could see the drive, the front door, and the boarded-up side cellar entrance. Of course, the boards were spaced to keep out humans, but any furry critter could scurry through. As always, a halogen light shone on the front of the yard but left the side and back in shadows.

Twenty more minutes, and I'm out of here. Okay, back to . . . *where it all began.* Her eyes held more grit than a Texas-sized backhoe. Her shoulders slumped. She'd never admit it to Big Chief Lassiter, but she'd truly been afraid to stay alone after the break-in. Her evenings had lost big chunks of sound sleep without him nearby. He would understand, but he'd also treat her to a big-sized dose of teasing about feminine heebie-jeebies.

She put her head down between her knees, holding the sides of her mask with both hands. Oh, for just a half-hour solid snooze. The kaleidoscope circling and fragmenting would stop . . . just for awhile. She breathed the night air and leaned back on the bush behind her rocky seat. Ah, heavenly to change positions.

Talk about changing. Sammie Yannich certainly had changed into something akin to one of those backasswards roller coasters. In the high school Mall, she'd bragged to the aide about *something good coming her way.* Everyone took that to mean her relationship with Bernie Burkhalter. Willi groaned. Poor woman. If she only knew. Ah, but people do change in some ways. At any rate, Sammie was ebullient about that, and then nervous—no, more than nervous—scattered emotionally. Scuttlebutt was she feared Burkhalter was going to back out on some deal with her. Marriage? What else could it be? Perhaps she really did have a panic attack, and this murder was the catalyst.

Willi blinked and executed a jaw-popping yawn. She leaned forward with her elbows resting on her knees. Hmm. Strange, Sammie held together just fine until the attack on the fireman, Vic Ramirez. Since then she'd had her roller-coaster bouts of silence, jerked back over to her motor-mouth mode, and seemed to switch back to mute again.

Willi shoved her sleeve back. Oh sleep, she needed sleep. Hortense had said the last word Tessa spoke was *señor.* That didn't make sense at all. Either Hortense was

too panicked and *thought* that was what Tessa said, or
Tessa, as many in their last moments do, yelped out sense-
less ramblings. No, no, that didn't work, either. Tessa had a
lawyer's mind.

A shadow flitted across the clearing. Willi gasped. She
reminded herself she would not confront, merely determine
who the intruders were and try to get some proof to show to
the sheriff. She congratulated herself on this very mature
stance, one not likely to get her into trouble for a change. A
black and waddling creature with a white stripe scuttled
toward the basement. "Oh, for heaven's sake."

Willi whispered, "Please, little skunk, don't go down into
my cellar, please. Amble on, furry friend. Take your perfume and go toward the woods."

She couldn't see far enough into the shadows to tell, but
hoped she'd not be in for what Lassiter would refer to as
Skunk Medicine. Well, guess he'd be right. Skunk had the
ability to attract or repel, and when you wanted to do either,
you called upon this Medicine. She definitely wanted to
repel whoever trashed her cottage. Perhaps this sighting
was a good sign, not a bad one.

The purr of a motor took her attention back to the front
of the cabin. She spread a few leaves apart to see better. A
yellow Cadillac pulled to a stop.

"Well, who'd have ever figured?" She clamped a hand
over her mouth. *Be quiet now.* They couldn't get in. The
locksmith had taken care of the front and the cellar
entrance was boarded up.

Burkhalter got out, ambled to the door, and knocked.
When he received no answer, he shook the doorknob.
"Damnation. That meddling Gallagher woman has locked
it up again. *He* gonna be able to find that key again?"

Willi grinned. *Damned right she did, and whoever he is
won't find the key.*

Sammie Yannich pushed out of the passenger side. From
this distance, Willi couldn't tell if she had color back in her
cheeks or not, but now she really didn't give a rat's
whisker. Sammie grabbed Burkhalter by the elbow. "Baby,

let's just forget the deal. Something isn't right. Let's go. Maybe she told her boyfriend or his uncle."

He moved her aside, not unkindly, as Willi thought he might, but with a gentle turn toward the car. "Honeybun, your nerves are all shot. You get back in the car. Have another sip from that Jack Daniel's Black. By and by, you'll feel some ease. We'll have a little fun later, yes we will, sweetie pie."

She stumbled, and he walked with her. She said, "Maybe it's a trap."

Willi pulled the shirred edge of her mask more tightly beneath her turtleneck. These were the romantic couple invading her cabin? Please, where were the punji sticks for her eyes?

"Hush, honeybun, now hush. Papa will take care of this." He tapped on the back window of the Caddy. The black glass rolled down. Willi strained but couldn't tell who spoke. A few words drifted from the interior. "Relax . . . be here soon . . . business then . . . rain's let up."

Willi frowned. Maybe he said, "Pain's let up." Either way, no matter. Obviously, the Oxhandlers weren't involved. Thank goodness. Guess one of these sickos had taken one of the Oxhandlers' girlie mags. Maybe couldn't chance one of their upright and uptight rears to buy one.

Sammie refused to get in the car. She lit one of her cigarettes. Even at this distance, Willi caught the scent of tobacco. Sammie tilted a flask to her lips a couple of times, too. Her hand shook, and she dropped the metal flask. Burkhalter picked up the hooch. "Honeybun, that's okay, Baby. Here. Papa got the goods for you. Doesn't your papa always take care of you, sweetie pie? Even got you new see-through nighties. Be able to get you diamonds, soon."

Where the hell was a barf bag when you needed it most? Willi shut her eyes tightly and wished she could do the same to her ears for a moment. She swallowed. Might be, she'd stepped into more Texas caca here than she ever imagined. That third player in the backseat proved a nasty touch. A threesome? Oh, yeah, she would need an American Airlines barf-sized bag. And . . . they were expecting more. Oh my dear Lord, orgies going on in her Mama and Daddy's cottage. . . . Oh, they'd both not only be turning in their graves but doing the dervish dance. Well, not graves. Both had opted for cremation and the scattering of their ashes in the *Paja Sapa*—the Sacred Black Hills. More her mother's than her father's wish, but he never denied his true love anything. Willi whispered, "And you sorry slime are not going to desecrate their special place. Not *again*."

A gray Mercury town car drove into the lighted area. The new super, Jarnagin Ventnor, emerged from the passenger side. Eldritch, the school board member always shadowing him, worked his way out of the driver's seat.

No way. The old super, the new super. What in blue blazes and saddlehorns was going on here? Obviously, not what she'd first imagined.

Viola Fiona's soon-to-be ex snapped his fingers, and Eldritch, after rubbing his thick-lensed eyeglasses off, opened the Mercury's trunk. Finally, the Cadillac's last occupant emerged. Vic Ramirez snapped open the caddy's trunk. Willi fell off the rock with a soft plop into the muddy grass. Every head swiveled in her direction. She didn't move an eyelash for the count of ninety seconds.

Sammie Yannich's voice broke the unbearable silence. "A raccoon, nothing but a raccoon or skunk or something. Get the exchange over with." Her words slurred, but she took another drink from the flask before lighting a smoke.

Ventnor and Burkhalter sauntered toward the cases taken from the cars' trunks. Both nodded and shook hands. The aluminum cases were changed from one boot of the car to the other. Willi stayed crouched, mud seeping coldly through her black jeans.

Great. Just great. A drug-money exchange was going on here, and where was Big Chief Lassiter and Sheriff Tucker? They were enjoying the lap of the lake's waves against the bank, probably getting to watch herons alight while she viewed the knuckle-dragging, nasty excuses for men in Nickleberry. *Well, don't leave out Sammie. Hope she chokes on the next swig of Jack Daniels.*

Willi eased back up on the rock so she could see better between her curtain of leaves. A light drizzle started. With the exception of Burkhalter and Ventnor, the group got in the cars. Those two moved within two feet of Willi. She did her best imitation of a rabbit trying to elude a raptor by holding so still she forgot to breathe for a moment.

Burkhalter tapped Ventnor on the chest. "Leave Baby and me out of your tricks to rid yourself of that wife of yours, or we'll call it quits on the deals now."

Jarnagin Ventnor placed a hand on Bernie's shoulder. "No sweat. That's over anyway, due to that damned Gallagher woman helping Viola. Now *there's* the little woman who ought to be taught a lesson. You didn't warn me I was getting a damned snoopy broad on the faculty along with the job. She could mess up a sweet deal about to be sweeter with kids coming to school in a few days."

Burkhalter sighed. "She's always been a pain in the ass one way or another. But we can't move on her now, not with all that Tessa Aiken mess going on. What was all that about, anyway?"

Ventnor stepped back. "How the hell should I know? You're the one who dealt with Aiken."

Both men eyed each other with obvious suspicion. Willi swallowed. Jeeze, she'd never been popular with superintendents because she didn't let them run over her, but who'd have thought she'd be on a double super hit list. The idea was as cold as the icy raindrops coming down in earnest.

Burkhalter pulled his collar up. "We'll talk later."

Ventnor stepped in front of him. "She's not the only one. Sammie is falling apart. Nervous people make me nervous. Know what I mean?"

"I'll take care of my Sammie. She'll be fine. The Gallagher woman is in your playground, Ventnor. You deal with her."

When the last taillight disappeared, Willi rose from the brambles. She needed warmth, a towel to dry off with, and then she'd head back to the farmhouse. She ran to the cottage door, unlocked it with the new key, and entered. She switched on a one-bulb ceiling fixture and startled a figure before her who jumped.

He lowered his head to run her down, yelling, "Now I've got you!"

CHAPTER

16

When he roared out, "I've got you now!" she froze as if all the raindrops clinging had turned into one ice cube. Her mind worked, but her limbs refused. He must have torn off boards on the cellar, snuck in, and replaced them so it looked undisturbed from outside. Oh, those drug-dealing cretins had known all along she had hidden and watched. He'd been the first shadowy figure, no doubt, the one preceding the furry friend. Perhaps the phone call to warn her had been a trap, a trap to take care of that nosy Gallagher woman once and for all. Only a nanosecond actually went by, a moment when she recognized the booming voice as an Oxhandler's. He held a blue-capped bottle in his hand. Water? She doubted it. His loudness upset another on the premises that ambled up behind him and waved its perfumed tail. Willi yelped, stomped on Oxhandler's foot, and bolted out the door. Her adversary received the full blast of the noxious spray.

The storm, in renewed fury, roared. Lightning flashed. Electricity made her hair crackle beneath her hood. Disoriented, she stopped a moment to get her bearings. Impossible.

She had run too far from the cottage to see even the halogen outdoor light. The skunk odor made her wrinkle her nose long before she heard Neeper's or Dan's breathing to one side. She pivoted around a tree to hold a strong limb back with all her strength. When she turned it loose, the resounding smack and subsequent cursing proved she'd hit the mark.

She rushed forward and, within the illumination of another flash from the sky, stopped short of a barbed wire fence. She scrambled between two bottom wires and left a tuft of her turtleneck as a calling card. She stumbled away from the grotesque scent only to face a gigantic and misshapen monster. Willi screamed. The creature veered closer. Bulging eyes and flaring nostrils evoked satanic images. It bellowed from a cavernous mouth. Its horns brushed down and past Willi to cut into her jeans. Now, more of the 800- to 1,200-pound animals surrounded her.

Well, hell. The Orlandos' dairy herd. The lightning had frightened them, but her presence pushing against one and then another as she worked her way through seemed to calm them. She took a few jagged breaths. Here among the lowing herd, she'd hide from the Oxhandler cousin. Thunder clapped and changed her moment of comfort into panic. Four hundred strong, the cows twisted, kicked, and turned about.

Skunk scent, unmitigated by rain or herd, rose nearby. She worked her way against muscle and bone toward the edge of the herd and hoped Oxhandler got the worst of the hooves and horns. By then she'd been treading mud so long, she felt like an extra in the story of Moses's *Ten Commandments*. When lightning once more lit the area, she chanced a look behind her. A calf chose that moment to ram into her midsection, catapulting her over into the sludge. A surreal glance upward revealed her feet overhead. Feet, no tennis shoes. Mud-encrusted *feet*.

She landed into an unspread truckload of manure, now a muddy hill of seepage. On hands and knees she clawed her way through but only seemed to get into thicker sludge. She fell face forward. Oh gosh, the stench. With a hand now bare of glove, she wiped muck away and blinked. *Light, oh thank you, Lord, thank you, there's light.* The Orlandos' barn lay ahead of her.

She grasped the handle of the barnyard gate. A rasping breath and stench behind warned her of Oxhandler's presence. He grabbed her arm, swinging her around to face him. Through the holes of her ski mask, she looked at a similarly clad figure.

He roared, "By Damn, you won't get away this time!" His anvil-shaped fist swung like a sledgehammer.

The impact popped her head back. Pain shot along her jawline. Her knees buckled before she tilted and thudded onto her back in the barnyard refuse. Nausea attacked her, but she managed to peer out of one eye. Dang mask must have twisted. She couldn't see anything from the other opening. The barn door swung wide to allow light to stream out and around the brawny silhouette.

Lay still or try to run? Only five feet separated her from Oxhandler. She raised her head. Wooziness assaulted her. She opted for Opossum Medicine and closed her eyes.

A tug on her turtleneck sweater lifted her upper body from the mud. She peered cautiously through the one slit. Oxhandler knelt over her, his legs straddled across hers. He bared his teeth in a feral grimace. With one hand holding her up, he used the other to heft a large bottle capped in blue. One flip of his thumb and the lid would pop off.

No, no. Bottles just like this sat in the science labs. *Not acid, ohmyGodmyGod, please no.* No one was going to throw acid in her eyes. She used her last strength to push Oxhandler back, yelled, and raised her knees into his groin. With a groan he rolled over. She scrambled to her knees and clamped her hands on both sides of her head, since it seemed to be floating some two feet above her. Her bare feet slipped in the slimy sludge. An iron fist held her bare ankle. Oxhandler rolled over. "You . . . uh . . . aren't getting away. The rest did, but not you." He jerked, and she splatted down face first. She twisted around and pummeled his chest. Out of the corner of her eye, more lights registered.

The Orlandos . . . yes, they had awakened from the storm. Willi bent her head back and screamed.

"Damn you. Just quiet down. I just want to talk."

Right. And Bad Bart just gunned down one man. The bottle stuck out of the mud. She grasped the neck, pulled it underneath her, as the Oxhandler brute turned her over again and pinned her down. When he let up for just a moment, she butt-bucked him backwards, flipped off the bottle top, and flung the liquid into his face. She scrambled upward and a few feet away, fell to her weak knees, and covered her eyes.

"Oh, God. How's that feel, you sorry excuse for a man? Oh, I can't believe I did that. Oh, jeeze." Everything was silent. Even the rain stopped. "Why aren't you yelling in agony, like . . . like . . . she did?" Willi peeked between her fingers.

"I always carry water. *Water*. What did you think?" he asked.

A circle of legs surrounded Willi. At first, she thought she was seeing double, triple, and beyond. The Orlando farm hands, *mojados*—wetbacks—stood with hands in their jeans pockets. Some of them scratched their heads underneath worn hats. One with a big belt buckle stepped forward. *"¿Qué pasó aquí, hombres? ¿Están representando como Zorro en el lodo?"*

In Spanish, Willi answered. "No, we're not playing the role of Zorro in the mud. Grab him. He's a criminal, a *matador*—a killer."

Another one, dark eyes gleaming, bent down on his haunches. "Looks like to me, you both got the mask of a *ladrón*. Maybe so, you both trying to steal the herd of our *patrón*. We see when the sheriff he come."

"You called the sheriff?"

"Sí, thief with the voice of an angel. We call the *jefe."*

There was a Mexican laborer on each side of her and Oxhandler as well.

Willi pulled her mask off. Her hair tumbled around her shoulders. "Now, see here. I'm your neighbor. I was laying in wait for this jerk. He's broken into my cottage before and again tonight."

"Willi Gallagher?" Oxhandler boomed and pulled his mask off to reveal Dan.

The belt-buckled hombre said, "She's a thief *muy bonita*. Little wild, too; she's *muy simpática*. Maybe so we see what else she have before the sheriff comes?"

"You get your hands off me. I'll kick you so hard your *cajones* will be *cacahuates* for the rest of your life."

Another, obviously the foreman who had the name Chopo embroidered on his collar, stepped up and said in English, "Hernando, you don't talk to any lady like that, thief or not, and I've heard about Ms. Gallagher. She is a *señora,* an unusual one who does some strange things, but a lady despite wanting to turn certain parts of your body into peanuts."

Hernando looked sheepishly at his belt buckle and mumbled, "*Lo siento mucho. Perdón, señorita.*"

She pointed at Dan. "He's the one who is the burglar and worse."

"Not me, Willi. I was laying in wait for the gang, dirtbags who've burglarized my boat twice now. And I followed them here on two other occasions. Been keeping a watch on the place for a couple weeks. Just ask Neeper. Why, he thought the other night he'd caught one of those who'd broken in our place. Followed them home, but he must have lost them and followed you home instead. Didn't want to worry you until I was sure what was going on, Willi."

"Uh . . . what does Neeper drive?

"A Dodge Ram with cab lights on top."

"Black?"

"Sure. Only color he'll ever get."

"He scared me to death one night following me home from the lake."

"Well, he felt right funny when the car turned into your drive, too."

Willi sighed. Thank goodness. At least, he didn't know she was actually the one who had broken into the boat. "Wait. You said two times?"

"Right."

Chopo said, "It's okay. We'll get it all straightened out when the deputy sheriff arrives." He said to Hernando, "You did call 911, right? It's taking them a long time."

Hernando's eyes grew as big as tortillas. "*Nueve-uno-uno?* I maybe did *nueve-cero-cero* and a couple of numbers after. I get *muy* nervous on the phone, but the lady who answer say, sure I'll be the cop, so I gots the right *número,* right? She *muy* nice to me on the phone. That is why I long time."

Chopo sighed and addressed Willi, "I will explain to him later."

"Tell you what," Willi said, trusting her instincts and what she knew of Dan. He was an idiot and a knuckle-dragging bubba sometimes, but he wasn't a bad person. She repeated, "Tell you what. No sense calling the sheriff now, since I know Dan is telling the truth, and you all know we weren't after your cows. In fact, many a time, I've brought strays back to your side of the fence."

Chopo grinned. "This is so. You trust this man, then, *señorita?*"

"Yes. So, could one of you give us a ride in your pickup back to my place?"

"*Sí, señorita.* Hop in the back." When she and Dan opened the door and pulled the handle forward to climb in the backseat of the double cab, Chopo said, "No, no. In the back." He thumbed toward the truck bed. "You, barefoot little *señorita,* are covered in *lodo,* and your friend, he smells like *una mofeta.*"

At the farmhouse, Willi made Dan strip down in the mudroom, run outside to drape all his clothes on the fence line, and make use of the enclosed shower beside the washing machine. Meanwhile, she ran up to the third-floor attic, scrounged around in the roll-around clothes hangers to find some of her daddy's old khaki outfits. She showered and changed into a white pair of jeans and a pink sleeveless pullover. Barefoot, she ran back to the kitchen.

Charlie Brown chased her upstairs and down, woofed at

the door of the mudroom, and generally made a nuisance of his little hairball self. She settled him with a warmed bowl of oatmeal mixed with his Ukanuba dog food.

"Now that the four-legged has a full tummy, it's time to see to the two-leggeds."

While she worked on chopping up smoked sausage and onions, she turned her kitchen radio on. "You Light Up My Life"—a double play of Boone's followed by Rime's rendition—mellowed her out some but made her heart long to have one irritating special investigator in the house right now, not Dan Oxhandler. How ironic. Lassiter was scoping out the *Comanche Raider,* while right underfoot she had the renter of the floating domicile.

Dan entered. Her daddy's clothing was tight around the shoulders and too long in the leg, but he had had sense enough to roll up the pants cuffs. "That smells great."

She stirred the meat and onions before pulling the boiled eggs off to place them under running cold water. "I must say your aroma has also improved."

He reached over and turned the radio station to hard rock. She slapped his hand away with the dish towel. "What are you doing?"

His loud voice bounced off the walls. "Changing the station. I hate country western."

"Well, I like it."

"I guess Quannah does, too."

"As a matter of fact, yes." Since he made no move to stop the noise of some group with nine-inch nails, she switched it back. A ditty played with lyrics, "Kiss . . . kiss this and I don't mean my ruby red lips . . ." Willi grinned, cracked and peeled the eggs. "Here, make yourself useful. Use a spoon to scoop out the yolks and mix them with that mayo, mustard, and chopped pickle. Salt and pepper are there, too."

Dan grumbled but deftly mixed.

"*We* like golden-oldies rock 'n' roll, also." She smiled at her use of *we.* He might be one irritating, sometimes chauvinistic man, but she'd now defend Lassiter against all comers.

Including one former student and present-day colleague, Dan Oxhandler.

She placed the frying pan of steaming smoked sausages and onions in the center of the table alongside the deviled eggs. Sliced tomatoes with an herb sauce completed the midnight meal. She pulled a cold beer from the fridge for him and poured iced tea for herself. Allowing him to finish his first helping, she remained quiet, listening to "Battle Hymn of Love" segueing into "The Waltz of the Angels." She frowned. She loved that song, but that had to be the fifth time she'd heard it in the last forty-eight hours. She glanced at the frying pan. "Well, hit me up side the head."

"Hm?" Oxhandler managed around a belch.

"Thinking of angels. Angels' knots. Killing knots. Love knots. Hmm."

Without comment, he scooped up another helping.

"Aren't you a little curious? Angels' knots. Love knots? Killing knots?"

"Duh-uh. Why? Your mind is always off on weird things. Sometimes I swear I can see smoke rising from the heat up there."

She smirked. *Why not? Anything that didn't affect him personally . . . just didn't compute.* "Before you get a puppy-tight tummy, want to talk about it?"

He raised his hands in a questioning gesture.

"Tonight, Dan, don't play games."

He leaned over, opened the fridge, and got himself another beer. "I worked at Tyler ISD for awhile. Maybe you know."

"Yes, someone mentioned that."

"You may not know that Bernie Burkhalter and Jarnagin Ventnor also worked up through the file and rank there."

She made the give-me, give-me hand motion.

"While there, I was accused of things. Totally untrue— all of them."

Hm. Guess he's referring to the junior high girl's accusations.

"In getting back to the root of those things, I got to fig- uring someone nailed that on me to get attention off what they were doing. Burkhalter had been in the Nickleberry ISD for ten, maybe twelve years, but he and Ventnor stayed friends . . . and what . . . they was doing—"

"*Were* doing." Willi clamped a hand over her mouth.

Dan grinned and took the correction as if still in her classroom. "And what they *were* doing was trying to bring a drug syndication to the kids in Tyler. At least, that's what I thought. When my situation got headlines, folks forgot about them."

"I need more details. And not another drop of Budweiser until you give them up."

"I'd gotten a young lady to help me get some info on the two. Before I could turn around twice, I was brought before the school board. When I told them my plan, they really thought I was crazy and gave me the *choice* to resign and save my career. Soon afterward, I got my contract accepted here, and Burkhalter let me know he'd better never hear a word spoken about such things. This was my last chance. I didn't want to mess anything up."

"So . . . what changed your mind?"

"Tessa's death. She had some connection to those creeps but would never tell what exactly. There's something really wrong about her dying in Burkhalter's Caddy. Can't believe they released it to him."

"Why did you think, Dan Oxhandler, that I had something to do with those creeps?"

"I never thought that until I pulled off your mask. When you're faced with a fact, you have to take it in . . . and so . . ."

Willi tapped the tabletop. "Well, hang on to that thought when I ask you this. Why in blue blazes was your *Playboy* magazine in my folks' cottage? Hmm?"

"Uh . . . well, a man has to have . . . something to while away the time when he's on . . . surveillance." At what must have been her narrow-eyed, murderous look, he offered more. Both hands outward, he said, "Hold up. Wait. Bits and pieces I overheard told me someone was using your place for a meeting spot. I'm sorry I left the magazine. They came in earlier than I'd planned one night, and I think I just stuffed it under the couch and hid in the cellar stairway. That's the way I went in tonight, too."

"Don't ever do it again."

"What?"

"Enter my folks' cottage, my property, without permission." She felt her own cheeks flare with heat. What a hypocrite she was. The strains of "The Stripper" wafted around the empty cells of her brain. And she really wanted to ask him a question without revealing she'd trespassed on *his* property. "Uh . . . do you remember Tessa wearing a bright green and white scarf the day she died?"

"While we were out at the lake. Sure. She was teasing her aunt about wearing her part of the Irish Fling Festival. It was something Irish. What about it?"

"When . . . when she was found that afternoon, she had on her bathing suit and robe, her sandals, but no scarf. What might have happened to it?"

"Not a clue."

"Hmm."

"Hmm?"

"Just wondered. I guess in the struggle, she could have knocked it partially off, it could have blown out the window or . . . or something."

"A thousand things could have happened to it. She could have given it back to India Lou. I think it was part of some quilt they were finishing up to give away on the last festival night."

"There's a possibility." Or someone who wanted to get Dan blamed could have taken it and later stuffed it down between the cushions of Dan's sofa.

"You said you and Neeper live together?"

"At the marina on a cool boat, the *Comanche Raider*. That's Neeper's name. It's really his boat. I pay rent. You'll have to come out sometime. I'd like to give you the grand tour."

Willi put half a deviled egg in her mouth to keep from responding in an unladylike way. When she finished chewing and swallowing, she sipped her iced tea. "Did Tessa get to visit?"

"Oh, yeah, we'd fry up a batch of crawdads whenever she came in. She loved those." Tears welled in his eyes, and he took a swig of his Bud. "She didn't visit that last day. We all met out at the swimming area, went sailing awhile, swam, lazed around, and talked."

"She wasn't on your boat that day at all?"

"Naw, now get off that, Willi. Hey, you'd like the boat. Real rich wood, lots of red."

"Hmm. Wow."

"Saralee York, the new teacher, came out that night and had a beer with me. She knew we all were classmates. Figured Neeper and I'd be upset. Brought Nestlé's Tollhouse cookies. That was real nice of her, wasn't it?"

"Yes, and it seems like something she would do."

He leaned across the table toward Willi. "You think maybe?"

"Think?"

"You know. Her an me, maybe?" He shrugged.

Roy Orbison's heart-touching ballad, "Joni," ended and was followed by "Distant Drums." Willi sucked in her bottom lip and slowly released it. "Oh, uh . . . I don't know." Willi remembered seeing Officer Piedra holding Saralee's hand beneath the parking lot light at the late-night faculty meeting. Also, she suspected she could guess the identity of one Stetson wide-brim that Saralee quickly pushed out of eyesight. There was after all, some reason Officer Jon Piedra was running up the stairs toward the young teacher's apartment when she and Sheriff Tucker headed toward the call at the high school. Willi grinned. She'd bet the two Klondike bars she grabbed from the freezer, he was going to retrieve his sombrero left as a calling card—a warning to other males on the premises: My hat, my woman. Another of those ways modern two-legged Texas males of the species marked their territory.

"You're grinning and saying yes, I might have a chance?" Dan sat up straighter.

"Oh, no. I don't want to get your hopes up in that arena."

"She's only been here a few weeks. Who could she know but Neeper and me? And he's not partial to brown-eyed redheads. Think they ought to only have blue."

"Well, that's certainly a criteria. But . . . but she does have blue eyes."

"Nope, nope. Neeper and me had this here argument already."

"Okay."

"Me and Neeper, we agreed to disagree. I don't care what color she has. She's real nice. And I learned a lot from dating you, about thinking before I speak, about friendship and what it means to be one, about what the ladies expect."

"We were *not* dating. We went out a few times as colleagues."

"Yeah, well, I guess we'll just agree to disagree about that. May I have another beer?"

"No."

"Willi! I asked."

"Yes, you did, but I just thought of something I wanted you to see—to see clearly."

"Then the beer?"

"We'll see. Meantime finish your Klondike bar while I run upstairs and get some books."

He rolled his eyes. "You and your books. Willi, you've got enough learning in your little noggin for five teachers. Why are you still reading? Jeeze."

"If I didn't know you were kidding me, I'd be upset. You know, Dan, just because you grew up in small-town Texas doesn't mean you have to keep that bubba attitude." She pushed the button on the coffeemaker as she left the room.

Downstairs, with the school annuals in hand, she flipped on all the lights in the living room and chose the couch to settle both her and Dan. "Here," she said, placing a steaming mug of coffee on a coaster in front of him. "I want you to put that scientific, analytical part of your mind to work."

He glared at her.

"What?" she asked.

"Making fun of me?"

"I . . . most certainly am not. What do you mean?"

"Everybody knows the brains went to Neeper. That's why I teach first-year biology. I can only stumble through the higher math and sciences."

"Well, I truly didn't know that. You seem to do a commendable job. You get great evaluations and honest ones from Wiginton. The kids respect you in the classroom and on the field."

"Yeah?"

"Sure."

"So, I'm not too dumb and bubba-brained to approach Saralee?"

Willi blinked. She didn't want him hurt, but his ego needed gentle encouragement right now. "You know what Stuart Little says?"

"We are talking that little white mouse, right, Willi?"

"Yes . . . and his motto is, 'Never say die.' Never give up. Now, let's get your thinking cranking on this." She tapped the first book.

He sipped the coffee, grinned, and peered at the page she'd opened before him. "Oh, yeah, this was my senior year, your first year of teaching. Look at you. You look younger than half the kids. And you're shorter than anyone in that class."

"Actually, I started teaching when you were a junior. I came in the spring term beginning in December. Took over for some pregnant teacher. I didn't have you guys until the next year." She wanted him to just ease down memory lane and see if anything—anything jelled or led to her constant messages about *where it all began.* She encouraged him with a word here and there and let him ramble as they perused the pictures.

He said, "There's Edmonds as super. Guess it was a few years after our high school graduation when Burkhalter got to move up to super."

"Right. About five. He's lasted quite awhile for a super. Almost five years."

"Kassal Heberly was picked as class favorite along with Vic Ramirez. Boy, look at that hair. Styles sure change, huh?"

"And there you and Neeper are—the class clowns. Those long cowboy dusters and black hats. What a dress statement that was. You *look* like someone who'd like country western music."

He grimaced. "I'd forgotten. They'd never allow kids nowadays to wear those."

"Nope. The Columbine tragedy changed high school dress codes around the nation. No yellow slickers, certainly, nor cowboy-style ankle-length dusters."

"Here we are—the whole gang," he said.

Willi read the caption. "Setting up for the junior-senior prom, these seniors help before heading for tuxedos and cummerbunds, corsages and swept-up glamour do's." On ladders, Dan and Neeper attached streamers from one end of the rented hotel ballroom to the other. Tessa Aiken was taking a moment to teach Vic Ramirez dance steps. Margarita Uriegas, in red sweats, stapled roses and vines around a trellis for the photos later in the evening. She was engulfed with them around her body and they trailed behind her. A policeman tried to unwind her, looked over his shoulder just as the bulb burst in his surprised face. A much younger Officer Jon Piedra grinned.

"What was he doing there?"

Dan said, "He's always been cool. Real quiet, but he took . . . Neeper and me over to do the decorating. Uh . . . we had both had our licenses suspended for a couple months."

"Uh-huh. That was nice of him."

"Yeah, he's about two, maybe three years older than you, but like you, he fits in with all age groups. How do you do that?"

Willi, surprised at the sincere groping for knowledge, stared at him. "I don't know. I guess, for one thing, I don't see age, like I don't see color or a particular religious bent as being the person. I just enjoy folks. Probably Piedra does, too."

She refilled Dan's coffee cup and glanced at the clock: 1:45 A.M. Jeeze, that could be why her eyes seemed loaded down with twelve yards of pea gravel. She blinked to bring some moisture to the surface. "I chaperoned that prom dance. I don't remember seeing him that evening as our peacemaker."

Dan yawned. "Nope. He got mad about something. Can't remember what, maybe at Neeper and me being— as you'd say—bubbas. He was gonna take us and our girls in his cruiser, even had it okayed by Sheriff Tucker. Then he didn't show. We had to get Tessa and her date to pick us up."

Dan picked out a few other faces in the work crew and closed the book.

"Wait," Willi said. "What about the prom pictures?"

"Willi, they didn't have any back then. Nowadays, they do an addition to the annuals, but we didn't ever get our prom photos in the yearbook."

"Oh, that's right."

She was about to call it quits but hid a yawn and took a sip of her own coffee. She handed him the *Coup Counting* annual, wild warrior leaning down over the side of the Nickleberry mascot, that yellow horse with the bright blue paint markings. "This was your junior year."

"I can't believe I'm saying this, but it's really late . . . or early . . . and—"

Willi grimaced but offered, "Okay, how about that other beer?"

"Naw. This coffee is fine."

"Huh?"

"But, I'd take another Klondike bar, if you're going to force me to stay."

She had to get some answers, and by damned some of those entwined knots had to be unraveled somehow in the *Coup Counting* books. "One Klondike bar coming up."

When she returned, Dan had a strange look on his face and flipped quickly past the page he was on.

She sat and said, "Go back. I missed those first pages."

"Nothing important on them. Just our class photos. We were such dorks."

She shuffled back to the black-and-white photos with names, clubs, and awards listed underneath. "You weren't dorks. You were all so cute." She did laugh upon seeing Dan and Neeper Oxhandler, pictures next to each other. Slender faces, the Oxhandler shoulders far too bony for the name they carried, the boys had on overalls and T-shirts. He groaned. "Everybody wore them that year."

"Evidently. Boys and girls. Looks like the farmers' convention." She moved her finger forward to find Victor—not Vic—Ramirez's picture. He was all brown eyes—dark eyes bigger than his mama's tortillas—and a shy little grin.

Dan shook his head. "Sure hope the scuttlebutt about him being involved with Burkhalter and Ventnor aren't true."

Willi stared at him. Oh, so from the cottage he couldn't see who got out of the cars in front. He didn't know Vic was very much involved. Well, she was a liaison for the sheriff, so she was to gather, not divulge, info. She flipped back a few pages to look at Tessa Aiken's photo. All grin and shining eyes. What a promising life she'd had before her. Willi's eyes teared up this time, and she flipped back to the last class page. "Oh, there's Margarita Uriegas."

"Yeah, that's about five years after her having her daughter. Probably wearing all those tight red clothes had something to do with—"

Willi raised an eyebrow and pursed her lips.

Dan stuffed his last bite of ice cream in his mouth.

"I have the greatest admiration for that young lady."

"She's come through okay. Through some tough times, that's true." Dan turned to the clubs section. "Here's the whole gang again." At first he smiled, then frowned and tried to turn the page, but Willi held it down. "You were all in the science club. Makes sense. Neeper sitting up on the lab desk. You *standing* above the sink and acting like you're Dr. Jekyll and Mr. Hyde about to drink the potion. Tessa Aiken holding on to your pants leg and begging you not to take it."

"Notice, though, she's smiling straight at the camera."

"That's our Tessa. If she'd lived, no doubt she'd have moved from practicing law to political office," Dan said.

"Who's this beside Vic Ramirez, and what is that contraption on his head?"

"A precursor to his fireman's helmet. This one held six cans. See the straws coming from each one leading down to the one single sipper for the mouth? That was too cool. I remember one time we took it out and filled those Coke cans with beer, and even Officer Piedra didn't know. Cruising and drinking and no tickets in sight, oh man it was—"

Willi sighed.

He said, "Uh . . . I guess you had to be there."

"Who is that beside him?"

"That's . . . oh . . . that's Sunny. Mrs. Yannich's daughter. She'd gained a lot of weight there, you know, I guess because . . ."

"Because?"

"Sunny was just like her name. Happy and helpful and just cute as a button."

"Doesn't sound like a reason to gobble goobers, do a malt meltdown, plunge into a pita and pizza party."

Dan frowned this time. "Sunny, Vic, Tessa, and me and Neeper, we did everything together from ninth grade on. But . . . after the accident, Sunny changed. Well, we all changed. Look at us now. If the names weren't underneath some of these pictures, I wouldn't have a clue."

"I remember. She helped move the lab materials up to the second floor."

"Yeah. Girls. She was stupid."

"Dan Oxhandler!"

"Naw, I meant she wore those real high wooden, open-backed shoes and was climbing stairs . . . and holding all kinds of ingredients and glassware. When she tripped on the stairs, there was glass embedded all up and down her arms, her neck, one leg, and she had horrendous scars, not just from the cuts but from acid the kid next to her was carrying. She fell against him and both went stumbling down those concrete stairs. Wasn't his fault."

Willi snapped her fingers. "I do remember. That's when I thought Sammie Yannich was so cruel to her daughter."

"Both parents. They wouldn't let her be operated on, 'cause they wanted her victimized arm and leg to show in court. Photos weren't good enough. They were going for the gold. Wanted the scars on her face to be there for the jury to see. Don't know how it turned out."

"I don't recall either."

"It dragged on until at least two years after we graduated. By then we'd all gone our separate ways. Even the Yannichs split up. I think he died before they actually got divorced, though."

"What happened to Sunny?"

"She gained so much, no one recognized her by the time we graduated. She dropped out of all activities. Vic invited her to the prom."

Willi said, "She wasn't in the photo of you all decorating in your senior yearbook."

"Yes, she was." Dan picked up the senior book and pointed to the photo. "See, there to the left of Officer Piedra."

Willi got her magnifying glass. "She's blurry and in shadows. Damn. I can't remember her."

"Like you said, you'd come at the second half of our junior year. After that, you saw all of us together—all of us but Sunny. No reason you should remember her."

"Well, I'm glad she got to go to her prom. That was wonderful of Vic to ask her, considering she'd dropped out of so much."

Dan's shoulders slumped. "You know that night we cruised with the beer hat? Uh . . . that was the night he asked her."

"So?"

"So . . . hey, Vic was the school's star quarterback, you know? You can't blame him for something like that."

"Like what, Dan, like what?"

"He lost his nerve at the last minute. He couldn't take a

scarred girl to the dance. He told her right after we finished decorating."

"What a jerk."

"Yeah, kids are . . . and we were kids then. Vic felt badly; we've talked about it. He's not proud of it, even tried to get in touch with her through Mrs. Yannich, but even Mrs. Yannich didn't know where Sunny went after the court proceedings ended."

Willi rubbed the back of her neck. "That's all the input I can handle. Sleep calls."

Dan said, "This couch looks comfortable. I could just—"

"Not on your life—well, maybe if you were still full of beer—but otherwise, not on you life. Get 'em up, head 'em out, Oxhandler."

After he left, Willi locked up, turned off lights, and let the mighty fighter of tigers—Charlie Brown—stay in his downstairs basket. She checked her messages when she got into bed.

Quannah's voice was on the third one. "*Winyan*. It's a little before midnight here. I'm sure you're already in dreamland, but I had a five-minute woods break. Nothing going on out here at the lake and the boat. Sometimes stakeouts are like that—more boring than watching dirt daubers spit on their nests. Hope you had a much-needed restful evening. If you do hear this before you're tucked in, remember that star twinkling is me . . . winking at . . . my lady."

She grinned, blew a kiss to his framed photo on her nightstand, and instantly fell to sleep—sleep interrupted by nightmares about vines and acid, Irish dancers and frogs. Sleep from which she was constantly awakened to listen to creaks and wind. Each time she'd get up to check for intruders, but only a loose shingle or a coyote howling could be discerned. When she arose the next morning, her eyes no longer felt like cement, they were more like Highway 67's crater-filled and roughly patched asphalt.

"And what in Hades and Hell is that commotion downstairs?"

CHAPTER
17

Elba hollered upwards. "Laze abed, come on down when you're ready. Your housekeeper of the day is here and already at work."

Willi smiled. Thank goodness. Showered and dressed, she stepped into a roomful of the aromas of frying bacon and eggs: a stimulant for the gnawing in her stomach. "Smells wonderful." When she rounded the corner, her smile widened.

Quannah munched on a buttered biscuit. He winked and pulled out a chair for her. "Don't blame me. Elba invited me for breakfast."

"Fine by me. I want to know what's new on the case, any-hoo. What did you and Sheriff Tucker find out last night?"

He splayed a hand across his chest. "It's nice to see you, Lassiter. I hope you were in no danger, Lassiter. How are you this morning? Elba, she doesn't want me around except for tidbits on cases. Can you believe?"

"Fool woman, if so." Elba set plates of eggs before both of them. "Good for a body to have a man around the house. A young woman without a man is like—"

"Elba, don't you start." One of the things she loved about him was the light repartee that flowed so easily between them. However, he was right. She *did* want to know what happened, whether they'd identified the sneaker's owner. Whether they saw anyone board the boat who shouldn't have been there. Of course, she wanted to know. She looked up from her bacon to catch a glint in Quannah's eyes. "What, Lassiter?"

"Maybe," Quannah said, "we ought to let Elba in on next weekend's plans?"

"Might be best." Willi toyed with her hot tea. "Uh, Elba, there's something we should tell you."

Elba laid a set of keys on the table. "Here. Me and Aggie done made an extry pair for him."

"You knew?"

Quannah held both hands up in that don't-ask-me mode.

"Me and Aggie both did reads—me with the crystal, her with the cards—and both showed your true love coming to stay, Willi. Also showed you was gonna be a trial to him and he to you, at times. But . . . him being here makes sense besides. A woman getting along in her years like you— thirty-six or so—"

"Thirty-two, Elba, thirty-two."

Elba folded her arms underneath her bosom and frowned. "This don't mean me and Aggie is losing our jobs here, does it? Seeing as how there's two of you, seems like there ought to be twice as much work, right?"

"Of course, you don't lose your jobs."

"Certainly not," Quannah agreed. He got up and gave Elba a big bear hug and sound pats on the back. "I need all the help I can get to keep this woman in line."

"That's what I was thinking. And, there's plenty for a man to turn his hand to here. Things the three of us . . . uh . . . ladies . . . can't seem to get to for one reason or another."

"Not a problem. After another helping of eggs and bacon, I thought I'd clean out that corner bedroom upstairs. Isn't that the one, Gallagher, you wanted for an upstairs office?"

Hades and blue blazes, there he was in her head again. She

knew daggum well she'd never once mentioned that to him. "Well . . . yes, for . . . for *you.* I thought you'd like some space to call all your own . . . like my nookery is for me."

He hugged her from behind her chair, bending down to touch his warm cheek to hers. "Yes, I will need someplace to hide when you decide it's scalping time, and I won't intrude into . . . your needed space. That was one of your fears, right?"

She frowned. "I don't recall ever saying such a thing."

"You didn't." He winked.

Infuriating man.

Elba said, "Yep, you two will keep life interesting one for the other. This ought to be fun."

Willi slapped her napkin on the table and ignored Elba. "Sit and eat, Big Chief. If you'll tell me all that happened out at the lake, I promise no scalping today."

He sat and salted and peppered his eggs. "Ah, *Winyan,* you're very focused this morning. Any particular reason?"

"Inquiring minds want to know, Lassiter. Not another strip of bacon, Elba, until the frijoles start jumping—that means—"

"I know," he said, "until I give up the news. You're going to be disappointed."

"No way, José." She shoved her plate away. With both elbows on the table, she leaned toward him.

"Nothing happened. Neeper Oxhandler showed us the shoe from the break-in."

Willi removed her elbows and folded her hands tightly in her lap. "Shoe?"

"One tennis shoe. Looked like a woman's, probably about your size."

"Oh?"

"Or a kid, maybe twelve, thirteen. Whoever they were came in an open window, played with the buttons on the . . . uh . . . bedroom console."

"Console?" asked Willi in her most innocent voice.

Quannah scratched his chin and looked up at the kitchen ceiling fan. "Control panel that operates . . . uh . . . radio . . .

music . . . somehow. Anyway, they couldn't say anything was taken, but there'd been a number of petty crimes out that way, so it was worth checking out."

"I thought you said it might have to do with Tessa Aiken's murder?"

"Just a hunch on Uncle Brigham's part, being as the Oxhandler cousins were good friends of hers. Not every hunch works out, or the *Comanche Raider* could later prove to have something to do with the murder. But last night's vigil didn't turn up anything." He picked up his plate and Willi's to set them on the counter beside Elba's sink of soapy water.

"Guess," he said, "you had a quiet evening?"

Oh, dear. She wanted info, but she really didn't want to share her escapades with thunderstorms, cowherds, skunks—four-legged and two-legged variety—and her mud wrestling adventures. Or, at least, not until she tied them in some way with the murder. For all she knew, the exchanged metal cases could have been notebooks and files, not drugs nor money.

"Gallagher?"

"Huh?"

"You had a quiet evening?"

"Well . . . "She really did need to tell Sheriff Tucker about the exchange, and he, in turn, would certainly share with his law officer nephew sitting before her.

Quannah leaned back, stretched, and raised an eyebrow. "So . . . not such a quiet evening?"

"One little teensy thing of interest might have happened, which I have to touch base with your uncle on as . . . as his liaison. So, how about this? You clean the room, I'll run a few errands, and we'll meet Sheriff Tucker for lunch. Then I'll tell you both at the same time. Won't be like I'm report- ing to someone else behind his back."

"*Winyan,* you are a wise lady. And you are absolutely right. I have no official interest at all. I'm only concerned about your safety, and seeing as how Uncle Brigham has placed boundaries for you on this case, I have no problem.

I trust you to let me know all the important things going on in your life."

"And . . . and you'll do the same?"

He stared at her a long time, his hooded eyes boring into her. "We will both try. I want you to share all you can. Always, there will be a core that neither can reach in the other. Sharing should be a comforting and mutual outpouring, not forced."

"Perhaps it will take time and practice and patience to learn to share all?" she asked, hoping for that patience from him and vowing to give the same to him.

"Yes, *Winyan,* so . . . we will both remember *Mastincala Cistila Kin*—the little Rabbit."

"*Mahsh-teen-cha-cha* what?"

"Pronounced, *Mah-sh teen cha la . . . cheeshe-tea-la . . . keen.* Rabbit Medicine will get us through many decisions about how and when and what to share."

She smiled and hugged him. "Drop the fear."

"Yes, drop the fear. It is okay to trust each other." With one strong finger, he traced the delicate outline of her jaw.

She shivered and blushed. Her heart seemed to soak up the flashes of sunlight coming through the kitchen window. "I'm off then. Elba will help you locate anything you need. I'll see you at Pulido's at noon."

By lunchtime, she had that once-a-month, have-to-have-it-or-die urge for Mexican food. She somehow wanted to tell about the first part of her evening up to the skunk episode. She still had too many questions to ask some folks before she could really explain about the rest. There were definite clues within all the information, but she needed time to regroup again. Sheriff Tucker arrived at Pulido's Restaurant first.

When she arrived, he pulled out one of the chairs painted in floral colors of purple, pink, yellow, and teal. Aztecan and Mayan pottery stood between plants on the windowsills. Sheriff Tucker's head hit against a red, green, and white piñata—a representation of the Mexican flag.

He pushed her chair in and glowered at the parrots and

burros, the *caballos*—horses—and eagles covering the ceiling. "They got a papier-mâché zoo overhead, by dang. Seems like it might be a fire hazard."

"Sit down, Sheriff. They're pretty. I love the bright colors."

Linda Ronstadt's version of "Palomita de Ojos Negros" sweetly filled the background as Juliet Mata took their drink order. "I know what you want, Ms. Gallagher. Dr Pepper with lemon, yes?"

"Works every time."

"I remember our English class *pachangas*—fiestas."

"Juliet, never fiestas."

The dark-eyed petite Juliet giggled. "Ah, yes, never *pachangas* or fiestas because in your class we never broke the school rules of no parties in the classroom, right?"

"Absolutely."

"So"—Juliet winked at Sheriff Tucker—"Ms. Gallagher called them cultural experiences. I just never understood how we got away with studying *Macbeth* and having chimichangas and guacamole together in a cultural experience."

"I'm sure I wrote *multicultural* experience on the board."

"Works for me. I'll bring your salsa and chips right out."

Ronstadt's song about the "little dove with black eyes" hit the section where she held one note for four or five measures. When the song finished, Sheriff Tucker waved at Quannah. "Come on over here. Watch that dang menagerie overhead."

After they ordered and while munching on the hot tortillas crisp taco chips and hot sauce, Willi told about her escapade.

Sheriff Tucker and Quannah both exploded at once after only a few sentences into the tale. "You *staked out* your cottage in the rain, knowing that someone would be there?"

Quannah put his hands on his legs and his mouth became a thin line. Sheriff Tucker wiggled his finger beneath his bulbous nose. "Miss Willi, Miss Willi, I told you not to take any chances, not to go out anywhere on this case without—without telling me first where and for what."

On her right-hand side, she heard a rumbling, perhaps growling from deep in Quannah's chest. She shoved a chip into the salsa and broke it. "Just a cotton-picking, chigger-biting minute, fellas. I have every right to be on my property, every right to protect my property, and every right to do so at my discretion."

When both opened their mouths, she held up her hands, palms outward. "Hold those galloping tongues one more minute." Very slowly she said, "I . . . did not know . . . anything more than that vandals were going to be snooping around. And, Sheriff Tucker, you told me, remember, at the break-in at my house, the culprits were probably kids. Didn't you? Now, I did *not* breach any agreement here, okay?"

Tucker worried his left earlobe. Quannah's breathing sounded less like a bull's. He filled his mouth with a buttered and rolled tortilla. "I see how you reasoned that out, Gallagher, but did you think to call and let someone know just in case something were to happen?"

"As a matter of fact, Big Chief Hot Tamale, I did. You two couldn't be reached."

Grumbles and mumbles came from both sides, effectively cut off by stuffing their mouths.

She put an open hand on her chest. "I called dispatch to let you know. Did they not inform you when you came in?" She stared at Sheriff Tucker.

He pulled out a sky blue with white clouds bandanna, turned his head, and sneezed. "Mayhap, that wasn't on the top of them pink slips I checked this morn. Most important goes to the top."

"Gallagher, what happened after you hid behind the bush?"

While the lively Mexican mariachi polka, "La Adelita" played, she told them about the meeting between the former and the incumbent.

"So, Miss Willi, you think we can put pressure on Jarnagin Ventnor through Viola Fiona and get him to give up the others?"

"Makes sense. He's been spending all the monies of Viola Fiona's he can get his hands on. When he can get no more without doing her in, he tries that. Now, he's into some sort of exchange. With the info I brought back from Tyler, lots of things point to both of those creeps—Ventnor and Burkhalter—being involved in drugs. They tried to get it started in Tyler, Texas, and may have succeeded. The authorities there will have to dig a little deeper to find out. But certainly, they weren't exchanging Tupperware treats last night. And they made reference to getting on campus here at the beginning of school. Reaching a lot of kids."

"Speaking of which," Quannah said, peering at her. "Aren't you all having in-service today?"

"Yes, but when we got through working in our rooms this morning, we could do lunch off campus. We're supposed to go back by one-thirty or so." She smiled, failing to mention she planned to do a bit of snooping . . . uh . . . investigating before returning to campus. Or she might call the principal and beg off. Yep. That sounded like a better plan. She sighed with relief. The explanation of her adventure had been given and accepted, thank the elastic on Granny's garters. No reason to mention her encounter with the crazed killer—Dan—nor her terror among the stampeding herd or the mud wrestling. Life was good.

Sheriff Tucker slammed his fork down. "After scarfing down these here vittles, I'll get right over to Viola Fiona and get her cooperation. Mayhap we can squeeze the sorry wimp enough for him to talk. I sure do hate to hear about Vic Ramirez's part in this; I sure do."

Quannah's hooded eyes opened slowly as he stared at Willi. "Yep, Uncle Brigham, sounds like you got *some* of the skunks out of the woodpile."

Willi shut her eyes a moment. *Get out of my head, Lassiter.* She wasn't yet willing to share about her adventure with skunks, seeing as how it would make her look like such a fool in front of the two men she wanted most to impress this side of the Rio Grande. Juliet Mata placed steaming plates of enchiladas and side dishes of cool guacamole on the table. The next few minutes were busy with appreciative munching. She finally relaxed and smiled.

Quannah chose that moment to ask, "Was there a skunk near the house last night outside the mudroom?"

Okay, don't look him in the eye. Just concentrate on the chip full of guacamole. She chewed slowly and dabbed her napkin on her lips. "Might have been. I didn't hear Charlie Brown fussing, though." All true statements. There could have been a *real* skunk near the house. There had been many times and would be in the future. And Charlie Brown hadn't made a fuss about any critter *outside* the house. Daggum Lassiter's lawman's intuition.

"Just wondered. Elba found a mask in the mudroom she said smelled to high heaven and back of skunk scent."

"Hmm. I wore a mask. I told you. Must have been mine." Damn. Oxhandler must have picked hers up when he left. She didn't like not telling Quannah, but was that necessary about every tiny thing in her life now? Could she keep her own council about nothing without feeling guilt? She'd need more practice with this sharing concept, obviously.

"Hmm." He grinned, picked up the check, and gave her a kiss on the lips—a sweet kiss. "I have a feeling there's a story behind that skunk scent, and knowing you, it's got to be one with a lot of Coyote Medicine—the humorous part—in it. But only when you're ready to share. And, remember, you owe me a good tale."

"Why?"

"I gave up all dignity and danced the jig for you in a green leprechaun outfit, may Great Spirit forgive me."

"That you did. Tonight, by the by, is the last evening of the Irish Fling Festival. We have to be at the lake by eight o'clock."

He squeezed her shoulder. "Wouldn't miss it, not if you're leading the Wednesday night festivities."

At his words and his touch, her tightened shoulder muscles relaxed. He was saying, *You be first. Share with me as we live and learn together.* As he started to rise from the kiss, she pulled him back for a tender one of her own, one full of promise for later. Elba's words skipped through her mind. *This could be fun.*

"*Ay, ay, ay, ay, canta y no llora.*" The song now playing had good advice: sing, don't cry, because in singing our hearts are happy. "Cielito Lindo" was one of Willi's favorite traditional Mexican songs. She hummed it while heading toward the Nickleberry City Library. The booths at the Irish Fling Festival grounds would be closed until this evening, so she couldn't make good on her idea of checking info there.

But by Coyote's eyes, she could use her favorite mode of research, the city library, a three-story brick building she'd been tramping to since she could walk. There she'd discover more about the strange cards left in the yellow Caddy, in her fish tank, and briefcase. She glanced at the car's digital clock. Plenty of time. *No problema.*

Inside the polished wood walls of the building Marilyn Pinn presided, as she had for eons, with her five brooches pinned to her blouse. A silk, high-necked blouse, of course with covered buttons. When Willi greeted Marilyn, Miss Pinn fiddled with the brooch containing a lock of hair. Since Willi and her best childhood friend, MacKenzie Francis, could remember, Miss Pinn always wore that one at her neck. The other four might change with the seasons and her whims. Neither then nor now did Willi have the chutzpah to ask to whom the lock of hair belonged.

In her whispery voice, Marilyn said, "Forgive our mess." She pointed to the Hall of Horrors, a long corridor of stone literary figures embedded within its walls. Every few years a bevy of new characters would be added. "I'm sure you got one of our newsletters about the new additions."

Willi said, "No, Miss Pinn, you've told me that the last two times I've been in, but I've yet to receive one. That's okay since you've personally kept me in the loop."

Poor Marilyn. Her age couldn't be cited as a reason for her forgetfulness. She'd always been this way but blamed others for the supposed lapse on their part. Like folks in town, Willi accepted this eccentricity as a lovable if sometimes exasperating part of Miss Pinn.

Miss Pinn waved a hand toward the Hall of Horrors. A sculptress and painter worked now on the front part of a bloodstained and dented car, obviously meant to be one made famous by Stephen King. Peeking out from the backseat was the saucer-eyed sorcerer, Harry Potter. "I'm sure you don't want to go down the Hall after your experience some months back."

Willi recalled frightening moments when she was locked into the darkened corridor with all the creatures and one murderer. "You're right, Miss Pinn. I wonder if you could direct me to the special section of books you pulled for the Irish Festival display."

Miss Pinn closed her eyes and smiled like Mother Teresa blessing the poor. Of course, Mother Teresa probably didn't pat the brooch at her neck while doing her blessings. "Right over here. We had two cases full of Irish and Celtic materials. Not bad for a small-town library. Our city coffers have been most open with us for these special occasions. Anything in particular you need?"

"Celtic mysticism about trees." Willi rubbed her hands together. Finally, she'd get some easy answers for a change.

"Oh dear, oh dear." Miss Pinn brushed the enclosed lock of hair with nervous fingers. "Those seem to be of interest to a lot of folks."

Hell's bells. "I don't suppose you could tell me who?"

"Absolutely not. Against policy."

Willi smiled, remembering a past ruse or two she'd used to get Miss Pinn to divulge information. The city librarian's mouth seemed to be in a determined mode today, though. Willi brushed dark tendrils back from her face and sighed.

Three hours later and Willi sighed down to her toenails and back up. Her eyes were gritty, her head felt full of cotton, and she'd not gained any insight into what she needed. She slammed the last of the seventeen books back into the shelves. Her stomach growled. She couldn't believe after enchiladas only four hours ago, it would dare complain ever again.

"Now, now." Miss Pinn patted her arm and grabbed her by the hand as if she were eleven years old. "Nothing in the books about the trees? I know someone who might help with that information. Good librarians know their sources beyond their own library, you know."

"What source? Another library?"

"A friend of a friend's daughter." Miss Pinn shook her head. "Or a daughter of a friend's daughter . . . which I guess would make her a granddaughter of a friend . . . or—"

"And her name is?"

"Can't recall, but . . ." Miss Pinn tweaked her Rolodex to the *L*s. "Ah . . . here we are, Andrea Landis."

"The daughter or the granddaughter who's going to tell me about Celtic wizardry concerning trees?"

"No, the friend. Just one moment."

Willi snapped her fingers. "The Landises' cousin. Neither Elba nor Agatha have been able to reach them."

Miss Pinn made a commendably businesslike call at the end of which she asked, "Can you meet her now? She's resting her hands, you know."

"Resting her . . . well, uh . . . yes. Where is she *resting* . . . uh . . . *her hands?*"

Miss Pinn scribbled on a large sticky pad sheet for a few minutes. "Here's a map to Andrea Landis's place seven miles east of town. She's hosting one of her cousins, the harpist—"

"Ah," Willi said, "who's *resting her hands* for tonight's—"

"Program. Exactly. You were always one of my favorites, Willi. So quick to catch on to things."

Willi shook her head and sighed. "Miss Pinn, you're sweet to go to this trouble, but I don't need to know about Celtic/Irish harp music, I need—"

"Information about the mysticism associated with the trees of Ireland. And this woman is the very one who can tell you quickly. Her name is quite enchanting, don't you think?"

"Andrea Landis?"

Marilyn Pinn looked liked she were sucking on the one

sour grape in a cluster. "You were quicker as a child, Willi, dear. Now, when I've told you a name, you should try to remember it."

"But Miss Pinn, you didn't tell—"

Miss Pinn shook a finger in Willi's face.

"Could you tell me once more?" Willi asked.

At the stern look and frenzied patting of the twinkling brooches, Willi added, "Please?"

"Joni McDonald. Now that's J-O-N-I pronounced like *Johnny* and then the hamburger place. You can remember it now, I bet."

Willi peered at the clock on the polished wood wall. "I'm going to have to get a move on if I have to go that far. You're sure this . . . uh . . . Joni McDonald . . . can answer my questions about—"

"The Celtic—"

"Trees?"

"Yes, Willi. Now, run along. I'll send you a newsletter about the renovations in the Hall of Horrors."

"Really, there's no . . . oh, okay. Thanks."

Willi loved to drive back roads as long as she could just meander and adventure. When it came to finding an actual place, she hated squinting at tiny county road signs, most hidden behind overgrown brush. After two turns down the wrong roads, one that ended in dried teeth-jarring ruts, she finally located County Road 493. She drove through a cattle guard and faced one of the oases the Texas landscape offered up in the least likely spots. Lush green fields courted both sides of the long drive marked off by white iron fences. On the left, longhorn cattle grazed: on the right, a little burro opened his lips to reveal characteristic teeth to her. Obviously, a family pet and trained to entertain newcomers.

The drive, over a mile long, led to a circular bricked drive large enough for carriages and four or a couple of Mustangs, a Porsche, and a BMW, which now faced her. She looked up at the immense set of curved steps—and, of course, counted them. Ah. Thirty-four. Not being divisible by thirteen, according to her daddy's rules of superstition, they were *safe* steps. These were lined on each side with sixty-eight pots of pink and red geraniums and ivy. She rang the doorbell.

Andrea Landis, tennis outfit on, answered the door. "You're Willi Gallagher. Delighted to meet you. You've done a wonderful job with the prep on the Irish Fling. Cousin Joni will join you on the terrace. Hope you've not done supper yet. I took the liberty of having something prepared for you all. I've got to run. Doubles and martinis at the club call, then a pool party."

Willi could only smile at the fourtyish woman who smelled of lemons and soap. Her enthusiasm for life was contagious, and her words were said with such warmth that Willi grinned. Only one way to take an Andrea Landis of the world: at face value. One of those folks Willi instantly wanted to be around more because she was downright pleasant. "Thank you. I hope we get to know each other another time."

"Works for me. Make yourself to home. Straight through and out the French doors to the left. When you see the waterfalls, you've arrived."

Willi glanced at a Jeffersonian clock as she entered. Okay, she still had a few hours especially since Principal Wiginton had given her the time off. Somewhere on her path today had to be answers about those dang knotted cards. She pushed open the French doors, walked out under a canopy of lattice and leaves some sixty by sixty feet. In one corner near a seven-tiered natural rock waterfall, a table and chairs waited. The waterfall emptied into a series of pools surrounding the latticed patio. Twelve-pound koi fish swam languidly. Oh, she missed Chaucer and Beowulf. The thought made her more determined to find out why they had to be sacrificed to the mind behind the unusual calling cards.

An ethereal figure in layers and layers of filmy blues—all the seven colors in the ocean—drifted toward the chair opposite Willi. A cool breeze seemed to enter with her. When Willi looked upward, she eyed automatic air conditioners hidden here and there among the foliage. Ahhh, an oasis indeed. Joni McDonald had a mass of baby-fine hair. Its silver color caught the flickering sunlight coming through the latticework. Being as it was long enough to sit on, she waved it aside as one would a cape before she sat down. It settled slowly in light layers around a wisp of a woman.

"I'm Joni McDonald and you are—?"

"Willi Gallagher. It's kind of you to see me on short notice."

"Not at all. I've been a guest of the Landis household all week, and feel I've been quite a burden. I'm a distant cousin. When I got the invite to play for the festival for a week, Andrea and Webb kindly invited me to stay here. I've played the harp music during the day at the festival. They gave time off to get ready for the last of the festivities tonight. I needed to rest—"

"Your hands."

"Yes, my fingers and wrists needed recuperative time."

"I've not been out to the lake during the day, so I've missed hearing you," Willi said. "I'll remedy that tonight."

"Wonderful. Ah, here's our limeade." The Landis's maid set umbrella-topped, ice-frosted glasses before them. "Lovely," Joni said. "We're ready anytime you're prepared to bring out the salads, Evelyn." To Willi she said, "You wanted to know about some trees, is that right?"

Willi gulped down half of the limeade and pulled out a plastic baggie holding the two cards. "What can you tell me about these?"

As if she wanted to use her hands as little as possible, Joni kept hers in her lap and said, "Lay them on the table, please, and give me a moment."

While Joni McDonald considered the pieces of cardboard, Willi soaked up the comfort of the world surrounding her. Diving in and out of the orange and purple trumpet vines, hummingbirds gave a performance. A black and white koi spashed his tail in the pond for attention. Serene. So calm.

She sat on the warm rocks and let her naked legs dangle

*in the cool back splash created by the waterfalls. Her wet
hair lay cool upon her shoulders and back, some locks
curling between her breasts still beaded from water from
her swim. A fish jumped and flipped its tail. She laughed
with the pure joy of being out in sunshine and air, in verdant growth and sparkling water. She rubbed coconut oil
on her skin before picking up her comb. She flipped her
hair over her face and bent down to comb it forward.*

*In the water a face stared back, but not her own. A young
woman, dark of skin, opened her mouth like a fish. No
words came out. Willi threw her own hair back and over to
one side to see better. The ebony-skinned beauty tried
another time to speak, shut her eyes, and when she opened
them, her eyes were blue. Again and again, she tried to
speak. Each time her mouth opened her eyes changed color.
Enough. Willi dove into the clear waters to help the girl.*

*Where did she go? Willi twirled to the left, to the right,
and back. The waif had disappeared. Willi's hair grew
longer, twining and floating out in the water in thick tendrils,
floating back toward her, wrapping around her arms, her
torso and legs, never quite choking her but never allowing
her enough freedom to work her way to the surface. She
didn't mind. All was so serene. So calm.*

The koi flipped his tail and dove into a watery cave. Evelyn set a salad of Mandarin oranges and pears before her.
"Enjoy, ladies. The catfish will be out in a few minutes."

"Thank you, Evelyn," Joni said. While they ate, Joni
filled Willi in about the two cards. "Not knowing what you
really want, I'll just ramble on until a specific question
comes to mind."

"Works for me," Willi said.

"These cards are from a set called the Celtic Tree Oracle. It's one of many popular systems of divination, a
method of learning to concentrate on a higher source, a
way of focusing on improvement—"

Where did it begin?

"Uh . . . could you give me a little background of the
belief system? Assume I know nothing."

"Certainly. Would you like more sesame seed dressing?"

"No," Willi said. "No, thanks. This is great as is."

Joni stared up at the latticework a moment. "Long before the Romans invaded Britain, the Celts had tribal groups."

"Much like our Native Americans?"

"Yes, very similar. The Celts, like the Native Americans, lived a life concerned with all aspects of nature, of the elemental forces in the world." Joni tilted her head and smiled. "Interesting, now that you've got me thinking along those lines."

"What's that?"

"The ancient Celts, like the Indians, had wise elders of the tribe. They had the responsibility of memorizing events and passing them along."

Willi agreed. "Sure. Many of the plains tribes called those historians and storytellers Twisted Hairs. Go on."

"In the case of the Celts, the wise ones were the Druids, Ovates, and Bards. Oh, well, you don't need to know about all those, I guess. As far as these go"—she tapped the cards—"the Druids were philosophers and judges. Somewhat like the shamans of the plains tribes, the Druids saw human life as a special pattern and used symbolism to teach and remind people who they were and from where they and their beliefs came. They developed a special and secretive alphabet used to communicate and used to teach through questions and answers."

Willi snapped her fingers. "That would be the very early Irish *Ogham* alphabet. Yes, I've heard of that."

"Exactly. Oh, here's the catfish. Lemon?"

"Yes, thanks. Oh, those new potatoes look delicious, too. I feel like royalty."

Joni laughed. "Me, too. In case I forgot to mention it, I'm the *poor* distant cousin of this clan. This week has been a treat. Now, where was I?"

"The *Ogham* alphabet."

"I hope I can explain this well. Let's see. In this alphabet there are twenty-five letters. Each of these, due to the Celts' nearness and dependency upon the elements of nature, has a name of some plant, tree, or maybe some part of the sea."

"Okay, I'm still with you." Willi tasted the catfish, a divine melting upon her tongue.

"Trees were so intricate and important to the ancient ones. Makes sense, seeing as how oaks could be hundreds of years old and yew trees have lived to be thousands. Everything was, of course, cyclic in the thirteen months of the old calendar."

Willi choked for a moment and wiped her mouth on a sea-green napkin. "Thirteen? Did you say *thirteen?*"

"Yes, anyway, each of the thirteen months used one of the *Ogham* symbols for its name. Through the passage of time, the *Ogham* became known as the Tree alphabet."

"Ah," Willi said, "Native Americans call them the Standing People . . . uh, the trees, I mean. Sorry, go on."

"Oh, interrupt as you want. Standing People. I like that. The early Celtic or Culdee, the early church, hid the alphabet for special symbolic use and teaching. These cards depict the letters and the symbolism. I guess you'd like to know what your two cards in particular represent?"

"Exactly."

"This one, coll-hazel, is connected to an ancient who could take on the form of animals, among them fish. According to Liz and Colin Murray's *Celtic Tree Oracle Cards,* he swam as a salmon beneath the hazel tree's branches from which fell nuts of wisdom. The legend goes that the salmon swallowed and used the inspiration. Land disputes such as boundaries are associated with the card."

"Yes, Agatha had remembered something about boundary and land issues."

"She's one of your neighbors I've heard so much about. I'd love to meet them sometime."

"We'll see if we can't make that happen."

Joni said, "If one receives this card, it might be that they are, like the hazel branches, one who transforms others' thinking, helps others to bring their ideas to the surface of murky waters, so to speak."

"Like . . . like a teacher would do?"

"Absolutely right."

Willi set her fork aside and leaned toward the wispy-voiced harpist. She shared the circumstances of finding the card with her skewered finny friends. "Under those circumstances, what might you further deduce?"

"I'm not a profiler, Willi, but my guess would be that this was simply a message. Must be from someone who has had or has you now for a teacher. Now, wait a minute. It could be from an instructor or someone who sees himself as part of the educational process, someone trying to *teach* you a lesson. Certainly, it's a warning that all your collected wisdom from the hazel tree of life won't protect your most intimate space—your home—nor you."

Joni McDonald used both graceful hands to pull her floating layers of silver hair off her neck. "Willi, you should turn this over to your local authorities. I would be frightened if I'd been the recipient of this card in the way you described, and you should be, too."

Willi sat back in the cushioned chair. "I am . . . a little. What about the second card?"

Evelyn whisked their plates away and replaced them with tiny silver cups of homemade vanilla ice cream with a caramel topping and strawberries. "Will you ladies be needing anything more?"

Joni raised an eyebrow in Willi's direction. Willi shook her head. Joni said, "No, Evelyn. Everything was lovely. Thank you so much."

"My pleasure."

"The second card," Joni said, "is *ohn-furze*. The furze has a strong scent of honey, and the flowers are yellow. A person receiving such a card might be like a magpie, flitting hither and yon, gathering things for a certain goal." Joni stared fiercely at Willi. "That's what you've been doing—what you're doing now—isn't it? Gathering together information? Cousin Andrea said you were someone involved with the Irish Fling Festival as a co-coordinator, but there's more to it than that, right?"

"I'm afraid so."

"Be very careful, Willi Gallagher. Around the honey-scented furze shrub are swarms of stinging bees."

"One more question. Around the edge of each plant are drawn the intricate knots."

"Ah, yes, the work of the angels."

"I knew they were called that, but why?"

Joni folded her napkin to set beside her empty ice cream dish. "Those monasteries where they used the tree alphabet had monks with more time than they knew what to do with, obviously. Also, those ancient times were an age where beauty was appreciated, no matter the amount of time needed to create it. Thousands of hours were spent in creating beautiful manuscripts with intricate Celtic knot work. Different knots meant different things, each type having a history of its own. Because these were done as a labor of love and devotion for a higher power, the artwork became known as the work of the angels. For what my two cents are worth, I don't think the knot work has much bearing on the message being sent to you."

"Why do you say that? I've received so many messages to the contrary."

"Be that as it may, Willi, on the cards, the same pattern is used on all of them. That doesn't mean the person who left these doesn't have his own particular sick meaning he's giving to them."

"He? A man. I think of the cards, for some reason, as a feminine mode of communication."

"Not necessarily. Some of the most profound and insightful readers of the cards are men. Don't rule out a man, Willi Gallagher." Joni pushed her chair back. "Please stay for as long as you like. That's an invitation directly from Cousin Andrea, but you'll have to excuse me. I want a nap. The last night's festivities will last well into the wee morning hours, I'm sure."

Willi said her good-byes to Joni McDonald's back, the silver hair floating along behind, lifting and settling as her passing created a stir of breeze. Willi swallowed. Even the baby-fine tresses reminded her of knots tightening around her throat.

"Oh, no, I forgot." She jumped up and followed Joni McDonald into the house and caught up with her on a winding staircase. "Forgive me," she said to the ethereal figure that seemed to float on the riser. "The third card was found with . . . with a woman. A blackthorn, I believe."

"Oh, dear."

"Oh dear?"

"A violent card, the *straif,* one that indicates strife, struggle. Usually a fierce struggle of long duration. Such a fight can create an angel or a demon."

"That would make a sick kind of sense. What else can you tell me?"

"The blackthorn or *straif* has mean thorns. The blackthorn's wood was used for a weapon of death, the shillelagh."

"Shillelagh?"

"An Irish cudgel. At the fair there's a booth on the same row as mine. I'll point it out to you, tonight."

"Appreciated, but you'll be busy." Besides which, Tessa Aiken didn't die by any stretch of the imagination by cudgeling.

"One more thing comes to mind," Joni said. "The blackthorn is a harsh and driving influence, meaning there is no choice and no escape from its fierceness. A person using only the negative of this influence will only damage themselves in the end."

"There is a redeeming side, right?"

"Of course, Willi, but . . . it doesn't apply here, does it? The card was found on . . . on a dead woman, wasn't it?" Joni turned and floated up the stairs. Willi put one heavy foot in front of another and plodded downward and out into the unmerciful Texas heat. She'd gotten what she wanted all right. Info about the cards' meanings, but by hades and hell if she didn't feel even more entwined with vicious vines full of leaves—each leaf an unanswered question. Even the green fields and the hee-hawing burro failed to lift her spirits.

At least one thing had been accomplished. She knew what her next step would be. If all of these cards were tied to the murder, and the murder was connected to the acid from the high school labs, then the attack on Vic Ramirez fit into the picture somewhere. Yes, Vic was involved with whatever shenanigans went on between Burkhalter and Ventnor, but that was separate from the murder. Well, maybe.

There was one easy way to prove part of a nebulous theory growing in what Lassiter would no doubt call her "fertile imagination." Since it should be easy to prove, that probably meant she'd not be able to locate what she needed, but she had to try. And there wasn't any reason to tell Sheriff Tucker. After all, she was simply going to run by the high school. Might be good to let Principal Wiginton see her make an appearance, if only a brief one.

She grimaced at her watch. Yeah, yeah. She'd have time. She knew she was close to getting some answers. Her nose itched, and she could almost touch those answers in the darker corners of her mind. Where better to bring them to the forefront than those hallowed halls of learning? Perfectly safe place if she didn't go hunting around dark labs.

CHAPTER

18

Willi rushed into the high school. As she passed the glass-enclosed office, she tapped on the window and said hi to her principal. Sammie Yannich, on the phone, looked as pasty as a ghost. Until Sheriff Tucker decided to make a move about the exchange between the groups last night, Willi had to pretend she knew nothing. The secretary broke a pencil in the electric sharpener and threw it on her desk. Luckily, Willi only had to greet, not stop and talk to Sammie. Many teachers milled about. Evidently all were behind in preparation and were pulling some late hours.

Around the corner, she peered at the janitor's closet door. With care, she opened it. She moved step by step closer, looking all around before entering. She switched on the light. Mops and brooms, cleansers and water pails shared space with rolls of paper towels and toilet tissue. Willi looked behind each item, lifted those she could and pushed things aside.

Blue blazes and saddle sores. Nothing.

"What you doing, Miss Willi?" India Lou's ebony figure, all six feet of it, loomed in the doorway.

"Yikes!" Willi clutched her neck. "India Lou, don't sneak up on a person like that. Jeeze."

"I be very sorry, but bottom line is, what you doing in this here closet?"

"Shush. Looking for a clue."

"I done sniffed every bottle of cleaner in here. Ain't no blue stuff where green ought to be, and ain't no green where yellow ought to be. 'Nuther words, no acid."

"That's not what I'm looking for." Willi explained what she was after before getting down on her hands and knees to check the baseboards. "Might have fallen down here when the acid spilled."

India Lou searched the tops of the shelves. "This you lucky day, Miss Willi, sure is."

"You found it?"

India Lou held out a piece of cardboard. "Is this it?"

Only a corner of the Celtic card showed. "Wonder what happened to the rest of it?"

"Oh, Lawdy, that's gonna be on my head. Remember now, Vic Ramirez, he and the sheriff said it was just kids heard about the murder and copycatting?"

"Right?"

"So's there weren't no reason a body shouldn't clean up after the accident, right?"

"You recall, India Lou, sweeping up something like this piece?"

"Bottom line is, I sure do. Thought it was some playing card out of a deck of fifty-two."

Willi added the torn section of the Celtic card to the other two in the plastic bag. "Not to worry. This is enough. At least, I know that Vic Ramirez was a target, not a perpetrator in this instance. I'm not quite sure how, but that's important in . . . unraveling all these twisted vines. India Lou, don't mention this to anyone, you understand?"

"You gonna tell the sheriff?"

"Yes, when I have one or two other things cleared up, but not yet. He's working on another aspect of the case . . . or maybe, at least, a related case."

India Lou stuck a cleaning rag in her apron pocket. "Tell your Aunt Minnie I'm ready to come back to my regular job, would you? I got to stay busy, and just between us, my old knees just can't take this high school work no more."

"I'll tell her . . . and you don't tell anyone anything. I haven't even been in this closet."

India Lou grinned as she shut the door. "What closet?" She went down the hall humming an old hymn.

In her car, willi turned the ac on high along with her golden oldies station. "Do You Know the Way to San Jose" and "I'm Henry VIII, I Am," two of her least favorites, played through while she mulled over what to do next. She took deep breaths and wondered what Quannah would do. She groaned. Yeah, she could just imagine his instructions: *Figure out where it all began.* Well, Hell's bells and damned bats' tails, that's what she was *trying* to do.

Tie up all the loose ends. When all the little things are out of the way, the important things will stand out.

Great, so what did that mean at this point? She suddenly felt a great need for his counsel if nothing more than just to play the devil's advocate, make her think and reason it out. At The Apothecary Shoppe, the old-fashioned malt shop and drugstore, she stopped and ran in to use one of the three ancient enclosed telephone booths.

After opening sweet pleasantries and banter, she asked him, "Remember how you are all the time saying 'When all the little things are out of the way, the important things will stand out'?"

"Yes, *Winyan,* it is a basic in problem solving."

"Exactly how do you go about doing that on a case . . . I mean theoretically, of course?"

"Why do you ask, Gallagher? What are you doing? Where are you?"

"I asked the first question." She waited for a full twenty seconds, having to start on the twenty-one Mississippi before he finally relented with a huge sigh.

"If I'm working on a case, I write down where I've been, what I've seen, then highlight those items that raised my hackles. Ninety percent of the time those amount to worrisome things, taking up unconscious energy. Once those things are questioned and marked off, they need no longer take up your thoughts, thus—"

"Thus freeing your mind to consider only the more important. Okay. A list. I made one the night . . . but not with this perspective. Got you."

"Gallagher, is there something you need that—?"

"Did you get your office space cleared yet?"

"Close to it. Thought I might move in a few items this evening . . . if that's—"

"Oh, that's perfect. Yes, perfect . . . and Lassiter?"

"Uh-hm?"

"I'll have some things to . . . *share* with you when we meet at the festival tonight."

"Looking forward to it . . . I think. Gallagher, you will be careful and—"

"Don't be a worrywart. It's unbecoming in you, Big Chief."

"Okay, *Winyan,* you get all your school preparations ready. Want me to just pick you up there on my way?"

"Uh . . . no." Not a good idea since she wasn't going to be at the high school for the next half hour or so. "No, I'll want to come home for a shower before tonight's festivities. I'll meet you at the clubhouse."

"Gallagher, where are you?"

"Didn't we just go through that? Got to run. Lots of work to do."

"Stay safe, sweet woman, stay safe."

"Lassiter, sometimes I really love the way you say things." There was a lump in her throat.

When she got in the car this time, she switched from golden oldies to a country western station. Buck Owens sang out, "I feel a trembling in my knees . . ." and something about turning cloudy days to blue skies. Tammy Wynette belted out lyrics to "Stand by Your Man," something Willi fully intended to do but not give up her own identity in the process, thank you very much.

In fact, if her hunch worked out, she'd be able to clue him and Sheriff Tucker in about who killed Tessa Aiken. The drive to the marina end of the lake took only two songs more, one about "working on a feeling called love" by someone in the Cash family of singers and Mac Davis's "I Believe in Music." She drove into the marina parking lot and walked up to where the *Comanche Raider* berthed. About two hours of daylight left.

Okay, time to get answers about the small things. She rang a rope bell on the pier and waited. Neeper stuck his massive head out. "Ms. Gallagher. Come aboard, come aboard." He got her seated with a Dr Pepper in hand and yelled into the master bedroom, "Dan, Ms. Gallagher's here, and I got to go." To her he said, "He's in the shower. Be out in a few minutes. I hate to run, but make yourself to home."

"No problem. I know my way—" She smiled. "I'll just sit right here until he gets out. A question before you go, though."

Neeper's broad Oxhandler shoulders filled the cabin's doorway. He placed a Paul Bunyan–sized foot on the first riser of the stairs. "Yes, ma'am?"

"I'm just trying to tie up a few loose ends because India Lou asked me to."

"Oh, sure, and the sheriff, too, I bet." His eyes twinkled.

"Well, maybe." She shifted uneasily on the sofa. "That day out at the beach. You all were with Tessa, right?"

"Yep, sure. Me and Dan, Vic, and what's-her-name, uh . . . Saralee. Don't know how I forgot her name even for a minute. She's sure a pretty blue-eyed doll."

"You mean brown-eyed?"

Neeper rolled his eyes. "Trust me. You and Dan both must be color blind."

"I'm pretty confused, and it's not even an important thing. You could be right."

Neeper tapped his massive foot and stepped up one more riser.

"Neeper, you were my student the same year you were a student under Principal Bernie Burkhalter back then. You find it obviously easy to address him by . . . by Bernie, but you . . . still use Ms. with me."

Neeper grinned. "Purely out of respect, Ms. Gallagher. I don't want you to think that I think . . . well, you know, you and Dan . . . weren't you all going out for awhile?"

"Only as colleagues."

"He saw it differently."

"I know, but it wasn't."

Neeper stepped back down and hovered over her. "You want me to stay? Until you talk to him . . . I don't want you being—" He peered at his watch and worry lines etched his forehead. "I don't want you to feel uncomfortable."

"Neeper, no. Go ahead. Dan and I are fine. No problem. One more thing. You remember the scarf Tessa wore out at the beach that day?"

"Naw, but I'm not good at things like that. I guess I'll run."

He did. Faster than a roadrunner. Willi ignored the risqué periodicals and chose *Time* magazine to thumb through. Politics, sports, and world tragedies weren't what she was concerned with, though. She tiptoed to the bedroom door, put her ear to it, and heard the shower and Dan's humming.

She shoved the magazine of world tragedies away and concentrated on the homegrown variety. What common tendril held this tragedy together? Obviously, Vic could be such a connection. He had a commitment to something nefarious—drugs probably—and he knew Tessa. Also, he'd almost suffered her fate.

Well, the same could be said of Bernie Burkhalter. He had a triple twining of vines around him. First, the Tyler, Texas, connection with Tessa Aiken. There'd been accusations—well, proof in Dan's eyes—of a drug problem that might very well be linked back to those junior college days. Then the ugly exchange last night, which Burkhalter had a share in, didn't paint a pretty picture of the former superintendent. With two fingers, Willi pinged her forehead. And don't forget Burkhalter's death machine, the yellow Cadillac.

Willi crossed one leg over the other and toed the table of magazines. Damn, if all this didn't want to make her cry. So many of her students ending up dead or implicated. Sure, implicated.

Willi rubbed her temples. Tessa murdered. Vic Ramirez into a possible drug ring. Even Sammie's daughter was lost to her family and friends forever due to stupidity. Brown-eyed, dark haired girl of simple features in a family of redheads, she'd been no outstanding beauty, but she made up for it, according to Dan, in intelligence and sweet disposition. But Sunny wasn't in the picture anymore. The four fast friends now were Tessa, Neeper, Vic, and Dan.

Willi swallowed and bit her bottom lip. She just couldn't get her mind to wrap around the right details. Those tendrils would need pruning slowly and a layer at a time. She bent over to straighten the magazines she'd pushed hither and yon. When Dan walked into the area, topmost in her hand was one titled *Playgirl.*

He said, "Glad to see you admire the male . . . uh . . . *virtues,* Willi."

She threw the magazine down with *Playboy* and other such periodicals. She stood to face him. "There are some in you I don't admire at all."

He put one of his baseball caps on backwards. "What's not to love?" His voice ricocheted off the walls.

"Stop with the clowning. I want some straight answers, Dan Oxhandler, and I want them now."

"Okay, okay, what's the beef, Willi? Why are your undies in a wad?"

"To make sure you understand how serious this is, first of all my undies are absolutely none of your damned business, and from this point on you call me *Ms.* Gallagher. Straight on that?"

Dan gulped and twisted his cap around so the bill hid part of the hurt she saw in his eyes. Too bad, but he had to get past the bubba stage of his life sometime. "You told me the other night you remembered the Irish quilt square Tessa wore that day at the beach."

"Right. We kidded her about it." His voice was turned down to a less intensive volume.

"Neeper didn't remember."

Dan shrugged. "Told you before. Neeper's the smart one as far as books go, but the everyday little details bore him. Why is this scarf so important?"

"It's one of those niggling little things that have to be cleared up, okay? So, what happened to the quilt square, Dan? Any ideas?"

"Naw, how would I know? I guess it was in the Caddy where Tessie . . . where Tessie . . . died."

"You called her Tessie."

"Well, yeah, we did sometimes."

"Hmm." Willi wrinkled her brow. "Someone else . . . oh, well, that's not important right now. When did you last see the scarf?"

"Willi, this is getting old. On her head at the beach."

"Did she come by here—the *Comanche Raider*—after you all went swimming?"

"Naw, she didn't approve of our . . . *literature* any more than you do, Will—uh—*Ms.* Gallagher. Didn't we just have this same conversation last night?" Dan pulled his bill up a little. "She wore it in swimming, and it didn't come off. I don't think I could have wrestled it off her head."

"Dan, what if I were to tell you I know for a fact Tessa's Irish chain quilt square was here on this boat after . . . *after* . . . Tessa was murdered?"

Dan's eyes narrowed. "I'd say your source was lying through their teeth. I may not be the most noble of the male species, *Ms.* Gallagher, but I'm not a bad person. I live my life open and honest." He waved his hands around to indicate this. "If someone found such a thing here— and I'd sure like to know *who* and *when*—then the scarf was planted here by someone other than me or Neeper, I guarantee. You better check on the honesty of your source."

Willi's cheeks burned. "Uh . . . just who all was on your
boat right after Tessa's death?"

"I believe I answered those questions the other night
when we looked at the yearbooks, and I don't want to and
don't have to answer anymore, *Ms. High-and-Mighty Gallagher.*"

She sighed. "Sorry. We're colleagues. Please forgive me
for that outburst. Of course, you can continue to call me
Willi."

Dan grinned. "Well, shootfire. Sure. You're probably
just suffering from a bad hair day. Womenfolk do now and
again."

She bit the inside of her mouth and managed not to
growl. She left and headed toward the high school again.
She did need an hour or two to prepare things in her classroom. Once there, she began cutting, taping, tacking, and
stapling bulletin board displays, a basically mindless task,
which left her gray cells free for more important considera-
tions. Picking up where she'd left off before on her mental
list of suspects, she probed the idea of Vic Ramirez again.

Obviously, after last night's rendezvous and exchange,
he was involved with drugs. This was a second connection
to Tessa—Tessie Aiken. He also had access to the school
by his own admission. As he was the fireman responsible
for updates and spot checks, he had a master key to each of
the district's campuses. If he had a master key, then he
could have access to the labs and the acid.

Willi stepped down from a footstool and admired the
display about the era of Camelot. Needed straightening.
She stepped up again. Hm. If Vic Ramirez had access, he
could easily have gotten acid and used it to mutilate Tessa.
He'd been part of the group on and off at the lake that day.
Willi shut her eyes to picture a scene of Vic attacking the
petite Tessa. Being a fighter, she would have struggled
madly to escape. Willi sighed. Yes, Tessa would run toward
people—the parking area, but perhaps in passing would try
door handles. Finding the Caddy unlocked, she would—

No, no. She was in the Caddy before someone got to her.

Someone whom she trusted sat beside her. Either a passenger got in at the lake or at the high school.

Willi again shook her head. The trellis pictured around the castle of Camelot seemed to swell, and the vines writhed. Willi put her hands to her head. That could have been Vic Ramirez. Or Neeper or Dan. Anyone at the lake or school. And here she was again full circle with questions, questions, questions. Hell's bells. For numerous reasons, Tessa could have been in the Caddy and for just as many reasons someone could have ridden with her. Most likely unless the killer told, no one would ever know how Tessa came to be attacked while in Burkhalter's Cadillac. Willi opened up her stapler and slammed it smack-dab in the middle of the castle.

Someone screamed. Willi dropped the stapler, stumbled off the stool, and ran down the hall toward a general melee of folks gathering around the office. Saralee stood at the edge of the group and tried to see over the heads in front of her.

Willi asked, "What's going on?"

Saralee's smooth voice, in contrast to her fiery curls, uttered, "I can't see. I think someone said . . . someone said . . ." agitation make her normal voice crack ". . . said she was dead."

"Who?" Willi pushed her way through the crowd. "Come on."

"No, oh my God, what if—"

Willi peered over her shoulder to see tears in Saralee's eyes. She put a comforting arm around the younger teacher's shoulders. "It's best to find out the worst. Then we can deal with whatever it is. Stay with me."

A white-faced Mr. Wiginton looked out of his office and signaled for Willi to follow him inside. She pulled Saralee along for moral support, and because she looked like she might faint any moment if Willi turned loose. Wiginton shooed the others away, closed the blinds, and locked the doors. He said, "You two have cool heads. Help me deal with this. Saralee, call 911. Willi, help *her*." He pointed to Mrs. Yannich seated at her desk.

Willi rushed over. "My gosh. She's had another collapse." Well, no wonder. Out until the wee hours of the night, trespassing, trafficking in God only knew what, and drinking herself into a stupor. Nevertheless, Willi bent down to the woman who lay with her head on one side of an open ledger. The side Willi viewed had fresh welts, created in the same manner as those of Tessa Aiken. Willi gasped and covered her mouth. No matter what the woman had been up to last night, she didn't deserve this happening to her. Willi used her fingers to probe for a pulse. There was a strong one.

"Can you hear me? We're getting help."

Willi leaned closer. Mrs. Yannich's lids fluttered, and she peered lucidly into Willi's eyes. She whispered something at the same moment sirens blared outside the building. "What? Try again. I'm so sorry. Help is on the way." Her babbling wasn't helping the poor woman. Willi patted her shoulder. "Never mind. Don't talk. The ambulance will be here any minute. Right, Saralee?"

The young woman at her shoulder, never robust in coloring, seemed ghostlike. Tears streamed down her heavily made-up face. "Yes . . . oh, yes, I called."

The secretary grabbed hold of Willi's arm and pulled her down again. She even scrabbled and pulled on Saralee's long sleeve. She whispered, "Sun."

"What?" they both asked in unison.

Ambulance attendants pushed both women out of the way. Within a few moments, they had Sammie strapped to a cot. They tied tubes and bottles every which way while Wiginton bustled himself and them outside the office to stand with the rest of the faculty. Saralee's cool and in-control facade had completely melted away. She shook so hard, Willi feared the paramedics might be needed for her. Saralee said, "I've never seen anyone . . . anyone. Did you understand what she was trying to say? I couldn't. I wanted to, but I couldn't."

Wiginton spoke in a fatherly but stern voice. "Pull yourself together. You did a commendable job in there. Both of you. Don't fall apart on us now. We've enough to deal with." He patted both of them kindly on the shoulder.

Willi again hugged the younger woman. "No, I didn't understand either. Unfortunately, this isn't my first experience with such things. I can only tell you folks say the most idiotic and nonsensical things in what they consider their last moments. Something to do with the brain's synapses misfiring. She had a strong pulse. She'll be okay." Bile rose from Willi's cavorting stomach. She went to the water fountain and used her hands in the spray to pat her hot cheeks. She stood for the longest time staring into the flowing water fountain, seeing each individual little droplet in the sunlight. She had no idea how long the moment of déjà vu held her in its embrace. Neeper stood at her elbow. "Okay, Willi?"

"No, I'm not okay. I think it's time we talked about that venison pie."

"What do you mean, Ms. Gallagher?"

"The day of the murder. You were out at the lake. Then you had a late-afternoon lunch at Oxhandler's Barbecue and Emporium."

He took her elbow and guided her outside the front doors. He said from the corner of his mouth, "All that's correct. What's bothering you?"

"You can't be that forgetful or worse."

"It's hard to defend myself if I don't know what you're after."

"Your Uncle Ozzie never serves venison in any dish."

Neeper frowned at her. "And what does that have to do with the price of jalapeños in Texas?"

"You told Sheriff Tucker and me . . . and . . . what's-his-face . . . uh . . . Officer Piedra you had venison."

"Humph. I don't know what I had. Guess I just said the first thing that came to mind. Didn't think the food I ate had importance as far as Tessa's mutilation and killing were concerned."

Willi narrowed her eyes and sighed. "Maybe you just didn't notice what you ate, seeing as how you were across from some beautiful little number."

"Huh?"

"According to Ozzie Oxhandler and Margarita Uriegas."

"Margarita of the red, red jeans. Ah, well, she always had a good memory. Could remember that elements chart easy as that." He snapped his fingers.

"Neeper!"

"Don't know why you're so upset over what I ate and who I ate with."

"Because, you stubborn man, you're my coworker and friend. I really don't want your ornery hide considered as a suspect."

His eyes opened wide as if he'd never considered such a possibility.

Willi said, "Typical absentminded professor." She shook her finger in his face. "Maybe absentminded and infatuated with a new young teacher, huh? Ozzie said she was a red-head. Saralee, right? I should have thought to ask her in the first place. She *would* remember what you all ate." Willi turned and opened the door.

Neeper removed her hand and shoved the glass door closed. "Whoa, Miss Marple of the range. You've got your Colt .45 half-cocked."

It was her turn to say, "huh?"

"Haley Himes kept me company that day."

Willi eyed him and shook her head. "Don't remember her."

"Why should you? She's a paramedic I met in Fort Worth. She called me on her cell phone on a return trip from delivering a patient to Houston. She didn't want to eat alone." He pulled out his billfold, riffled a couple of cards, and pulled one out. "Here, Miss Marple of the range, is her business number so you can set your mind at ease."

Willi pretended to blow smoke from the end of the Colt and holster it. "Thanks. I'll do that." Took her only a few sentences with Haley Himes to confirm his story and to determine that they ate Oxhandler's regular fare that day.

As they went inside, she frowned and said, "And just what do you mean, Miss Marple of the range?"

He just shook his head and said, "One of Quannah's phrases for you, not mine. Poor man."

CHAPTER
19

Another round of interviews occurred within the next two hours. Sheriff Tucker, Willi, and Officer Jon Piedra used the upstairs teachers' lounge again. Willi kept glancing at her wristwatch. She wanted time to run home, do a facial of cool cucumbers and honey, shower, and change into her costume for the evening. She'd need a few minutes to go over the little speech she had to give to thank all the participants. Oh, let's see, and then there were the special gifts she'd gotten for the committee officers. Mustn't forget to put those in the car. She rubbed her eyes and tried to concentrate on the questions—the same questions over and over again—being asked those at the high school.

The good news was that only one person now held a key to the new lock on the lab doors. That dubious honor belonged to Principal Wiginton until school officially opened and until the case was solved. The bad news was the acid could have been procured before the new locks were done. The worst news was anyone in the building could have done the deed. When the last person—Saralee York—shut the door, Willi sighed.

Sheriff Tucker eyed his deputy. "Officer Piedra, that Miss York seems a right nice young lady, but—"

Jon Piedra's face, always a mask of strength, froze. "Sir?"

Sheriff Tucker stifled a sneeze long enough to pull out a bandanna with purple and green squares on it. "Not to worry, not to worry. Last case here in Nickleberry is where I met my Aggie. Just going to tell you, they don't come along but once in a lifetime. Word to the wise, that's all, word to the wise."

"Thanks, Sheriff. I've known her a long time."

Willi stiffened. "She's only been here this summer."

Piedra nodded. "Right." The man of few words paused. "I met her once in Tyler when she worked there. They called in extra help from all over for a rave get-together. She protested having the rave but helped set up security since a lot of her students were going to be present."

"Like I said, a right nice young lady." The sheriff folded his bandanna and put it away. "Now, Miss Willi, let's touch base on what's going on. For instance, your trip to Tyler with your Aunt Minnie. Your visit to Oxhandler's Emporium. And . . . and a certain *tennis shoe.* Let's start with the papers, okay?"

"About those papers, Sheriff, uh . . . they were taken . . . but . . . *but* . . . Aunt Minnie said the archives lady is faxing them again to me today. In fact, she even found more, from some hospital. Maybe having to do with drugs taken from there or someone being admitted for drug rehab. I'm not sure. Aunt Minnie does get facts mixed, but I'll have them all for you tomorrow."

"What happened to your first set?"

"Well, they were stolen from my briefcase . . . here at the school during a meeting we had one night. At least, I think so." She sighed down to her toenails. For some reason to which she could put no name other than *uneasiness,* she didn't want to discuss the details of the Irish chain quilt square, the Celtic cards and their convoluted meanings. She wanted things clearer in her mind before she brought those to the forefront. "I can tell you about the

Oxhandler Restaurant situation. They don't serve venison, and Neeper Oxhandler is an absentminded professor." She went into more detail. For the jillionth time, she glanced at her watch. Okay, forget the cucumber and honey facial. She'd just take a quick shower.

"Ah-choo!" Sheriff Tucker punctuated her last sentence before grabbing his bandanna again. He snapped his fingers in front of her face. "Earth to Miss Willi. Now, about the tennis shoe?"

"Tennis shoe?" Willi opened her eyes widely. "I've no idea what you're talking about. Is that a clue in the case?" *Oh, no. What was there about that dang shoe that could have connected it to her?*

This time Sheriff Tucker sighed and pulled his earlobe. "Mayhap, mayhap." He eyed her for a half-dozen heartbeats. Her own cantered somewhere near fifty rpm's, but she kept her nonchalance. Jon Piedra, a quiet shadow in the corner, shifted and put his pen and paper away.

Willi used the small distraction. "Sheriff Tucker, I do have lots of things to tell you and to show you." *Like three Celtic Tree Cards. Like nebulous thoughts concerning the coterie of Neeper, Dan, Vic, and Tessa. Like a growing suspicion of just what was meant by "find out where it all began."* "But, could we postpone the discussion until tomorrow? I'm to be out at the lake for the last night of the Irish Fling Festival. And, I believe, a certain Agatha Kachelhoffer will be waiting for her feller, too."

Sheriff Tucker stiffened and pushed his Stetson back on his graying but red-tipped banty curls. "Now see here, Miss Willi, *bidness*—law business always comes first." That point made, he added, "Course if you held anything pertaining to the identity of the murderer, I know you'd tell me that now, right?"

"Of course, but I don't know. In fact, all I've gotten are more questions."

"Sometimes," Jon Piedra offered, "it's best not to ask so many questions. Answers will come when you just sit and think about things."

Willi raised an eyebrow. "Typical man, hm? Trying to keep the *little lady* from nosing around too much."

Jon Piedra touched the brim of his hat. "Not at all. Sheriff Tucker trusts you to be a liaison, and I respect that. I just hope you've not gone beyond those bounds. Loose lips sink ships, that's all. I've seen many an informant end up with busted kneecaps and worse. I don't even want to think of you in such a condition, Ms. Gallagher."

"Thanks, I think. My lips have nothing of import to divulge. Yet."

"She's a stubborn lady, right, Sheriff?"

"Now, you're beginning to know her, Piedra. Okay, Miss Willi, we'll go over all your *questions* tomorrow. Don't seem like I've got any answers about the attacks against Tessa or Mrs. Yannich right now, anyhoo."

Willi nodded. *Or the attack on Vic Ramirez.* Hm. She'd have to remember to add that to her discussion tomorrow. Right now, she had a date with a bar of creamy Irish Spring and a steamy shower. She'd make a call from the office and get Elba and Aggie to pick up the gifts. "Okay, I'm out of here. See you both at the lake. And remember the motto for tonight: Dress in Green for the Fling."

As she went out the door, she could have sworn they both growled. "Men—go figure."

After showering and shampooing, she dressed in her Irish maiden-of-the-castle costume. Full skirted and short to reveal green and white striped panties and lots of bristly petticoat, it cinched in at the waist with crisscrossed ties. The low-cut blouse with tiny cups for sleeves, revealed above its lacy edge more of her bosom than had ever seen daylight in even her bathing suit. Her hair, crimped and curled, fell in cascades from a ponytail. Her black hose matched the edging on her buckled baby doll heels. She peered in the mirror. Ah, well, no time left. She'd have to do.

Quannah rang the doorbell. She leaned out the window. "Use the key, knave."

He pounded up the stairs. "Knave?"

"Knight? Whatever, sounded right at the time."

He stood at the doorway a moment, walked around her, and eyed her up and down. As he winked, he let out a wolf whistle that ended in his throwing his head back and howling.

Her cheeks grew pleasantly warm, and she slapped at the vest of his jig costume. "Hush, you'll have every coyote in the county yelping." She lowered and locked the window. "What are you doing here? I thought we were meeting at the clubhouse."

"We are . . . if I let you out of the house . . . hmm." He grabbed her around the waist, bent, and laid of row of butterfly kisses along her neck. Finally, he touched his lips to hers. Drawing back with obvious reluctance, he said, "Where are they?"

Somewhat cross-eyed and mellowed by the nearness of him, she murmured an inane, "Huh?"

"The tickets for the gifts. That's why I'm here. Elba called and said she couldn't pick them up. I volunteered, but I need the receipts or something."

"Or course." She took a steadying breath. "They're here . . . somewhere . . . uh . . . no, downstairs in the nookery."

"In the nookery? In which of the thousand little places should I look?"

"Beside the computer. On the desk. Maybe in front of the fax machine?"

"*Winyan,* I'll find them. Run along. I'll catch up."

She grinned up at him and batted her lashes. "*Pilamaya ye.*"

He clicked his heels and bowed. "You're very welcome." He bounded down the stairs as fast as he'd come up them. As she more carefully stepped down, she peeked into the room he had cleaned out. My gosh, he already had a desk and a leather couch and . . . and other manly looking details strewn about. Even a saddle in the corner. She smiled. *This weekend. Yes. It was going to happen. This weekend.*

In the car, Willi opted not to turn on her radio but instead to use the twenty minutes' travel time on the winding Licorice Lane to mull over what she'd learned the last few days. The Kachelhoffer sisters' readings, right on the mark, had said she'd be lied to by many women. Samantha Yannich had certainly not told all the truth about any number of things. Perhaps even something that might have led up to a sadistic killer attacking her. Rain flashed from the sky with no warning. Just a soft drizzle, barely enough to justify the windshield wipers.

"No, not tonight." Well, it could stop as suddenly as it started. She felt a sickening pull from her steering wheel. Whoa, slow down. She wasn't ready to join the angels, not just when her life was opening up to some wonderful possibilities.

Her wonderful possibility honked his horn behind her and indicated she was to pull over.

"Not the best of places, Lassiter," she said as she got out. He signaled her to get on the far side of the vehicles away from the road. She pulled an old sweater over her head. In the bushes and tendrils, she tried to keep from tripping.

He handed her a fax. "This came in just as I picked up the receipts. It was about one of your teachers, so I thought it might be something you needed for tonight."

She glanced at the name at the top. "Hmm. Must have been that little extra Aunt Minnie was so excited about finding, but it doesn't mean squat to me right now. But . . . thanks. I'll study on it later."

"Guess I was wrong. Maybe I just didn't want to see you out gallivanting in that pretty outfit. Figured you'd need protection." He patted her on the butt.

"Quannah Lassiter, people we know do pass along this road. Stop that." She giggled and pushed him. He lost his balance, caught her hand and for a millisecond she thought she'd saved him from falling. In the darkness neither had seen the edge of the steep ravine covered with those damned vines. His slick dance shoes gave way, and he crashed backward. She stood pigeon-toed in a Betty Boop stance. Crashes and curses reached her ears. She grimaced. When he rose up, shook himself, and started the climb upward, she backed up.

Hands together in prayer she said, "Oops."

"Grrr."

"Now, let me just get that branch off your head. And here's something inside your vest."

With her tender ministrations the vest ripped down the back, and her hands came away with two pieces.

"Double oops?"

"Gallagher, Gallagher, Gallagher."

"You're alive. Uh . . . gotta run this way . . . you have to go back that way. See you." She jumped in her car just as rain started in earnest, gunned the motor, and roared out of sight. In the light of the dashboard she glanced again at the fax sheet, a release form for Saralee York from a Tyler hospital. The words *reconstructive surgery* caught her eye before she threw the sheet onto the seat. "Aunt Minnie, why you'd think that was important, I don't know. So many young women opt for boob jobs and tummy tucks and what have you."

She slowed the car to the posted thirty miles per hour around the many switchbacks and curves. Willi sighed. This weather was going to make a twenty-minute trip take half an hour. So, back to considering the facts. Maybe even Hortense had fibbed . . . well, perhaps had just not quoted Tessa correctly. Hard to believe her last words would have been about señor somebody or other.

A roadrunner raced in front of her tires, Willi braked, and the car slid. She corrected the wheel, gulped, and slowed down more. The rain was so hard she couldn't see more than two feet in front of the car. Hmm. Wait a minute. What if the last words were to give a clue as to the killer, not some nonsensical rambling? That just made more sense with Tessa and her lawyer's mind. What if the words had to do with *senior* or *senior year* or something along those lines? Yes, that would make sense. *Win. Señor.* Maybe a part of a sentence like *when* I was a *senior.*

That had to be where all this began. Everything seemed to point back to the years past. Okay, okay. Willi squinted to see the road. Go with that idea a moment. Those attacked were Tessa Aiken, Vic Ramirez, and . . . Sammie Yannich. What did those folks have in common from ten years ago? High school graduation. Sammy's kid was one of the graduates.

Ohmygod, ohmygod, oh my God. She knew the common denominator. It'd been right there in the yearbooks she and Dan looked at. Yannich's daughter. Acid accident. Willi could barely breathe as the kaleidoscope of ideas shifted, remolded, and shifted again. Motive? Yes, a young girl who felt her life had been ruined by the accidental mutilation. How many psychology books, how many Maury and Oprah and other shows were filled with people who'd held grudges over smaller things all their lives?

She'd come back to take revenge. Yes, but after years of changes. Samantha's daughter, Sunny, was the Nickelberry nemesis. Willi just as quickly dismissed the idea. How stupid. No one had seen her around. Surely, Sammie would have said something if her long-lost child had come home.

Not if . . . not if she didn't know.

Willi's stomach lurched. Not if she weren't recognizable. Not if reconstructive surgery had hidden the facial scars and such. Hell's bells. That meant others were in danger, others who had caused the girl grief. Tessa had stopped running around with her and had even been one of the nominees for prom queen. Vic Ramirez—ohmygosh—had stood Sunny Yannich up on the most important date of a girl's high school years.

Sure, her parents had refused to let her have a timely operation to keep her from suffering those indignities. So, she'd suffered at their hands, too. Burkhalter was now Sammy's heartmate so by reason of proximity to a hated one, would be a target.

Sunny couldn't make her dead father pay, but she could get back at her mother's present-day boyfriend. Easy to get him implicated with the use of his yellow Cadillac. Then she went after her mother. If she'd stoop to killing her own mother, she wouldn't think twice about her past classmates . . . and . . . the teacher most responsible. But he, too, had passed away. Yes, the science teacher whose materials were being moved from lab to lab that day had died only a few months ago. Dan and Neeper and Vic, too, would be in possible danger.

Why had Willi alone received the warnings, then? Thunder boomed and scared her so badly she jumped and hit her head on the car top. Willi had been the only one who had comforted the girl, even though she hardly knew her, barely remembered her, in fact. But Dan had reminded Willi about her own kindness. Willi was the one searching for clues and getting close. Or, at least, Sunny thought she was close, so Willi was warned off. Sunny had stolen books from the school library and from Willi because those were the two places Willi would consider looking and might put two and two together. Everything added up. Now, who the hell was Sunny and how could . . . how could she fool everyone?

A black pickup with spotlights on top of the cab rode up on her bumper. Willi gunned the motor to give him room. Obviously, he just didn't see her in the darkness and rain. Her wheels squealed as she took a corner too fast. The dark monster bumped her car this time.

"What in blue blazes? Neeper?" That had to be him. What did he think he was doing?

She sped up a bit and moved to the right side as far as she could to let him pass. He hit her again, tilting her car into a circle. Her heart literally in her throat, she managed to straighten the wheel. "Are you crazy, you son of a bitch?"

As she got a little ahead of him, she glanced down at the sheet, which had floated onto her lap. As she shoved it away, she gulped.

"It's not Neeper. No, it's *her.* Oh my dear Lord."

Willi finally put all the colorful pieces together and glanced at the fax of the hospital bill. "Reconstructive surgery. Saralee York. Sunny Yannich. She hadn't even changed her initials, but she changed her appearance."

Of course, Neeper saw her as brown-eyed. When Dan saw her blue-eyed as Willi had, Sunny—Saralee had worn

contacts. The long sleeves, the high-necked blouses covered scars that surgery couldn't completely obliterate. The
thick makeup. No mousy brown hair. Saralee's bright red
locks reminded her own mother of a cousin. Was that when
the secretary had her breakdown, when she realized that
her child had come back to kill?

The truck roared around a corner and raced across the
slick road. Willi swerved onto the left side of the yellow
line. The pickup followed, breathing down her bumper
again. Willi braked. In the expected reaction of the truck
doing the same, she sped away, putting space between
them. If she could just get on a straight section and off
Licorice Lane, she'd have more control. She rolled down
the window to see better. Rain splattered inside, but she
could view the edge of the road more clearly. The droplets
and wind blew that damned sheet onto the window. Just as
the Tyler hospital fax sheet floated outward, the name of the
person paying the bill registered. The black racing truck
crashed hard into the bumper, then into the side of her car,
just as she'd seen a hundred times on *COPS*.

Her car barely missed a huge oak tree, but the Standing
Person cut off her exit on the driver's side. She scrambled
out the passenger side. Up on the slick tarmac, the truck
squealed to a halt and turned. The top cab lights searched
along the road edge and finally held her in their beams. Her
mouth was so dry she couldn't swallow, and tears streamed
down her face. Her heel caught on the bottom of the door-
jamb. Oh, no. She didn't want to die like Tessa Aiken, half-
in, half-out of the car. Shit. She pulled and pulled. The
damned buckle caught on twisted metal.

She bent down. Her fingers shook so badly she couldn't
feel the leather strap much less the buckle.

"Where *is* he?"

Not Saralee York at all. No, it was the one who'd paid
finally for her surgery, the one who had known her a long
time. Jon Piedra, who'd been a young cop when he met the
beautiful Sunny, who'd witnessed her pain and agony but
still loved her. Oh God, yes, he was, as Sheriff Tucker said,

of the perfect cop mentality. He wanted to help those in need. And Sunny Yannich had needed him. *Knots of the angels. Killing knots. Love knots.*

The truck lumbered slowly.

"Damn you to Hell. Think you've got me trapped. Take your time, you son of a bitch."

She finally freed the buckle and hobbled away with one shoe on. Vines wrapped around her legs, pulling her, tripping her, until she rolled down the embankment, into muddy water. She pulled at the tendrils around her legs.

A pickup door slammed, and crashing behind her increased her efforts. He easily jumped around her and in front. He stood there in the beam of the pickup's headlights. Quiet. Quiet and steady Jon Piedra. With a blue-capped bottle in his hand.

He said, "The pain doesn't last long if taken directly down the throat."

Willi shut her mouth tightly and tried to back away, but the vines held her in place. Wind picked up, the oak tree's branches above swayed and bent furiously.

"Up to eighty-mile winds predicted for tonight. What with the rain and all, you ran off the road. Would have been good for you if it could've ended that way. I'm sorry."

"You won't get away with this. Quannah will hound you to the end of your days. He will know. One way or another, he will know."

"But he's a lawman. He'll need a body for proof. There won't be one."

"Why?" she screamed. Maybe someone would pass, would see the truck, the crashed car with motor still running. Keep him talking.

She moved one foot, eased it from the vines. A branch fell from the oak tree and hit her arm. "Damn."

"If someone sees the vehicles, no problem. You'll be dead, Willi, and it's easier if you accept that now. It's ten times harder on Samantha Yannich. She didn't see me attack, but she knows someone has to come finish the job. So, you see, we have to hurry. I've a lot to do tonight before going to the Irish Fling Festival. Hey, you should be happy. I wore green."

"You sick . . . son of—" She changed tactics in midsentence. "Sunny couldn't want this, she wasn't that type of person." She had to yell above the increased wind, and both she and Piedra were dodging small limbs and leaves. "She was a teen, frightened and scared when she made such horrible verbal threats years ago."

"Sunny is beautiful. Inside and now . . . outside. I take care of her. She doesn't know I'm protecting her. I don't want her to feel stifled. She's suffered enough. I'm here to see she never has to face those who ridiculed and tormented her and drove her from her home."

The rain stopped, and for a moment, total quiet reigned. Willi's stomach churned, and bile rose. *The eye of the storm.* In more ways than one she was in the eye of the storm, her adversary far stronger than she, and she was going to . . . no. *No!* She was by damned not going to die. She fell and rolled forward instead of back as she thought he'd expect. Sure enough, he dove right over her as she continued rolling down the embankment. The wind roared over her head. A fence post with barbed wire flew near her, ripping skin from her arm as it flew on past. Behind her, such a rush and roar resounded she figured lightning had hit and blown up the pickup. She scrambled up, searched up the hillside, but could not see Piedra. She turned tail to run up the other side of the embankment but only went a few steps before she was slammed toward the roots of a tree by the strongest wind she'd ever encountered. Her head contacted the ground. She tasted blood and mud.

Oh, the light hurt, what in blue blazes were all these leprechauns doing in her dreams? And with that light. She brushed it away. A cacophony of voices rose around her.

"Well, is she gonna be in this dangblame world anytime soon, Doc? This is enough to scare a body's innards, enough to make a lady lose control of her senses, might near made me lose control of my dang bladder. Lord knows that oak tree splitting in half and killing Piedra might just as easily have landed on her."

"Elba?" Willi managed to whisper.

"Sister, she's trying to speak. Hush and listen." Agatha's peacock colors and her huge, round earrings registered before Willi shut her eyes. Agatha's voice continued above her. "Yes, it's just a shame, he had that bottle of acid in his hand. To have to go to your grave with no recognizable face. Tragic, all so tragic."

A warm and strong hand held hers. *"Winyan."* Lassiter seemed to choke up on the word. What was wrong with him? "Gallagher, can you hear—?"

Willi popped open her eyes again. Oh, that light.

"Gallagher, you're going to—"

His words were cut off by a huge nurse who pushed everyone back. Willi peered for a moment straight into the eyes of Nurse Rufflestone. *Hell. She was in Hell. With leprechauns and gypsies, her sweet chieftain and the nurse who gargled with sulfur.*

Another voice broke through the miasma. "You'll not be taking the care of this one under your devilish wings, that you won't. Unhand the girl. Quannah Lassiter, stop that woebegone sniveling act and demand another nurse. Be quick about it, or Viola Fiona—and that would be me, you know—will be kicking your backside back to the very Black Hills, sacred though they may be."

A night in the hospital under the care of a private nurse did wonders for her. The evening of the next day, she sat on her front porch, rocking beside her visitor, India Lou. Her dark skin glowed in the porch light. "Thanky, Miss Willi. We can lay ghosts to rest, now. My, my how lives do turn out and around and about again."

The scent of late roses filled Willi's nostrils. Everything seemed to smell sweeter the last forty-eight hours. She figured near-death experiences made small things in life very precious. "Very true, friend. I'm glad Viola Fiona's lawyers convinced Ventnor to spill the frijole pot all over himself and Burkhalter. Guess the ending of this tragedy explains all those dreams about the white and black wolves trying to work things out. I certainly had fed the darkness more than trusting in the innate goodness of folks."

Elba and Agatha on the porch swing nodded. Elba said, "Them drug-pushing crooked superintendents is out of the picture, thank goodness. Hope the school board can hire a decent man or woman. Bet they'll double-check credentials this time around."

Agatha piped up. "Oh, I'm sure. I'm still a little peeved with Brigham."

"Why?" Willi asked.

"He could have saved us all a lot of worry if we'd known Vic Ramirez was not only a fireman but occasionally worked undercover on drug stings."

"True," Willi said, "but I suppose that might have jeopardized his cover, so to speak. I know one young lady who is really glad he's on the right side of the law."

India Lou rocked and nodded in time. "That wouldn't be a little lady down to the Oxhandler's Emporium, one what wears them tight red jeans?"

"You're in the loop, India Lou," Willi said. "Margarita Uriegas is a wonderful person and deserves the same. And so does Sunny Yannich. No, she legally changed her name to Saralee York. She really had no idea what was going on until the attack on her mother. Got to give it to the girl. It took all she had to even think of her one defender as the perp and to tell Sheriff Tucker about her suspicions. She and Sammie need each other now. Sunny—Saralee had come home to work her way back into her circle of friends and family slowly. She was going to eventually reveal herself as her psychiatrists told her to. She'd no idea of what her love for Officer Piedra and his for her had made him plan for all these years and finally act upon."

"And you can be sure by all that's green, the good will come to the surface, that it will." Viola Fiona rounded the corner. Following her, in all their Irish garb, were the Oxhandler cousins, Vic Ramirez, and Quannah sans his vest. Margarita Uriegas, in a red Mexican skirt, placed a cake on the side table. Hortense made room for her salsa and tortillas. In their black and white, the Horsenettle twins, offered up steaming enchiladas and quesadillas. Guess after a week, everyone had grown tired of Irish fare, delicious as it was. Quannah and Dan placed a harp at one end of the porch. Joni McDonald, her Landis cousins, a guitarist and a flute player joined the growing crowd.

"What's going on?" Willi asked.

"We're having a little bit of the celebration that you missed a few nights ago. I'd planned to do this then . . . but maybe we'd better get used to the unusual in our lives together. Would you stand a moment, *Winyan?*"

Sweet harp music drifted through the gathering. Willi stood beside Quannah. They faced Viola Fiona. She said, "Oh, it's a pleasure you're giving me to do this honor for the family, so to speak. Willi, it was Quannah's request that you both accept all aspects one of the other. He wants you to honor the Native American, but you've also the Scotch-Irish. This, too, he wishes to honor. So . . . tonight I tell you the tale of the Claddagh Rings."

"Cladda?"

"That's the correct pronunciation, it is. Later we'll go into the history, if you've a mind."

Quannah held out a box with two rings of different sizes.

Viola Fiona said, "As you can see, they're cast in the form of two clasped hands, symbolizing faith and trust—what any relationship must have to grow. They are rings to be exchanged between friends and lovers—another two important elements of a darling relationship such as we'll be wishing for you both. If you wear such a ring with the heart forward, it means you're heart-whole and fancy-free. If facing you, your heart is taken, one by the other, signifying you're trusting each other with faith and love, friendship and loving. Love and loving being a bit different, as no doubt you'll be finding out."

Tears choked back anything Willi could say. Her heart was too full for words. She merely smiled while Quannah placed the ring on her finger. She managed, despite her trembling fingers, to get the other one on his strong hand. He looked into her eyes for a long moment.

"Well, be kissing the girl. What are you waiting for, the drum rolls from Killarney?"

Quannah proved he could follow directions well, in the kiss and in the dancing afterward. At the end of the impromptu festivities, he held his arm around her waist as everyone left. He tugged a very tiny second box from his shirt pocket and held it out.

"What's this? I can't take in any more happiness tonight, Lassiter."

"Open it, *Winyan.*"

A set of white feathers so small they had to be from baby birds resided on blue velvet.

He said, "Eventually, I will make you a medicine pouch to put them in along with your *Tunkasila* teaching stone."

"Do they stand for something special?"

"Yes, two hearts coming together. A more native way of saying faith and trust."

"That's beautiful. You have your moments, Special Investigator Quannah Lassiter."

"You're beautiful. And you have your moments, too, Miss Marple of the range. In fact, I need your help on a wrap-up on a case. Has to do with a size five tennis shoe."

"Oops."

MARGARET COEL

THE SPIRIT WOMAN

Coel returns to her bestselling mystery series featuring Arapho lawyer Vicky Holden. A missing archaeologist echoes a similar disappearance from twenty years earlier—and both are tied to the legend of Lewis and Clark's guide, Sacajawea.

❏ 0-425-18090-5

THE GHOST WALKER

Father John O'Malley comes across a corpse lying in a ditch beside the highway. When he returns with the police, it is gone. Together, an Arapaho lawyer and Father John must draw upon ancient Arapaho traditions to stop a killer, explain the inexplicable, and put a ghost to rest.

❏ 0-425-15961-2

THE DREAM STALKER

Father John O'Malley and Arapaho attorney Vicky Holden return to face a brutal crime of greed, false promises, and shattered dreams.

❏ 0-425-16533-7

THE STORY TELLER

When the Arapaho storyteller discovers that a sacred tribal artifact is missing from a local museum, Holden and O'Malley begin a deadly search for the sacred treasure.

❏ 0-425-17025-X

THE THUNDER KEEPER

The apparent suicide of a young Arapaho on sacred ground shocks the populace of the Wind River Reservation. But strange events following the death lead Vicky Holden and Father John O'Malley to suspect foul play.

❏ 0-425-17025-X

THE SHADOW DANCER

With the disappearance of a young mand and his old friend Vicky Holden accused of murder, Father John O'Malley must prove his huncg that both events are connected to a dangerous sect leader known as Orlando.

❏ 0-425-19127-3